THE HANGMAN'S BELIEF

A TRIALS OF THE SERVUNDAY NOVEL

CHRISTOPHER HARVARD

FREE MOUSE, LLC

Dedicated to my mother
She probably would have hated this book
But said she loved it anyway

CONTENTS

PROLOGUE

WHEN FACING IMMINENT DEATH, what are the final thoughts that occupy one's mind?

A comforting slideshow of cherished memories? Maybe a list of regrets that remain unresolved? Perhaps thoughts of loved ones soon left behind?

In the case of Ed Bayliss, it was all the above.

He saw a montage of his greatest victories, in which he found the perfect reaction meme to decimate his opponents in an online argument. Ed cursed with regret at how he had yet to post his critique of a Naruto fan fiction he found online—stern, but fair. His heart sank when he thought of the girl he had matched with on his dating app that never responded to his generous slew of dick pics—only somewhat doctored.

But in the end, none of that matters. While those thoughts do itch away at you, they pale in comparison to the only one that matters.

Is this going to hurt?

Fear of pain pushed Ed beyond breaking as he sprinted down that dusty road, though saying he sprinted is being rather generous. A light drizzle had begun, and the smell of asphalt rose from the ground so thick he could taste it on his tongue. His purple windbreaker, soaked from a mixture of rain and sweat, clapped against his skin with every desperate step he took.

The sharp sting in his chest, side—pretty much everywhere, really—forced him to take a knee. As he huffed through his open mouth, he worked up the courage to look behind him. To his relief, he saw nothing but the line of trees as they curved around the road.

Where had it gone?

He could have sworn it was at his heels as he ran in search of help. Maybe it was afraid to be in the open? A spark of hope ignited within him to cry out that this was all just the tail end of some horrible nightmare.

Unfortunately for him, the nightmare was only beginning.

The trees next to him splintered and crashed to the ground as his pursuer burst forth from the woods. The 'Tryst' landed on all fours before rising to tower over its cowering victim. This lupine monster stood over seven feet tall with jet-black fur on its upper body that receded to brown at its waist before culminating in solid white feet drenched in mud and debris.

Ed screamed and fell backward as he tried to shout for help, but his voice failed him as a few inaudible chirps escaped his throat.

The Tryst took a heavy step forward as its prey began to beg. "Please, p-please don't hurt me!"

The beast squatted down, dipping its head low so that its eyes met his. Its fur seemed to shine in the moonlight as its brown eyes glowed with excitement. As it observed him, a wicked grin curled up its muzzle, showcasing a row of razor-sharp teeth.

"What do you want?" Ed received no response as the creature tilted its head, taking delight in his fear. "I can give you money! Here, take everything! I won't tell anyone. I swear to God, your secret is safe with me!"

Ed held up his wallet for the beast to see as tremors rocked through his arm. To his surprise, the beast reached out to grab the wallet as he nodded it on with encouragement. The glimmer of a smile faded from Ed's face when the beast wrapped a hand around his own and flicked the wallet away with a thumb.

The Tryst caressed Ed's palm with its elongated fingers, similar to a parent touching their newborn child. It was transfixed on their embrace, relishing the difference in size between their hands. A sharp stab in his chest made Ed realize he had not taken a breath since the beast had started fondling him.

"That's right. I'm your friend. We're friends, see?" Ed managed to choke out. "Do you like my ring? My mom gave it to me. It's real gold! You can have it!"

The Tryst looked back up into Ed's eyes and gave him a wry smile, leading him to return a hopeful grin of his own.

Without warning, the Tryst enveloped his hand in its own and squeezed. Ed's digits popped from the top of its fist with a sickening squelch like a can of Vienna sausages under a hydraulic press.

Despite its irregular features, there was no mistaking the look of pure glee that sprung to the Tryst's face as Ed cried out in pain and fell backward, cradling the bloody banana peel of skin that hung from his wrist.

The Tryst stood and licked up Ed's fingers from its fist like salt before a tequila shot, masticating them as its eyes rolled back in pure ecstasy.

The monster could barely believe what it had just done! This body possessed so much power! What else could it do?

Much to the Tryst's chagrin, Ed continued to squeal at its feet, spoiling its sinful decadence. The Tryst's eyes settled back on its prey. There was still plenty left.

Perhaps another test—something a bit harder.

The Tryst slotted the wrist of Ed's remaining hand in between its ring and middle fingers. With only the slightest tug, it pulled Ed to his feet as it gaped at its own inhuman strength. The Tryst then closed the two fingers together as it watched Ed's painful struggle with his own frail mortality.

It was like cutting through warm butter as it crushed Ed's bones into powder. The only thing the monster could feel was the heat of his blood as it pooled in its palm. With a twitch of its finger, Ed's hand popped free and went sailing into the dirt with a dull thud.

Amazing!

Exhilarating!

Better than sex!

Ed had reclaimed his spot on the ground as he mumbled something unintelligible to himself. Thankfully, he had gone into shock; it was a mercy granted by his own body to make these final moments free of torture. The Tryst deduced this was the case when Ed did not even react as it stepped on his foot, flattening it into an empty wrapper of human meat.

This wasn't fun anymore, which meant it was time to complete the sacrifice.

The beast bent over and wrapped its massive hand around Ed's neck and lifted him into the air. It turned its free hand sideways and jammed it through his stomach and out his back with a spray of blood and bone. Suspending Ed on its forearm, it wrapped its other hand around him to the opening in his back. In one swift motion, it tore him in half with no more resistance than a damp tissue. Each section of his body fell with a viscous splash, followed by a rain of viscera that slapped against the asphalt like wads of wet paper towels.

Ed's eyes went milky white, the spark of life gone in an instant.

The Tryst's entire body was covered in blood and emanating a calm steam that dissipated into the night air. It looked at the chunks of flesh that dripped from its claws, reveling in the capability of this holy gift.

Spurred on by powerful emotions and some fundamental understanding only it could comprehend, the Tryst began to dance. It held its arms aloft as if it were cavorting with a partner in an illustrious ballroom while an audience in fancy dress applauded the display. By the end, its white 'socks' were stained red from the gore it had unleashed as it bandied about to its own satisfaction.

After finishing on a pirouette, the Tryst clapped its hands together as it searched for a place to leave its mark. It found the perfect canvas in the form of a gnarled tree with a large vertical branch that reached up toward the heavens.

The Tryst skipped over and shoved its thumb deep into the bark. It then carved lines leading into the hole from multiple directions with the claw on its index finger. Upon completion, a sudden downpour blanketed the entire area like a falling curtain, signaling the finale to the Tryst's morbid performance. This was truly a gift from above—it would make cleanup so much easier.

The Tryst looked toward the heavens and let the cleansing waters wash away the filth. Its body was now clean, but its soul still felt tainted.

This was not enough—not even close.

The Tryst looked down upon its fresh kill, watching as the lifeblood dissolved with each drop of rain.

The beast licked at its maw with one final thought.

Time to get rid of the body.

CHAPTER ONE

THE ROSE HILL MOTEL

THE SUN FELT AMAZING.

Hangman sat with his arm outside the driver's side window as he enjoyed the warmth of the day and the rush of wind against his face. He gazed up at the overhanging trees that spotted the road with shade, creating shimmering pools of light along the road's surface.

His phone rang, causing him to tap his fingers against the side of his truck in step with the catchy melody before answering. "Scriptor, what's up?"

The hands-free call blared from his truck's speakers as Scriptor spoke, his voice muddled by static. "Just wanted to see how you were doing."

"The same since last you checked," he snapped back. "About to come up on the place here soon."

"Okay, good. You didn't happen to see the crime scene on your way there, did you? Remember, it should be right there along the road next to a big tree."

Hangman craned his neck to the side. "Big trees are about all I've seen for the past hour. Been trying to spot some crime scene tape or something, but no luck so far. Seems kind of weird that they would have cleared it already."

"Well, we are a little late to the party on this one. Besides, you are getting out into some country-ass shit. Who knows how they operate down there."

Hangman scanned the road once more. "No big deal. I'll figure it out once I get to whatever this place is."

There was a pause before Scriptor spoke again. "What's the name of this 'place'?"

Hangman's eyes darted about the cab as he tried to recall, causing him to swerve.

Scriptor gave a disapproving grunt at the silence. "Hangman, you told me you had the case file memorized front to back."

"And I do," Hangman stalled. "Which means that the formal designation of this venue that I am advancing toward is most assuredly: Uhh…"

Something caught his attention from the periphery of his vision, forcing him to slam on the brakes and bang his sternum into the steering wheel. He cursed under his breath and waited for the pain to subside before putting the truck in reverse.

"Hey, you okay?" Scriptor asked.

Hangman rubbed his chest as he looked at the peeling letters on the faded wooden sign that kissed the road. "The Rose Hill Motel," he answered. "That's the name."

"Good job," Scriptor congratulated with a hint of sarcasm.

"Hey, I'm almost there, so I'm gonna hang up, all right?"

"Okay, cool. But just don't forget, from this point forward you go by your code name. 'Hangman' doesn't exist anymore."

"Yeah, yeah." Hangman huffed. "I've been using the damn thing for years, but it still feels off. Why couldn't I use a different one this time? It's my case. I should be able to use what name I want."

"Don't know, don't care," Scriptor responded. "Usually, the person running the show makes this crap up. But for some reason, she was adamant that you were not allowed to come up with names…ever. I've got a feeling you know why."

"No idea," he lied.

"But at least you got to create the backstory and everything for this one. I hope it's nothing too outlandish."

"Nope, I gave this one a lot of thought," Hangman said before clearing his throat. "My name is Frederick Ferdinand Fleet. I'm an unemployed electrician traveling south looking for work because all the construction jobs in my hometown have dried up. I decided to stay the night since I've been driving fourteen hours and need a break. When I go to leave tomorrow, my vehicle will 'mysteriously' fail to start. This will give me an excuse to stay here as long as I need."

"I didn't ask for an explanation, but that sounds pretty decent," Scriptor said with a sigh.

"I read a ton of manuals just in case anyone questioned my profession," the newly christened Fleet stated with pride. "I even learned what a 'ballast' is."

"Neat," Scriptor mumbled over the speaker.

Fleet continued unprovoked. "My friends all call me 'Fleet,' but only family calls me 'Freddy.' Once, when I was ten years old—"

"Amazing. What a vivid picture you have painted. Moving on," Scriptor interrupted to Fleet's chagrin. "Now, I want a report on your findings tonight regardless of how much or how little that may entail."

"Yeah, sure. You got it. I'm rolling in now. Later," Fleet replied.

"Wait!" came one final plea from the phone.

"What is it?"

"Are you nervous?"

"Hell no," Fleet lied, trying to sound cool. "I'm a Servunday, after all. This is what I do."

"Big talk from the man on his first solo. But I'll take your word for it," Scriptor said. "Just...ful -ou -thhh -lo..."

Fleet crinkled his nose at the garbled audio. "I think I'm losing you. Can you hear me?"

The phone made a few inauspicious beeps to signify the call was dead.

Fleet looked at the screen to discover that he was down to zero bars. Calls would be impossible out here, though a text might make it through if he was lucky.

He was on his own.

Fleet slid the phone into his pocket as he looked up at the motel.

The driveway was a gauntlet of muddy potholes that led up to a compact building that served as the main office. Farther back was a couple of adjacent two-story buildings with a set of open-air stairs connecting them together. The doors to the rooms were a dingy green, painted to match the roof and awning, all of which had faded to the same shade after so many years of neglect.

Fleet twisted the wheel and pulled into the drive, wincing as he hit the first deep pothole. His truck bounced and shook, threatening to fall apart as he made his way up to the central building. Finding no designated spaces, he pulled up adjacent to the only other car in sight: a cherry-red SUV with a California license plate.

Fleet exited his vehicle and took a deep breath before stepping up onto the wooden porch. The aged timber groaned under his weight, scaring the flies away from a bowl of cat food that sat perched on the edge.

A screen door was the only thing that separated him from the interior of the main office. He peeked through the mesh and took notice of a young woman with glasses attending to her phone, oblivious to anything else.

It required a surprising amount of effort to open the door, as it had warped into the frame. The hinges sang as the door fell back with a loud clack that made him jump. Despite the door's protest, the attendant sitting behind the counter remained unaware of her new visitor.

The front office itself was small; one might even say cozy. Though the wall space was limited, it was almost impossible to tell what color it was due to all the pictures that decorated it. Fleet looked them over, hoping the attendant would notice him in the interim.

Most of the pictures involved a trio: a man—had to be the dad, a woman—gotta be mom, and a pie-faced little girl that Fleet assumed was their daughter. Now and then, Fleet noticed a man in a sheriff's uniform pop up as well. He stopped when he got to a picture of those two men standing next to a young woman dressed in graduation robes, holding up a diploma like she had just carved a chunk from the moon itself.

Fleet turned back to the attendant when he noticed the similarities, at which point he also realized she still had not looked up from her phone. Fleet scratched his nose, accepting the fact that he was going to have to make the introduction.

"Excuse me," Fleet said as he approached the counter.

There was no response as she continued to be absorbed by the screen, all sound blocked out by a pair of corded earbuds. He then noticed a call bell in front of her and gave it a ring, only for it to return an inaudible hiss. With a sigh, he thought about the best way to approach this delicate situation. Using two fingers, he pushed the call bell to the edge of the counter and flicked it over with a meager flourish.

The clatter from the bell caused the poor woman to squeal as she tossed her phone in a panic. It bounced off the counter before crashing to the floor underneath the stool where she sat.

With a sharp gasp, she ducked down to retrieve it and inspect the device for any signs of damage. Finding her phone unharmed, she let out a sigh of relief and made to stand back up, cracking her head on the bottom of the counter in the process. The force of the impact caused her glasses to fall into a dingy corner of her desk. With a dainty groan, she rubbed the back of her head before retrieving her spectacles and placing them back on her face, oblivious to the large dust bunny that clung to the bridge.

She righted herself and gave a start when she saw the man standing wide-eyed in front of her.

Fleet grimaced and held out a hand to her. "Are you okay?"

She blushed as she choked out in quick succession, "Oh my gosh! I'm so sorry! I didn't mean to ignore you!"

But all Fleet could do was study the large deposit of dust hanging from the end of her nose. He pointed to his own face. "You got a little—"

Before he could even finish, the young woman unleashed a powerful sneeze, one so mighty that it sent her glasses flying over the counter. She managed to cover her face; unfortunately, she used the hand that held her phone, leaving the device coated in spit with a thin string of snot that connected to her nose.

She put her phone down, wiped her nose, sank back onto her stool, and shielded her face with both hands in an attempt to hide her embarrassment. She gave a pathetic whine when she realized there was no chance to salvage what was left of her dignity.

Muffled words escaped from between her fingers. "That didn't just happen, did it?" Hearing no response, she spread her fingers to peek through.

"Sorry about that," he apologized with a grin, holding out her glasses. "Didn't mean to startle you so much."

She took them from Fleet with her thanks. "It's my fault," she said, countering his apology by taking the blame upon herself as she slid the glasses back on. "I should have been paying better attention. I got wrapped up in this podcast and..." Her words drifted off and her jaw fell as the man standing before her came into focus.

She gazed at him in reverent silence, like she was absorbing some prestigious masterpiece in a museum. It took a concerned look from Fleet for her to realize what she was doing. The woman turned away and fidgeted, picking at her nails as she tried to regain her train of thought.

"So, what can I do for you?" she sputtered.

He gave a small shrug. "I feel like that's a rhetorical question, right?"

She deflated at his response. "Oh. Okay. How long do you plan to be here?"

Fleet was caught off guard by her sudden change in demeanor. "Only the night, I'd think. I'm actually just—"

She looked up at him with genuine surprise, interrupting what was going to be an elaborate tale. "Are you serious? She never lets anyone stay that long."

He cocked his head to the side and gave her a puzzled look.

She returned a skeptical one of her own. "So...that's not why you're here?"

"I don't think so? Maybe it depends on who 'she' is supposed to be?"

The woman fumbled her words as she stammered, "She? The...umm...the cat! Patchy! She can be real picky about who she lets stay here. You know how cats can be, right?"

He raised an eyebrow. "I'll try my best to make it into her good graces."

Not to linger on the subject, she explained the terms of his stay in rapid succession. "So, it's going to be fifty-five bucks a night. I'm pretty lax about check out time since it's not like people are fighting for rooms. There's an ice machine in between the buildings which I lock at sundown, so if you want ice, get it before it gets dark. I know it's inconvenient to lock it, but you would be surprised what people have put in there. The room phone only does local calls or nine-one-one in case of emergency. If you need toilet paper or something like that, just ask me. I try to keep everything stocked, but I'm just one person, and um..."

Her words slowed as her voice took on a nervous tone.

"I don't do a continental breakfast or anything, but if you get up early enough, there is a diner in town that I frequent, you know, if you're hungry. We could go together, or whatever."

She adjusted her glasses and looked up at him. Fleet just stood there, holding a black credit card in between his middle and index finger.

She flinched and apologized, "Sorry, we don't take cards."

"Then what's that?" He pointed at a card reader next to the cash register.

"It's broken," she responded.

"I don't have that much cash on me."

"That's okay, I'm sure you can get it. You can just leave your driver's license with me until you get the money," she said, then added with a hopeful inflection, "There's an ATM near the diner I told you about."

"Wait, how am I supposed to get you the money if I can't drive anywhere?"

Lowy had to stop herself from laughing. "Trust me, that won't be an issue. It's miles of empty space between here and the downtown strip, so the police never bother to come out this way unless it's an emergency. You'll be fine."

"Is that right? Gotta say, this is awfully trusting of you."

She gave him a smile. "I guess you just have a real trustworthy face."

He chuckled and pulled out his driver's license. "Well, let's hope I don't destroy your faith in humanity or anything," Fleet quipped as he handed it to her.

She took the license from him and looked it over. "Frederick Ferdinand Fleet." She paused for a moment. "Your initials spell 'FFF.'" She punctuated his initials by making a sound like a deflating air mattress.

"Yeah, I get it," Fleet responded, rolling his eyes. "My initials sound like somebody windsocked a fart. I heard that one enough in school to last me a lifetime."

She apologized, fearing she had slighted him. "No! I promise I wasn't making fun of you! I was just making a stupid observation and—"

He held up a hand and laughed. "Hey, don't worry about it. I'm just messing with you. I promise I'm not mad or anything."

She gave a nervous laugh as she calmed herself.

Sensing the awkward moment had passed, Fleet extended his hand to her. "And before you start calling me Freddy— which I hate—I want you to know that all my friends call me Fleet, and I'd appreciate it if you did the same."

She stood up and wiped a sweaty palm on her pants before extending her hand in kind. "My name is—"

Fleet tried to recall what he had read as she spoke, *Harlow R-something...*

"—Harlow Rowshell, but you can call me Lowy if you want. That's what my friends call me. Like you said. Like you meant when you said, not that..." She caught herself, giving a quick exhale to right the conversation. "Nice to meet you! I know it says Rose Hill out front, but my parents took some liberties with our last name when they christened the place. It just looks prettier on a sign when you're driving by; more romantic, I guess."

Close enough, Fleet thought, taking the meager win.

He shook her hand. "Clears up that mystery. Well, it's a pleasure to meet you, Lowy."

Lowy giggled at his reply for some reason and nodded, letting the handshake linger just a bit too long. She continued to smile even as he retracted his hand. They stood without speaking for several seconds with Lowy grinning at him the entire time.

Fleet felt a need to break the silence. "So, which room am I going to be in?"

She snapped out of her daze, seeming disappointed the moment was over. "Oops, let me just take a look." She turned to the cork board behind her where several keys hung. Based on the number of hooks, there were sixteen rooms in total. "I'll put you in room 102. It's our deluxe suite!"

Fleet thanked her despite his doubts. "Wow, I appreciate it!"

"No problem! And if you wouldn't mind, please sign the guest book while I get the key."

Fleet obeyed, taking a moment to scroll through the other signatures and give a stifled huff of amusement at the juvenile names others had written. "Should I make up a name?"

Lowy turned around as she was reaching for the key hanging from the wall. "No, put your real name. Why would you make one up?"

Fleet shrugged and then added his chicken scratch that he had rehearsed for hours on end to make it so consistent.

Lowy returned just as he finished and proffered him a key. "Here you go. C'mon, I'll show you where the room is."

She started to walk toward the back exit but was interrupted by someone struggling with the screen door. The mesh was able to hold the man back, but did little for the sound of his lamentations. "I can't believe she didn't listen to any of my suggestions. When I walked in the door, I should have been greeted by clean linens with a chocolate mint on top. Instead, I walk in and I'm greeted by a syphilitic cockroach that wants to sell me meth."

A gruff but dulcet voice chimed in. "He seemed pleasant enough to me."

"This isn't funny," the annoyed one continued. "All I'm saying is why should anyone spend money to stay here when they could just roll around in medical waste for free?"

"You might want to watch your volume," the baritone responded. "I am pretty sure she can hear you."

"Perfect! It will save me some time of having to repeat myself."

The upset guest struggled against the door one more time. "Damn it! Could you help me out, please?"

The other man pulled the door and it swung open with ease, but he waited as his partner walked in first before stepping in himself. Fleet watched as the second man had to duck and twist to make it through the opening. This burly man dwarfed everyone in the room; a solid jump could put his head through the ceiling.

Fleet heard Lowy curse under her breath. Based on what they had just heard, she was about to have one hell of a confrontation.

Lowy steeled herself and spoke to them. "Hey, Oreen. Hey, BJ. Is there a problem with your room?"

Based on how she greeted them, Fleet could tell that the small one with the complaint was Oreen. Perhaps small was not the right way to describe him. Oreen was about the same height as Fleet, but when compared to the giant who came in behind him, it was an easy mistake to make.

Fleet took a moment to assess the two men and was struck by the contrast between them. The irate one was somewhere in his late twenties or early thirties. He had neatly styled hair, and he was wearing business casual clothes with nary a wrinkle in sight. It was obvious his appearance was very important to him; what was even more obvious was that his companion did not share this sentiment.

The only thing louder than Oreen at the moment was the bright Hawaiian shirt that the large man wore; it could very well double as a gaudy tarp for a picnic table should the need arise. The first few buttons of his shirt were undone, and a tuft of peppered chest hair poked over the top, matching the strands atop his head that peeked from underneath a red cap embroidered with galloping horses on the front and back. He wore cargo shorts that were splotchy and frayed from years of frequent use, keeping in theme with his sandals that had worn down to the sole.

From what he was wearing and the calm expression on his face, Fleet deduced he must be a gentle giant—at least he hoped, given the circumstance.

Oreen approached the front desk with resolve, ready to unleash his fury. Fleet glanced back at Lowy with pity. Perhaps he could at least try to defuse the situation somewhat.

Oreen slapped his hands down on the counter but was cut short when Fleet spoke up first. "I'm sorry, but Lowy here was just about to show me to my room. So, if you don't mind, could you and your buddy wait your turn?"

"Technically, I was here first, so I should be addressed first," Oreen responded. "If you have any complaints, feel free to take it up with 'my buddy.'"

Fleet never fancied himself a coward or one to back down from a confrontation, but when he craned his neck to look up at BJ, there was just no fucking way.

He gave Lowy an apologetic shrug and mouthed sorry.

Secure in his victory, Oreen turned back to Lowy with a huff. "Lowy, I have to say I'm disappointed in you. I gave you explicit instructions on how you should prepare rooms going forward. So when I come back here and I see…"

His voice trailed off and his expression softened as he watched her. She looked like a frightened puppy recoiling from a rolled-up newspaper.

"I'm sorry," Lowy apologized to Oreen. "With everything that's happened, I just forgot. I'll be better about it, I promise!"

The face she was making forced Fleet to struggle with the urge to jump over the counter and give her a hug—and from the looks of it, he was not the only one.

Oreen struggled to find the proper words before he could respond. "No, forgive me. I'm not being considerate. We can work on the room stuff later. I'll even help you!"

"That's great!" Lowy shouted, clapping her hands together. "I can get you started on cleaning out all the grime in the bathrooms!"

Oreen groaned and rubbed his face; he knew he'd been got.

Behind Oreen, Fleet swore he heard a short guffaw from the man known as BJ. Lowy had already perked up and was having a rather civil conversation with Oreen.

From what Fleet could gather, they had some sort of prior relationship, but he could not discern the extent. Either way, it seemed like she had the situation covered, so he decided to check out his new quarters.

"Lowy, I'm heading out to my room! Thanks for your help!" he yelled over their voices.

"Are you sure you don't need me to show you the way?" she responded through her exchange.

"There's not that many rooms, I think I can figure it out."

He gave her a small wave before nodding at the two men as he left through the front door.

CHAPTER TWO

ROOM 102

FLEET STOOD IN FRONT of the entrance to his room; it was on the ground floor in the building to the left. The first two numbers on the door had fallen off, leaving only a silhouette of the preceding '1' and '0.' He unlocked the door and was hit by a musty stench that reminded him of an abandoned building. Fleet exhaled to clear his nostrils and studied his new accommodations from the threshold.

The ceiling was covered in brown water spots that bled into the floral wallpaper. A small CRT television sat on top of a washed-out credenza on one wall, and two black nightstands stood on the opposite side a few feet apart from each other. Fleet shook his head at the sunbaked manila phone that sat proudly atop the stand closest to him; he could not remember the last time he had seen one of those. Before entering, Fleet dragged his foot across the greenish brown carpet where it latched onto some dried gum that had been ground into the fabric.

The room was tiny, yet surprisingly spacious. It took him a few moments to figure out why: there was no bed in sight.

Deluxe suite, huh?

He made his way to the back of the room and found a small closet; opposite that was the lavatory. The bathroom was bigger than he had expected and filled with all the basic accouterments, though they were a bit dated.

In the porcelain sink, brown streaks had formed around the spigot that intertwined into a murky trail leading down to the rusty drain. He turned the handle labeled 'H' and listened as the pipes shook and sputtered before it spat out a stream of lukewarm water. He flipped it back off with a judgmental snort and went to inspect the shower.

Fleet pondered the odd design choice on the curtain before realizing that the splotchy black pattern was actually mildew that had settled there years ago. Rust stains decorated the outside of the old clawfoot tub, and the bottom was worn down smooth to expose the metal (probably lead) underneath the paint (probably lead). A turn of the handle led to him being sprayed by cold water as the showerhead shot streams in all directions.

The only destination left was the toilet, so he headed over and reached for the lid.

Nope.

He turned around and left the bathroom.

Something caught his eye off to the side—a sort of metal bar set into the wall opposite the television. He slipped his fingers around the mystery handle and pulled. Painful squeaks and groans echoed throughout the room as a fully made Murphy bed fell from the wall and slotted between the two nightstands.

That same vacant stench from earlier made a reappearance, making it clear that this bed had not been used in quite some time. A few hard slaps to the mattress sent bursts of dust sailing through the air as Fleet swatted at the particles in a futile attempt to keep himself from inhaling any. With the bed now laid bare, the illusion of space the room presented earlier had been broken.

He edged his way between the credenza and the bed to put his hand over the large vent in the room's corner just below the ceiling—nothing. He wiped his hands and attempted to peek farther inside, but its position in the room kept its interior away from any light.

Perfect size. Hard to get to. That could work.

Fleet went outside to his truck that he had parked in a space closer to his new dwelling. The cab opened with a groan and Fleet pulled out a black backpack, which he tossed through the open door of his room. He then jumped into the truck bed and unlocked the metal toolbox.

Inside the container, he pulled a hidden handle that was concealed under an emergency road kit. Fleet lifted the base of the toolbox and slide it over to reveal a large black duffel bag. He made a fake struggle of sifting through the box's contents to give him an opportunity to check his surroundings. The place felt deserted. There were no signs of life, and the blinds were shut on all the visible windows.

Figuring he was in the clear, Fleet lifted out the heavy bag with a grunt, shut the secret hatch, and locked the toolbox, but not before grabbing a Phillips head screwdriver.

He returned to the corner of the room and placed his burden below the vent, then took out his screwdriver and set to work. The screws had been painted over, which made them difficult to turn. Fleet had to put both hands on the screwdriver and force all his upper body strength into it before he heard a faint crack as the screw turned.

One down.

He placed the screw in his pocket and wiped some sweat from his brow before he began the same process on the next one. Just as it showed signs of movement, his knuckle slipped and caught the sharp edge of the vent. He spat out a few expletives as he shook his hand in annoyance at his own carelessness.

Slight cuts ran down his pointer finger; they were not deep, but he was bleeding. He cursed one more time before unfastening the screw.

The next two screws were set on the top of the vent out of his reach. With a spark of ingenuity, he grabbed the nightstand to use as a makeshift stool. He brought it over to the wall and then stepped up on top.

The nightstand wobbled, but it was tolerable. He set to work, and with great effort, he unfastened the final two screws. The grate slid off with little resistance, and he jumped down to retrieve the duffel bag. He hoisted it onto his shoulder and stepped back up onto the nightstand with a grunt as the heavy bag weighed him down. As he had assessed earlier, the large vent was the perfect size, and it slid in almost as if it had been made for this purpose. The metal tiling within popped as he shoved it an arm's length deep inside.

Satisfied, he put the grate back on and reinserted the two screws at the top. He shifted the nightstand off to the side before setting about inserting the bottom ones. He placed one in the bottom-right hole and grabbed the screwdriver.

A knock on the door startled him—so much so that he dropped his faithful tool.

A voice came from outside. "Fleet! It's me, Lowy! Can I come in for a second? I want to check and make sure you are stocked on toilet paper!"

"Yeah! Sure thing! I'll be there in a sec!"

Shit! This will be hard to explain away if she sees what I'm doing! Gotta just finish up quick.

As soon as he thought that, he heard a click as the door opened.

I forgot to lock the fucking door!

He sprinted over to greet Lowy before she entered the room. He stopped the door from opening all the way by leaning on it to block her line of sight.

Lowy was startled, but still greeted him with warmth. "Hi!"

"Hey, you," Fleet responded, his mind racing for a possible excuse just in case.

They both stood smiling at each other for several seconds before Lowy spoke, sparing him reason to lie. "So, umm, what do you think? About the room, I mean?"

Fleet rubbed his chin as he struggled to find the right words for this delicate question, unintentionally exposing his cuts to her.

Lowy's eyes shot wide, and her mouth fell agape. "What happened to your hand?"

He had already forgotten about the injury to his finger. Granted, it looked much worse than it was now that a small trickle of blood had run down to his palm.

Fleet responded without hesitation. "Oh, that. Yeah, my wallet fell in between my car seats, and when I was reaching down to grab it, I cut my finger on something down there."

"That could get infected! Let me go get my first aid kit!"

Lowy darted off before he could respond.

He waited for her to be out of sight before he rushed to the vent and began frantically reinstalling the screws. He made it to the last hole only to realize that he didn't have the last piece.

Shit! I must have dropped it! Where the hell is it?

He got on the floor and began searching, running his fingers through the grimy carpet all around the base of the nightstand.

Shit! Shit! Shit! Maybe she won't notice?

He tilted the nightstand up, but no luck. As he placed his impromptu stool back in its original spot, something hard poked into his heel. He tapped the front of his shoe on the floor and felt a tiny object move up to his toes.

It's in my fuckin' shoe! How the hell does that even happen?

He pulled off his shoe and shook it, causing the errant screw to fall onto the carpet. He installed the last piece and shoved the screwdriver into his pocket just as Lowy came to the door.

Fleet backpedaled away from the vent and turned to greet her.

"Okay, I got the kit," she said, holding the item aloft. There was a brief pause as she studied his foot. "Why do you only have one shoe on?"

Fleet raised an eyebrow and looked down. In his hurry to take off his shoe, the sock had gone with it as well.

He wiggled his toes before he responded, "Oh, I was just changing my socks. If my feet get too moist, they break out in a smelly rash, ya know. I've had to burn some footwear because there is just no saving them once that happens." Fleet finished with an awkward laugh. "Want to avoid that if possible."

Lowy returned a subdued nod. "Sorry to hear that. I bet it gets expensive."

In an attempt to validate his statement, Fleet walked to his book bag and began searching through it for a pair of socks. Not finding them quick enough, he took the bag over to the credenza and dumped its contents into the top drawer.

He rifled through the clothes as Lowy chided, "Stop that! You're going to get blood all over your clothes!"

Preoccupied by his chicanery, he had forgotten about his injury once again. Lowy walked over and sat down on the creaky mattress with the first aid kit in her lap, then patted the spot next to her. "Come over here. Let me take a look at your boo-boo."

"A boo-boo?" Fleet feigned concern. "Now, I don't know all them fancy medical terms like you, but that sure sounds serious. Just tell me straight, Doc: can you save the hand?"

Lowy hid her amusement by donning a veil of forced authority. "Sit down! If you don't hurry, the best I can do is a pinky!"

Fleet sighed and took the seat she offered. The cuts on his finger were too awkwardly positioned for a normal bandage, so Lowy applied some disinfectant and wrapped them in a thin gauze.

She finished up and gave him a small pat on the knee. "All done! Now, doesn't that feel better?"

"Yeah, it does. Thank you." Fleet gave her a small but appreciative smile. "You do this often?"

"Not really," she admitted, but Fleet detected an air of longing in her words. "I've always liked this kind of stuff. Some basic first aid isn't much, but it's something I know how to do. And thanks for letting me work on you. Most people don't like untrained strangers putting their hands all over them."

"Well, you did excellent work," Fleet complimented. "So, feel free to put your hands on me whenever you want." He paused for a second. "You know what, I apologize. That came out wrong."

Lowy grinned before she turned her head and muttered under her breath, "I'll hold you to that."

"What was that?"

Lowy coughed and stood up. Looking for a distraction, she walked over to the credenza where Fleet had dumped his things. "I said that if you just leave your clothes like this, they're going to get wrinkled."

Fleet balled his hand into a fist a few times to test the elasticity of his bandages as Lowy began pulling out his clothes and folding them into neat squares where applicable. Having her rummage through his things was a bit awkward, but it was keeping her preoccupied, so he let it slide. She found two socks and tossed them over her shoulder.

Fleet caught them by reflex and began putting them on. "Thanks, Mom."

She gave a small chuckle and continued to fold until she found something metallic hidden under a well-worn shirt. She pulled it out for closer inspection to find it was a little red car. The toy's paint looked worn, as if someone had rubbed it off with sandpaper.

She held it up for him to see. "What is this?"

Fleet leaned back to study what she had in her hands. "Oh, that's just my good luck charm. I take it with me everywhere."

She walked over and handed him the bauble. "What makes it so lucky?"

Fleet paused before shrugging. "You know, not a damn thing. It's difficult to say now that I think about it."

He rubbed the little car tenderly with his thumb. Fleet's voice seemed to drift away as he spoke, like the only person who was listening was himself.

"No matter what I do, I can't bring myself to get rid of it."

He set the car down on the nightstand and looked up at Lowy.

"You don't have anything like that?"

She thought for a moment. "I can't say that I do." She then jumped to another topic, as if the subject was a bother to her. "Oh, that's right! I almost totally forgot why I came here. I wanted to invite you out back to a little bonfire that I'm having. It's been a while since I've had this many people stay here at once, so I was kind of hoping I could get everyone out for some, you know, camaraderie."

"I thought you were here to see if I had enough toilet paper?"

"Oh, yeah, that too. Anyway, we are all meeting outside in about thirty minutes. I will be super pissed if you don't come, okay?" Lowy seemed almost giddy as she darted from the room. She stopped just outside the entrance to lean back in one last time. "Thirty minutes! Don't be late!"

Fleet tapped his wrist. "Thirty minutes."

After she was gone, Fleet rubbed the toy car with his thumb before setting it aside. His eyes lingered on the bauble as he returned to the bed, mentally bracing himself for whatever Lowy had in mind.

Chapter Three

CAMARADERIE

Fleet decided it was time to make his way out to the bonfire like he had promised.

Had he promised to do that?

Either way, this could be the perfect opportunity to investigate the tenants. He locked his room on the way out and took a moment to familiarize himself with the layout of the area.

There were two separate buildings connected by a single roof, both of which had two floors. Four rooms were on each floor, making a total of sixteen apartments. All the rooms faced toward the road, so it made it easy to read the large metal numbers, or at least what was left of them.

The bottom floors started at 101 through 108, and the top occupied 201 through 208. The buildings separated at rooms 104 and 204. In the center, there were two sets of stairs, one for each building, with a breezeway in between them. A rusty metal divider sat along the edge of the stairs and the second-floor pathway to ensure that nobody fell to their doom in a drunken stupor.

Even before Fleet started down the center pathway, he heard a roar echoing from between the buildings like a dragon guarding its hoard of gold. He soon discovered the source upon entering: a generic soda machine and a leaky icebox competing to see whose struggling motor could output the most irritating racket. Despite the audible assault, the allure of a sugary drink was too much for Fleet to ignore.

Luckily, he had a small cache of pocket change that he eagerly inserted before selecting his beverage. He waited for the sound of his can flailing through the inner machinations of the contraption, but all he heard was that same annoying hum.

Fleet gave the machine a swift kick. "Come on, man."

The soda machine's light blinked in protest as it refused to acquiesce. Fleet grabbed the sides and gave it a firm shake and found that the latch was not engaged. He glanced around before opening the front cabinet.

"I did pay for it," he said to justify himself.

Fleet grabbed his soda of choice and gave a disappointed sigh when he felt the can's lukewarm temperature. With a defeated shrug, he cracked it open and took a hardy swig. He enjoyed the burn of the fizzy libation before going in for another sip, but then spat it out all over the front of the machine.

Something had rubbed up against his leg during the last gulp, catching him by surprise. It took him a moment to realize who was the culprit: a rather brazen calico cat.

"Scared the shit out of me, little guy."

The cat seemed perturbed by his reaction, but continued to circle around for a turn at his other leg.

"You must be Patchy." Fleet reached down to pet the cat, but recoiled when the beast gave a mirthful hiss and swatted at his hand. "Only you get to touch. Got it," he said as the cat brushed between his legs once more.

For the sake of his ankles, he decided it was best to let the cat lose interest on its own before he made a swift retreat. Thus, Fleet continued to drink his soda while the lower half of his body remained immobile for the cat's oppressive delight.

This continued for longer than it should have until something caught his eye: a person near the entrance of the walkway peeking their head around the building.

As he turned his head toward them, the figure ducked behind the brick wall. Finding this new target more interesting, the cat abandoned its march around Fleet and trotted over to them. It sat down and meowed until the stranger reached down to pick it up, letting Fleet catch a good look at the stranger.

She was a young girl, perhaps early or middle teens. She was wearing a long-sleeved shirt several sizes too big for her that fell past her hands. Her thin face framed her sunken eyes, which were accentuated by the dark circles underneath. Her posture was meek and hunched like some wayward woodland creature, afraid of human contact, but also curious at the same time.

She wrapped her arms around the cat and brought it close to her chest, the extra fabric of her shirt acting like a swaddling cloth. The cat did not fight or even growl; it seemed content to be held like this.

"Is that your cat?" Fleet asked, making his voice sound as kind as possible.

The girl took a step back behind the wall, though her eyes remained locked on him as if she expected an attack at any moment.

He took a sip and continued. "You must be best friends if he'll let you hold him like that. Never been too good with cats myself."

He received nothing but that same empty stare.

"So, what's your name?" he asked.

She did not respond.

"Come on, kid. You've got a name." He scratched at his neck. "I bet it's a flower one, like Rose or Lily."

They stared at each other in silence.

Fleet sighed. *This is a waste of time. Why am I even bothering with this kid?*

It was as he was taking another sip that he noticed how fixated she was on the can.

He looked at the soda for a second, then pointed at it. "Would you like one?"

While it may only have been the most minuscule of movements, he was positive that he saw her nod.

"Okay, what flavor do you..." Knowing full well what her response would be, he formulated a compromise. "How about this? I will point to all the different flavors, and you just let me know which one's for you."

Fleet swung the front panel open far enough for her to see and then moved his finger down the buttons one at a time. While she made no discernible confirmation, he did notice her eyes go wide at one point.

He looked to where his finger had stopped. "Orange. Nice choice."

He reached in and plucked one of the lukewarm beverages from the machine and held it out to her. At his gesture, she took a quick step backward with the cat kicking at the air in annoyance.

"I'll just put this right here," Fleet said as he set the can on the concrete. "You can come grab it whenever you want." Fleet closed the soda machine and gave her a wave as he headed to the back of the building. "You two take care."

He did not turn around to see if she came out to retrieve her gift as he walked into the open air.

The area behind the building was just a flat plot of land thirty yards in circumference surrounded by dense woods. Off to the right, Fleet noticed a dirty green hatchback parked close to the building.

At the center of the backyard was a large tire well sitting atop two cinder blocks that served as a makeshift fire pit. A couple of small logs, some lawn chairs, and what looked to be an old stadium bleacher served as the seating.

Lowy stood next to the pit, drenching its contents with some liquid from a metal can.

Once she realized he was there, she gave him an exaggerated wave and a hearty smile. "You made it! Come on over. I'm about to light the fire."

"Quite the soirée you've got going here?" Fleet mused, noting the distinct absence of any other guests.

"Well, you are a bit early. The caterers haven't even showed up yet," she responded with a smirk and a squeeze of the can.

"Fair enough." Fleet took a seat on the rusty bench. "But it better be an open bar or I'm out. Hope there's orange soda if the kid is coming."

Lowy set the can down with a hollow thunk. "Kid? Do you mean Jill?"

Fleet shrugged. "I guess so. Met her coming up here. Real shy. Wouldn't even speak to me."

"Yeah, that sure sounds like her. Don't take any offense at it. It took a long time for her to get used to me, and even now, I wouldn't say we're friends."

Fleet raised an eyebrow. "How long has she been here?"

Lowy picked a lighter from the ground and tapped the nozzle in her palm as she thought. "I guess it's been about six months now, give or take."

"Six months?" Fleet repeated in surprise. "That seems like a long time to stay in a place like this. No offense."

Lowy narrowed her eyes at him. "Why would I be offended?"

"Uhh, no reason." He changed the subject. "You gonna light this thing or what?"

He tapped his chin as he thought about what she said. *Six months...that means that the girl should have been here when it happened,* Fleet reasoned. *Why wasn't she in the report? You'd think she would have been interviewed or at least mentioned.*

"Here you go," Lowy called as she tossed him the lighter, catching him off guard. "You can have the honor of lighting my fire."

"It would be my pleasure."

Fleet flicked the long-neck lighter to life and crouched down. As the igniter touched the soaked wood, there was an explosion of flame, and they were both hit by a burst of incredible heat. Fleet fell backward onto the ground, cursing as he knocked over the bleacher while Lowy stomped on small patches of fire that dotted the ground.

"Holy shit, how much did you use!" Fleet exclaimed.

"Just half the can," Lowy said, swiping at the smoke.

"Can of what?"

"The old lawn mower fluid I never use."

"That's gasoline!"

Lowy backed away, coughing from the acrid smoke billowing from the fire pit as Fleet patted his face to see if his eyebrows had become a casualty of the homemade fireball.

She ran over and kneeled next to him. "I'm so sorry! Are you okay?"

"Yeah, I'm good," he mumbled with wide eyes as his brain fumbled over the alternatives. *Barely an hour into my first assignment and I have to be carted off to the burn ward. They'd never let me live that down.*

Lowy righted the fallen bench and helped Fleet sit down, brushing the dirt off his back. "I promise I didn't mean for that to happen. How about I make you a nice breakfast tomorrow as a sincere apology? Bacon and eggs! That'll make you feel better."

Fleet looked up at her with an exasperated expression. "Are you trying to keep me from suing you by bribing me with a continental breakfast?"

Lowy pursed her lips. "Umm..."

"Yeah, that sounds good," Fleet said with a groan. "I've waived my rights for less."

"That's great!" Lowy shouted. "I haven't made a real breakfast in a long time. This will be fun!"

"Yay," Fleet moaned, though he had to admit the thought of a hearty breakfast was enticing.

Behind them came a gruff voice, catching them off guard. "Is breakfast for everyone?"

They both turned to see a Sasquatch in a Hawaiian shirt shuffling over to them.

"Hello, BJ!" Lowy greeted him with a wave. "Everyone's invited!"

BJ rubbed his hands together as he developed a deep and genuine smile.

"And just like that, you've found the way to his heart," Oreen said, stepping into sight from behind BJ's imposing frame.

Lowy ran up to give him a big hug. "Hey, Oreen! Glad you guys could make it!"

"I wouldn't miss it!" Oreen returned her embrace. "Even despite the current company."

Fleet looked around and halfway closed one eye. "Are you talking about me?"

Lowy clapped her hands together, cutting Fleet off. "That's right! You were never formally introduced." She stood up and held out a hand to Fleet. "Oreen, BJ, this is Frederick Fleet, but you can call him Fleet."

"Good to have a name to go with the face," Oreen said, his smirk tinted by a hint of vitriol. "Sorry if we got off on a bad foot earlier, but I hope that's all in the past."

Fleet waved it off. "No problem."

Oreen put a hand on his hip. "So, Fleet, where are you from?"

Without hesitation, Fleet responded, "Delaware."

"Delaware? How interesting! You're such a long way from home." Oreen nodded and then pulled out his phone. "Where in Delaware?"

"Why do you want to know that?" Fleet asked with some trepidation.

Oreen pointed down at his phone. "Sorry. I was just looking at the Delaware sex offenders list, but it seems I need to narrow it down a bit. What's your address?"

Fleet took a deep breath and squinted at Oreen. "Yeah, I'm not going to tell you that."

"Got quiet real quick; certainly not something an innocent man would do," Oreen remarked with a huff as he put his phone away. "Lowy, you need to be pickier about the level of clientele you let stay here."

An unfamiliar voice barged its way into the conversation. "Now if she did that, I'd still be sleeping on the street."

Everyone turned toward the origin of the intrusion and found that it belonged to a woman holding a half-empty whiskey bottle. Her hair was dark, short, and unkempt, with green highlights on the ends. She wore a small crop top with a skull motif and cut-off jean shorts that were unbuttoned at the top. It looked like she had worn the same makeup for two days straight; her smeared black eyeliner lending credence to the fact.

The woman finished a pull on the whiskey. "That would be a goddamn shame for a fine lady such as myself."

Lowy noticed Fleet tilt his head in confusion. "Fleet, this is—"

"Call me Dash. That's the name all my friends use," she interrupted, "and I can tell we are going to be very good friends."

She took a swig from the bottle of whiskey and sat on the bench next to Fleet, sliding in close to press herself against him. She offered him the bottle with a sultry smile, but Fleet waved it off as he scooted away.

"Making a girl drink alone? Chivalry is dead." She tilted her head back for another long swig.

Fleet couldn't help but watch as a small stream of alcohol escaped her lips and slithered its way down her neck. The whiskey continued its downward journey between her breasts until it found a trench formed by her toned stomach. From there, it flowed farther on, where it pooled in her belly button before finding a home somewhere under the fly of her unbuttoned jeans.

She gave a small convulsion before wiping away the liquid from her chin. A smirk accompanied her seductive giggle. "Mmm. That's the good stuff." Dash forced the bottle into Fleet's hand and whispered, "Are you sure I can't tempt you?"

Fleet felt his heart bashing against his ribcage like an angry gorilla. He needed something to calm his nerves, or so he told himself.

Without a word, he turned up the bottle of whiskey and chugged it like cold water on a hot summer day, enticing Oreen to say, "Aww, you guys! It's a match made in trailer-park heaven."

Fleet did not adjust his stance and instead responded with a silent extension of his middle finger. He lowered the bottle with a powerful sigh and used his forearm to wipe the excess whiskey from his mouth. He handed the bottle back to Dash, and she accepted it with a smile.

"Looks like I found a new drinking buddy," Dash chirped as she placed her hand on Fleet's knee. "And a cute one at that."

"S'mores!" Lowy suddenly shouted out to the group. "I got everything for s'mores..." Her voice tapered off toward the end as she lifted a bag of unopened marshmallows.

"Fuck yeah!" Fleet shouted as he stood up and took the bag of marshmallows from Lowy.

He sat back down on the bench farther away from Dash, yanked open the bag, and devoured a handful of the fluffy confections.

Oreen kicked at a marshmallow that had fallen near his foot. "I don't think you quite comprehend how s'mores are supposed to work."

"To each their own," Lowy responded in Fleet's defense as she grabbed the chocolate and graham crackers.

She passed them around, and everyone took what they wanted with both Fleet and BJ taking enough to make multiple.

"Take a seat, you guys," Lowy encouraged Oreen and BJ.

Oreen grimaced at the weather-worn log that was being offered to him. BJ lifted his heavy piece of wood and sat it closer to the fire pit before taking his rightful place. After seeing BJ sit down, Oreen sighed and reluctantly sat on the log next to him after brushing it off and rubbing his hands together in disgust.

Lowy had brought some old coat hangers that had been straightened out to roast the marshmallows on, though Dash and Oreen did not take part. Those with hangers roasted their marshmallows, letting the sweet smell encapsulate the area.

Fleet's marshmallow caught flame, causing him to yank it out of the fire. After a few quick blows to cool it, Fleet popped it between two graham crackers and chocolate before taking a satisfying bite. He made a content 'mmm' as the creamy goo danced across his palate. Lowy smiled at his reaction and watched with similar delight as BJ bit down on his own double-stacked creation.

Her smile lingered as she crafted a sugary sandwich of her own. "This is nice." As she was about to take a bite, something caught her eye. "Jill? It's okay. Do you want to come and have s'mores with us?"

Everyone turned to find Jill standing alone in the walkway, the cat rubbing against her legs.

"They're good, I promise. You can make one if you come out and join us," Lowy coaxed in a cheerful voice.

Perhaps enticed by the alluring smell, Jill made her way to the campfire at a weighted pace. Dash picked up the materials and began roasting her marshmallow on the fire before turning her full attention back toward Jill's approach. Everyone at the fire went silent as Jill timidly approached the empty lawn chair, where she sat down in a ball with her knees touching her chin.

Being the closest, Fleet put a marshmallow on one hanger and held it out to her. After a few moments, she accepted it with caution and tilted it over the fire, looking around at the group as if seeking assurance.

Dash nodded in confirmation. "You're doing great."

Fleet wasn't sure, but he could have sworn he saw Dash's bottom lip quiver as she spoke.

They all sat in reverent silence as they roasted their marshmallows until Fleet noticed Jill had let hers slide down a bit too close to the fire. As someone who considered himself a s'more connoisseur (and perhaps swayed by the alcohol), Fleet could not allow such sloppy technique to go uncorrected.

"Jill, you need to hold it higher. Like this."

Fleet leaned forward to reach for the hanger. Jill gasped and jerked back as he got close, sending the marshmallow flying. The flaming ball of goo found its way toward BJ, where it slapped against his neck just under his Adam's apple.

The fire from the marshmallow licked at his chin for a brief second before he placed his hand over it to extinguish the flame. BJ scraped the charred mess off his throat and studied it.

Jill was in tears, overcome by the fear of how BJ would react to her unintended assault. Everyone else seemed to have a similar reaction; tension kept their eyes locked on the man.

Fleet felt his muscles tighten and his teeth clench as he readied to jump to Jill's defense. *Please be a gentle giant. I do not want to get my ass kicked today.*

BJ stared at it for another second before he looked over at Jill. He then put his hand to his face and took the messy goop into his mouth, followed by half a graham cracker and a whole chocolate bar.

After several seconds of mastication, he covered his mouth and said, "Thank you. That was delicious."

Fleet felt a wave of relief wash over him as he let out a deep sigh; next to him, Dash did likewise. Across from the two, he saw Lowy wearing a big smile. Oreen seemed uninterested in the whole situation.

Jill had returned to an upright position and was wiping tears from her eyes. BJ waved his hand as he smiled and nodded to show there were no hard feelings.

Fleet laughed. "Not gonna lie. I was kind of worried there for a sec."

"Oh, please," Oreen scoffed. "He wouldn't hurt a fly—unless it crossed him."

Oreen narrowed his eyes at Fleet, who didn't even notice as he put another marshmallow on the hanger and handed it back to Jill.

"Jill, watch me. See how I'm holding it? Close, but not too close. It all depends on how you like your marshmallow: crunchy, soft, or—" His instructions derailed as something in the distance caught his eye. "The hell is that?"

Fleet tilted his head and squinted as he pointed toward the disturbance, spurring everyone to follow his gaze.

One of the windows on the first floor was open, with a man perched on the sill. He tried to jump, but his foot caught the bottom of the window, sending him face-first to the ground outside with a painful thud. Everyone just watched while he moaned as a small cloud of dirt swirled around his lithe frame.

"Is he like a robber or something?" Fleet asked, confused by everyone's lack of urgency.

Dash spoke up to address his concern. "No, that's not a burglar. That's...shit. What was his name again?"

"Gary?" Lowy answered Dash's question as she called out the man's name.

"Gary! Yeah, that's Gary. Good ol' Garrison," Dash said, thanks to Lowy's help.

Gary looked up from the ground with dirt smeared across his face to see who was addressing him. He struggled and coughed as he tried to climb back to his feet, stalling as he propped his hand on the wall to catch his breath.

He gave a defeated wave to Lowy, accompanied by a weak greeting. "H-hi, Lowy. Good to see you."

"Dash, not another one," Lowy moaned in disappointment.

Dash feigned surprise at her words. "What? I got no idea what you're talking about."

Lowy shot her an annoyed glance before turning her attention back to Gary. He had slunk over to the driver's side of the hatchback that Fleet had noticed earlier.

"Gary! Do you want to come join us? We've got s'mores!" Lowy called to him.

Gary opened the door to his car and shouted back at Lowy. "No, thank you! I have some, uh, stuff to do! Good seeing you! Bye! Hope all is going well!"

Before he even finished talking, he had started the engine. He backed up, doing a seven-point turn, and peeled off in a hail of gravel. The engine sputtered as he sped around the outside of the building and out of sight.

Lowy sighed. "Dash, it might have been a little awkward, but you should have asked him to come."

"Nahh." Dash shook her head. "Didn't you just see the man struggle? No way he has the stamina to come twice in one day."

"There is a child right here!" Oreen yelled his objection, holding both hands out toward Jill. "Aren't you like her mom or something?"

Jill did not respond to any of this; her attention was settled on mastering the proper marshmallow roasting technique.

"Do I look like a mom to you?" Dash scoffed, taking another swig and finishing with a belch into the back of her hand. "Lowy, before I forget, I've got rent for the week."

Dash reached into her shirt and retrieved a wad of soggy bills.

Lowy accepted the payment, trying her best to hide a grimace. "Oh, thank you."

Dash noticed her apprehension and held up a finger. "In my defense, they were like that when I got them."

Lowy dropped the wad onto the ground and wiped her hands on her shirt. "I'll just leave them here to dry for a bit."

Dash shrugged and took another hit before letting out a hiccup as she stared into the fire with a blank expression.

Oreen leaned forward and mock-whispered to Fleet, "To think, you just drank from the same bottle as her."

Fleet licked his lips in modest disgust as Lowy chimed in to change the subject. "Does anyone know any good campfire games?"

"Lowy, honey, even Jill over there is too old for campfire games," Oreen informed her as gently as he could.

"Sounds like someone's scared of getting their ass kicked," Fleet chided.

Oreen held up a hand. "First, I would laugh at your poor attempt at peer pressure, but that would insinuate that I consider someone with the maturity level of an eight-year-old to be my peer. Second, bitch, I would wreck your ass at duck-duck-goose."

"I'm not even going to address the audacity of that last part," Fleet countered with a wave of his hand. "But an eight-year-old? I mean, I like boobs, so that's at least got to push me up to puberty age. Though, the one thing I think we can all agree on is that it doesn't matter how old you get, farts will always be funny."

"Here, here!" Dash confirmed with a hiccup.

BJ nodded, but ceased when Oreen gave him a sideways glare.

Oreen turned his attention back to Fleet and shook his head. "Typical. I had you figured out the second I saw you."

"The fuck does that mean?" Fleet leaned forward and scowled. "You don't know me."

Oreen held out a threatening finger. "No, you don't know me!"

"You don't know me!" Dash parroted for no real reason.

"You're all right!" Lowy interjected before anyone else could claim to be unknown. "We don't know each other that well, but this is the perfect time to remedy that, especially

Fleet. For his benefit, let's all go around the campfire and talk a little about ourselves, okay?"

Oreen was the first to object. "Pass."

"Ditto," Dash concurred.

"Yeah, I'm not feeling it," Fleet added, for once putting them all in agreement.

BJ and Jill remained silent, though Lowy never expected much from those two.

Lowy assaulted them for their lack of enthusiasm with a heinous insult. "All right, you bunch of sour grapes. I'll break the ice and start, then you guys can join in when you feel comfortable."

Fleet held up his hand.

Lowy pointed to him. "Oh, uh, go ahead."

"Did you just call me a 'sour grape'?"

"Yes. Yes, I did."

Fleet crossed his arms over his chest. "How dare you."

Lowy grinned before getting back on topic. "Where to start. So, I was born and raised right here in this town with—"

"Brrrrraaaantttsssss," Dash brayed, using her thumb to press an imaginary buzzer in her hand. "I love you, but you're an open book, girl. We've all heard your story."

"What sound was that?" Oreen asked.

His question went unheard as Dash continued. "If we have to talk about ourselves, let's at least make it truth or dare. That way, we can skip the boring shit and get to the fun stuff."

"That sounds like a fantastic idea," Oreen complimented before taking over. "I'll go first."

"I want to go first. It was my idea," Dash argued.

"No." Oreen wrote her off. "Fleet, right? Truth or dare?"

"I never said I was going to play," Fleet stated.

"Please, Fleet." Lowy clasped her hands together. "Once you start, I bet everyone else will want to play."

"Fine," Fleet agreed with a sigh before turning to Oreen. "I'll go with truth since I don't want to end up with some of these hot coals up my urethra."

"Smart move." Oreen leaned in and narrowed his eyes. "Tell us about yourself."

Fleet had to fight back the urge to smirk as he thought, *You got it, buddy. I put a lot of depth and nuance into my backstory. It would be a shame to waste all that hard work.*

"Okay, if I must." Fleet grunted with feigned annoyance. "But where to begin?"

"How about your job?" Lowy suggested. "I bet you do something important."

This elicited an overplayed theatrical scoff from Oreen. "What in the world makes you think that?"

"Not sure." Lowy shrugged, her enthusiasm dampened by his outburst. "I guess I just saw the black card you had earlier, Fleet. I know they just don't hand those out to anyone."

Fleet froze as if his brain had glitched out. *Holy shit, she's right. The hell is a struggling electrician doing with a credit card that has no fucking limit! What was I thinking? I haven't even been here two hours, and I've already fucked up my backstory before I could even tell it!*

"That's very perceptive of you," Fleet stammered out.

His reaction hadn't gone unnoticed to Oreen. A wicked little grin manifested on his face that complimented a mirthful chuckle. "Oh, I get it. I know exactly what he does."

Fleet's palms began to sweat. It was impossible that Oreen could know the 'real' truth, yet he still struggled to maintain a calm demeanor.

"Please, enlighten us," Fleet challenged in a cool voice.

Oreen leaned back and wagged a finger at him. "You don't do shit."

Everyone else seemed confused, none more so than Fleet.

Oreen took their silence as a prompt to explain his theory. "You're just a spoiled little brat, aren't you? I bet you have never worked a day in your life. Your parents have been footing the bill for you, buying you anything and everything you want. You probably even have a nice little trust fund set up."

Fleet's mouth fell open as Oreen continued.

"But why are you here?" Oreen asked his rhetorical question. "I'll tell you why. Living in that big house of yours must be boring. Perhaps to curb your ennui, you grabbed daddy's black card and decided to go slumming before you get cut off and have to go back, tail between your legs with a boatload of STDs."

Oreen indicated Dash with a flourish of his hand.

Instead of being offended, she stuck out her tongue, closed one eye, and pointed back at him as she wavered about on the bench.

"Case closed," Oreen declared, leaving no room for rebuttal.

Lowy turned toward Oreen and demanded, "What do you mean by 'slumming'?"

Oreen's attitude changed as he attempted to remove the foot from his mouth. "No, no. I didn't mean here, necessarily. It's just that seeing this place from the road, one might think, 'Oh, hey. That sure looks like a fun place to score some illicit substances.'"

Lowy crossed her arms and stared him down.

That's a hell of a look, Fleet thought. *So, she isn't all sunshine and lollipops. This place must mean a lot to her.*

Lowy's eyes narrowed as Oreen interlocked his fingers and tapped his thumbs together. "But once you come in and see just how wonderful and loving this place is, you realize just how wrong you were," he said. "I'm sure that's how he felt when he came here. Right?"

Oreen turned to Fleet with a pleading smile. Fleet stared daggers at his accuser, subverting the fact that in his mind he was singing Oreen's praises.

You beautiful bastard. You just gave me an amazing backstory, even if it makes me look like a douche. Based on what I just saw—and if I play this right—I might have just found my segue into asking about the murder. Okay, here goes nothing!

"You know what, Oreen? You are right. About everything." Fleet clapped his hands on his knees and stood up. "I know that I'm spoiled rotten. I do get everything I want. Know what else I get? People who pretend to be my friends, people who act like they give a shit about me just because my family has connections. Can you blame me for wanting to once in my life find something authentic?"

Fleet puffed out his chest when he noticed everyone watching him with rapt attention.

"I figured the best thing for me was to get away from it all. To just get in my car and drive. That's how I found this place. Pure impulse made me pull in here. Like you said, this motel isn't much to look at, but deep down, I knew there was something special about it."

Fleet made a theatrical sweeping motion with his hand.

"This was to be the first stop on my road to self-discovery."

Fleet turned from everyone and grimaced where no one could see.

Was that too melodramatic? Maybe I should reel it in.

He turned back around to see them staring wide-eyed, hanging on his every word.

I guess not. Time to go all in.

Fleet paced back and forth, punctuating his words with expressive gestures.

"Then I got here, and as it turns out, it's just a cheaper version of what I ran away from. If I had wanted to be accosted by hookers and random assholes, I would have just stayed in the city. Know why? Because at least there, you can find shit to do. Because despite everything else, that's this place's biggest sin: It's so god damn boring!"

Fleet grabbed the handle of whiskey from Dash and turned it up, taking several swigs before coughing into his arm.

"I'm—It's not boring!" Lowy stammered in defense. "You almost blew up earlier, remember? That's pretty exciting, right?"

Fleet slammed the bottle back onto the metal bench. "Backyard related mishaps, huh? Sounds about right. Next, you're gonna tell me about the time Mrs. Johnson's donkey bit off her husband's big toe. I'm sure the whole town talked about that for weeks; might have even had a candlelight vigil. Gonna have to do better than that, Lowy."

Fleet sat back on the bench with a thud just as Dash finished her swig and held out the bottle. He took it from her as he watched Lowy from the corner of his eye. Her hands were balled into fists and pressed deep into her upper thighs as she glared at the ground. Oreen was biting his lip as the others stared into the fire.

What seemed like an eternity of awkward silence passed before Fleet realized his acting had been for naught.

I gambled and lost. It was worth a shot.

He ran a thumb along the neck of the bottle with a sigh as he apologized. "I'm sorry. I shouldn't have said those things. I just—"

"There was a murder," Lowy blurted without looking up.

"I...I'm sorry. What did you just say?" Fleet tried to be coy, all the while thinking, *No freakin' way. Did it work?*

Lowy continued with trembling hands. "I'm the one who discovered it. When I was out jogging, I found—"

Oreen crouched down beside her, put his hand on hers, and whispered, "Shhh, Buck, it's okay. I'm here. Don't worry, we can do something else."

Did he know about it? Fleet wondered. *Did everyone here know? None of these people were brought up or even alluded to in the report.*

"Holy shit. I'm sorry you had to go through that," Fleet said, accompanied by an empathetic shake of his head. Then, a bit too over-eager, he followed with, "Where did you find it?"

"Are you serious right now?" Oreen shouted as he shot up.

Lowy unclenched her fists and wiped her sweat-drenched palms on her pants. "I'm okay. I promise."

Finding that severed hand must have had a real impact on her, Fleet thought. *What am I saying? Of course, it did. I remember how I felt my first time. But no matter what, I have to see this through. That's my job.*

Fleet cleared his throat. "Since I just went, that makes it my turn. Lowy, truth or dare?"

"Could you stop being such an insensitive twat for one second and think about someone besides yourself?" Oreen protested.

Fleet nodded, saying 'right, right' under his breath. He then looked over and addressed the large man. "BJ, was it?"

"Only if you ask nicely," Dash purred in a low voice as she put her shoulder on his.

Fleet closed his eyes and exhaled in annoyance before continuing. "Truth or dare." He did not wait for a reply. "Truth? All right. BJ, is your son always this much of a bitch?"

"First off: fuck you," Oreen answered for him. "Second: he is not my 'dad.' He is my husband."

Oreen held up his left hand and flashed a diamond ring.

Fleet's jaw dropped in disbelief as his eyes darted between the two men. "How the hell does that work?"

Oreen let out an angry scoff. "It works quite well you ignorant little—"

"Can you two please stop shouting insults at one another?" Lowy interjected.

"I'm sorry, Lowy," Oreen apologized. "I'll stop yelling."

With a smirk, he then turned to Fleet and moved his hands in an animated fashion. Fleet immediately recognized these precise gesticulations as sign language. The motions roughly translated into:

-We've been married three years, you stupid asshole. Now, go fuck yourself-

Fleet's hands danced in response with a silent insult of his own.

-I would, but your mom has me booked up for the foreseeable future-

Fleet could not help but smile at the circumstances. Sign language was one of the first things they had taught him in his training; to think that he could use it like this was beyond gratifying.

Oreen was left speechless, not so much by the childish rebuttal, but at Fleet's apparent mastery of sign language.

Sensing his next question, Fleet made up an explanation. "My grandmother was deaf. She pretty much raised me since my parents were always busy or never wanted to bother. Granted, I had to look up the swear words on my own."

Fleet savored Oreen's reaction for a moment before he continued. "So, BJ. The question I asked was inappropriate and I apologize, so let me rephrase it: is your *husband* always this much of a bitch?"

Looking dejected, BJ scratched his chest and responded, "It's hard to explain. He just sorta—"

Before he could finish, Oreen spoke up against Fleet. "You took the modicum of respect I just developed for you and crushed it like a baby bird in your greasy palm."

"Forgive me, Oreen. You're right to be disappointed," Fleet apologized, his words ripe with sarcasm. "I should never have asked a rhetorical question in a game of truth or dare. It defeats the purpose. Let me start over."

The flames crackled and licked at the air as Fleet studied the faces around the bonfire. Lowy smiled in quiet anticipation despite the distant expression on her face. Jill was enamored by the charred marshmallow that she poked with a finger. Dash took another swig from the bottle, still miffed she wasn't the center of attention. Oreen continued giving Fleet the stink eye. BJ remained pretty much the same.

"Lowy, truth or dare?"

It surprised Lowy that he had chosen her despite Oreen's prior warning, but that only made her more excited to play.

"Hmmm..." Lowy picked at her fingernails as she thought. "Dare. No one has done one of those yet."

"That a girl."

Fleet paused to build tension, but Oreen put an end to that. "You don't have to do anything he says, Lowy."

"Lowy!" Fleet raised his voice to regain her attention and drown out Oreen.

She gave him her full focus. Fleet looked deep into her eyes with an unwavering gaze, testing her resolve. Lowy's breathing became audible as she waited on Fleet's request.

Finally, he spoke.

"I dare you to show me where the murder happened."

CHAPTER FOUR

INTO THE WOODS

"YOU DON'T HAVE TO do this, Lowy. We can always turn back." Oreen had been parroting this or something similar since the group had made their way to the street, but each time Lowy reassured him she was fine.

"I'm telling you, I'm all right," she retorted, restraining her annoyance. "It's true I might not have done this on my own, but I feel safe with everyone here."

"Really?" Oreen questioned, looking back at the others.

Though the original dare had only involved Fleet and Lowy, Oreen had barged his way in. Dash had also accompanied them with neither provocation nor invitation. She meandered just behind them, occasionally taking drags from the glass handle. Jill and BJ had opted to stay by the fire; they were more enticed by the thought of the delectable s'mores than the impromptu adventure.

"This is good for her," Fleet said, trying to justify their jaunt. "She needs to face her fears, and what better way to do that than with the help of her dear friends."

"Shut it," was Oreen's response.

The four of them continued in a weighted silence, broken periodically by the sound of sloshing alcohol. Fleet looked behind him and found that he could no longer make out the hotel through the slits of the trees.

"You said you run this far every day?" he asked Lowy.

"I wouldn't say every day, but most of them," she responded. "Need to stay healthy somehow. It's also a good chance for me to clean up the road a bit."

"That's quite the public service," Fleet said.

Lowy shrugged. "I guess, but the truth is it also saves me some work. I've had a lot of cars recently show up at the motel with a flat or two after running over something around here. Plus, you'd be surprised how many people don't know how to change a tire. I've gotten pretty good at it from all the ones I've done now."

Fleet realized something. "Wait, isn't that counterintuitive to your business model? Why not feign ignorance and charge them for a night at the motel while they wait on a tow truck?"

"Because she isn't a sleazeball like some people," Oreen grumbled with a frown that showed he wanted to point fingers.

"That's not a hundred percent true," Lowy corrected with a sheepish grin. "At first I did that, but not because I wanted to cheat them or anything. I just didn't know how to fix a flat. They usually showed up so late in the day that the nearest auto shop was closed. Them staying a night until it opened the next day just made sense."

Fleet lauded her acumen by holding out his arms. "See, that's just good business."

"You'd think, but most bailed before checkout in the morning. I guess they got a hold of someone from out of town to tow them somehow. That's why I just looked it up on the internet and would fix it for them to save me the headache."

"Why didn't you charge up front or take their license like you did with me?" Fleet asked.

"Some did pay, but most people only have credit cards. I took their license, but I guess it's cheaper to just get a new one than to pay your tab. I've amassed quite the collection."

"Sounds to me like you just need to fork out for a new card reader," Fleet said.

"Do you know how expensive those things are? That's not even including the fees," Lowy countered. "Does it look like I'm made of money?"

Though he questioned her logic, Fleet nodded in agreement. "I hear that."

"Would you not do that?" Oreen interjected.

Fleet looked at him with confusion, wondering what newest offense he had inadvertently broached.

"Going 'I hear that,' or 'that's crazy'; it's rude and patronizing. It's a slap to the face that shows you have no interest in the conversation or the feelings of the one speaking. If you're going to shit out one of those canned responses, you may as well remain silent when the other person is done talking."

Fleet nodded in agreement. "Yeah, that's crazy."

"Oh my God," Oreen moaned, clenching his fists in front of him.

"If you two don't cut it out, I'm going to turn around!" Lowy scolded the two, though the grin on her face betrayed her true feelings. "Besides, we're almost there; it's just a little farther by that tree up there."

Fleet looked ahead and saw only more trees just as innocuous as the countless ones that he had passed on the drive here. "How do you know this is the place? Everything looks the same to me."

"How do you know your right hand from your left?" Lowy replied, turning to face him.

For a brief moment, Fleet was caught by the question and looked down at his hands.

Oreen laughed at him. "That's adorable. He's like a child." His tone then somehow became even more mocking as he answered for her. "It's because you see them every day."

Lowy smiled and touched the tip of her nose. "Exactly what I meant, minus the attitude."

Fleet gave a deep bow. "Forgive my brevity. I was not aware I was in the presence of Harlow: Queen of the Forest."

"Know your place, peasant, lest the trees claim another!" Lowy finished with a haughty laugh.

Annoyed to have lost the upper hand, Oreen huffed in aggravation. "Well, we're here. The dare is complete. We can go back now."

"Hold on," Fleet said, holding up his hand. "We just got here. Let's look around."

Without waiting for the others, he made his way toward the tree that just four days prior had been the scene of a diabolical slaughter—or at least a body dump.

There was about a six-foot gap from where the asphalt ended and the thicket of wood began, which was filled with a mixture of dirt, gravel, and a random assortment of plant life. With so many people around, investigating the ground wasn't feasible even though a cursory inspection didn't show anything of particular interest; not to mention that all the primary evidence had already been collected by the authorities.

The tree Lowy had spoken of was rather large and grew close to the road, the roots causing the asphalt to bow up and crack. A thick branch on the tree's side jutted horizontally from near the base before shooting straight up; it looked as if it would make a decent throne for a forest queen.

This is it. This is the place.

The 'throne' was what did it for him. It had been in the crime scene photo where it stood out like a sore thumb, though not as much as the actual thumb of the severed hand that lay just underneath it.

Fleet began walking closer to the tree. *Running this way, this tree would be in a place where she would have to either go into the woods or onto the road to get by. If she jogs this way every day like she said, there's little chance she'd have missed the severed hand. That means the killer dropped the hand the same day that she discovered it.*

Fleet congratulated himself on the logical deduction with a hidden smirk.

Just as he was about to turn around to ask Lowy for more details, something on the tree caught his attention. Almost eye level with him was a small circular hole cut deep into the bark with what appeared to be scratches leading into it.

He tilted his head and poked his finger into it.

"Why are you fingering that tree?" Oreen blurted with concern.

Fleet yanked back his finger as Dash plopped onto the tree's large chair-like limb.

"Gonna stick your woodpecker in there?" Dash joked.

"You people got a lot of growing up to do," Fleet admonished before indicating the indention. "But it's weird, don't you think? It doesn't look like a natural formation. Kind of reminds me of like an artistic depiction of a sun, or—"

Dash chuckled before blurting out, "It's a butthole! You've been fingering the tree's butthole!"

She doubled over with laughter until she choked, nearly falling from her organic armchair.

"It's not a butthole," Fleet retorted, unsure of why he was defending himself. "If anything, it's a belly button."

"Why do you think that makes it better?" Oreen lamented with a scowl.

"You're missing the point," Fleet said as he turned back toward Lowy. "We came out here to help her with—"

Fleet stopped short when he noticed Lowy had backed away from the group. They all fell silent as Lowy looked toward the ground at Fleet's feet.

"It was right there," she almost whispered, a slight tremble in her voice. "Right where you're standing."

Fleet looked downward, picking up one of his feet to examine the sole of his shoe as if he'd just stepped in something.

Fleet backed away and pointed at the spot. "This is where you found the body?" he asked, taking the extra precaution of referring to it as a 'body' and not a 'hand.'

"It wasn't a body, just a piece of one," she corrected. "All I found was a hand."

She continued with her story under no additional encouragement or coaxing, like she needed to get it out in the open.

"I was doing my daily jog when I came across it. People throw their trash out here all the time, so I just pick it up and throw it away myself. When I saw it, I just assumed someone tossed out one of those tacky plastic hands you see at Halloween."

As she recounted the events to everyone, her eyes never strayed from that inauspicious patch of dirt.

"I didn't want to carry the thing for my whole run, so I decided to just grab it on the way back. When I came around again, I went to pick it up, and..."

Lowy faltered for a second before she could continue.

"I smelled it."

She stopped there, which left her listeners casting pensive glances at one another in anticipation.

Unable to contain himself, Fleet spoke. "What did you do then?"

Lowy gave a quick start and looked up as if she had just awoken from a trance. "Well, I did what any rational person would do. I poked it with a stick."

Fleet nodded in agreement. "Of course. What did that tell you?"

He saw Oreen begin to protest but just as quickly back off; perhaps he was a victim of his own morbid curiosity.

Lowy relived the moment in vivid detail as she pantomimed the entire gruesome encounter. "I stuck the tip deep into the wrist and tried to lift it off the ground. The skin just curled over the bone like uncooked bacon. Mountains of maggots started pouring out, wriggling all over, covered in some brown liquid that—"

Lowy gagged, unable to finish her story. Oreen rushed to her side as Fleet looked down at his feet, comparing her story to what he remembered of the crime scene photos. *That's spot on. She saw it without a doubt. No wonder she's messed up.*

"Once you realized what it was, that's when you called the police?" Fleet asked.

Lowy swallowed and righted herself. "Y-yeah. I called Uncle Denvis."

"Uncle Denvis?"

"Oh, he's the sheriff," she clarified.

Fleet nodded in understanding. *I remember that name. Sheriff Denvis Callman, or something like that.*

Lowy looked back toward the motel and continued. "That was four days ago, and I've tried running twice since then. But whenever I come to this tree, I freak out and turn around. That's why I'm grateful you guys came with me today. It's helped a lot to be able to confront it like this."

"I'm proud of you." Oreen congratulated her with a comforting hug. "Maybe it was a good thing we came out here after all."

Fleet gave Oreen an approving nod, causing him to roll his eyes over Lowy's shoulder. In conjunction, Dash hopped from her seat and tripped as she took a stance in front of the tree.

"No worries, Lowy!" Dash shouted before draining the last bit of whiskey from the bottle. "I'll teach this tree not to scare you anymore!"

With those words, Dash flung the bottle at the tree, shattering the container and sending tiny shards of glass shrapnel flying everywhere. Though everyone got a share, Fleet received the brunt of it. He shielded his face just in time, but not before he felt a swift sting as a piece hit his nose. He had to force back a sigh of relief after he rubbed the affected spot and inspected his fingers to see there was no blood.

"What the hell is wrong with you!" Oreen cursed at her.

She slumped to the ground as Lowy yelled out her name. "I'm drunk," Dash chirped between hiccups.

"Dash, there's glass everywhere!" Lowy said, unable to hide her annoyance. "What if someone gets hurt?"

"That's what shoes are for," Dash countered.

"That's not the point!"

Dash waved a hand in the air, her words slurred and erratic. "Fine, you let...you me...handle it."

She crawled and wobbled around, picking at the larger pieces of glass with little success.

"This is just sad," Oreen said as he watched her struggle.

Lowy bent down and grabbed Dash's shoulders. "Stop that! You'll hurt yourself!"

Dash shrugged her off and continued her work, sweeping swaths of earth and glass into a large pile with her hands. Lowy sighed and bent down to pick up the pieces that were out of her reach.

"See!" Dash proclaimed, proud of the dirty mound that she had created. She clasped her hands together under the pile in an effort to pick it up in one fell swoop.

Once again, Lowy protested. "Stop, Dash!"

This time, Dash listened to her advice. She stopped and bent over to scrutinize her handiwork. Her face was now only inches away from the pile of debris. She slid her fingers across it and shifted away the top layer of the pile until she pulled a clump from within. Dash brought her discovery close to her nose, examining it as her body continued to sway back and forth from her inebriated state.

A panicked yell escaped Lowy's mouth. "Dash, you're bleeding!"

Sure enough, her whole right hand was covered in blood from a deep cut on her index finger. Dash unleashed a series of expletives as she studied her gushing finger. She rubbed the bloody hand on her shorts before bringing it back up to stare at her open palm. Blood flowed down her arm and dripped from her elbow when she made a fist, though she showed no sign of pain.

Dash managed to stand despite her constant undulations. "See? Dun hurt."

Something had caught Fleet's eye throughout this entire display, but he couldn't be certain what he saw.

Did she just slide something into her back pocket?

Lowy grabbed Dash's wrist and pulled it close so she could get a better view of the injury. "This cut is deep. Not to mention you've been rubbing it around in the dirt. We've got to get you home so I can clean it before you get an infection."

"Lowy, be careful! You're holding a fountain of gonorrhea!" Oreen shouted in a concerned voice.

"Oreen, this is not the time!" Lowy snapped at him. "I need one of you to help me carry her home."

Oreen pointed to Fleet. "Let him do it. I'm sure he's got all the same diseases anyway."

"I'll stay here. Someone still needs to clean up this glass," Fleet volunteered in opposition.

"Holy shit. You really do want us out of here so you can fuck that tree," Oreen retorted.

Fleet huffed at him. "Fine. I'll take her, and Oreen can clean up the glass. Looks like it's just the two of us, Lowy. All alone. In the dark. Far away from—"

"I'll get her home." Oreen moved into place. "Lowy, I'm sorry, but you need to take the bloody side since you've already been exposed."

Oreen took Dash's left arm over his shoulder with a cringe, and they lifted her up to begin the trek back to the motel.

Lowy turned and yelled to Fleet as they made their way. "We'll see you back at the motel! Don't take long!"

Fleet smiled and gave a thumbs up as the trio trudged away. He pretended to pick at the glass until they had hobbled far enough down the road, then he set to his real mission.

CHAPTER FIVE

GUMSHOE

IN ORDER FOR FLEET'S unit to be called into the field, there first had to be the possibility that a 'Tryst' may be involved. This meant that one of two guiding factors predicated their intervention: a high number of disappearances in the same geographical area, or a murder that was so brutal and malicious it raised doubts that a human could have accomplished it.

It was the latter of the two that brought him here today.

This has worked out better than expected, Fleet thought, rubbing his hands together. *I have a legit reason to get some alone time with the crime scene without looking suspicious.*

Fleet squatted and ran his hand along the ground, looking for any divots in the soil. The first and most obvious sign that a Tryst has been in the area are claw marks carved into the surroundings. With their raw power, these remnant scars can happen if the Tryst is not paying close enough attention, or perhaps is too inexperienced to control its movement.

Is this one? No, there's no way to tell now, even if it was. The report said it has already rained twice since they found the hand. Stone or wood is one thing. Dirt? This long out, it's a waste of time.

Fleet looked at the asphalt, hoping to find the telltale markings, but came up empty.

If someone was killed and eaten right here, then the Tryst didn't attack from the road. It would be almost impossible to prevent marks unless they were running like they just had their toenails painted. He chuckled to himself, unable to repress the mental image.

Fleet lay on his stomach, being extra careful to avoid the glass, and scanned the ground in what he knew would be a futile effort. He wasted little time on the search but figured he would get grilled on it later if he did not try.

No hair either. Not surprising.

Another indicator is hair that the Tryst may have left at the scene, though this was rare. Fleet had learned this the hard way when his superior handed him a bag of fur and told him to pick out every one that belonged to a Tryst. He had spent hours sifting through it like a jackass, only to be told later that there were none; 'She' liked to screw with him like that. He was later taught that for a Tryst to lose its hair it had to be ripped out, which was beyond the strength of a normal person.

There's not much to go on. Actually, there's nothing to go on besides the hand itself, but even that doesn't make sense.

He looked down to where Lowy said she had discovered the hand and shook his head.

Lowy told us she went jogging every day, taking special care to pick up any litter that she sees. It seems unreasonable that she would have missed the hand there for several days. That means it must have shown up sometime after her last outing.

Fleet got back up and dusted himself off.

But if I'm right about the time, why was it so decomposed? I'm not an expert, but there's no way it could have gotten that bad in less than a day. It had to have been dumped there after being stored somewhere else.

Fleet kicked at the dirt and walked to the opposite side of the tree.

But if it was a Tryst, why even bother with that? They could have just eaten it and gotten rid of any evidence. Why toss it here of all places? Did they know Lowy ran that route and would discover it? Was it a threat against her?

Fleet snickered and shook the thought from his head.

No way. I can't imagine anyone holding a grudge against her. She seems to have quite the fan club around here—could be that's the problem. But even if some stalker or ex did the deed, it doesn't mean that they're Tryst.

Fleet rubbed his hands together, this time speaking aloud to himself as he compiled the facts in his mind.

"If I take all that I've learned into account, everything points to this being a 'balk.'"

He'd always liked this slang term that had been a part of the departmental lexicon long before he joined the unit. A 'balk' references a case that is so far removed from the unit's purview that one's superior will balk when you ask them for additional time and resources.

Almost all his cases have been balks. In fact, over ninety-five percent of investigations come back as unrelated to Tryst activity; it looked like this time would be no different.

Well, this was all a waste of time. Can't complain, I guess. At least I'm not getting thrown to the wolves on my first solo. That would suck. So, what do I do from here?

Fleet walked back to the other side of the tree.

I still need to get my license back. Sure, I can get a new persona with no trouble, but having my picture left behind is no good. And I still need to get my stuff. Might as well stay the night and cut out early tomorrow. No reason to feign any car troubles now.

The soft crunch of a broken shard brought Fleet's attention back to the earth.

Oh yeah, I was supposed to pick up the glass.

He bent over, but stopped when he realized he had no way to carry it.

I did not think this through.

Fleet grunted as he stood up and walked onto the road to find something that he could use as a makeshift carrier. To his surprise, something white was flapping in the stiff breeze about twenty yards up the road.

He leaned forward and squinted. "Is that a shopping bag?"

He confirmed his suspicions a few minutes later as he pulled the opaque plastic bag from a low-hanging tree branch. Fleet inspected it for holes, but found it to be in good condition.

"This'll do."

He started his trek back, but stopped as a look of mild disgust crossed his face.

There's all kinds of garbage around here. The flat tires make sense now.

He had not noticed earlier, but there was a decent amount of refuse littering the roadside. Out of either respect or pity for the poor woman, Fleet picked up garbage and placed it into his plastic bag, which was a step beyond his initial chore.

He talked to himself as the time grew longer.

I've been on the road for over an hour and haven't seen a single car. How does this much crap even get here? I guess there could be so much garbage 'because' no one comes here; they don't have to worry about being caught. Or it might just be one douchebag who doesn't care and tosses it all at the same time. Or maybe...

Fleet crafted several more mental threads before having the realization that his self-imposed quandary was either too philosophical or too stupid to pursue any further.

He continued about his monotonous task of picking up the various bits of garbage. His collection included an empty bag of chips, Styrofoam cups, beer cans, a used condom, and waxy cotton swabs (they were grosser than the condom).

However, there was one piece that made him stop and inspect it. The object in his hand was some kind of trading card, at least that's what he thought. It was larger than normal with the art on the front depicting a man in tights hanging from a tree by his leg. That was the best he could make out considering the card had been torn in half down the center.

Fleet's curiosity soon waned, and he tossed the card into the bag. With his work done on the area, he gave a self-satisfied huff and walked back toward the tree to begin the laborious process of picking up all the broken glass that Dash had left for him. He was careful not to rip the bag, which held up thanks to the garbage he had collected earlier acting as a cushion.

"Never thought this is how my first solo would go," Fleet mused as he reached for a shard that was underneath some dead leaves. He brushed them aside to find that they were all connected on a branch that was impeding his search.

He gave it a yank and discovered that the branch connected to a dead sapling that had fallen from inside the thicket. Another quick tug showed that the tree was not alone. It shared the ground with at least four of its brethren, all of them dried out and crispy to the touch.

Out of simple curiosity, Fleet put down the bag and pushed through the blanket of tall grass and Queen Anne's lace to the other side.

"What the hell?" he mouthed as he stepped into a modest clearing past the foliage. While not well defined, there was without a doubt some kind of trail that led deeper into the woods. He backpedaled out of the brush with an expression of concern and confusion intermingled on his face.

"This is just a coincidence," he said, trying to convince himself.

Fleet turned toward the gnarled tree, his eyes locked on that suspicious hole he had noticed earlier. Just in case, he took out his phone and snapped a quick picture of it. He then grabbed his bag of garbage and steeled himself before hopping back into the woods.

"Okay, where do you go?" he muttered to the forest as he trudged along the makeshift path. It reminded him of an old deer trail; however, the ground was still overgrown. All around the trail, the foliage was matted and broken as if something had barreled right through it. What Fleet found most interesting was the way the smaller trees had fallen: all of them were facing toward the road, showing that whatever had made this trail must have started from the other end—right where he was now headed.

Fleet felt his muscles tense up as a foreboding sense of paranoia sank in. He walked slower, checking in all directions as he progressed.

Before long, he glimpsed something between the slits of the trees as the forest thinned. He tilted his head while he walked, as if trying to peek around an imaginary bend. His pace quickened until he burst through a small opening hidden behind a large tree into a wide-open area.

Not far from him, the campfire where everyone had once sat was now unattended as it sputtered in its final throes. BJ and Jill were nowhere to be seen; once the supply of marshmallows was exhausted, they must have lost their common ground and parted ways.

Fleet stood by the trail entrance, the wind jostling his bag as he considered this new revelation. Just a few minutes ago, he was ready to write it off and call it a day.

But a severed hand sitting right next to a hidden trail? This new discovery changed nothing based on the evidence, but that's what was eating at him—it was just too much of a coincidence to ignore.

Fleet caught himself wishing 'She' were here; he'd get no end of shit for it, but at least he would have some answers, some clarification. He realized he was pining and suppressed a deep growl as he balled his hands into fists.

I'm trying to find something that isn't there. This is my first solo case, and I'm just nervous that I'm going to screw it up. That's what this is. But I'm not. No way. This one's all me, and I'm gonna kill it.

"Like a fuckin' boss."

Fleet marched over and looked down into the dwindling fire, hoping that the heat would melt away his apprehension, yet still it pervaded, clinging to his every thought. No matter what he did, he just could not shake the feeling that something strange was going on here.

He let out a tepid sigh of defeat.

"Looks like I'm extending my stay."

<hr />

Shortly after the trio left, Dash went rag doll on them, which had made the trek back a difficult one. She continued to mumble something indecipherable, often followed by a loose spit take; the majority of which just dribbled down onto her chin.

"I don't like this, Lowy," Oreen complained over the sound of Dash's dragging feet.

"Same," she agreed, taking a second to regain her grip. "But we can't just leave her out here." She caught Oreen flinching as Dash flopped against him. "I really appreciate your help with this. I know you aren't her biggest fan."

"And you're welcome, but that isn't what I'm referring to." Oreen peered over Dash's dangling head at Lowy. "I'm talking about you and that guy."

"What do you mean?"

"Come on now," Oreen said with a sniff, insulted she pretended not to know. "I've seen the way you've been stealing glances. Laughing at his lame jokes. Trying to be all prim and proper. It's like the beginning of a bad fan fiction or a good Jane Austen novel."

Lowy scoffed. "That's not true! If this were like any of the fanfics I've written, we'd be at the butt stuff already."

"That's what I mean!" Oreen groaned as he adjusted his grip on Dash. "Have you let any nuggets like that slip out while he's been around?"

"Of course not!" Lowy balked at his accusations. "You're acting like my mind's always in the gutter. Besides, you've gotta get to know a person first to understand their sense of humor before you can say things like that. I don't want to offend him with anything too crass."

Oreen pointed at Dash with his free hand. "The man drank hooker backwash. I doubt his standards are that high."

The moment he finished speaking, Dash projectile vomited. As she started to wretch, Oreen dropped her, causing Dash to swing toward Lowy and coat her midsection in gastric fluid.

Lowy tightened her lips, closed her eyes, and stood in silence as she fought the urge to puke herself.

Oreen held up his hands in forgiveness. "That's my bad."

Lowy opened her eyes but refused to look downward. "Can we just go?"

Only nodding, Oreen took his station by Dash's side once again, and they continued onward to the motel.

Dash's 'outburst' had brought a cessation of all conversation as they continued toward the main office. With no little hardship, they wrangled Dash through the front door of the building and propped her up against the front desk so Lowy could tend to the injured finger with her first aid kit.

First, she disinfected the cut with hydrogen peroxide. Next, Lowy grabbed a butterfly bandage and tried to fit the large strip over the awkward cut as best she could. For the final step, she wrapped Dash's finger in gauze like a miniature bloated mummy.

"This is all I can do for now," Lowy stated, satisfied with her efforts. "But that cut is even worse than I thought. It needs stitches, but knowing her, she'll fight that tooth and nail."

Oreen watched the entire procedure in reverent silence, partially because he still felt a little guilty, but also out of respect for the way she took care of her patient.

Lowy returned the medical supplies to their box before asking, "Oreen, mind helping me get her to her room?"

"Of course," he responded with forced exuberance.

Roused by the treatment, Dash could now support her own weight to a degree, which made the walk to her room much less strenuous.

Lowy pushed her way in through the unlocked door toward the fold-out bed in the center of the room. They laid Dash down on the mattress, where she moaned, picked up a pillow, and put it over her own face.

Lowy smiled as she left to meet Oreen at the opening to the door. After she closed it behind her, she thanked him for his help.

"You're welcome," he said, fighting the urge to say anything about the state of Dash's room. "You know, it reminds me of the way you tended to me when I slammed my thumb in the car door."

"All I did was put some ice on it."

"I just meant how you go out of your way to help complete strangers. I think it's a good personality trait," Oreen complimented.

"You know what else is a good personality trait? Not smelling like puke," Lowy said with a laugh. "I'm going to put out the fire right quick before I go change. If I see BJ back there, I'll send him your way."

"Sounds good," Oreen said, but something was nagging at him. "I know you've had a lot going on, but have you given any more thought to what I said?"

Lowy gave him a confused look, unable to recall.

"About finding something else, remember?" Oreen reminded her. "The first aid was pretty good. Maybe something in the medical field would—"

"I really need to finish up here, Oreen," Lowy interrupted, shutting him down.

She gave Oreen a small wave and left him standing in the thoroughfare as she hurried toward the backyard, eager to finish her last chore so she could get out of her soiled clothes. With a grimace, she stretched out the bottom of her shirt to get a better view of the chunky mass that had congealed there.

This is so gross. I have to get changed before—

But her thoughts were cut short when she looked up and saw Fleet standing opposite her by the fire pit. She let go of her shirt and it flew back against her stomach with a wet slap that made her jolt.

"Fleet! Hey! How are you?" she stammered in embarrassment.

Fleet pointed toward her shirt, ignoring the greeting. "What's that?"

"This? I'm just trying out a new look." She gave a quick spin, sending small chunks flying about as she did. "What do you think?"

Fleet returned an agreeable nod and said, "I think it suits you. The bits of corn really complement your eyes."

"They say jaundice is in this year."

Fleet stifled a laugh. "Then I'd say you are red-carpet ready."

Still blushing, Lowy joined in the laughter. After the moment passed, she continued to smile as she stared down into the fire.

She didn't look away until she heard Fleet jingle the bag of broken glass and say, "I got everything I could find. Even picked up some other random crap, too."

"Thank you so much for doing that. That's one less thing I have to worry about now."

Fleet waved off her gratitude. "No problem."

She put on a grateful smile that soon faded into a frown of consternation. "How did you get back here without me seeing you?"

"I took a hidden shortcut through the woods."

He studied her as she responded, "A secret path? Where?"

Though his expression remained unchanged, Lowy felt as though his eyes were probing her. After several seconds, Fleet threw up a hand. "Come on. I'm joking. I have no idea why you didn't see me."

"Yeah, I've been busy," Lowy said, waving her hands over her shirt.

"I would say so."

Lowy gagged as the smell of vomit became more pronounced, caused by the embers of the fire baking it against her skin. "I'm gonna grab a shower real quick," Lowy said as she peeled the shirt away from her skin once again. "Can you do me another favor and put out the fire?"

Fleet nodded. "Can do."

"Thanks. The hose is on the side of the building over there." Lowy indicated the direction by nodding her head.

"Got it. Enjoy your shower."

Fleet dropped his bag on the ground as they both walked away from the fire. After a few steps, Lowy stopped and turned toward him, but he was already facing away from her. She made to speak, but hesitated as a sudden surge of anxiety bit at her throat. She lowered her head with a sigh and continued onward.

"Hey, Lowy," Fleet called out, catching her by surprise. "I'm sorry for putting you through that. I could tell how tough that was for you."

Lowy shook her head and smiled back at him. "It's fine. I'm actually feeling better about the whole situation now. I'm glad we went."

Fleet wiped at his brow and made a *phew* sound. "That's good. I'm relieved to know that—as always—I continue to be right about everything."

He gave her a playful grin as he turned to go fetch the hose.

Emboldened by their last exchange, Lowy called out to him one more time, though her voice cracked just a bit. "But you know, if you *really* want to make it up to me, you can take me out to dinner."

Fleet stopped and turned back around. "Well, I do still owe you for rent."

"What the hell? You can't do that!" Lowy yelled back. "This is supposed to be your penance for traumatizing me. You can't just lump it in with your current debt."

"Damn, you changed your tune with a quickness," Fleet said, lifting an eyebrow.

Lowy turned away in a huff. "Fine. Be that way. Guess I can just skip my bath and cleanse myself in a shower of my own tears."

Fleet couldn't help but laugh. "You lay it on thick. All right. I'll buy, but only if it's just the two of us."

Lowy couldn't believe he had accepted, but more importantly—'just the two of us'? This was now officially a date. She wanted to squeal and jump in delight, but she also didn't want to freak him out. Instead, Lowy reeled in her excitement with a tilt of her head.

"Cool."

"I'm not just saying that because I'm cheap," Fleet said. "I got a feeling Oreen will want to tag along, and I've had about enough of him for one day. Dude's got a real hate boner for me for some reason."

"We can do that, but we might have to be sneaky about it."

"That's what makes it fun, right?" Fleet said. "Now go on and do your thing. I'm starving, and I need you to pick us out a good place to eat."

"Yeah, just give me a bit," Lowy agreed as she turned away, hiding the broad smile that had just come to her face.

After she was sure he could no longer see her, Lowy skipped in delight as she pondered what she was going to wear, somehow ignoring the shirt slapping against her.

CHAPTER SIX

CHICKEN AND WAFFLES

"ALL YOU CAN EAT literally means all you can eat, right? I don't want you guys tapping out once I get on a roll," Fleet said.

"Yep," responded their distant but affable waitress.

"You heard her, right?" Fleet turned to Lowy with a serious glare.

"I did," Lowy replied, somewhat disconcerted by the intensity of his question.

"See, I'm going to hold you to that. I've got a witness," Fleet claimed, smiling at the waitress.

"Mmm-hmm," she hummed in return.

Their waitress poured them two glasses of sweet tea before retreating to the kitchen to relay their order. Fleet downed the drink in front of him and swirled the remaining ice around in the glass. "This is like drinking straight syrup."

Lowy took a meager sip from her cup. "They like to load up their sweet tea here. Sorry, I should have warned you about that."

"Nah, you miss my point. I judge a place based on their sweet tea. And looking at this, I should be in for a treat," Fleet reasoned, rubbing his hands together in anticipation.

Despite Lowy's recommendation for a fancier locale—at least the fanciest of the three restaurants available in town—Fleet had vetoed any suggestion she made when he found out that this particular greasy spoon served unlimited chicken and waffles.

As a local favorite, the entire place was packed out with hungry patrons. The waitresses buzzed about, taking and delivering orders with a level of efficiency bordering on absurd; though the one exception was their own server, who maintained the same casual saunter between tables. The lively conversations and clatter of dinnerware made it difficult to hear, so Fleet adjusted the volume of his voice in kind as he spoke.

"Do you know all these people?" he asked while looking around the restaurant.

"Kind of." Lowy peered over the crowd. "I've seen them in some fashion over the years, but I never got to know any of them beyond names. This is a small town, but I've always been kinda secluded."

Based on what Fleet had seen, Lowy wasn't kidding about the small-town part. The town proper was just a strip of road populated by local shops on either side, culminating in a brick building that served as all facets of the local government.

"Oh, I do know them." Lowy nodded toward an older couple a few tables down. "Those two over there are the parents of the guy who took me to prom in high school, but I can't remember their names to save my life."

Fleet tucked his chin in mock disbelief. "You made it to prom?"

"What's that supposed to mean?"

"Nothing at all. Just interesting."

"For your information, Joshua and I had a wonderful time that evening. What about you? How was your prom?"

Fleet nodded and gazed at the ceiling. "It was pretty cool. The hardest part was getting a date."

"For a stud like you?" Lowy joked.

Fleet shrugged. "Oh, yeah. There was this one girl I had my eye on. I had to work up the courage to ask her out for an entire week. Finally, I just said the hell with it and walked straight up to her and said, 'Mom, will you go to the prom with me?'"

Lowy choked on her drink.

Fleet chuckled. "I was the coolest kid there. I even went back to her place afterwards."

Lowy covered her face with her palm and started laughing. "Oh my God, you are so dumb."

As Fleet reveled in his own joke, their waitress came back and sat a strawberry milkshake in between them.

"I'm sorry," Lowy apologized, "but we didn't order this."

The waitress turned and pointed to a corner of the restaurant. "Courtesy of the gentleman in the booth."

They both turned and saw a man sitting in a circular cutout booth all by himself. The mysterious benefactor held aloft a milkshake of his own and gave them a slow, deliberate wink.

"Who's that?" Fleet asked.

"I'm not sure, but I feel like I've seen him somewhere before." Lowy was hit with a sudden burst of realization. "I do know him! He stayed at the motel a while back. This must be his way of thanking me for my awesome service."

"Or maybe he just thinks you're cute?"

"Well, who could blame him?" she remarked with a hint of arrogance.

Lowy picked up the milkshake and waved to the man.

"That's not for you," the waitress corrected her. "It's for him."

"Do what?" Fleet asked, raising an eyebrow.

"It's your lucky day." The waitress left them with that flat statement and sauntered off once more.

Fleet turned his head and gave the man a rather concerned nod. At this distance, he couldn't make out the man's implicit features, but it was impossible to miss the broad smile stretched across his face.

"This just got weird," Fleet said just before taking the milkshake out of Lowy's hand.

"You're going to drink that?" Lowy asked.

Fleet repositioned the straw. "I'm not one to waste a good milkshake. Besides, who could blame him, right?"

"Fine." Lowy grumbled at the quip thrown back in her face. "But why you?"

Fleet waved a hand over the front of his torso. "When you cast out the net, you never know what you're going to reel in."

Lowy just stared at him.

Fleet felt the need to elaborate. "To clarify, my smokin' hot bod is the net and—"

"I get it, you dork," Lowy interrupted, though she couldn't hide a playful grin.

"But for real, if I pass out or something from this, please make sure I get home safe," Fleet asked after a long drag on his straw. "And don't take advantage of me, either."

"I will do my best."

The front door to the restaurant jingled to signal a new arrival. Fleet cocked an eyebrow, but he did not relent from sucking his straw until it collapsed in on itself. "Did it just get real quiet all the sudden?"

Lowy looked toward the floor as she listened. Sure enough, it was as if all sound had ceased; even the shuffle of the busy staff had halted. One after another, heavy footsteps clacked on the linoleum floor. Fleet leaned out of the booth to get a better vantage, and Lowy turned around to follow suit.

The footsteps of the rebel who had broken the eerie silence belonged to a stocky man wearing a beige uniform and a black Kevlar vest. At his side hung a radio and pistol that swayed along with his every step. Pinned to his chest was a golden badge set above a small name tag that read 'D. Callman.'

Lowy popped up and wrapped the man in a hug. "Uncle Denvis!"

"Buck! I wasn't expecting to run into you here," he drawled in a gruff yet tender voice after releasing his side of the embrace. "How are you holding up?"

"I'm doing just fine." After noticing Denvis' sudden nonverbal acknowledgement of Fleet, she said, "Oh, this is Fleet. He's one of the guests staying at my motel."

The sheriff gave him a cordial grunt.

Fleet extended his hand in greeting but stopped short when Denvis asked Lowy, "You always take your guests out to eat?"

"Not really." Lowy considered his odd question before shelving it. "Come on, have a seat and we can talk."

She grabbed Denvis' wrist and pulled him toward her booth. She was surprised when he pulled away from her grasp and shuffled himself into the seat next to Fleet, forcing him up against the windowsill.

"Remember what I said about a wide net?" Fleet said as he struggled to find a comfortable position.

Lowy ignored him and cleared her throat. "Big D, I haven't heard from you in a while? How have you been?"

Denvis frowned at her. "Please don't call me that in public." He then tipped his wide-brimmed cowboy hat in apology. "But I'm real sorry about the blackout. Work's been keeping me busy, especially after the...you know." He shot Fleet a sideways look. "But that's no excuse. I should have checked in on you more."

"No worries. I know how tough your job can be," Lowy said. "But I wish you would swing by, or at least call me every now and again. It feels like you've been drifting away recently."

"I'll be better about that. I promise." He held up a hand to get the waitress' attention. When he made eye contact with her, he just shouted 'the usual' and left it at that.

Fleet managed to carve out a space and asked, "So, 'uncle,' is it? On what side?"

Without looking his way, Denvis grumbled, "Her ma's."

Fleet pursed his lips and nodded. "Neat."

What followed was an oppressive blanket of dead air as Lowy looked between the two of them before taking it upon herself to break the silence. "Since you two are in such rapt conversation, I think I will take this opportunity to visit the restroom."

As she got up, Fleet pleaded with her by shaking his head. She either did not notice or chose to ignore his plight, leaving him to be crushed by the imposing sheriff—both literally and figuratively.

"What brings you to town?" Denvis asked as Lowy slipped from view.

"Just passing through."

As Denvis talked, he maintained an ominous straight-forward glare. "How much longer you going to be here?"

"Not sure."

"I'd advise you to head on out of here soon as you can."

"Why's that?"

Denvis lowered his head. "Nothing personal, mind you. It's just that we don't care for tourists very much around here. I just wouldn't want to see anything happen to a fine young man like yourself. Understand?"

Fleet nodded to make sure the sheriff saw, despite his angle of view. "Sir, I just want to thank you for helping me cross something off my bucket list..."

The sheriff's eyes narrowed as Fleet explained.

"Ever since I saw Bonanza as a kid, I've always wanted to be threatened and run out of town by the corrupt sheriff. It's my favorite cowboy trope."

The sheriff turned to him, anger welling in his eyes.

Fleet clasped his hands together. "If you're willing, could we go for the hat trick and play some piano as you toss me through the saloon doors?"

Denvis shifted his lower body, pushing Fleet farther up against the wall. "Listen here, you little shit. I'm doing you a—"

"Wow! You guys sure look like you're having fun," Lowy interjected as she returned to her seat.

Denvis flipped back around. "A friendly argument, is all."

"About what?" she asked with an innocent tilt of her head.

Denvis' eyes widened. It was clear that he did not want Lowy to see the side of him he had just shared with Fleet.

With a smirk, Fleet decided he should come to the rescue. "We were just arguing about which macrame knot is the best. He said it was the square knot, so naturally I called him a basic bitch."

Lowy tilted her head. "You're kidding, right?"

Fleet knew his gamble had paid off when Denvis bit the inside of his lip and nodded.

"I didn't know you guys were into that," Lowy said. "I also don't know what that is."

"Sports. It's sports," Denvis grumbled, trying to regain a bit of his manhood.

Before any follow-ups could be asked, their waitress came back to the table with three plates balanced precariously on her arm. Her free hand somehow held both a canister of whipped cream and a syrup dispenser like a pro.

A delicious aroma wafted over the table, creating an unspoken truce.

The waitress dropped the containers on the table and slid a plate in front of Lowy and then the sheriff, forcing Fleet to stare at their meals as his stomach growled with discontent.

The sizable portion of crunchy, light-brown chicken bubbled and hissed, proof that it had just been pulled from the fryer. It lay on a golden pillow of waffle, sinking ever so slightly as butter oozed forth underneath like the approaching tide. Fleet ignored all pretense as he grabbed the whipped cream and waited for their waitress to deliver unto him such glory of his own.

However, his childlike glee soon faded as he watched the waitress tilt her head, give a loud honking snort, and hock an enormous wad of phlegm right into the center of the plate balanced on her arm. Fleet's smile deflated in tandem with the mucus as it ran down the sides of the fried chicken like a viscous avalanche.

My chicken... Damn, the sheriff wasn't kidding when he said they really don't like—

Fleet's thoughts stumbled as the waitress slid the last plate she held into the one already on the table, pushing the fresh one in front of him and leaving the one she had violated with the sheriff.

Fleet looked up and saw that Lowy was just as shocked by the entire display as he was; Denvis did not convey the same emotions, instead sporting a dejected grimace. The waitress gave the sheriff a condescending smile before trotting off once again. The restaurant soon filled with restrained chuckles and judgmental whispers from the other patrons at the sheriff's expense.

Fleet had many questions, but he was too dumbstruck to ask them. Thankfully, Lowy took the lead. "Uncle Denvis, what did you do?"

He gave defeated sigh. "Sometimes it's what you don't do."

With that, he stood up, grabbed his plate, and gave Lowy's hand a quick squeeze. "Think I'll take this to go. Talk to you later."

He then walked off toward the register.

After he was out of earshot, Fleet leaned forward and whispered, "What the fuck was that?"

Lowy continued to stare at Denvis' back, blinking at odd intervals before letting out a loud gasp. "I think I know!"

The spontaneous drama had caused Fleet to forget about the bounty before him. "What? Tell me!"

Lowy leaned back and scanned her hands about as if writing in some unseen playbook. "He's had a crush on our waitress for the longest time."

"The loogie lady? Seriously?"

Lowy nodded as if she had just stumbled upon the world's juiciest gossip. "Yes! I could always tell when we came here that he was sweet on her. Maybe they started dating and he did something to make her angry, so they split up. He's depressed, that's why he's been so distant. When he gets sad or upset about something, he holes up and buries himself in work."

"Poor guy." Fleet could sympathize with that. "Between you and her, it could explain why he was being such a dick."

Lowy gave him an apologetic look. "I figured he had said something crass to you. He can be a little overprotective."

"No worries." Fleet dismissed her concerns. "Nothing I can't handle."

He took a long sip from his milkshake, which made him recall his mysterious admirer. He had forgotten about the man thanks to the encounter with Denvis.

Fleet felt uncomfortable in a way he couldn't quite understand. "Lowy, you've got the better angle. What happened to the guy who gave me the milkshake? Is he still there?"

She didn't even need to check. "He's still there. The guy hasn't taken his eyes off you this entire time. It's kind of creepy."

Fleet could sense the man's gaze burning into his side; it felt like he was sitting too close to an open fire.

Figuring it best to ignore the whole thing, Fleet unwrapped his silverware and unfolded the napkin onto his lap. "Well, if nothing else, I can't say that hanging out with you isn't interesting."

Lowy's brow furrowed as she poked at her food. "I'm sorry. I didn't expect it to go down like this."

Fleet waved a finger at her. "No, no, no. If anything, I should be apologizing to *you*. I accused you of being boring. Clearly, I was in the wrong there."

Lowy shook her head. "But none of that was me."

Fleet wrinkled his nose at her. "What do you think 'boring' is? That you have to do a backflip every thirty seconds or jingle your keys to keep me entertained?"

"Well, I—" Lowy started.

Fleet cut her short to make his case. "You're never bored if you like the person you're with, and if I may be so bold: Lowy, I find you to be very pleasant company. Now let's eat because I'm starving."

With no further ceremony, Fleet sprayed an abundance of whipped cream over his plate and sectioned off the meal, taking care to get both chicken and waffle on every forkful. Lowy looked down at her plate and prodded the chicken with her utensil, an enormous smile on her face.

Fleet cleared his throat. "Hey, do you think I'd look like a goober if I asked for a cherry to put on top?"

Lowy cut into her waffle.

"Totally."

CHAPTER SEVEN

SEPARATION

THE REST OF THEIR meal had gone without incident, and to Fleet's relief, the mysterious benefactor had left before they were done without ever approaching them. Lowy was still in awe that Fleet had put away three and a half servings before he decided to throw in the towel; she had only been able to finish one with a bit left over.

"Thanks for driving, by the way," Fleet said before holding up a fist to his mouth as his cheeks inflated. "I. Am. Stuffed."

"Yeah, I think you had them sweating back there in the kitchen," Lowy said. "I thought after the third order, our waitress was going to ask us to leave."

"I gave them fair warning." Fleet then shook his head as he remembered the waitress. "I still can't believe she spit in his food. That was nuts."

"Poor Denvis," Lowy said as Fleet fiddled with the silver knob on her radio.

She drove a green 1984 Crown Vic that her father had called 'a beaut,' but it was now a dilapidated mess with cracked and faded wood panel siding. Fleet had insisted she drove because his truck was too messy—which was the truth—but he also did not want to risk a run-in with the law since he was without a license; this was now doubly true after his last encounter with 'Big D.'

Fleet continued to swivel the dials, but he was rewarded only with static. "Can you get any stations out here?"

"No, and even if it could, it would probably be gospel stuff."

Fleet flipped off the radio. "We're in that part of town, are we?"

"Big time." Lowy laughed. "In fact, my old school was next door to the church. Back then, you didn't have one without the other. We said our prayers before the pledge of allegiance, before we ate lunch, and before going home."

Fleet whistled. "One of those, huh? I'm guessing they always put that extra emphasis on 'theory' when talking about evolution?"

"Oh no, they taught it," Lowy corrected him. "But it was less a 'theory' and more a fact that Darwin was a crazy person, if not the devil himself."

Fleet winced. "Damn."

"I know, right?" Lowy said. "It was the same thing with dinosaurs. I was infatuated with them when I was a kid. I used to set up my dolls and hide in the bushes like I was a raptor waiting to ambush them."

Fleet nodded and tried to choke back his laughter. "Clever girl."

Lowy smacked his shoulder with the back of her hand. "Shut up! I'm an only child. Give me a break."

"I'm sorry, please continue," Fleet encouraged with a smile.

Not to disappoint, she said, "Anyway, you can imagine how I felt when one of my teachers told me they were a lie and that Satan put their bones in the ground to trick people into doubting God. I just remember going home and bawling my eyes out for days."

"That's terrible." Fleet's grin twisted into a sneer. "What did your parents think about all that?"

Lowy shrugged. "In truth, they weren't that religious, and they hated what they were teaching me in school."

Fleet cocked an eyebrow at her. "Then why did they let you go there?"

Lowy shook her head. "No choice. If you didn't go to church, or at least pretend like you believed those things, then you were at best a social pariah, and at worst..."

She trailed off into a heavy silence.

Fleet waited a moment before he asked, "Why didn't you all leave?"

"The motel," she answered with a weighted sigh. "My parents poured their heart and soul into it. It was their dream. They'd never abandon it."

A morbid possibility flitted through Fleet's mind, but he decided it was not his place to inquire about it.

"Well, fuck that school," Fleet cursed, shifting the conversation. "I can't believe they still let them do that kind of shit."

That seemed to garner a smile from Lowy. "Doesn't really matter since it's closed now. The state found out and threatened to pull funding if they kept it up, and that's saying a lot considering our state. The school board did not oblige and tried to take the school private, but nobody could afford that, so it closed down. A new school was built a town over, and the kids were shuffled off there."

"What about the church you mentioned?"

"Without the extra funding, it went under with the school," Lowy said. "Plus, nobody wanted to drive this far out only for the church. Everyone just found something closer."

Fleet thought about what he had just heard. "What do you mean 'this far out'?"

Lowy pointed a finger up the road. "They're not much farther this way."

Fleet found himself confused. It was a lengthy drive from Lowy's place to town, and based on his earlier drive to the motel, it was just as long as the other way to reach any sort of civilization.

"They built a school and a church all the way out here?" he asked.

"To be fair, there used to be a lot more people who lived out this way. It was a big hunting town for a while. That's how we made most of our income. People came for whatever was in season and stayed with us since we were the only place around."

Fleet had noticed that on their drive. Even if it was sparse, dappled all along the side of the road were derelict houses, a few of which might have even been businesses at some point. Nature had already reclaimed the buildings in some form or another, though their skeletons remained as a bleak reminder of what once was.

"So the school is just abandoned?" he asked.

"Yep," Lowy confirmed.

A large abandoned building in the middle of nowhere that happens to be near the scene of a murder.

Was this another coincidence?

At that moment, a memory in the back of Fleet's mind forced its way up from the darkness; a recollection often confused with a waking nightmare. Something about this shook him. A trauma that had never healed was leading him to a possibility that he could not overlook.

Lowy continued on, unaware of what was stirring in his brain. "Well, mostly abandoned, I guess. I hear teenagers like to go out there to drink beer and fool around."

Fleet turned to her. "Lowy, I think we should go there."

Lowy choked on her spit, leading into a short coughing fit that left the car shaking as she drifted off the road. She corrected the vehicle, this time keeping her eyes forward, though her knuckles were wrapped tightly on the wheel. "What do you want us to do? I'll do it, I mean, but..."

"Nostalgia," Fleet responded after a brief pause.

Lowy let out a disappointed exhale. "That's nice, but haven't you been paying attention? I don't have much nostalgia for that place."

"That's what I'm saying!" Fleet exclaimed, hoping his reasoning would sway her. "I think you need to confront your past, ya know? Just go up there and give it a big ol' FU." Fleet looked toward the road and extended both middle fingers. "Let it know you got out of there and you're better off for it. It'll be a cathartic type of thing."

"Sure, let's do it!" she responded, bouncing in her seat.

Fleet had thought his excuse was rather lame considering how quickly he had come up with it, but she seemed eager to try. Maybe she did need to get something off her chest.

Before he could congratulate her, Lowy squinted at the trees and said, "It should be coming up here soon. Is that it?"

Lowy slowed the car to a crawl as they came up on a small gap in the woods. The only indication that this was even a path was some scattered gravel and two broken posts that must have once supported a sign.

"Yep, this is it," she confirmed. "I'm glad it's not dark yet, or I'd have never found it."

The foliage scratched at the car as they bounced and shook down the untended drive. The road itself was overgrown yet clear enough to follow, though you would be hard-pressed to fit more than one vehicle on it at a time.

Fleet sat in an uneasy silence, but Lowy did not notice; she was too focused on dodging the more dubious potholes that dotted the way. Two minutes passed before the woods cleared, exposing a large open area with two buildings at the center.

The school was a large brick building with a flat roof that stood three stories tall. There was a walkway leading into another area that was only a single floor but taller than normal; based on the layout, Fleet assumed it must have been the gym. All the windows on the ground floor were boarded up, and rusty chains held the doors closed to trespassers.

Connected by a walkway, and a stone's throw from the school, was the church. Much smaller than the school, it had a slanted roof with a steeple that sat prominently on top. The white paint had long ago chipped away, and most of the windows were broken down to only a few jagged remainders of colorful glass. A paved walkway with low-centered chain railings connected the entrance of the school and the church, ensuring that no one was lost on the trek betwixt the two.

In the distance, nestled up next to the tree line behind a neglected playground, were rows and rows of cars in various degrees of disrepair. Even from afar, one could tell they had been used for target practice based on the caved windshields and bullet holes that afflicted most of them.

It's possible this could be a hideout, Fleet thought to himself. *If I were going to pick only one place, this would be it. I'll need to come back later and check it out, just in case.*

Realizing he was being self-absorbed, he remarked, "Damn, you weren't kidding about them being close."

While Fleet had been studying the layout, Lowy had leaned over and popped open the glove box without him noticing. He jumped when Lowy dropped a flashlight onto his lap.

Fleet took hold of it and asked, "What's this for?"

But there was no one there to respond; Lowy had already shut the door to the car before he could finish his question. Fleet whispered a few curses as he watched her jog up to the building. He shoved the flashlight into his pocket and exited the car after her.

"Where you going?" Fleet called out as he took off after her.

Lowy looked back at him. "Going to get me some of that catharsis, like you said."

"I think you can do that from inside the car."

Lowy ignored him as she walked around the building, forcing Fleet to quicken his pace to keep her in sight. She had stopped by the second window and was pulling at the warped plywood barricading it.

"Hold on, I don't think that's safe," Fleet cautioned.

Lowy pulled at the slab of wood like she was on a mission. "Just don't touch the rusty nails and you'll be fine."

"I mean breaking in." Fleet pulled up next to her. "This place is closed for a reason. It's structurally unsound. Probably has black mold in the walls or something."

Lowy didn't stop. "If a bunch of kids can do it, so can we."

"Hey, if you want to be like the kids, I think I see a teeter-totter back there behind the building. We could have a go at that, huh?" Fleet attempted to compromise.

Lowy stopped to give him an accusing look. "Are you scared? Didn't figure you for being such a weenie."

"I'm not a weenie, goddamn it!" Fleet yelled. "I simply have respect for people's personal property. But if being a law-abiding citizen makes me a 'weenie,' I accept the title with pride."

"That's fine," Lowy said. "But can you at least hold this board while I go in so it doesn't swing back and give me tetanus in my butt?"

Fleet was getting desperate. "Is this because I said you were boring? I already apologized for that. You don't have to prove anything to me."

Lowy closed her eyes, tilted her head back, and sighed. "I'm doing this for me, okay? I'm going in, end of story." The next words she spoke were delivered in an innocent and saccharine tone. "But if there *is* something bad in there, I sure could use a big, strong man to protect me."

"Eat shit." Fleet spat out the words, defeated.

There was nothing else for it. He couldn't drag her back to the car and make her drive home. She was dead set on going in, so he might as well accompany her—this was his fault after all. Besides, the chance of this place being dangerous was slim.

At least, he hoped.

Lowy shrugged and turned back toward the window. As she started to climb up, Fleet stopped her and said, "Okay, fine. But I'm going in first."

Lowy smiled and stepped back, holding the plywood so he could enter. The window was devoid of glass, meaning this had to be the main entry point others were using to break in.

Fleet pulled himself up and over the sill, ending with a crunch as he landed on shattered glass. He sat in silence to see if he could hear anything from the interior. Hearing no reaction to his entry, Fleet pulled out his flashlight and gave the area a once-over.

He had landed in some kind of classroom, one for small children from the looks of it. Miniature desks sat in a semicircle where abandoned toys intermingled with empty beer cans, cigarette butts, and used condoms. Laminated bubble cutouts of the alphabet reflected at him from the walls alongside a parade of labeled animals, forever frozen in their march toward a construction paper ark.

Fleet reached out the window to hold back the barricade. "Okay, come on."

Lowy followed suit and was soon brushing herself off inside the classroom.

"Well, you're in." Fleet kicked at a beer can by his foot. "Now, what was it you planned on doing?"

"I don't know," Lowy wondered aloud, flicking on her flashlight. "Figured I would vandalize the place a little. Break a few windows. Might even poop on the floor."

"Smells like someone already beat you to that," Fleet groaned, holding his nose as he walked around the room. "This is like a kindergarten class. How many grades did you have in this building?"

Lowy took the opposite direction from him. "Pre-school all the way up to middle school, and I was in every one of them. I can almost remember who taught this grade. It was Mrs. Gee-something."

Lowy's light scanned the wall until she found letters on a pin board that read 'Mrs. Goodman's Class.'

"Goodman!" she shouted. "I knew I was on the right track."

Lowy went silent as the beam from her flashlight lingered on the wall. "No way."

Fleet's light joined hers up on the board. Underneath the words 'Mrs. Goodman's Class' was a large smattering of drawings done by the students; there were so many that the cork beneath was completely obscured.

Lowy walked up to it and ran her hand over one picture before yanking it down. She held her flashlight over the doodle, studying it.

Fleet walked up and glanced over her shoulder. In her hands was a simplistic drawing featuring three stick figures: one with a triangle waist labeled 'Mom,' a taller one whose entire midsection was just a large circle with the label 'Dad,' and a small one in the middle with no midsection at all labeled 'Me.' Off to the side was a square with lines inside of it that seemed to represent a building. On top of the square was a small cross.

"I drew this," Lowy admitted, choking out the words. "I can't believe it's still here after all these years."

She rubbed the picture between her thumb and index finger, making the laminate squeak at her. Fleet heard Lowy swallow in the darkness as she continued to stare at her handiwork.

"They look just like you," Fleet joked in an attempt to lighten her mood. He relaxed a bit when he heard a soft chuckle from Lowy, so he asked, "Is that the church in the corner?"

"That's the motel," Lowy corrected. "I learned how to game the system when I realized that if you put a cross in your drawing, it was much more likely to go up on the board."

Fleet clicked his cheek at her. "Not even out of pre-school yet and already a shyster."

He saw her smile from the reflection of her drawing. She folded the paper in half and shoved it in her back pocket. "Come on, I'm not done yet."

Fleet had already resigned himself to her adventure, and thus followed her obediently into the hall. Outside the room, stalls of blue lockers lined the walls. The only gaps were filled by doors to another classroom. As they shone their lights down the hall, they saw the dust swirl and dance around the refuse left by students and faculty from long ago.

However, the one thing that stood out the most was the horrific stench; it had only grown stronger, changing from a cloying distraction to a full-on olfactory onslaught.

Lowy gagged, overtaken by the smell. "That is horrible. Let's keep moving and see if we can get away from it."

"Lead the way," Fleet replied, shaking his head as if it would ward off the odor.

Lowy pointed her light ahead. "If I remember, this way will lead back to the entrance." She turned the light the other way. "Over here is the stairwell, and if we hit the end of the hall, it should take us down to the gym."

Lowy strode downward, pointing her flashlight in each classroom as she passed, calling out their grade and homeroom teacher. Fleet followed at a close distance, a strange sense of unease clawing its way into him.

Lowy stopped at a room. "This was Mr. Spangle. He taught third grade, I think."

As they passed Mr. Spangle's class, Fleet glanced in, but walked past the room until something in his brain demanded a double take. He shot backward and held his flashlight up to the small glass window. There it was, right on the chalkboard: the exact same symbol he had seen carved on the tree. Crudely drawn with chalk, it was a large circle with lines poking into it from various angles, but always oriented to the center.

There was a connection between the two sites. But what could it mean? His palms perspired around the flashlight as he racked his brain, trying to make some logical conclusion. He threw open the door and stepped inside, scanning the room for some kind of clue.

"Another one," he said aloud, not even realizing it.

Sure enough, there was a second copy of the symbol underneath the first one.

His paranoia was getting the better of him. *Is it their crest? Are they plastering it everywhere to mark their territory? What if there are Tryst here now? Lowy. I brought her into this. Fuckfuckfuck, what am I gonna do?*

Fleet's hands shook as he continued to assess the board.

There was more.

Next to the two symbols was a large oblong shape filled with lines that stretched out across the board, culminating in chalk dust that resembled some sort of arterial spray. Was this a warning of some kind, or maybe...

Fleet drew his lips to a line as if he had eaten a spoonful of salt.

"It's a penis."

What he had considered as symbols were actually two hairy testicles. The oblong oval was the shaft with veins thrown in for good measure. Though the true instance of creativity shone in how the artist used the erasers to form ejaculate bursting forth at the end.

Fleet walked backward until he collided with a desk and sat down. He brooded in the darkness—hoping it would hide his shame—before realizing that his light was still on. Fleet smacked himself in the forehead with the butt of the flashlight several times, causing the light to flicker on and off. He wasn't bothered by the fact he had been wrong; any other time, he would have had a good laugh about it after.

It was how he reacted.

The first hint of danger and he had panicked. "I told her I wasn't ready. Just a couple more and I'd be golden."

He put his hands behind his neck and pulled down his head.

"What's wrong with me?"

He sat there in silence, contemplating his recent failure, his only companion that horrible stench.

Then it hit him.

He realized what had been making him feel so paranoid since he entered the building: it wasn't the haunting atmosphere or the looming threat of attack.

It was the smell.

With that rotting, heinous stench came parity; it dredged up those awful memories of 'that time,' something he had never been able to forget despite his best efforts.

Fleet gritted his teeth and dug his nails into his skin. *Stop. Stop. Stop. It's nothing! You're overthinking again! Some rats—a lot of rats—probably just croaked under the floorboards. I have to stop seeing shadows everywhere I look. It's not the same! It's nothing like back then!*

He breathed through his mouth, in part to calm his anxiety, but mainly to halt that smell. He sat there in silence for a time, letting himself be drawn in by the quiet.

Quiet.

Quiet?

Too quiet.

His head shot upward. "Lowy!"

There was no response.

He ran to the door and called out again.

Somewhere in the distance, he heard a rhythmic *thunk* that seemed to permeate the halls. He walked with his head to the side, trying to discern the sound's origin, which led him to double doors at the end of the hallway. He pushed on the metal bar, and it creaked open, echoing into the space beyond.

Something rammed hard into his hand, sending the flashlight clattering to the floor. Fleet hit the ground, grabbed the flashlight, and rolled to his feet as he braced himself to use the butt as a blunt object against his assailant.

The only thing that assaulted him was the sound of laughter. "What was that maneuver?"

Fleet's eyes adjusted to the ambiance of the room, where he saw Lowy staring at him with her hands on her hips. It was then that Fleet noticed a basketball rolling away at his feet.

"Don't be jealous of my sweet moves," he chuckled as he shook his stinging hand. "But why the hell did you throw a basketball at me?"

"It's called a pass, and I told you to think fast before I threw it."

"Like hell you did!"

Lowy went to retrieve the ball. "I meant to." She pushed down on it with both hands before picking it up. "It's a little flat, but still usable."

Fleet breathed a sigh of relief. He had been worried about her, but now he was just grateful that she had continued with her nostalgic tour instead of staying behind to see him freak out over a drawing of a huge dong.

They were in a large gymnasium that now doubled as a graveyard for abandoned office and exercise equipment. Off to the sides were several rows of stacked bleachers that presented themselves as a trophy case for beer bottles of all shapes and sizes. Fleet flicked off his flashlight after realizing that the gymnasium was being bathed in the soft luminescence of the cresting moon from a skylight in the roof.

Lowy had backed herself up to a large metal table with a glass top in the middle of the court, one of the few open areas on the floor. She dribbled twice before taking a shot, sending the ball passing through the naked hoop.

"Like riding a bike." Lowy did a fist pump in celebration. "Mind grabbing that for me?"

Fleet retrieved the ball from behind a dusty file cabinet. "I didn't take you for a B-baller," he said as he passed the ball back to her.

"It was my favorite thing about school. Everyone always wanted me on their team." Lowy took another shot, and while it wasn't as pretty as her last, it still found its way through the hoop after a modest bounce.

Fleet retrieved it for her but stopped mid-pass when he noticed she had moved over to a seat on the bleachers.

"This was their seat," Lowy reminisced, wiping some dust from the space next to her. "Rain or shine, they never missed a game."

Fleet couldn't help himself. "Considering this is indoors, I don't see how that's an accomplishment."

"You know what I mean!" Lowy snapped back. "We didn't play other schools or anything, but I always remember them sitting right here, cheering me on so loud that the other parents filed a complaint with the school. I was so embarrassed."

A wistful smile came to her face while her eyes explored every nook and cranny of the gymnasium, replaying memories of a time long ago.

Fleet walked to the center of the gym and sat down on the glass table, reclining back to gaze up at the stars through the skylight. "It's good to revisit the past every now and then." His voice lowered as he continued. "Just make sure you don't get stuck there."

Lowy came over and stretched out next to him to share his view up at the sky. "Such wisdom from the wayward vagabond, wrought from the many trials and tribulations of the open road," she mused, adding extra flair to her words.

"I don't know about that," Fleet said as he got back to his feet. "I think it's more like a 'those who can't do, teach' sort of thing."

Lowy propped herself up with her elbows and gave him a quizzical look.

"I'm just talking out my ass." He gave a stilted laugh as he came up with a way to change the subject. "What happened to your glasses?"

"I switched to contacts." Lowy sat up and crossed her arms. "How did you not notice until now?"

Fleet stared at the young woman awash in the pale glow of the filtered moonlight. She seemed nervous, unable to return his gaze for more than a few seconds at a time.

"What!" Lowy screamed, no longer able to endure his optical torture.

"I don't know. I guess I miss the glasses," Fleet remarked before deciding to cover all his bases. "But you look pretty either way."

Lowy looked to the wall to hide her smile as Fleet congratulated himself on the diversion.

"Well, I think that is enough fun for one evening," he decided for them both. "Are you ready to head out?"

Lowy shot up from the table. "Not yet! How about we play a game of DNA before we leave?"

"DNA?"

"Deoxyribonucleic acid." Lowy pronounced it phonetically to check for accuracy. "It's like horse, but longer and more confusing since no one knows how to spell it."

"No way in hell! That sounds like it would take hours!"

"Okay, just horse then."

"No!" Fleet's objection echoed through the building.

Lowy continued to bargain. "One shot. Winner take all."

"Can we leave afterward?"

"Yes."

"Fine," Fleet relented, tossing her the ball. "You first."

Lowy held up a finger. "Wait. What's the bet?"

"What bet?"

"The winner gets one favor from the loser that they can't turn down."

Fleet rubbed the back of his neck. "That seems pretty open-ended."

Lowy spun the ball on her finger. "That's because it is."

"What if we both make it?"

"It cancels out and we go home."

Fleet looked between her and the hoop. "I just saw you make two in a row from half court. I feel I'm at a disadvantage." As he pondered the situation, Fleet caught Lowy looking him up and down with concern. "What is it?"

"Oh, nothing," she mumbled, shaking her head. "I noticed you were slouching, which makes sense considering you have no spine."

Fleet pointed to the backboard. "Shoot the damn ball!"

Lowy abided with a grin and sent the ball sailing through the hoop once more. Fleet cursed under his breath as he walked over to retrieve the shot.

As he made his way back to her, he felt he needed to clarify something. "If somehow I don't make this, you can't use the favor to make me stay here and play more, got it?"

Lowy nodded in agreement, the anticipation getting the better of her. "Of course. Now you have to shoot from right here."

"I know how to play the damn game," he grumbled at her as he took his place.

He flipped the ball over several times in his hands as he lined up the shot. Holding his breath, he bent his knees and sent the ball sailing toward the hoop.

The basketball rebounded off the top left of the backboard, bounced off an old mahogany desk, and into a pyramid of beer cans sitting atop a folding table. Cans clattered to the ground, sending a deafening echo throughout the building. The only thing that drowned out the clamor was Lowy's laughter.

"It's too dark in here. I couldn't see the backboard," Fleet complained.

His excuse just made her laugh harder.

Fleet waited for her uproar to dissipate. "You done?"

Lowy nodded as she took a few deep breaths to steady herself.

"Fine, you win," Fleet admitted. "Now let's go."

"Wait, I still have to figure out the favor," Lowy protested.

Fleet cocked an eyebrow. "Right now?"

Lowy didn't respond; she was already deep in thought. She picked at her nails as Fleet watched a gambit of emotions play out on her face, leaving him more concerned by each shift of her expression.

She eventually let out a defeated sigh before putting on a smile and revealing her demand. "You can be my maid for a day."

Fleet gawked at her. "Your maid?"

"We can call you a janitor if it makes you feel better," Lowy compromised. "I would say butler, but that sounds too fancy for what you'll be doing."

"How did I get into this mess?" Fleet rubbed a hand down his face. "Okay, whatever. We can go now, right?"

Lowy gave a quick nod. "Sounds good. The stink in here is getting to me, anyway. Kind of smells like a wet dog rolled around on rotten crab meat."

Fleet chuckled at her observation. "Personally, I think it smells more like someone ate asparagus and peed on a dead skunk."

Lowy let out a shrill laugh before she contested, "I think mine was better."

Fleet made a resigned gesture. "I already lost to you once. Can't you let me have this?"

Lowy gave in. "Okay. Fleet, I think yours was better."

"I don't need your damn pity!" Fleet held up a finger as he started for the door. "Especially since you're going to lose the race back to the car!"

"You ass!" Lowy yelled as she followed after him.

They ended up play-fighting to see who got through the door first before sprinting down the hall. With his recent failure softened by their childish revelry and creative similes, he felt no scorn as he raced past the classroom that harbored that monstrous unit.

Chapter Eight

Helping Hand

Lowy leaned on the hood of the car, grinning at Fleet as he closed the passenger door.

"Thank you for a very interesting evening," he said.

"You're welcome," Lowy responded, her smile growing. "I had a lot of fun. I don't get out much, so this was a treat."

Fleet walked backward toward the door of room 102, bowing to her as he did so. "Glad I could be of service, but all good things must come to an end."

He fished the large keychain from his pocket and unlocked the door, but he did not enter. Instead, he turned his head toward Lowy, who was now standing beside him, arms behind her back and rocking on her feet. Fleet looked around before turning his attention back to her.

"What are you...?" he began before realization creeped into his expression. "You want it, don't you?"

"Yes!" Lowy blurted out before she stammered, "Well, I mean, if you want, I could totally...yeah, if it's cool with you? No pressure or anything."

Fleet patted his hips before turning his head toward the ceiling and shouting, "Shit! I forgot to get you your money."

Lowy backed away and croaked out, "No, it's fine. Don't worry about it."

"But that was the whole point of us going out."

"I suppose..." Lowy trailed off for a moment. "Umm, how about this: since I kind of hustled you into being my janitor, we can call it even after you do the work?"

Fleet's shoulders dropped. "Are you actually going to hold me to that?"

"A bet's a bet," she confirmed, regaining her composure.

"Fine," he said as he turned back to his door.

Lowy patted him on the shoulder. "I'll come get you tomorrow once I get everything straight. Goodnight, Fleet."

"Night," Fleet returned as he entered his room, but he stopped short when he caught sight of Lowy in his peripheral vision walking off toward the woods. "Lowy! Where are you going?"

She turned around and yelled, "I'm going to sleep!"

Fleet pointed in the direction she was heading. "Over there? I thought you lived in the motel?"

"No! I've got my own spot back here!"

"It's pitch black that way!" Fleet yelled. "Aren't you afraid of coyotes or something?"

Lowy turned back to look where she had been headed. The trail ahead was prone to early darkness thanks to the thick foliage that prevented most external light from reaching the path.

But Lowy wasn't afraid; never had been.

She had walked this path a thousand times, often in some form of darkness. Most of those trips came from when she was a child on her lonesome, off to play in the creek. In fact, she didn't even need to see at all. She had memorized the path to the point she could do it with her eyes closed, avoiding every tripping hazard along the way.

However, she saw an opportunity to take advantage of Fleet's misplaced chivalry.

"Yes," she drawled, still in the early stages of her plan. "I am terrified of coyotes…and the night."

"I can walk you down there if you want," Fleet offered out of concern, somehow forgetting that it had been her idea to break into an abandoned school in the middle of the night.

"That would be great!" Lowy thanked him, turning so he couldn't see her smile; she hadn't even had to suggest it.

Fleet ran to join her as he enabled the flashlight on his phone and held it aloft, motioning for her to continue. There was little conversation because the walk was so short, leaving Fleet looking rather silly for thinking she needed an escort.

Sitting in a clearing farther back was Lowy's place: an old mobile home that had long since given up said mobility. A satellite dish sat perched on the corner like a concave gargoyle, encircled by Christmas lights that snaked their way around the roof.

A small area next to her abode had been sectioned off by chicken wire into a quaint little garden that was thriving with tomatoes, squash, and eggplant. The metal walls of the home were washed and grunge-free, and the open area had been swept of fallen leaves and debris.

"Wow, pretty neat little spot you've got back here," Fleet said as he put away his phone.

Lowy nodded at his compliment. "My parents always kept this place for when the motel got busy and they needed to stay overnight. After I sold our old house, I just kind of made it my new home."

"Very economical," Fleet commended.

Lowy walked over toward the entrance and put her hand on the metal siding. "It's not much, but I like it."

She took the concrete steps up to the door but paused before she went inside. There was a question in the back of her mind, but she wrestled with the moral implications of whether she should ask it.

She was fighting a burning desire to jump down into his arms and wave the awkward pretext in between, yet she couldn't even muster the courage to look back at him while these thoughts swirled about within her mind.

Ask him to come in. What do I have to lose? Worst case, he will just say no, right? I mean, we aren't that close, so it isn't like it will ruin our friendship or anything. He isn't going to stay anyway, so even if it gets awkward, I won't have to deal with it for long. Then I can at least say I tried instead of wondering what could have been. I'm doing it.

Her quick flash of internal bravado was soon dulled by several pervasive factors.

Wait a second. I'm not on the pill. Does he have any protection? Hold on. If he always carries protection around with him, does it mean that he has sex with a lot of women? Is that a bad thing, or does that mean he's good at it? My God, I could use something good right now. I mean, I was already going to use 'it' tonight, but the batteries are dead, so that makes this like a necessary evil, right? Not that it's evil. Not at all. I'm not taking advantage of him. We are both in full control of our faculties, so I won't have anything to be ashamed of in the morning. I am in charge here. I am the one asking, and I can handle whatever comes next. It's decided. I can do this. Here goes.

Before she could even move, her muscles tensed as she had a dark realization.

Wait a minute? Did I leave 'it' out from last time? That's right! I got frustrated when the batteries died, and I threw it on the floor. Maybe I can rush in before he sees and hide it somewhere. Or maybe I shouldn't. He'd walk in and go, **'What's this?'** *I would be all, 'Oh my God, I'm so embarrassed.' He walks forward.* **'Lowy, I didn't realize you were such a sexual creature.'** *I look away. 'I'm no different from any other. I have these basic lustful* *urges that must be satisfied.' **'Then be rid of this mechanical imposter!'** He slaps it off the bed and pulls me in close. **'Such modern trappings cannot satisfy your desires! We must be more...primal.'***

Lowy swallowed hard and her hand gripped the metal door handle tight. Even though she realized how cringe-worthy and unrealistic the dialog was, it still led to a possibility that wasn't just mired in fantasy.

This was it.

This was her opportunity to make it happen.

There would be no withdrawal and no regrets.

Emboldened by her poorly contrived erotica, she turned and propositioned in the most seductive voice she could manage.

"Would you like to come in?"

Lowy let go of the handle as she swung around, waiting with bated breath for the confirmation she longed for. Her gaze fell on the gathered trees surrounding the clearing, their sways and brushes echoing the murmurs of an audience admonishing an actor who misspoke their lines.

Unfortunately, Lowy was unaware of just how much time she had spent embroiled in her sultry mental gymnastics. She never noticed that Fleet had departed back to his room some time ago when he took Lowy's extended silence as an awkward way of telling him to leave.

When she did not find Fleet, she continued to swing her body about in search of him. This caused her to lose balance when her foot slipped off the top step and sent her face-first into the dirt.

She rasped and struggled as the air returned to her lungs. Once she realized she was not going to die from asphyxiation, she said a silent prayer in thanks that no one had witnessed what just transpired.

There was a sharp pain in her chest as she hobbled back to her feet, cursing under her breath. Lowy staggered back up the stairs, taking deep breaths intermingled with even deeper sighs. She had decided that if she was going to sulk, it was best to do it indoors.

Fleet plopped down onto his musty bed, causing a swathe of dust particles to wash over him. The day had been far more eventful than he had planned for, and he found himself drained.

Fleet pulled the contents from his pocket and splayed them all out on the nightstand next to his bed, causing the toy car to roll dangerously close to the edge. He leaned over with a grunt and caught it before it tumbled to the floor. He lay back down and held the car above his head as he attempted to rotate that one stubborn wheel with his thumb.

A sudden rap on the door surprised him enough that he lost his grip and dropped the car onto the bridge of his nose; it turned out to be more painful than one would think. Fleet grabbed his face, and after a muted 'damn it' to ward off the pain, he sat up in bed. He waited a moment before calling out, concerned at the ferocity of the knock.

"Who's there?"

There was no response. He walked toward the door and asked again. Still nothing.

Fleet pushed the curtains aside but was greeted only by a lone support beam standing in the dim light. He heard the knock again, but this time fainter, as if the source had moved farther away. He waited another few seconds to see if it would happen again, and sure enough, it repeated, but this time he could pinpoint that it was coming from somewhere to the left.

He cracked the door open and peeked outside. Mired by shadow farther down was a figure leaning against the next door over. Fleet took a step outside and called out to them. When he received no response, he repeated it a bit more forcefully. This time, he earned some recognition as the person turned toward him.

He cursed aloud once he realized who it was.

"Drinkin' buddy! There ya are," Dash slurred, pushing the words through a wet belch. "Knew I fine you if I jess kep' on knocking."

She pushed off the door that held her upright and made her way over to Fleet. She steadied herself with her hand against the wall as she walked, creating a horizontal streak of blood as she did.

"How are you still moving?" Fleet asked, more out of amazement instead of concern. "You need to go to bed."

Dash shook her head, causing it to fall forward and increase her pace.

As she pulled closer, Fleet noticed the crimson trail she was leaving along the wall. "Shit, that's bad. I'll go get Lowy. She'll know what—"

Dash pushed him out of the way with her clean hand, cutting him off. She then used the door frame to swing her way into his room, leaving the outside looking as though someone had been abducted from next door and dragged inside.

Fleet put both hands on his head as he walked outside to study the gruesome scene. "Holy shit. What the hell are you thinking?"

He walked back into the room to admonish her further, just in time to see Dash slide her shorts down around her ankles.

"No. No, no, no. Stop right now," Fleet commanded, but Dash was already going for her shirt.

As she lifted upward, her top clung to her breasts, lifting them until they broke free, undergoing but a split second of freefall before gently colliding with each other as they bounced off her chest. But the low-effort seduction came to a quick halt when Dash tangled her arms in the shirt as she pulled it over her head.

Her playful giggling warped into exasperated grunts as she struggled against her cotton confinement. She swayed back and forth, cursing at the shirt as though offending the clothing's sensibilities would somehow make it loosen its iron grip.

She lost the battle—along with her balance—and tripped over her own feet, slamming headfirst into the wall with a heavy thwack. From there, she twisted face-down onto Fleet's bed with her legs hanging off the side.

After taking a few seconds to process the situation, Fleet asked, "Uhh, you okay?"

She didn't respond.

Fearing the worst, Fleet leaned over to check on her, keeping his distance. He gave a sigh of relief when he realized she was still breathing. His concern was now co-opted by annoyance. He kicked her shin a few times as he called her name with increasing volume at each strike.

She never broke from her slumber.

"My first day. My first god damn day," Fleet mumbled with irritation. "Get the hell up!"

Dash only groaned at him in response before her breath deepened into a coarse snore. Fleet decided it was in his best interest to just go ahead and seek help on this one. As he looked over the scene, he hoped that Lowy would believe him. It was going to be difficult to explain this one away, and the kicker was that he didn't even have to lie about what happened.

As he headed out, he stopped short and held his hands out in an exasperated fashion when he noticed Dash was bleeding through her shirt, spreading a stain of crimson onto his pillow. In the heat of the moment, he had forgotten about her injury, which was still gushing a steady stream of blood. The wound had been dribbling down her torso throughout that entire ordeal, leaving a spotty trail that ended at the shorts crumpled around her ankles.

The seat of her pants was still covered in dried blood from the incident earlier. But the thing that caught his eye was how there looked to be dirt around the right pocket. It was then that he remembered: he saw her take something as she was picking at the glass earlier.

He looked at Dash, still snoring away in her inebriated hibernation. He knelt down, fighting the urge to look at the bare ass that was now at eye level.

Please don't let anyone walk in on this, he begged the universe as he turned the pocket inside out.

An odd clump fell to the floor, accompanied by a shower of dirt.

"I knew it!" Fleet whispered in triumph as he picked up his prize.

The ball was a mixture of dirt and blood that had congealed around something oblong and metallic. Fleet scraped away at it with his thumb, squinting in wonder at what he was excavating.

"Is this...a ring?"

Fleet stood up, holding the item flat in the palm of his hand, trying to justify his diagnosis. It looked like it was a ring—at some point. Now, it seemed to resemble a slip of metal after an unfortunate encounter with a steamroller. He flipped it over with his index finger after bringing it closer to his face.

"An inscription?"

It could be some sort of writing, but without a thorough cleaning, there was no way to tell. Fleet slid the item into his pocket and turned his attention back to Dash.

"You gotta go."

Ignoring Dash's groans of dissent, he yanked her shirt back down over her chest as best he could from such an awkward position. He then attempted to pull her pants back up but gave up with a shout of 'fuck it' when he failed to get them over her buttocks.

He grabbed her by the wrists and hoisted her up to her feet. She mumbled something at him, but he cut her off.

"Thanks for stopping by and all, but I got a long day tomorrow."

Dash stumbled as Fleet pushed her outside before slamming the door and locking it shut. The gentlemanly thing would have been to at least ensure she had not cracked her head on the pavement, but he was far too focused on his recent discovery to even consider that.

He rushed to the bathroom and shoved the item under the faucet, scrubbing it clean. He shook the water from it before he studied it again, confirming his deductions: it was definitely a ring, though it had seen better days.

The ring was gold but only plated; it had been scratched enough that the copper underneath was showing through. Three small stones sat in the head, which was about twice as thick as the shank. There was a clear fracture in the band that made the ring look as if it could function as a pair of ostentatious tweezers.

Fleet bent the two halves apart to better examine the writing on the inside. Squinting in concentration, he read aloud as the letters came into focus.

"To Eddy, Mommy's Favorite."

Fleet grimaced at the writing before shaking his head.

"I don't get it."

He had been hoping against hope that this would be some sort of revelation. A magical little gewgaw that would clear up all the inconsistencies and doubts and wrap everything up in a nice little bow.

But this wasn't it. This ring only raised more questions.

A ring near a hand can't be a coincidence, right? But there's no way this could fit on that hand in this condition. Why didn't the investigators find this? Does this mean it got there after Lowy found the hand? Who the hell is Eddy? Why did Dash take it? Was it just something shiny that piqued her drunken interest, or was she trying to hide it?

"Why is this shit so fucking hard!" he cursed in frustration.

Fleet put a hand to his temple. To his chagrin, a loud banging was coming from the front door that seemed to coincide with the throbbing in his head. He looked into the mirror and found he could not return his own gaze, instead focusing on the cracks and blackened edges of the glass.

"I think I'll call it a night," he said, more as an order than a statement.

Fleet dropped the ring on the nightstand, exchanging it for the little red car before flopping back in his bed. He grimaced as he felt something wet on his ear. He pulled the bloody pillow from beneath his head and threw it against the wall.

In the silence, he realized that the banging from earlier had halted. Unfortunately, it had now been replaced with a rather unpleasant odor. Ignoring the smell, Fleet closed his eyes and let out a deep breath as he rolled the wheels of the tiny red car with his thumb.

◀▌▌▌▌▌▌▌▌▌▌▌▌▌▌▌▌▌▌▌▌▌▌▌▌▶

I've found the regrets from opportunities taken fade much quicker than those from opportunities passed.

Lowy's father had told her that once, but it never registered until now as she stood on the cusp of a realization that he was right—or at least she hoped so. With his insight as inspiration, she had persuaded herself to pay Fleet another visit. However, she didn't quite know how much her father would approve of this particular 'opportunity.'

She had taken the time after Fleet's departure to formulate a proper plan of attack before heading to his room, most of which was spent in bed with a pillow over her face as she cursed her prior inaction.

Lowy stood in front of the mirror, preening herself as she deemed necessary. She was still riding the wave of self-confidence from the night's events despite her recent miscalculation.

There was a surge of inspiration: Fleet had told her he thought glasses were cute. She removed the contacts from her eyes before slipping on her glasses to check her reflection at different angles, making sure all was in order for a right and proper seduction.

I got this. I just need to be more assertive. I thought about it too much and missed my chance. Not this time. Dash wouldn't let him get away like that. I have to think more like her. The second he opens the door, I'm just going to jump him. No words, only action. Hot, sweaty action.

Lowy pushed open the door with exuberance. Though her heart was pounding at the thought of what she was about to attempt, she broke into a modest skip as she made her way down the trail to the motel.

"I'll make you proud, Dad!"

Lowy was so overcome by this new personal breakthrough that it took her a moment to realize what she had just said. She stopped dead in her tracks and winced as she looked up toward the stars in the night sky.

"Mom. Dad. Maybe you could stop watching over me just for a bit? Or at least, you know, cover your eyes or something until morning—maybe noon."

It almost seemed like the stars were twinkling in response to her request; she wasn't sure if this was good or bad. Regardless of what it meant, she continued onward with renewed vigor, as if the result was a forgone conclusion.

Her pace slowed the closer she got to the building, but her feet never ceased their march—a victory in itself. She stopped at the trail's entrance, took a deep inhale, held her hands in front of her chest, and then let them fall as she exhaled.

She was ready.

As she reached the building proper, she heard a loud rapping coming from the front. Catching herself, she clung to the wall and peeked around the corner. She could just make out the silhouette of a person in the darkness as they slammed their fist against one of the apartment doors.

The shadowy figure turned in her direction as if they were aware of her presence.

Lowy ducked back behind the building, pushed by a wave of her own anxiety. She stood there, pressed flat against the brick, afraid to take even a tiny breath.

She choked when she heard a voice call out from around the corner. Inches felt like miles as she leaned back around like a shy child peeking from behind her mother's skirt. The tension faded when she realized it was Dash. She could tell because the figure had moved into the dim light that illuminated the front of Fleet's door.

Fleet's door! Lowy screamed internally.

Lowy leaned a bit too far and fell forward onto the walkway, but she went unnoticed. She could hear someone talking; it had to be Fleet, but his voice was cut short as Dash forced her way into the room.

She stole my move.

For the second time that night, she felt her heart drop, and this time it was so heavy that it brought the rest of her with it. Lowy's feet slid from under her, catching her shirt on the porous brick to expose her midriff as she huddled on the ground. She put her chin on her knees and gazed off into the distance, refusing to look into the night sky.

Of course he would. Who can blame him? I mean, even I was trying to be like her when I came out here. So why settle for an imitation when you can have the real thing?

She took off her glasses and let out a crackling sigh.

I'm not sure what I expected. It's just…

She spoke the last part aloud.

"I wanted something different."

Lowy sat there alone in the dark with the chilly night air biting into her bare stomach, but she couldn't bring herself to move. Several minutes of this passed until she was startled by a loud noise that caused her to drop her glasses. She picked them up and affixed them back to her face as she peeked around the corner.

There was Dash with one of her breasts hanging free and pants halfway down her ass, cursing toward Fleet's room at the top of her lungs as she slammed a fist into the door. Lowy strained to hear what she was saying, but before she could make out any words, she heard the one sound that mattered.

"Blerraghpfft!"

Vomit shot from Dash's mouth like water from an unclogged hose.

Damn it, Dash! Not again!

Lowy's anger swiveled to confusion as she continued to watch. Dash began beating on the door like she meant to chop it in half. Her every hit was filled with unrestrained anger and malice as she cursed the man inside with slurred insults. Dash then collapsed into a heap right in front of the door and began to sob.

What the hell happened in there? Is she all right? I should go help her, but what if Fleet hears me? Will he think I was over here spying on them the whole time like some kind of creeper? Maybe he'll just think it alarmed me because it was so loud and—

Guilt soon overcame her self-preserving thoughts as she watched Dash shed tears in a pool of her own vomit. Lowy sighed and made her way over, knowing full well she was going to be taking care of her once again this night.

"Dash, are you—"

Lowy couldn't even finish her sentence before she started to dry-heave from the smell. She stepped off the walkway into the gravel parking lot to regain her composure. A few deep breaths and several spit takes later, she returned to Dash's side. Dash had calmed down somewhat, or at least enough that she was open to suggestions.

Lowy put a hand on her shoulder. "Come on. We're going to bed."

Dash turned to meet her gaze, but found it a struggle as her upper body undulated like an unmanned firehose. She was half naked and covered in her own sick, a fine complement to the injury on her finger which was still bleeding like a leaky faucet. Dash put her bloody hand down to stabilize herself and push up onto her knees. This just led to her falling onto her back and hitting her head on the concrete.

Dash moaned, though she did not act as if she felt anything.

Lowy let out an exasperated sigh. "You have to get up. I'm not going to drag you there."

It seemed Dash only heard the last few words of what Lowy said when she raised her arms up into the air like a cursed mummy rising from its sarcophagus.

"I said no!" Lowy yelled through her teeth.

Dash let out a high-pitched moan.

"Fucking hell!" Lowy growled as she ran her hands down her face.

Cursing herself, she grabbed Dash's outstretched arms and hauled her like a cadaver. The process was slow since Lowy was carrying dead weight, but Dash didn't seem to mind being scraped along the concrete. They reached Dash's room, which was on the ground floor two down from Fleet's.

Lowy dropped one of Dash's arms so that she could try the knob. The door wasn't locked, saving her a trip to grab the key. With a strained grunt, Lowy dragged Dash's body over the threshold and through a layer of garbage into the bathroom. She removed Dash's shirt and dropped it on the tile with a soggy thunk before washing her hands.

As she dried herself with a crumpled towel from the ground, Lowy looked down at Dash's bloody bandage. "Guess I need to grab the first aid kit—again."

Lowy set off to her trailer to fetch the key for the main office where the kit was stored. After retrieving it, she made her way back to Dash, who had yet to move an inch from where Lowy had left her.

"I think I had used this kit maybe twice before you got here," Lowy said. "From now on, I might just leave it in your room for easy access."

Dash seemed to consent by lifting her arm in the air briefly before letting it slap back down to the tile.

Lowy wet a washcloth and cleaned the wound before redressing it. She then wiped down the other areas that were covered in bodily fluids. As the washcloth made it to Dash's cheek, her pace slowed as Lowy studied the pained expression on her friend's face.

What happened in there? Did he try to force himself on her? It doesn't seem likely from what I know about her. If that was the case, I should be more worried that Fleet's lying dead in that room. Could he have wanted her to do something so depraved that even she couldn't handle it? That might be the other way around, honestly. Do I bring this up with them tomorrow, or should I just mind my own business?

Lowy heard a gurgling sound coming from Dash down on the floor. Lost in thought, Lowy had stopped washing Dash's face but still had the wet washcloth pressed over her mouth and nose akin to a mild form of waterboarding. Even with the unintentional torture, Dash made no actual effort to escape.

"Oh my God! Dash, I'm so sorry!"

Dash's words were weak, bordering on unintelligible. "I can't take this anymore..."

"It was an accident, I swear!"

Dash's face held an expression of pure anguish as tears rolled down her cheeks. "I'm so tired. I can't..."

"I know, I know." Lowy consoled her with a sympathetic frown. "Let's get you to bed."

She finished cleaning all the blood and vomit from Dash and made one last desperate attempt to get her to stand of her own accord.

It failed, of course.

And so, she dragged Dash across the floor—hopefully for the final time this evening—to the side of her bed. After clearing off a spot on the mattress, Lowy heaved the top half of Dash's body up onto the bed. Then she braced her back against Dash to keep her from falling off so she could reach down to grab her legs.

It was then, in the periphery of her vision, that she caught sight of a figure standing in the corner of the room, shrouded in darkness.

Lowy screamed and backed away, dropping her burden in the process. Dash flipped off the bed and slammed headfirst into the nightstand. The figure remained prone; they made no reaction to her outburst. Lowy retreated toward the wall, never taking her eyes off of this unknown intruder until they stepped forward, exposing themselves to the light coming from the bathroom.

"Jill!" Lowy gave her fear a moment to dissipate. "What are you doing just standing in the dark?"

Jill did not respond as Dash groaned and shifted about on the floor. Lowy was used to being ignored by Jill, so she didn't take offense at her silence as she resumed trying to get her inebriated friend back onto the bed.

Repeating the process from earlier, she was able to flip Dash onto the mattress. She pulled back the dingy sheets and set them over Dash, who clutched them to her chest as she curled into a fetal position. Lowy backed away and stretched out her back, her job now completed.

In the interim, Jill had made her way to the bed and was looking Dash over. She pulled back the sheets and placed the tips of her fingers on Dash's bandaged hand. Sensing what Jill must be thinking, Lowy spoke up.

"She hurt herself earlier on a piece of glass and I bandaged her up. I think she should be good for tonight, but the cut's deep. She'll need new wraps in the morning, so make sure she comes my way first thing."

Jill sat down on the bed and stroked Dash's hair; every motion she made was tender and caring. Dash cooed like a baby as her body relaxed, sinking into the mattress.

"Well, if you have this taken care of, I'm going to get some sleep," Lowy said, fatigue now catching up with her. "Just try to get her to drink some water if she wakes up, and make sure she doesn't pick at the bandage, okay?"

Lowy turned off the bathroom light and made toward the door, but stopped when she heard Jill speak. The words were so fragile, as if Lowy's own breath might cause them to scatter about the room, yet they reached her all the same.

"Thank you."

CHAPTER NINE

B-BALL

A SMALL SLIVER OF light intruded through the drawn curtains and struck Fleet across his face, stirring him from his empty slumber. He wiped the sleep from his eyes as he went to check the time on his phone and discovered that it had died during the night. Not only did he forget to charge it, but he must have forgotten to turn off the flashlight feature, draining the battery.

He splashed some water on his face and dried himself on the scratchy hand towel he had been provided. As he was wiping his hands, he noticed that the bandage on his finger had fallen off into the sink.

The cuts had healed, leaving only a near imperceptible scar. The wound hadn't been that large in the first place; Lowy had probably already forgotten about it. He tossed the bandage into the garbage and went to grab his toothbrush.

It was then that he realized he had neglected to pack any sort of toiletries. He blew into his hand and gave it a quick sniff test, followed by a grimace. He gurgled water and hoped for the best, not that he had a choice.

After getting dressed, he picked up the ring he had confiscated from Dash last night. Pondering the thing had caused him a restless sleep, but it led him to the conclusion that he should ask Lowy about it. He would just say he found it while cleaning the site yesterday and wanted her opinion on the matter under the guise of returning it to its owner. Perhaps he could get some information about this 'Eddy' guy from Lowy's guest register, though he seriously doubted it.

As ready as he could be, he stepped out and locked the door behind him before heading toward his truck. His stomach growled as the sweet smell of bacon wafted by him on a gust of wind, mercifully overwhelming the stench emanating from the vomit Dash had left the night before. He shifted direction to the only place it could be coming from.

Fleet put his weight into the screen door of the main office, and it stubbornly swung inward with a metallic moan. The door to the back room was open and from it he could hear the alluring sound of sizzling bacon as it beckoned him like a greasy siren's aria.

Alerted by the sound, Lowy peeked her head around the door and smiled. "Hey! You can come on back!"

It turned out that the office contained a kitchen area with the barest of necessities: a range, a rack filled with assorted cookware, an industrial sink, and other various sundries all packed into a small area with minimal space between them.

"Is this my payoff from you trying to immolate me yesterday?" Fleet asked as he squeezed his way in.

"I had forgotten all about that," Lowy admitted.

"You have a very selective memory," Fleet said. "Then what's the occasion?"

Lowy waved a spatula in front of her. "Maybe I'm just trying to class up the joint. You know, add in some additional services that will take this place from a measly four-star motel up to a five-star luxury resort."

Fleet made to quip, but Lowy interrupted him.

"And before you say anything snarky, just know that how you answer will affect whether you get any breakfast."

Fleet did not hesitate. "Only five stars? A fine establishment like this must be in the double digits. They need to rethink their scale."

"Damn straight," Lowy agreed with a shake of her spatula. "So, how much do you want?"

"How much are you making?" Fleet asked, eyeing what she had laid out.

"I plan on at least one carton of eggs, some pancakes, and one package of bacon."

Fleet nodded. "That sounds like it should be enough for me."

"Don't be greedy," Lowy admonished as she prodded the contents of the pan. "With the new guest, I'm worried I won't have enough as is."

"Guest? Do you have someone else who isn't just paying by the hour?"

"I don't care for what you are insinuating, sir." Lowy scooped out some bacon and placed it on a paper towel lined plate. "And yes, he is paying for at least a night. He's out back with everyone else. See what he wants, would you?"

Fleet gave a small salute. "Yes, sir."

Lowy returned the salute with the spatula and slung bacon grease across the kitchen. Fleet stepped out the back door as she apologized to him for the unintended assault.

Outside, there was a tiny patio filled with a random assortment of aluminum furniture where Oreen and BJ had taken a seat. The one-sided conversation between them ended once Oreen realized who had come through the door.

Oreen shot Fleet a dirty but placid glance from the small table where he sat. BJ just offered a friendly nod.

Fleet gave his words a healthy dose of enthusiasm. "Good morning, gentlemen!"

"Morning," BJ responded.

"Hello," Oreen returned, his greeting laced with just a hint of contempt.

"Where's the new guy at?" Fleet asked.

Oreen ignored him, but BJ motioned toward the corner of the building. Fleet nodded his thanks and followed BJ's direction. Just as he rounded the corner, a pair of arms wrapped around Fleet, causing him to curse in surprise.

"Freddy!" the man shouted in his ear.

Fleet recognized him, but that didn't dull his initial shock.

"Scri-Curtis!" Fleet shouted, catching himself before he used Scriptor's real name. "What are you doing here?"

"I've told you a thousand times, brother," Curtis responded as he released his grip. "You can't run from me."

"A brother?" Oreen questioned, making the assumption based on Curtis' greeting. "Are you shitting me? There's more of you?"

Running with it, Curtis put his arm around Fleet's shoulder and responded, "That's right."

Oreen's eyes bounced between the two. "Is this a joke? You look nothing alike."

"Well, I keep asking our parents if he's adopted, but they just won't ever fess up." Curtis laughed and slapped Fleet on the back, much to his annoyance.

"We're...stepbrothers," Fleet clarified, now forced to play along with his game.

Just then, Lowy poked her head out of the door. "Fleet, did you...oh hey!" She noticed their one-sided embrace. "Do you guys know each other?"

"Go on..." Curtis urged Fleet.

"Yeah. This is my brother."

"No way!" Lowy yelled as she compared the two.

"Eeeyup," Fleet drawled in a despondent tone. "Stepbrother, anyway."

"That's awesome!" Lowy shouted. "Curtis, right? You said you were looking for someone, but I would have never guessed it was Fleet."

"Someone has to take care of this little guy," Curtis said as he gave Fleet's shoulder another squeeze. "Speaking of which, let me ask you something, Freddy. Did you perhaps forget something before you struck out on your own?"

"No," Fleet responded in a flat tone.

"Is that true?" Curtis hummed in a condescending tone. "You sure as hell forgot your toothbrush, cause your breath is pretty funky right now."

Fleet pushed Curtis away, though he avoided opening his mouth, now self-conscious of any possible halitosis.

"I had just assumed that was the norm," Oreen contributed.

"I didn't want to say anything," Lowy interjected, "but I'm sure after you eat breakfast it will get better."

Fleet just stared at her with a look of betrayal.

"And if he left his toothbrush, then he probably left his deodorant too," Curtis continued. "And that shit is prescription. There's gonna be hell to pay if he doesn't get that smeared on soon."

Curtis jumped away in defense when Fleet lunged for him, causing the metal furniture to clang as he backed into it.

"All right, let's stop picking on 'Freddy' before you hurt his feelings," Lowy chimed in.

Fleet sent her a death stare, but Lowy changed the subject by getting Curtis' attention. "I never got what you wanted for breakfast. I have bacon and eggs and pancakes and...that's it."

"I'll take three helpings of everything to start," Curtis replied.

"Are you sure you two aren't blood-related?" Lowy asked with a grin.

At the sound of shuffling rocks, they all turned to see Dash hobbling toward them. Without a word, she grabbed the metal chair next to BJ and Oreen. The legs scraped against the ground with a grating rumble as she slid her body into it. Once situated, she groaned and dropped her head on the table, spilling a glass of water from the impact.

"Could you sit somewhere else?" Oreen asked. "You smell like death."

"Sure," she responded. Dash then grabbed Oreen's left hand and asked, "But could you help me up? I'm kind of struggling right now."

"I'll save us both the trouble and move myself," Oreen said as he jerked his hand out of her grasp. "Now I have to find some sanitizer before my fingers rot off."

As Oreen made his way into the kitchen, Dash remarked, "That's just plain rude. I don't stink that bad, do I?"

BJ wrinkled his nose and hopped his chair back.

"Did you not shower after all that? And what about your wound?" Lowy asked as she walked over to Dash and took her wrist.

The bandages she had put on her earlier were once again stained with blood, and it looked to be spreading.

Lowy exhaled in annoyance. "Come on, we need to get you cleaned up. Fleet, you too."

"Why me?" Fleet asked.

"You hurt yourself, remember? I need to make sure it's okay."

Crap, Fleet cursed to himself. He was sure she would have forgotten about something so innocuous. He held up his hand and flipped it around for her benefit. "Oh, that? It's all better, nothing to worry about."

He dropped it to his side as Lowy leaned in to get a better look.

"I'm hungry!" Dash blurted.

"Not until I look at your hand!" Lowy yelled back, her attention now on Dash to Fleet's relief.

"Food. Now," Dash countered.

"If we don't clean it, you're going to get infected."

"Food!"

Lowy surrendered and dropped Dash's hand. "Fine!"

"How the hell are you even moving right now?" Fleet asked Dash after Lowy was inside.

She propped herself up on her elbow and pointed a finger toward him. "Do I know you?"

Just then, a loud outburst caused them all save Dash to turn toward the kitchen. "That bitch took my ring!"

"Whoops," Dash giggled through a snarky half smile. She raised her hand over the table and dropped Oreen's ring onto the surface with a soft *tink*.

"On that note, I'm going to have a little chat with my brother," Fleet said, hoping to avoid the backlash that was soon to follow.

Curtis gave them all a small bow before turning to follow Fleet across the gravel lot. Fleet waited until they were out of earshot before he railed at his 'brother.'

"What the hell are you thinking? You're breaking every protocol by being here." Fleet's expression hardened. "Did she send you to check up on me?"

"No, she didn't," Curtis answered before giving Fleet a stern frown of his own. "And if anyone is breaking protocol here, it's you. Like I said earlier, didn't you forget something?"

Fleet's gaze softened, and he considered the question. He then closed his eyes and moaned, "I forgot to report in."

"Forgot to report in," Curtis repeated. "Protocol demands that I come in to investigate your whereabouts and report it to next in command. And since protocol is so important to you..." Curtis pulled out his phone and pecked at the screen.

Once again, Curtis was right. On field missions, it was mandatory for them to check in at the end of every day, if not more; not only to relay information, but to let others know they were still alive. Phone calls are best, of course, but even a basic text message would work as well.

Though Fleet attempted to concoct one, he had no excuse. He put two fingers on Curtis' phone and gently pushed it down. "Ya know, I think we can let it slide this one time."

"Going against protocol? You're a rebel; a true wild man," Curtis mocked.

"Yeah, that's me," Fleet said with a subdued sigh. "But you should have called first. You could have blown my cover."

Curtis raised an eyebrow. "The electrician thing? Far be it from me to do anything to disrupt that riveting and well-thought-out narrative. Though in my defense, I tried to call, but there is zero service out here."

"Exactly! I'm in the same boat," Fleet said as the excuse presented itself on a silver platter. "There's no way I could have gotten in touch since my phone won't work."

"I gave you a satellite phone!" Curtis countered. "It can make calls from fucking anywhere, for literally this exact situation."

Fleet rubbed the back of his neck as a vivid mental image of a blocky phone sitting on the counter at his house popped into his head. "I might have forgotten to pack that when I left."

"No shit." Curtis flicked the corner of his phone as he walked backward. "Which brings us to the present. Since I'm here now, I might as well get all the details on your first day. Let's head over there."

Curtis walked over to the edge of the dense thicket where an old basketball hoop stood. Its net had long rotted off the rusty rim, and moss hung just low enough to cover much of the backboard.

In the tall grass nearby, Curtis found a cracked and worn basketball. He gave it a few test dribbles—each one coming up shorter than the last—before taking a shot. The ball made a loud smack as it slapped the plastic and flopped into the hole. Fleet walked over to retrieve it as the ball sloshed onto the grass.

"Come on," Curtis said. "Let's hear it."

Fleet picked up the ball and juggled it back and forth in his hands as he tried to process the best way to relay everything he had encountered thus far. Though he wouldn't admit it, he was glad Curtis had shown up; it would help to bounce ideas off him. Fleet had always found Curtis to be intelligent and logical, thinking five steps ahead and finding patterns where he was at a loss.

This duality between the two was one reason Fleet had picked him as a partner, the lack of potential candidates notwithstanding. To simplify it, Curtis was the brain and Fleet was the muscle. But it had been good fortune that their personalities were similar, allowing their working relationship to coincide with a deep friendship that had formed over the years.

Fleet balanced the basketball in his hand as he talked. "Okay, so I've checked out the area. I've seen where the body part was found, and I've got first-hand testimony—pun intended—from Lowy, who was the one that discovered said hand."

Curtis nodded. "Not bad for one day. So, what do you think overall?"

Fleet tried to steady the ball on one finger. "I don't have anything concrete, but there's been some weird shit, that's for sure." Curtis gave him a concerned look that encouraged Fleet to continue. "At the scene, there is this weird carving on the tree, right in its skin."

"Skin?"

"Yeah, the...the tree skin."

"Tree skin? You mean bark."

"Yeah, if you want to get all technical," Fleet said.

Curtis closed his eyes and groaned.

Fleet doodled the mark he'd found there in the air with his free hand. "Looks kind of like this. Sounds dumb, but it reminds me of like a sun, or a..."

Dash's comparison rang in his mind, and it slipped from his lips before he could stop himself.

"...a butthole."

Curtis' eyes narrowed. "A butthole?"

"It's hard to explain." Fleet patted his pocket. "If my phone wasn't dead, I'd show you a picture."

Curtis held out a hand. "Cool. But for now, let's just chalk the tree butthole up to nature doing nature shit. What else you got?"

Fleet held out his arm flat. "So get this: there's a trail in the woods."

"Amazing. I've never heard of such a thing. Go on."

"Shut up. Anyway, it goes straight from the scene right back over there behind the motel. You might even be able to see the entrance from here."

Fleet pointed behind the building, and Curtis leaned to follow his direction. Curtis looked as if he was considering this one, causing Fleet to crack a wisp of a smile.

"You're checking everything. That's good. That's what you should do," Curtis complimented. "Then onto the next question: did you find any sign that someone had used the trail close to the time of discovery?"

"Not really," Fleet admitted. "In fact, I kind of already figured out that no one had used that trail in a while."

Curtis nodded. "Nice. But for future reference, if you have already concluded that something is irrelevant, you don't have to run it by me. Trust your own judgment."

"Duly noted. But I've been saving the best for last." Fleet reached into his pocket and took out the broken ring. "This was buried underneath where the hand was found."

That was the truth—though he omitted *how* he got it. He just decided it was best to keep last night's events to himself and off the record.

Curtis was straining to see the bauble, so Fleet tossed it to him. He snatched it from the air and examined it. "What are you saying this is, exactly?"

"Clearly, it's a finger bracelet."

"Please stop that," Curtis moaned.

"Fine, it's a ring." Fleet noticed Curtis' combative attitude. "What's up your butt?"

Ignoring the question, Curtis picked at the bit of metal for a few more seconds. "Okay, so it's a ring; a messed up one, anyway. What's this got to do with anything?"

Fleet was getting annoyed; how could he not get this? Fleet used his hands as props while he gestured in frustration. "It's a ring next to a severed hand."

"Hey, look over there." Curtis pointed as he repeated the same gestures in mockery. "There's a tree next to a forest. Who gives a shit?"

Fleet held out his arms in defeat, unable to understand where this was leading.

Curtis balled his fist in anger. "Just because two things have some vague relation, doesn't mean they *are* related. Remember the report?"

Fleet squinted at him in confusion, trying to figure out where he was going with this.

Curtis held up the ring and pointed at it. "You saw the inscription, right? 'To Eddy, Mommy's Favorite.'"

He stopped talking as if that should have been the end of the conversation. When Fleet did not speak up, Curtis bopped himself on the side of the head with his fists.

"You don't remember. I watched you read the autopsy report. How the hell could you forget?"

Fleet was feeling anxious, like he had missed something important.

Curtis enlightened him of his failure. "The hand was identified as belonging to a female. There is no way this ring came from that hand."

Fleet went on the defensive. "You don't know that for sure. Maybe her name was Edna. Eddy is just her nickname."

Curtis nodded in aggravation. "Sure. Now let's say you're right and leave the inscription part out of it. What you are now saying is that the killer, or whoever left the hand there, went, 'Hey, I know! What if I took off this ring, ran over it about twenty times in a semi, then buried it underneath this hand because I get sexual gratification from pointless nonsense.'"

He had made a damn good point.

Fleet exhaled in defeat. "Shit."

Curtis let out a guilty sigh and explained himself. "Look, I would be right there with you if the hand had been crushed or run over or something. But it wasn't. It was cleanly severed and left out there with no other damage and no other physical evidence, remember?"

"Yeah," Fleet agreed in a subdued voice.

Curtis stepped forward and held out the broken ring until Fleet took it in exchange for the basketball. Fleet gave the ring a dejected once-over before tossing the meaningless bauble into the grass.

With the flick of a wrist, Curtis had the ball spinning on the tip of his finger. "I know this is your first solo case, and you want to do it right, but don't go getting a hero complex on me. You just need to think through things a bit more. I know you can do it, and I know you have the potential to be a great 'Servunday.' One of the best. Maybe even as good as 'Her.'"

Fleet gave him a passive glance as Curtis passed the ball back.

"Well, maybe not on her level, but at least in the same general area. After all, you got all the time in the world to get there. No rush."

Fleet chuckled and tucked the ball in his armpit. "That's true."

Curtis walked to his side and put an arm around his shoulder. "So, 'Servunday Hangman,' now that we've sifted through the evidence, what are your thoughts on this whole thing?"

Fleet exhaled and shook his head. "After going over the evidence on my own, and with no help or input from anyone else." He fell quiet and feigned a ponderous expression. "I have to lean toward this case being a 'balk.'"

Curtis nodded in agreement. "Yeah, man. I mean, if it happens, it happens. But that's a good thing. Less work for us."

Curtis backed away as he motioned for the ball, and Fleet passed it to him. He caught it, spun the ball in his palm, and took his shot. He let his arms hang in the air as he mouthed 'boom' when the ball sailed straight through the hoop.

Fleet kicked the cracked rubber ball up after it came to a stop and slapped it together between his hands, causing it to pancake. "But someone still died out there."

Curtis slumped. "Come on, man."

"I know, I know, it's just—"

Curtis walked forward and yanked the ball from Fleet and stated in an unwavering tone, "It's not our problem."

"But what if I leave here and something happens to..." Fleet waved a hand toward the motel. "Someone else."

"It doesn't matter. If it doesn't involve Tryst, we don't fool with it."

Fleet made to argue again, but he was cut short by an exasperated Curtis.

"Everyone here could be murdered by an ax-wielding maniac, and that is not our problem. They could all be ripped to shreds right now by a rabid chipmunk—which once again—would not be our problem. Hell, know what? That sweet girl in there making us breakfast could be a serial killer. It was her the whole time. Been chopping up folks for years. Got a jar of pickled foreskins under her bed. Might even be feeding the rest of the body to us as we speak, cooking it up with fancy spices and some TLC. But you know what? Can you fathom what that might be?"

Fleet was becoming more agitated as Curtis continued to craft colorful scenarios. "I get it."

"No!" Curtis made a gesture of finality. "You have to say it. I need to hear you say it."

Fleet's body tensed at his demand but faltered after a feeling of defeat washed over him. "It's not our problem."

"Good," Curtis said, satisfied.

He took a few steps back before tossing the ball underhand to Fleet and apologized in a morose tone, "I'm sorry I got like that, but this is dangerous work. Even being out here like this, we are putting ourselves and everyone else in danger. We have to stay hidden whatever the cost, which means we can't go chasing things that have nothing to do with us."

Fleet frowned as he looked down at the basketball, causing Curtis to sigh.

"You're a good guy. But we're not in a 'good guy' line of work. That's just what it is, man. Bottom line, the longer we stay here, the longer we risk exposing ourselves to the public."

"Yeah." Fleet nodded. "I just wish your mom had gotten that message."

"Right."

"Since she's always exposing herself to the public."

"I got it."

"Cause she's a ho-bag."

"I'm telling you said that about my mama," Curtis threatened. "I'm gonna tattle to your superior, and you are going to get in taaaaaa-rubble."

"Hey, she's not my superior anymore," Fleet said. "She's my colleague—or something. So you can just lick my left nut."

"That's uncalled for."

Fleet stepped back, positioned himself, then took a shot that bounced off the rim and rolled into the woods. He cursed under his breath as Curtis went to retrieve it out of pity.

"Why do I suck so bad at B-ball?" Fleet lamented.

"I think the fact you call it 'B-ball' speaks for itself!" Curtis yelled from the thicket, still searching for the errant basketball.

And that was it. Fleet's fears were assuaged now that all the mysterious evidence had been addressed and peer-reviewed by someone he trusted.

And yet...

Fleet jumped as the ball sailed at his face, catching it just in time. Curtis stepped from the tall grass but stopped when he saw the expression on his partner's face.

"What now?" Curtis asked, his shoulders slumping.

Fleet looked to the ground. "Nothing, it's just... I don't know. It just doesn't feel right."

Curtis was dismayed, but tried his best to hide it. "I get it. I get where you're coming from. But like you said: it's nothing. You're experiencing an overabundance of caution because you're afraid you'll miss something. You just need to follow your gut on this."

"Follow my gut, huh?" Fleet murmured as he thought, *You're going to hate me for this one, Scriptor.*

Fleet dropped the ball to his waist. "There's one last thing I need you to do, and then we can pack it up."

Curtis looked hopeful, but his voice held a twinge of doubt. "Is that right? What is it?"

Fleet rolled the ball over to the goal, not even bothering to shoot it. "Down the road that way about fifteen minutes, there'll be an old washed-out gravel driveway on your left covered by plants with an old signpost next to it. Head down that road and you'll find a derelict school with a little church next to it. I need you to investigate it from top to bottom and report anything suspicious back to me."

Curtis' expression morphed into a dead stare. "Are you fuckin' with me right now?"

Fleet knew admitting that it had been another pointless hunch that took him to that place would only make Curtis angrier—much less the fact a civilian had gone with him. In the end, it didn't matter what the cause was; Fleet was in charge of this investigation, and his orders were absolute—he just needed to remind himself of that.

"You can go after breakfast."

Curtis could not contain his disbelief. "Are you seriously making me do this? Why? What do you think is in there? Why do you even know about this?"

Fleet cut him short. "You let me worry about that."

Curtis' eyes narrowed as he tapped himself on the temple. "I know what you're thinking. But this isn't like 'that time,' all right? We knew well before we got there what a shitshow that was gonna be. There are no similarities between now and then. You're being paranoid."

"I sure hope so. But I'm following my gut, like you told me."

"Your gut's off, man. You need to eat some goddamn yogurt!" Curtis yelled at him. He was so loud that Fleet turned back to the motel to see if anyone had heard.

"Scriptor, I would hate to pull rank on you here…" Fleet's tone got more serious. "So just do as I ask and call up some of your people to help comb through it. With more hands, it shouldn't take you long."

The fight was gone from Curtis, but his response was still obstinate. "Yes, sir."

"And don't half-ass it." Fleet looked him square in the eyes. "Please, man. I need this."

It was the truth. Fleet had gotten next to no sleep the night before from the stress of the case. Though most of his 'evidence' had been debunked, he knew that if he left with this one last thought still on his mind, it would continue to haunt him long after he had departed.

Besides, he knew Curtis would cave.

"Okay," Curtis relented, rubbing the bridge of his nose. "I'll take care of it."

Fleet thanked him, already feeling better that the wheels were in motion, regardless of what that may entail.

CHAPTER TEN

BUCKEYE

BETWEEN THE SIX OF them, they devoured an entire week's worth of groceries in one sitting. At one point, Fleet volunteered to cook out of guilt after seeing Lowy return to the kitchen so many times to make more, though he did not feel guilty enough to stop eating.

The breakfast conversation was sparse at best, but that fit the overall mood of the hungry guests. Oreen and Lowy finished well before everyone else and waited as the others cleared out the reserves.

At the end, Curtis patted his belly and let out a deep, satisfied breath. "That was a five-star breakfast. Thank you."

Lowy smiled, glad to see they enjoyed it. "It was my pleasure." Her eyes drifted to the portion that had been set aside. "I'm sorry Jill missed out. I think she would have enjoyed it."

"It's fine," Dash responded. "She's not the best with crowds."

"But she was doing so good yesterday," Lowy said.

Dash shrugged and left it at that.

BJ let out a contented sigh. "Thank you for breakfast, Lowy."

"I wish to mirror that sentiment," Fleet added. "Need any help with cleaning?"

"I'll help with the dishes," Oreen volunteered over Fleet.

Oreen gave Fleet a snide glare as he gathered the plates. He took great care when he touched Dash's, using only the tips of his fingers to place it onto the stack before wiping his hands on a napkin. Lowy thanked him as he headed for the kitchen.

"It felt good to cook for someone else for a change," Lowy said. "I'm just glad the food came out all right."

"It was amazing," Dash complimented. "But next time, bring a little hot sauce. It goes a long way."

Dash made a slight gesture with her injured hand to emphasize her last statement. Without a word, Lowy reached out and took Dash by the wrist. She brought her in closer to see how the wound from the previous night was faring now that Dash had eaten.

"Hey!" Dash exclaimed before realizing what Lowy was trying to do. "It's fine. I promise."

Lowy pulled at the end of the bandage and carefully unwrapped it from her finger. A flap of skin had gotten caught on the adhesive, which caused the wound to open farther. Blood trickled down Dash's wrist and dripped from her elbow.

"Yeah, that is not okay." Lowy frowned with concern. "It needs stitches."

"Just try your best, I guess," Dash responded, unconcerned by the bleeding.

"Not me! A doctor!" Lowy shouted back.

Dash declined immediately. "Nope. Don't trust doctors. Just wrap it up, give me a shot of whiskey, and send me on my way."

"Why do I believe that is the first time in your life you've ever told someone to 'wrap it up,'" Oreen quipped in a sardonic tone.

"You wait here. I'm going to grab the first aid kit," Lowy instructed, dismissing Oreen's barb to his chagrin.

Curtis stood up and made a gesture to apologize for his noisy chair. "You guys seem busy, so I'll take the opportunity to check out my room and take my morning constitutional. Brother, care to join me?"

Dash made a disgusted face. "Gross."

"Don't you judge us!" Curtis clapped back with feigned indignation.

Dash looked over at Fleet accusingly, causing him to give a weak shrug. "I sing to him through the door and give him a hug after a successful movement. Real self-confidence booster."

"Then what does an unsuccessful movement entail?" Dash asked.

"You don't want to know," Curtis responded for Fleet.

"I want to see how this plays out. Can I come along?" Dash inquired, looking for an excuse to avoid Lowy's care.

Fleet held up a hand. "No girls allowed."

Oreen had grown tired of their shtick. "I think you kids all need to calm down a bit, though I do appreciate your commitment to the bit."

"Duly noted, good sir," Curtis said as he grabbed Fleet by the shoulder.

Fleet waved as he left the group. "Later, guys."

He strolled next to Curtis through the parking lot and up to the front of his motel room. They reached the door and Curtis stopped in his tracks once he saw the condition it was in. "This is your room?"

"Correct."

"What the fuck happened!" Curtis blurted as he pointed to the vomit and blood that coated the exterior like graffiti.

"Yeah, had a minor incident last night. Nothing to worry your pretty little head over," Fleet assured him. "Don't remember the puke, though."

Curtis rubbed his brow at Fleet's response, all the while muttering curses under his breath.

Changing the subject, Fleet asked, "You about to head out?"

"Yep. My boss gave me orders to check out this haunted house, after all. Better take care of that before night hits and the spooky monsters show up."

"The irony," Fleet added.

"And the sooner I get it done, the sooner we can leave, right?"

"That's right. And if it makes you feel better, I'll go ahead and start packing." Fleet got serious for a moment. "But like I said, don't half-ass it and drive down the road for a few hours so you can pretend you went or something like that, all right?"

Curtis looked shocked and gasped. "I would never!"

Fleet held up his hands. "I feel like a jackass for even saying it. Well, I got to take a piss. Give me a shout when you're done, and—" Fleet interrupted himself by snapping his fingers; seeing the walkway to the backyard area had triggered his memory. "Okay, okay. Last thing, for real."

Fleet could see the annoyance building within Curtis as he spoke.

"I know we were just talking about being thorough—you applauded me for it, in fact—so I wanted to inform you I collected some evidence from around the scene, and I think you should look it over, just in case."

Curtis shot him a questioning glance. "You collected evidence?"

"Yes, in a plastic bag that I found in a bush."

Curtis squinted at him. "The evidence is in a plastic bag...that you found in a bush?"

"That is correct." Fleet pointed over his shoulder with a thumb. "I left it out back yesterday and just remembered it now."

"You left it out back...overnight."

Fleet tapped himself on the ear. "I like this. I like the repetition. It shows you're listening."

Curtis ground his knuckles into his forehead. "Just to reiterate, you are telling me you took evidence that you believed at the time may be pertinent to the case and put it in a dirty sack you found in a bush, which you then proceeded to leave outside overnight?"

"I don't care for the way you're phrasing it, but that is exactly what happened," Fleet admitted. "In the bag it's mostly garbage, right—look out for the glass, by the way—but I know there is a used condom in there. I saw some kind of liquid in it. Maybe swab it for DNA and compare it to the hand? Could be a connection there."

Curtis looked like he was about to have a stroke. "Goddamn it. It was a woman. Sperm won't tell us—"

Fleet waved him off, not wanting to admit he had repeated his mistake from earlier. "Hey, science is your job, not mine. But don't worry, you can do it when you get back."

Curtis reached out toward Fleet's neck, his hands trembling with rage before transitioning into a salute as Fleet stared him down.

"Yes, sir," Curtis said, his left eye twitching.

Clenching and unclenching his fists, Curtis stepped into the parking lot and walked over to his black SUV that was parked a few spaces away from Fleet's truck.

"Don't have too much fun!" Fleet called to him.

Without a response, Curtis tossed a paper sack from the driver's seat over to his 'brother.'

Fleet caught it and opened the brown bag with skepticism. Inside was a brand-new toothbrush, body wash, deodorant, and five candy bars of varying brands. Fleet made to say something, but Curtis had already shut the door and started the engine. As he pulled away, he mouthed 'you're welcome' and peeled off onto the road.

Fleet grinned with a restrained snort; he knew Curtis wouldn't stay mad at him.

After unlocking his door, he threw the bag of sundry items onto his bed, but not before removing a candy bar. Fleet made his way to the bathroom and ripped open the wrapper with his teeth while unzipping his pants with his free hand. Fleet took a deep bite of the peanut sugar log as he relieved himself. He tilted his head back while he chewed to study the water stains on the bathroom ceiling as he considered the current situation.

On the one hand, if he finds something, it means I'm not going crazy, and I don't come off looking like an asshole. On the other hand, if he comes up empty, that means I am crazy, but at least it shows there are no Tryst here. But then on the other—foot, I guess—regardless of what he finds, it means there's still a murderer on the loose. It means that Lowy is in danger.

"This sucks."

His pondering and stream both halted when he heard a sharp rapping on the door. "Gimme a sec!" he shouted at the unknown guest.

After cleaning up, he opened the door to find Lowy awaiting him with an enormous grin on her face. With no stay of exuberance, she greeted him with, "Ready for your first day on the job?"

"First day on the..." he began before realizing what she meant. "Shit, I forgot all about that. You're really making me do this?"

Lowy feigned a stern expression. "Wow. I know you're nervous and everything about your new job, but I'm going to have to write you up for that. FYI, three write-ups and you're going to receive a verbal warning. Three verbal warnings and you will undergo an administrative review. After the fifth and half administrative review, you will receive a squinty-eyed look of disapproval that will segue into an interpersonal investigation. This could possibly lead up to or include a notice of termination which will require multiple signatures from management that ultimately culminates in shame and dishonor to you and your family."

Lowy maintained her stone-faced gaze as she finished her spiel.

Fleet shot her a squinty-eyed look of disapproval of his own. "Is this place run by the government or something?"

"I assure you, good sir, that I take my job very seriously."

"I want to talk to HR," Fleet demanded as he crossed his arms.

"You can't. They died."

"They died? All of them?"

"Yes," Lowy responded, fighting off the urge to smirk.

"That is unfortunate. But I guess that means there's a position open in HR. I've always considered myself a people person, and anything's better than what I dread you are going to make me do."

Lowy clapped her hands together. "Certainly. I would be glad to have you on board. We just have to talk to our hiring manager. Unfortunately, she's dead too."

Fleet conjured a dour expression. "I'm sensing a pattern."

Lowy put her hands behind her back. "It's true. The company retreat was a poor choice on my part. I thought a hot-air balloon ride would help build teamwork and foster a healthy work environment. Turns out, no amount of synergy can overcome a strong gust of wind and an angry windmill."

Fleet had to bite his lips together to maintain his façade. "I feel for you. It must hurt to lose so many people at one time. Is that why you have your flag flying at half-mast?" He pointed to a condom hanging from the windowsill of the adjacent room.

Lowy's eyes grew large as she realized what he was pointing at, but soon returned to her serious persona. "We each have our own ways of grieving, sir. And since you mention it, I believe enough time has passed. Your first official duty will be to lower the 'flag.'"

"Damn it," Fleet groaned, kicking himself for calling attention to it.

"Don't worry, I have everything you need right here." Lowy took a step to the side and wiggled her fingers like a magician's assistant. "Behold, your chariot awaits!"

Behind her was a typical gray cleaning cart in pristine condition. On the top sat rolls of unopened toilet paper, freshly washed towels, and folded linens. Pockets along the side were lined with various cleaning supplies that hung over a lever-activated mop bucket.

Fleet could only stare at it. *Thank God Scriptor isn't here for this.*

Sensing Fleet's lack of direction, Lowy spoke up. "First thing is to take care of this." She waved her hand over Dash's blood and vomit.

He couldn't help but gag. All the bodily fluids had dried in the morning sun and were now flaking off in small batches, though the more stubborn clumps were holding on for dear life.

Unbeknownst to Fleet, Lowy asked a partially rhetorical question. "So, what happened here last night?"

Fleet put up no fight and gave her a quick but truthful response—even if he omitted certain things. "Dash showed up shit-faced, took off her clothes, and propositioned me. I said 'no thanks' and kicked her out. She did not take that very well, but that's pretty much the end of it. I didn't know anything about all this until I stepped through it this morning."

"Wow, not many guys would turn her down." Lowy picked at her nails behind her back. "Got someone else you have your eye on? Back home, I mean."

"Only thing I got my eye on right now is this gross-ass wall." Fleet sighed as he slipped on a pair of rubber gloves, his eyes pleading with Lowy one last time in hopes she would change her mind.

She did not.

He stuck a sponge in the soapy water and got to work scrubbing off Dash's blood. The sponge was having a hard time, frequently losing small bits as it struggled against the porous brick.

Lowy watched like a hawk and would offer unnecessary words of advice like 'Yeah, that's good. Really get in there', and 'That chunk's putting up a fight. Don't let him get the better of you.'

It wasn't long before Fleet lost his patience. "Do you know what micromanaging is?"

"Yeah, obviously," Lowy said, crossing her arms. "Do you think I'm going to trust the guy who can't even remember to brush his teeth to know how to properly clean?"

"You know, I can't argue with that," Fleet admitted as he got back on his feet to stretch out his back.

Lowy stepped forward and examined his work. "Not bad!"

Fleet raised an eyebrow at her evaluation. There was still some bile in the corners of the door, and his scrubbing had chipped off even more of the already dwindling green paint, but he figured it was best not to disagree. At least it didn't reek anymore.

Lowy leaned toward the wall, squinting. "But I think you missed a spot."

"And I think you're enjoying this a lot more than you should be," Fleet said. "You could help, you know. It would make it go a lot faster."

Lowy waved a hand. "Cleaning isn't really my thing."

"Who'd have guessed?" Fleet mocked, rolling his eyes.

"I'm a supervisor! I look at the big picture. Blood and puke, they come to you. If you have questions, then you come to me."

Lowy's last statement caused Fleet to recall a random factoid he had stashed away from the day before. "Yeah, I got a question, boss. The sheriff called you 'Buck.' Now that I think about it, so did Oreen. What's that all about?"

It took a few moments for a response, but Lowy sounded withdrawn when she spoke. "It's only a stupid nickname."

"Kinda figured that. But how did you get it?"

"It's not important," she answered, looking away from him.

"Cool," Fleet replied, seeing how uncomfortable it made her. "It's none of my business, but if you don't like getting called that, tell them to quit."

"No, it's not..." Lowy stopped when she saw Fleet squat down and return to scrubbing.

There was a brief period of awkward silence before Lowy spoke again.

"It's short for 'Buckeye.'"

Fleet halted his work and looked up at Lowy, encouraging her to continue.

Lowy started to pick at her nails. "When I was a kid, my dad used to do this thing where he would keep a buckeye seed in his pocket and rub it for good luck. After a while, I guess all the sweat and friction from your hand polishes it. They turn jet-black and get super smooth. They were so pretty, like little jewels."

Lowy stuck a hand in her pocket, her unfocused gaze reflecting her nostalgia.

"He could have one all polished in about a month. Told me he made them so fast because you're supposed to touch it when you think about someone you love, and he was always thinking about me."

Her lips trembled, but it didn't stop her from smiling.

"He would give them to me because he said that each one was good for a wish. But not a big wish or anything. They wouldn't end world hunger or give me a pet dinosaur, but they could do simple stuff. My wish could make the rain go away so I could play outside, or get me an ice cream for dessert; though I always had to make that wish within earshot of my parents or Denvis."

Fleet chuckled and started scrubbing again. "That sounds like fun."

"For a kid, it really was." She gave Fleet a cocky smile. "At one point, I had it all figured out. If one is worth a small wish, a whole bunch must be worth a big wish. That's when I started saving them all in a jar until I thought I had enough."

"Economics 101 right there." Fleet continued his work, enamored by her light-hearted story. "I bet you've still got that jar sitting around somewhere, don't you?"

"I threw it out."

Fleet cocked his head. "Why'd you do that?"

"I figured out it wasn't magic when it didn't grant my wish."

Before he could stop himself, curiosity forced his hand. "What did you wish for?"

Lowy was quiet. It was like she was standing on the edge of a cliff, deciding if she should jump. Finally, she took the leap.

"I wished that Mom would get better."

Fleet ceased all movement, giving her a sympathetic side-eye before starting to scrub the door once more. "I'm sorry."

"My dad stopped making them after that."

She went silent.

Fleet racked his brain but couldn't think of anything comforting to say, instead choosing to continue his monotonous assignment.

Once there was nothing left to scrub, he asked, "What do you think?"

This shook Lowy from her stupor. "Oh, yeah. That looks fine. Grab some clean towels, and let's change them out."

Lowy pushed through the door past Fleet. She folded her arms as she stared through the bathroom and out the window, all the while giving him instructions on what he should do to make up the room.

She still had not moved from her spot by the time Fleet had finished, so he thought it best to apologize. "Hey, I'm sorry about all that. I should have seen where that was going and stopped prying before you had to dredge up those memories."

Lowy shook her head, still maintaining her position. "No, I've come to terms with that. It's just a part of life, right? I miss her, and it does still hurt, but that's not it."

Fleet picked up the old sheet and rolled it into a ball, trying to distance himself from the conversation. He felt as though anything he said would act as a catalyst to reopen some old wounds.

Damn, Lowy. Don't you have someone else you can talk to about this stuff?

This was going well past blending in and intel gathering. It wasn't his place to interfere; it went against everything he had been trained to do. And yet it made him ache. It felt wrong to walk away from this for some reason.

What was the right thing to do here?

Lowy took that decision away from him. "It was my dad. He was different when she passed. Not angry or abusive or anything like that. He was still my dad, he just... I can't explain it."

Lowy looked over her shoulder at Fleet.

"He felt so empty. Like he was only going through the motions."

Fleet stared back at her, his tensed hands hidden underneath the balled-up sheet.

She sat down on the newly made bed, where she picked up the small red car from the nightstand and ran her fingers over it. Clutching the toy in hand, she took off her glasses and said the words in a cracked voice.

"I could tell he didn't love me anymore."

"Don't you ever fucking say that!" Fleet shouted, taken aback by the heat in his own voice.

Lowy turned to him with tears in her eyes. "Then why? Why did he never tell me how he felt? Why did he always lie and say he was fine?"

She bent over, crying into her palms with the red car caught in the deluge.

"He didn't even think I was worth a note."

Fleet stood stunned, his mouth agape as he looked over at Lowy as she sobbed. After some time, she was able to strain out, "Didn't he know how much I needed him?"

Fleet's arms fell to his side, dropping his burden on the ground. He sat on the bed opposite Lowy with his back to her. "No, Lowy. I can see why you think that, but no. He was just sick."

It took several attempts to get words to form on his tongue.

"It's...like a darkness; heavy, but somehow hollow at the same time. It congeals inside you, coating your very being, replacing everything inside you down to the blood in your veins. Once it's claimed all of you, once there is no other place for it to go, it leaks out. It rips its way through, and once you're torn..."

Fleet cleared his throat as he gave a quick glance over his shoulder.

"Maybe it was brought on when he lost your mom. Could be it was always there; she may have kept it in check his whole life. But it got him. Just like any other disease, it got him. But that is not your fault."

Lowy continued to sob behind him, though she was hanging on his every word.

"I've...I've seen it," Fleet continued. "It's one of the worst things imaginable. But I can tell you with absolute certainty that he would never intentionally hurt you."

Lowy spoke up, desperate for clarification. "But how do you know?"

Fleet shifted on the bed so that he could look Lowy in her eyes. "Because a father will always love his daughter, no matter what. Of anything in this world, there is nothing I believe more than that."

Lowy sobbed once more, but this time her tears flowed past the corners of a smile. She turned back toward the wall to wipe at her face with a balled fist. "I hope that's true."

Overcome by a sudden urge, Fleet reached over Lowy's shoulder and put his hand on her fist. "I know it is."

A gasp escaped Lowy's lips as she felt Fleet's arm press against her cheek as it slid past. She closed her eyes as she leaned back into his chest and gripped his bicep, unable to control the thrill that surged through her.

She inhaled gently as Fleet pressed against her back, sending a wave of excitement down her spine that culminated as a pleasant tingle in her extremities. Clutching the tiny toy car to her chest, she reveled in the sensation of his contact.

This is it.

This was what she wanted.

However, this bore no similarities to the fantasies she had concocted on lonely nights. Her stories had all been a bit more fanciful, and usually didn't begin with snot pouring out of her nose.

But she was happy.

And she was ready.

Fleet's fingers dug into the fist at her chest, working themselves into her palm. She released her grip on the car as she squirmed against him, unable to monitor her heavy breathing. Lowy swallowed, taking her newly free hand to reach behind her and...

She fell backward.

Her head landed hard on Fleet's lap, her arm behind her back.

He looked down at her with concern. "You okay?"

She only managed to stammer short bursts of gibberish up at him. Without her glasses, everything was a conglomeration of muted blobs, but there was one thing she recognized: the small red car clutched in his hand.

That's what he wanted? His little toy? Not me. Just that fucking car!

Lowy's skin burned from the embarrassment. It was as if she were melting away, her ultimate fate to leave behind a scorched and charred skeleton that Fleet could use as an obstacle course for his tiny goddamn car!

Lowy sprang from the bed, grabbed her glasses, and marched her way to the door. Without looking back at him, she said, "Okay, I think we're good in here."

"I still need to change the pillowcases."

She stopped but still did not turn around. "It's fine!"

"Are you sure you're okay?" Fleet asked with concern. "Do you want me to come with you?"

Lowy pulled a ring of keys from her pocket and tossed it onto the bed. "Clean Dash's room now. I've got something I need to do."

"Like what?"

Anything, Lowy thought as she walked outside. *Anything to get out of here.*

CHAPTER ELEVEN

SOUL BRITCHES

LOWY CONTINUED TO WALK at a brisk pace until positive that she was out of view from Fleet's room. She gave a quick glance over her shoulder before she allowed her emotions to consume her.

Oh, God! What is wrong with me? Idiot! How am I this fucking stupid!

She thought the same, or at least similar, self-deprecating insults about herself over and over until she hyperventilated. Lowy bent over to catch her breath, which caused the glasses to fall off her face. She bent down to grab them and burst into tears. Instead of getting back up, she sat there and cried into her knees.

Soon, the sheer audacity of the situation—of everything—caught up with her. Intermingled between her sobs and coughing were small bouts of cynical laughter. She stayed like this for several minutes, unable to will herself to do anything else.

"Are you all right?" came a concerned voice from nearby.

Lowy looked over her knees to see Dash jogging her way. She kneeled and put her hand on Lowy's back, her face creased with concern. Lowy took a few more seconds and one last large sniffle before she could physically respond.

"I don't... I just can't... I can't follow everything that's going on in my head. I was sad, then happy. Then sad, then horny. There's so much shit in there, and it's all telling me different things, and I can't think," Lowy confessed through a wet and shaking voice.

Then, in a brief moment of clarity, she realized what it had to be.

"It's like my soul has food poisoning and it's coming out of both ends!"

Dash pulled Lowy in close and gently rubbed her back. "It's okay. I've shat my soul britches on more than one occasion myself. Just let it all out."

The two sat there for a while as Lowy attempted to reach some form of equilibrium. At one point, snot dripped from her nose, and Dash used her bandaged finger to wipe it away.

Lowy recoiled when she realized what Dash had just done. "You can't do that with an open wound!"

"It's fine. I didn't get any blood on you."

"No, I'm saying you can't let snot get in there," Lowy said, rubbing her nose. "C'mon, let's go."

Dash had avoided her first aid earlier, using the excuse that she had to go to the restroom, but Lowy wasn't going to let her get away this time. Lowy grabbed Dash's hand and began pulling her to the main office, relieved she had something to focus on besides her own failings. She forced Dash to sit down at the patio table as she walked inside to grab the first aid kit. She returned to find that Dash had made her way into the kitchen and was rummaging through the cabinets.

"What are you doing?" Lowy asked. "We need to change that bandage."

"In a minute," Dash responded over her shoulder. Lowy protested, but Dash cut her off. "Lowy, you're always looking after me. Let me return the favor for once. Sit down, all right?"

Spurred by the sweetness of her words, Lowy did as instructed and sat down outside to watch her work in the kitchen. Dash's efforts culminated in a light snack consisting of a bag of chips, a peanut butter and jelly sandwich, and one of the beers that Lowy let her keep in the fridge.

"Nothing like a PBR to go with your PBJ," Dash mused as she placed the paper plate on the table.

"That's a combination I've never considered," Lowy admitted.

Lowy smiled and took a bite; she wasn't particularly hungry, but she didn't want Dash's show of kindness to go ungratified.

"Don't knock it till you try it," Dash quipped, cordially cracking open the beer on Lowy's behalf.

Lowy took a sip, letting the opposing flavors war it out in her mouth.

She winced and put down the beer when Dash asked, "Okay, so tell me what's wrong."

"It's nothing," Lowy responded, taking a bite of the sandwich.

Dash sighed and opened the bag of chips, pulling one out and offering it up. "Come on."

Unsure whether she was talking about her lie or the chip, Lowy took the chip from her and crunched down on it. Dash was clearly not satisfied, so Lowy told her the truth.

"It's Fleet."

Lowy started as Dash leaned forward and said, "Did he do something to you? If he did, I swear I will end him. This isn't a joke. They will never find the body."

Lowy laughed at her friend's offer. "No, no, nothing like that. It's kind of the opposite, actually."

Dash's dour expression transitioned into one of playful curiosity. "Oh, really?"

"Yeah," Lowy said. "We've hung out a little since he's been here and...I dunno."

"You wanna fuck him."

Lowy choked. "No, it's not..." She looked meekly at Dash. "Maybe."

"Then go for it," Dash said, as if it were the easiest thing in the world.

"Yeah, that would be great," Lowy admitted. "He's just so easy to talk to. I can really be myself around him. It feels good." Fleet's blurry face holding the car flashed through her mind. "I just can't tell if he feels the same way about me."

Dash waved her hand in dismissal. "Hold up. You're talking about falling for the guy, aren't you? You're building all these prerequisites for banging him that don't need to be there."

"Is that wrong?" Lowy asked.

Dash pondered that. "Look at it this way. When you've got this old married couple that's been together for years and one of them says, 'I knew they were my soulmate from the first time I laid eyes on them.' It's sweet, right? Then there's your situation where you've known the guy a day, and you're thinking he's the one."

Lowy cringed, sensing where this was going.

Dash ignored her discomfort and finished her point. "One gets you a slideshow at the family reunion, and the other nets you a restraining order."

Lowy let out a long groan. "I know, I'm an idiot. I just had so much fun when I beat him at basketball last night and joked about all kinds of stuff. It felt like we connected."

"Wait a sec," Dash interrupted. "Your idea of foreplay was to emasculate him by beating him at basketball?"

Lowy raised her shoulders and lowered her head. "I didn't mean to."

Dash burst into a fit of laughter. "Well, some guys are into that, I guess."

"I don't think he was."

"Poor girl." Dash winced. "I bet he used that flat-ass ball over there as an excuse when he lost. Couldn't take a blow to his masculine pride like that."

"He did make some kind of excuse." Lowy grimaced at the realization before looking behind her to the old decrepit basketball goal. "But we didn't use that one. We played at the old gym."

"Gym?" Dash asked, her voice growing concerned. "Why did you go there?"

"Seemed like a good idea at the time."

Dash leaned forward. "Do not go there anymore. Promise me, Lowy."

"Okay," Lowy obliged before she could reason it out. "Thanks for the concern, but why? I didn't even realize you knew about that place?"

Dash sat back and shrugged. "I've heard stuff around town, is all. It's closed for a reason. I don't want to see you running in there and getting hurt or something. We'd never be able to find you."

"Yeah, I guess that's true," Lowy conceded. "But I didn't go in alone. I would have never done that, literally for the reason you just said."

"Instead, you took a guy you like to seduce him," Dash marveled, trying to segue back into the original conversation. "And instead of sex, you ended up kicking his ass and making him feel like a bitch. Oh, Lowy, you should have thrown that game."

"I know that now!" Lowy shouted. "The worst part is we made a bet. The winner could ask the other one to do whatever they want, and I thought about it before I chickened out."

"You thought about daring him to fuck you?" Dash asked for clarity, a smile crossing her face.

"Or at least make out or something. That would have been fun too."

Dash inhaled through her teeth. "Damn. I bet he would have given you some head if you'd asked."

"That would have been cool," Lowy admitted. "Instead, I got him to be my personal janitor." Lowy let her forehead bang down on the table, then in muffled words she uttered, "Which works out since it will be easier for him to hang out with garbage like me."

"Hey!" Dash shouted as she slapped Lowy on the back hard enough to make her jolt from the sting.

"What was that for?" Lowy grumbled in pain.

Dash grabbed Lowy's arm with her good hand. Her countenance was unwavering and carried a tone of absolute sincerity, something Lowy had never seen from her before.

"While that was clever, I never want to hear you say that ever again," Dash warned her. "You are an absolute angel, and there is no man out there who wouldn't be lucky to be with you. You have to understand that you're sweet, caring, smart—all those things rolled up into one beautiful little package."

Dash became misty-eyed as she continued, causing Lowy to do so in turn.

"This might sound weird, but you are a bright spot in my life, and I am so happy that you are here with me. And it's not just me. I know she doesn't say much, but Jill feels the same. You've cared for her more than anyone else ever has, and that means the world to both of us. I want you to be safe and happy because you deserve only the best and nothing less."

"You're going to make me start crying again," Lowy choked through a trembling smile, the warning coming a bit too late.

"As long as they are happy tears, I'll allow it," Dash relented with a big smile as she rubbed at her eyes.

"Are you okay if they are half and half?"

"Why only half? I thought my speech was pretty good."

"It's not that. Actually, that is the nicest thing anyone has ever said to me." Lowy wrung her hands in her lap as she looked down at the tabletop. "I guess it's because I am so happy that it makes me sad too, because I know you will leave someday."

Dash's smile faded from her face as Lowy spoke, but she brought it back before her silence exposed too much of the truth.

"If me and Jill run off somewhere else, who's going to take care of us? We'd be dead within the week," Dash joked, though she did not make eye contact.

"Yeah, you're right," Lowy agreed as she wiped a tear from her eye, the smile returning to her face. "Even though I know you're lying."

Dash lowered her head at Lowy's response.

Lowy leaned forward and wrapped her arms around her in a big hug. "Thank you. You're a good friend."

Dash was caught off guard but soon returned the gesture, holding Lowy tight. "Only the best for you," Dash managed to croak out through the lump in her throat.

They held the hug for a long while, neither one wanting to release the embrace.

"Are you feeling better now?" Dash asked.

"Yes, much better." Before Lowy could finish her sentence, she was overshadowed by Dash's growling stomach. "Wait, are you still hungry after that huge breakfast?"

"A snack wouldn't hurt," Dash admitted, eyeing the remnants of Lowy's sandwich.

Lowy happened to catch her gaze. "No, that's mine! You made it for me, and I am going to eat it. But go ahead and help yourself to whatever's in the kitchen."

"That is a dangerous liberty you're granting me. I'd feel bad taking advantage of you like that...again."

Lowy swallowed another bite of her sandwich. "Then think of it as a trade."

"For what?"

The question had been eating away at Lowy since last night. They were friends, right? What's a little gossip among friends? She took a swig from her lukewarm beer to calm her nerves.

"Can you tell me what happened last night?" Lowy was then overcome with the unnecessary urge to over-explain herself. "I'm not mad or anything, I promise. You didn't know how I felt, so it's not like you did it on purpose."

Dash slapped a palm to her forehead. "Did I do something stupid again last night? Whatever it was, I want to apologize, and I promise I'll clean it up."

"You don't remember?"

"The last thing I remember is getting to the campfire," Dash recalled, then threw up her hands in surrender. "Everything after that is gone until I woke up this morning."

"You don't even remember what you and Fleet did?"

At the mention of his name, Dash took on a worried expression. "What do you mean?"

Lowy took another sip of beer before she answered, which was enough time for Dash's demeanor to take on a hint of panic.

"I don't know the details," Lowy said. "I only saw the end of it when I took you to your room and washed you up."

"Tell me!" Dash shouted at her.

Startled, Lowy got straight to the point. "I saw him kick you out of his apartment, and you were screaming at him about something. I was worried about you."

Dash sat back, her eyes darting about as she tried to recall the events of the night.

Lowy attempted to calm her down by finishing her explanation. "I don't think you guys did anything, though."

"Really?" Dash asked, her voice hopeful.

"I mean, if you did, it was super quick," Lowy continued. "You were only in there a couple minutes. And if that's the case, maybe I dodged an awkward bullet."

Dash laughed so hard she struggled to breathe; it was like a weight had been lifted from her. Lowy watched, unable to read her actions until she finally broke her hysteria.

"That's...that's good. You had me going there," Dash finished with a relieved laugh.

"What was that about?"

"I just didn't want you to think I was trying to swoop in on your man," Dash explained. "Especially after that heart-to-heart we had. It would reflect poorly on my character."

"We can't have that." Lowy smiled. "But one reason I thought it was so odd was because I can't come up with a reason he would turn you down. If he said no to you, what chance do I stand?"

"Lowy, what did we just talk about?"

"Yeah, yeah, I'm a sexy goddess." Lowy brushed past her condemnation. "But why did he do it?"

Dash shrugged. "I guess he's a good guy and wouldn't take advantage of a lady. Which I think is good news for you."

Lowy smiled a bit when she said that.

Dash cocked her head and closed one eye as she thought on it some more. "Or he could be gay. It would explain the weird tension between him and the other guy this morning. Damn it, I always forget his name."

"Which one? Oreen or BJ?" Lowy asked, certain she already knew the answer.

"Not the big one, the little one."

"I hadn't thought of that," Lowy admitted, gripping the half-empty beer can. "It would explain a lot."

"I wouldn't take my word for it, though. Sorry I couldn't be more helpful on that end, but at least you know he's not a pervert or worse."

Lowy smirked. "That's a very low bar."

Dash tilted her head and shrugged. "Who am I to judge if you're that desperate?" She then got up and made toward the kitchen. "Speaking of which, I'm desperate to eat. I'll try not to clean out the fridge."

"It's fine. There's not that much in there. I need to go shopping for food." Lowy's head shot up. "Cat food! I forgot to put any out!"

Dash peeked around the door to the cabinet she was rummaging through. "You know, you can give the bag to Jill. She loves that thing, and I bet she wouldn't mind taking care of it."

"She really likes Patchy, doesn't she?"

Dash smiled with fondness. "Honestly, I think it's done wonders for her."

"That's great. I'd be more than happy to let her feed the cat."

Dash laughed to herself. "Or it might be more efficient to get your sexy janitor to do it for you and save us all some time."

Lowy shrank a little. "I don't think he is super happy with the cleaning I already have him doing."

Dash furrowed her brow as she leaned back once more. "Wait, for real? You were serious about that?" She laughed aloud. "Damn, I bet you *could* have got him to put out if he's willing to do that stuff."

"Yeah, well, this is nice too," Lowy said with a bit of buyer's remorse. "He should be finishing up with your room soon if he hasn't been dragging his ass without my supervision. Then I can set him on—"

Lowy jumped when she heard the slam of the cabinet door. Dash stepped into the doorway, gripping both sides of the frame, her nails digging into the paint.

"He's in my room!"

The sound of a siren from the parking lot demanded their attention. As they both turned to investigate, a car with flashing lights pulled up to the front of the motel building, right to the door of Dash's room.

Chapter Twelve

HIDING

"SHEEZUS!"

Fleet recoiled from the stench of skunked beer and cheap weed that assailed him when he entered Dash's room. He waved a hand in front of his face as he took a few cautious steps inward to examine the layout.

Almost every flat surface was covered in some sort of empty can or bottle of alcohol: whiskey, vodka, beer; there was even a green bottle of absinthe on the nightstand. Several ashtrays were stacked on one another in the formation of a precarious tower with the butts acting as a calk. When she had run out of trays, a red plastic cup had become the new container for refuse.

The Murphy bed was laid out and overrun by garbage, though there was a nook cleared out on the surface for her to sleep in. The only part of the room that seemed untouched by filth was a small path that led from the front door to the bathroom.

Sitting in contrast to the mess was a wall of beer cans that were meticulously organized by color and size and placed around the bottom of the walls like some kind of garish aluminum baseboard. Atop each one were wrappers color-coded to the can's label sticking out from the open mouth.

It would have been cute were it not so sad.

"What am I doing here?" Fleet asked himself.

It was a reasonable question. A good question. An amazing question, even.

While it was important to keep up appearances, was it necessary to go this far? All he was doing was waiting for Curtis to finish his meaningless investigation. The second he got the 'all clear'—which was inevitable—that would be it. He would just leave.

No goodbyes. No friend requests. Nothing.

Yet here he was.

"I did this to myself."

Fleet bemoaned his situation as he took the only path available to him, looking for a place to drop the rolls of toilet paper and fresh towels he had tucked under his arm. He arrived in the bathroom and found that it matched the motif of the bedroom.

He flipped back the shower curtain to find a familiar ring of grimy filth around the sides and drain. Fleet tipped the trashcan toward himself with his foot to see what was inside and found the saddest parfait of beer cans with a wadded-up ball of bloody gauze as the cherry on top.

The sink carried only the bare minimum of personal hygiene products and cosmetics. In fact, the only makeup Fleet could see were two tubes of eyeliner. Based on his limited time sharing a sink with a woman, Fleet found it a little sparse. But then again, what the hell did he know about all that stuff?

However, one thing stood out to him: a pocket knife sitting right next to the toothbrush. He recalled the times he had to take a knife into the bathroom. The reasons were never good, but the memories remained as drastic lessons of poor decisions that should not be repeated.

Of the few flat surfaces that existed, none were vacant or even marginally clean. But toasting his own ingenuity, Fleet kicked the toilet seat cover down and placed his sundries on the lid.

Fleet left the bathroom and stopped by the bed to remove the sheets, the second half of his assigned chores. While this meant he was half-finished, he did not revel in the fact when confronted with what that entailed.

It's not like I'm going to catch something. It's literally impossible. Still...

He pinched the edges of the sheet, slowly dragging them back to reveal a collection of stains that one might confuse for modern art should the mattress be hung in a gallery. As he untucked two corners, the sheet dumped a deluge of trash onto the floor.

With a quick yank, he exposed a pool of dirty laundry that had gravitated to the center of the soiled mattress. Fleet gagged but forced himself to continue, taking solace in the fact that this horrible time in his life was nearly behind him.

He let the sheet fall and kicked it into a ball; this took care of the top sheet, leaving only the fitted sheet and pillowcases.

Fleet bent to grab the next layer, but reflexively balled his fists and recoiled as the combination of human odors both natural and manufactured assaulted his senses. Feeling a rush of pure inspiration, Fleet stuck his hands into a couple of empty chip bags that made their home in the room's corner.

Now that he was fully protected—not to mention thankful for the overpowering smell of nacho cheese—he grabbed the sheets in his crinkly mitts and made for the door. Sadly, his plan failed when the sheets were snatched from his hands, causing him to tremble as they slid down his legs into a greasy pile.

Upon further inspection, he found the sheet had been caught underneath one leg of the bed, trapping it in place. A stern tug led to the brief sound of something ripping, forcing him to seek other means of removing it.

Cursing under his breath, Fleet grabbed the guilty corner with one hand and lifted. He failed miserably as the bed creaked at his pathetic efforts. He put a little more force into it. There were more metallic groans, but no movement.

Fleet stood back and rubbed his hand. The makeshift gloves he wore were now torn from the metal divots of the frame. His bed had been nothing like this. The mechanism that let it into the wall must have rusted over.

Fleet bent his knees and grabbed the foot of the bed with both hands. With great strain, he was able to lift the bed ever so slightly. He used his foot to slide the sheet from beneath its burden, but the post clung to it like a tent stake.

Annoyed, he stepped back and unclenched his hands, letting the chip bags fall to the floor.

It was time to get serious.

He realized how dumb this was, of course. It was an odd place to take a stand, but after everything that had happened, he desperately needed a win right now. And if it happened to be in the form of open defiance to some ungodly jizz-soaked sex coffin, then so be it!

Fleet bent his knees once more, took in a few deep breaths to pump himself up, and started the lift again. There was no holding back this time. The metal dug into his skin as he bellowed a feral screech of exertion.

He was doing it. As the frame rose inch by inch, Fleet readjusted his position to maintain the integrity of his grip. His muscles burned from the tension, but under no circumstances was he going to lose this one.

Soon, he had done it. The bed was high enough that the sheet was now free.

But no, that wasn't enough.

Stopping at mere victory would not do. This had to be complete and total domination—there would be no mercy this day.

Once again, pointless and dumb, but he felt oddly good about it. Besides, he was helping Lowy out, considering there was no way she could have done this on her own. He was simply loosening it up for her in the future or whatever.

Fleet stopped to catch his breath when he had gotten the base up to his shoulders. He inched his way forward, readying himself for the endgame while ignoring the nastiness that was now inches from his face.

One last push.

He set his feet and arched his back, ready to power-lift the stubborn frame over his head.

One.

Two.

Three!

The bed released a sorrowful wail of surrender as Fleet extended his arms. Letting out short and heavy breaths, Fleet stood there as his body shook from the strain.

Sweet victory.

Unfortunately, the sensation was short-lived as a horrible thought crossed his mind: he was now standing in the filth that was under Dash's bed. Now that his joints were locked in position, he looked down out of curiosity.

More wrappers, more bottles, a body...

"Shit!" Fleet cursed in surprise.

The shock of what he saw caused his strength to fail him, and he fell backward onto the floor. The bed landed with an angry crack, breaking both posts.

He hadn't gotten a good look, but he was positive it was a person. From his vantage, all he could see were legs, so he couldn't tell if it was a man or a woman in that brief interval.

Fleet jumped to the side of the bed closest to the unknown person and lay flat on his stomach. Though the head was turned away from him, Fleet immediately recognized them.

It was Jill—and she wasn't moving.

This must be one of her hiding spots to get away from everyone. But why hadn't she said anything when he was making his way through? Plus, there's no way she could have slept through all the racket that the bed frame made. But Fleet pushed those questions aside so he could focus on the what mattered.

"Jill! Jill! Are you okay?" Fleet called to her.

He reached in and lightly slapped her face with the back of his hand as he repeated her name.

She still did not respond.

The way the frame had fallen...did he crush her? Based on where she lay, her head should have at least been safe, but that didn't bode well for the rest of her.

Panic set in.

He grabbed her by the arm and tugged her from under the bed. Thankfully, she wasn't trapped, and her upper body slid out with relative ease. He looked her over to see if she had any immediate trauma, but didn't find anything obvious.

But there was clearly something wrong.

Jill's eyes were only white slits, the pupils rolled back into her head. She convulsed periodically, sending slight tremors throughout her body that accompanied stymied breaths.

What was wrong with her? Was this from the bed? Is it a concussion?

He had no medical training to make an accurate diagnosis. Why would he? First aid had been deemed a superfluous skill in his line of work, often being counterproductive to his goals. Not to mention that wounds involving Tryst would heal fast, even in their base form.

It was the exact reason he had written off Dash. Even though she had done something suspicious by taking that ring from the crime scene, the fact that she was still bleeding profusely the next morning proved her innocence, or at the very least, that she was human.

But the girl before him wasn't Tryst. She was a normal person, which meant she was in real danger, especially if there was damage to her brain from the falling mattress. Jill could die from this. She could have internal bleeding, or a collapsed lung, or—

Then he saw it: a needle dug into the crook of her arm.

The plunger was fully depressed, its contents now swimming through her veins. A series of bruises with blood that trickled from the center showed she struggled to find a vein, stabbing herself over and over again in the process.

He found no relief in the clearance of his guilt.

Did she overdose?

Once again, he had no idea. He couldn't tell if this was the intended result of whatever she had injected into herself, but just looking at her, he knew something was wrong.

There had to be something he could do. He knew what Curtis would say, but that was the furthest thing from his mind as he reached for his phone to dial 911. Even if someone tried to trace it back to him, he could always get a new number, a new phone.

She was more important.

As his fingers touched the top of the case, he stopped and let out a loud 'fuck,' remembering that his phone was still dead.

Wait, there should be one here.

Sure enough, in the same spot as his room sat that manila brick, reflecting the light from outside like some prophetic beacon of hope despite the layer of trash that entrapped it. He ran to the phone and said a silent 'thank you' as he heard the dial tone coming from the receiver. His finger clacked the tiny square with the emergency label on it.

A calm and reassuring voice answered. "This is nine-one-one. What is your emergency?"

Fleet's voice shook while he paced back and forth as much as the tangled cord would allow. "There's a kid here who I think has overdosed on something! I need you to send an ambulance right now!"

"I understand. Can you tell me your current location?"

"Yeah, I'm at the Rose Hill Motel." His mind went blank. "I can't remember the address. Do you know where it is?"

There was an uneasy pause on the other end. As Fleet blurted out a 'hello' to see if he had been disconnected, they responded, "Yes, I know where that is. I have an ambulance on the way. What room number are you in?"

He didn't know. Perhaps it was due to the current situation, but for the life of him, he couldn't remember.

"Hold on," Fleet said as he sprinted for the front door, still holding the receiver in his hand.

He jumped when the phone crashed to the floor. After a quick curse, Fleet held the receiver to his ear and called for the operator to no avail; he wasn't even getting a dial tone anymore. He ran back to the phone's base and repeatedly tapped the plunger down, attempting to reset it. After years of faithful service, the old girl had made her last ring.

Fleet slammed the headset to the floor, pausing afterward to take a deep breath. "It's okay. It's okay. She said that an ambulance was on the way. If I stand outside, I can flag them down."

He made for the exit, but stopped short when he heard a delicate whimper coming from under the bed.

"Angel?" He rushed back to her side and knelt down. "It's me. It's...Fleet."

What good was that? He was nothing to her. If anything, his presence was a detriment to her current state considering how uncomfortable she was around strangers. He should go find Lowy and—

Jill's hand drifted toward the sound of his voice. Fleet grasped it, holding it tight as he whispered assurances to her one after the other.

"It's all right. Everything is going to be fine. I promise."

Chapter Thirteen

House Call

FLEET BREATHED A SIGH of relief so deep that he almost fainted when he saw the ambulance pull up in the parking lot. It caught him off guard considering he hadn't heard a siren or seen any flashing lights, but at the moment, that was the last thing on his mind. He set down Jill's hand like a delicate flower, reassuring her one last time before running out the front door.

"Over here!" he called out in a panic, waving his arms around. "She's in here!"

Two men emerged from the front, both of whom lacked any sense of urgency. They meandered toward the building, looking around as if they were more interested in the sights than saving the life of a dying young girl.

"What the fuck are you doing?" Fleet yelled at them.

"Calm down. There's no need for all that," one man responded in a calm, almost serene voice.

The newcomer who spoke cut a striking figure, or at least one that was hard to forget. He wore khaki pants with his light green houndstooth vest, underneath which was a button-up shirt with the sleeves rolled up to his elbows. Perched at an odd angle on his head sat an off-white fedora with black trim, held aloft by the buoyancy of his bushy hair.

But what struck Fleet the most was the flute that the man carried in his back pocket.

"Just show us to the body and we'll take care of it," Flute-guy said.

Fleet did not take well to the rather glib joke—at least he hoped the man was joking. "She's not dead! She's in—"

"No offense, sir, but you're no doctor," interrupted the other EMT. "We'll be the judge of that."

This second man looked equally out of place, perhaps even more so than his compatri-ot. He wore a dark green military jacket decorated with metal pins and patches featuring the names of bands Fleet had never heard of. His jeans were skinny and tight, the hems clutching his ankles like a tattoo atop a pair of dirty Chuck Taylors.

"You're not doctors either!" Fleet shot back.

Skinny-jeans scoffed. "Is that so? Then why do I have this?"

He held up the chest-piece of a stethoscope that hung around his neck. He spoke no further, but his cock-sure demeanor showed he had awarded himself the victory.

"A stethoscope doesn't make you a doctor!" Fleet yelled, growing angry at himself for getting caught in this stupid argument.

"That's what this thing's called?" Skinny-jeans said, now studying the instrument with a careful eye.

The other "EMT" raised an eyebrow. "What did you think it was?"

Skinny-jeans lowered his head. "Now I don't want to say because I'll sound foolish."

"Worry not, my friend. There are no judgments here," Flute-guy encouraged, patting his friend on the shoulder. "Words are but labels, so why not conceive our own? Creativity should never be condemned, only encouraged."

The other nodded, looking at his friend like he had blessed him with some profound understanding. He looked at the stethoscope with confidence.

"I shall call it...a 'slap-wankler.'"

Flute-guy had to think about that one. "Very unique. I like it."

Fleet caught himself staring, his brain refusing to function. Were these two really EMTs? The only ones he'd ever seen were on television, and they were always much more professional. But this was a small town. Perhaps, like himself, there weren't any better candidates for a job that desperately needed to be done. But if nothing else, they could at least act with some semblance of concern.

"I don't fucking care about the stethoscope!" Fleet shouted, making the two men start.

"You mean the slap-wankler," corrected Skinny-jeans.

"Just go inside and help her!" Without waiting for a response, Fleet ran into the room.

He heard Skinny-jeans make a comment as he entered. "That was rude of him."

"He's in a bit of a state at the moment," the other responded. "And who can blame him, given the situation?"

"Well, he didn't need to yell."

Fleet knelt next to Jill, checking to see if her condition had deteriorated any further in his absence.

Flute-guy soon pushed him aside. "Stand back, sir," the man commanded, finally showing some initiative. "This looks serious."

Flute-guy looked her over before noticing the syringe in her arm. He pulled it from her skin and held it up to his face. He then thumped the empty shell twice before bringing the tip to his nose for a quick sniff. "This isn't good."

Fleet couldn't believe it. He knew there were only so many things that could go in a needle, so he had his suspicions on what Jill had injected, but to tell what it was from such a simple procedure? Perhaps he had underestimated these two.

Fleet leaned forward and asked, "What is it?"

The man turned to him and nodded toward the syringe.

"It's a needle."

Fleet's lips tightened as he stared at the man, unsure of whether he wanted to strangle or bludgeon him. While not one to shy away from humor, even Fleet knew there was a time and place.

The man was unperturbed by Fleet's death stare. He threw the empty syringe over his shoulder where it stuck into the wall. He nodded to his partner. "It's in your hands now."

"Leave it to me," Skinny-jeans responded.

The man belly-flopped onto the bed before flipping over the side onto the floor next to Jill. He grabbed the stethoscope by the bell, licked the diaphragm, and stuck it onto Jill's forehead with a wet slap.

"It's worse than I feared." He looked to his dapper friend with regret in his eyes. "Not an original thought to be found."

Flute-guy threw his fedora at the ground and clenched his fists in anger. "Damn it! Does their blasted influence know no bounds? Curse those Kardashians!" The man's anger quickly subsided. "It's a good thing you called us when you did. She's going to make it."

Flute-guy pulled the instrument from his back pocket and pointed it at his friend. "Inspiration. Give it to me. I believe she needs something classical to wash away her torpor."

Skinny-jeans tapped his fingers together in thought. Suddenly, his eyes lit up with an idea. "Romeo and Juliet!"

Flute-guy shot him down. "No, they both end up dead, which seems inappropriate given the circumstances. Perhaps something more abstract, less concrete."

Skinny-jeans ran a thumb over his lips. "The power of friendship?"

Flute-guy pooh-poohed the idea. "While the concept is sound, I fear you have fallen into rote territory, and I simply cannot pull inspiration from such a common trope."

"The Golden Girls?"

"While classic, I cannot improve on perfection. No fault on you, of course, but please try again."

Skinny-jeans frowned, but made one last attempt. "The dissolution of the Ottoman Empire?"

A smile formed on the Flute-guy's face as he nodded with wide-eyed exuberance. "Yes, yes, yes! You are my muse! I believe that will do nicely. There are so many facets, so many opportunities for creativity. You've truly inspired me this time, my friend. This shall be my greatest composition to date!"

The 'muse' pumped a fist to celebrate his success. Flute-guy put the instrument to his lips and played an odd, disjointed melody as he pranced about the room like the ancient god Pan.

"Right there, do you feel it?" cooed Skinny-jeans, holding a hand aloft. "The healing has begun." He then tapped along to the song on Jill's forehead, somehow able to keep up with the odd tune.

That was enough.

Before he could think it through, Fleet leaped forward and grabbed Skinny-jeans by the throat with his left hand and shoved him against the wall, far away from Jill. He chose him not because he found him the worst of the two, but simply because he was closest.

He had tried to stay calm—he really had—but this was too much. Their whole interminable charade had pushed him to the breaking point. He wanted to think this through and figure out some way to move forward for Jill's sake. But every time a rational thought tried to manifest, it immediately evaporated against the onslaught of his rage.

He had lost it.

Fleet's free hand joined the one at Skinny-jean's throat, lifting him up the wall, his feet kicking the air as he struggled for breath.

"Not a fan of holistic healing, I see," Flute-guy said as he slid the woodwind back into his pocket. "Fine, we'll do it your way. But don't blame me when she comes out worse than she was before."

Flute-guy pulled Jill from under the bed and lifted her up in his arms. "Please put him down. We're a team, after all. If he's incapacitated, the ride back will be incredibly boring without someone manning the playlist."

Fleet glared at the dapper man over his shoulder before releasing his grip on Skinny-jeans neck, letting his hands linger in the air as his victim choked for breath on the floor.

"I'm going with you," Fleet said, only now lowering his arms.

I shouldn't, Fleet caught himself thinking. *I should walk away right now.*

"Are you sure that's what you want to do?" Flute-guy asked with a surprising amount of gravity; it was almost as if he read Fleet's mind.

No. I'm leaving, Fleet thought, counter to what came from his mouth. "Yeah, I'm sure."

Flute-guy shrugged, causing Jill to bob. "As you wish. But it will be a very awkward trip after what you did."

As the man turned to walk away, Fleet heard a siren in the distance. He felt a small spark of hope pop within; maybe this was the real ambulance with competent EMTs to take charge from these goddamn clowns.

Fleet's dreams were dashed as he pushed past the dapper man and out the front door. A familiar face greeted him with a scowl from behind the windshield of a brown sheriff's car.

"Fuck me!" Fleet cursed.

Now he had the sheriff, who already hated his guts, and let's not forget the fact that he just choked a man, too. That weirdo could press charges and get him thrown in jail. How could this situation get any worse? Fleet knew Curtis was going to kill him, which would be a blessing if it meant 'She' couldn't get hold of him first.

"Fuck!" Fleet cursed again.

"What's going on here?" Denvis demanded, slamming the car door.

Fleet stepped forward and defensively held up his hands, trying to explain. "Okay, so listen. I called nine-one-one because I was in there and—"

"What the hell were you doing in her room?" Denvis questioned, his voice rising.

"It doesn't matter. Jill's in trouble and you need—"

Fleet found himself interrupted once again as Dash raced toward them. "The fuck is all this?" she cried out.

Before he could warn Dash about Jill, Lowy skidded to a stop behind her. "Uncle Denvis? What are you doing here?"

"Dispatch gave me a call," Denvis explained, not taking his eyes from Fleet. "Said that there was an emergency with a young girl over here. Figured I'd want to know about it."

Dash almost lost it at the mention of the 'young girl.' "Where's Jill?"

As if on cue, Flute-guy exited the room with Jill in his arms.

"What are you idiots doing?" Dash yelled as she ran over and clasped Jill's face in her hands. She put her ear next to Jill's nose, relaxing a little once she found her still breathing.

Fleet stepped forward and put a hand on Dash's shoulder. "I think Jill overdosed on something."

She slapped his hand away. "Mind your own goddamn business!"

Fleet recoiled as if she had just spat in his face, but before he could protest, Skinny-jeans stumbled out of the room, clutching his throat like it had been run over by a steamroller. "Officer, this man molested me, and I wish to press charges!" he croaked, pointing to his injury.

"The hell I did!" Fleet yelled.

"You mean accosted," Flute-guy corrected.

The entire group soon devolved into a cacophony of curses, accusations, and queries. As if to quell the verbal chaos, there came a shrill whistle, putting an end to the ruckus. The group turned toward the source of the sound to find a yet unnamed man leaning against the wall behind them.

This new participant looked to be in his late thirties, though the small patches of gray that peppered his brown hair might have been making him seem longer in years than he was. He sported no ostentatious jewelry or branded clothing to make himself stand out, almost as if he had put forth an effort to remain as nondescript as possible.

While he was handsome, he was also very unkempt; it was like the wasted potential of an unfinished work of art. In the corner of his mouth was a piece of red licorice that he removed and held like a cigarette, still chewing on the small bite he had already taken.

He lifted his head and gave them a smile.

No one moved. No one said a word. This stranger had taken center stage, and they all waited with bated breath in anticipation of his forthcoming announcement. The newest arrival seemed to enjoy the attention as he took another bite of the red candy rope. The smile widened across his stubbled face as he looked directly at Fleet.

A chill ran down Fleet's spine that ended in a burst of nausea. "Who the fuck are you?" he said. "Better yet, what the fuck is going on here?"

The stranger responded, but not to Fleet's demands, speaking in a unique accent that Fleet couldn't place, as if it had been muddied by many years of absence from its native land. "I would hate to see such a beautiful day marred by tragedy. I hope you take good care of that girl."

Flute-guy gave a small nod and walked to the ambulance, followed closely by his compatriot, who seemed to have given up on any legal recourse against his attacker. Skinny-jeans opened the back door of the vehicle, and together they slid Jill onto the interior floor, ignoring the gurney that was lying there.

After the musician stepped over Jill to get in the back, his eyes moved to Fleet for the briefest of moments before settling on the stranger. The stranger closed his eyes and returned an imperceptible shake of the head.

"The fuck are you doing here?" Dash yelled at the stranger, though her words seemed measured.

"Perhaps you should go with her," the stranger advised, without looking away from the ambulance. "It would be terrible if her condition worsened while you were away."

Dash snarled at the man, her mouth twitching. "Eat shit! You don't tell me what to do!"

The rebellious front she put up dissolved as she walked over to the ambulance and hopped in the back, shoving Skinny-jeans to the ground in the process.

"Well?" Dash shouted at Flute-guy.

He held up his hands and walked to the driver's seat. Skinny-jeans attempted to hop in with her, but a grim snarl from Dash sent him packing to the passenger's side. As Dash closed the rear door, she extended her middle finger to the crowd, taking special care to show that it was meant for the stranger and Fleet in particular.

But as they were leaving, she glanced out the back window at Lowy with a sorrowful expression that was lost among the shaking of the ambulance as it rumbled down the driveway.

"I do hope that child will get better," the stranger said before turning to the leftovers and giving everyone a placid smile.

Lowy's eyes popped with recognition. "It's Peter, right?"

"I am flattered you remember me after all this time, Miss Harlow," Peter said, giving her a small bow.

"I'm sorry about all this," Lowy apologized. "But I have no idea what's going on right now."

Peter chuckled and took another bite of his candy. "A feeling we all share, even in the best of times."

He didn't say anything more, so Lowy asked, "Is there something I can do for you? I'm happy to help you with a room in a bit, but I want to find out about my friend first."

Peter propped his foot on the wall behind him. "No trouble at all, my dear, as I have no need of lodgings. I happened to be on a walk when I noticed the ambulance and could not help but investigate. Curiosity often gets the better of me, unfortunately; one of my many faults."

Lowy's eyebrows crinkled. "You were walking? But there's nothing around here for miles."

"I am known to take excursions like this from time to time. Is that a problem?"

Lowy held up her hands in apology. "No, no! I didn't mean it like that."

Peter put his hands together and lowered his head. "Forgive me. Sometimes my mind wanders and my diction accompanies it. I should clarify. I meant to say: am I causing you any trouble by trespassing on your wonderful establishment?"

Lowy shook her head. "Of course not."

The man gave her another of those spine-tingling smiles. "Good. It would be rather difficult to contest my guilt with the sheriff watching over us."

Denvis did not respond to Peter's attempt to draw him into the conversation as he wiped at the sweat pooling on his brow with a forearm.

Peter found this amusing. "In truth, perhaps we should be more worried about this gentleman here." Peter looked Fleet up and down. "He seems to have stumbled into a rather traumatic situation."

Fleet was standing there in silence. He had watched the ambulance drive off, only now turning away to address the man speaking. Though Fleet seemed ready to give Peter some charged words, he faltered.

"Wait a minute, I know you," Fleet recalled, an expression of mild understanding on his face.

Peter looked almost giddy as he kicked off the wall and walked toward him. "From where, pray tell?"

Fleet held up a finger at the man when he was sure. "You're the guy who got me the milkshake at the restaurant."

The smile faded from Peter's face. "Yes, that was me."

"Well, nice to meet you, but I'm not in the mind-space to deal with whatever the hell it is you're trying to do here, so I'm gonna bail."

Fleet glanced at Denvis to see if he had any intent to protest, but he only stood there like a statue. Without another word, Fleet walked away from them toward the end of the building. Lowy called out to him but let slip only a chirp as Peter interrupted her.

"Do not worry about me," he said. "I am sure the sheriff will give me a ride home. 'Here to serve' and all that."

"It would be my pleasure," Denvis agreed as he wiped his brow once more.

Peter gave Lowy one last smile. "Off you go. Though, I do hope we will get the opportunity to chat more in depth one of these days."

"Uh, sure," Lowy said, backing away from the group. "Fleet! Wait up!" She took off after him, calling his name when he did not answer.

As she closed the gap, he did a quick turnabout and said, "What the fuck was all that shit?"

Lowy stumbled back, surprised by the ferocity of his question. "You were there. You should know better than me, right?"

"I guess that's the problem, isn't it!" Fleet objected, slicing his hand through the air. "You don't even realize that you're running some kind of fucking trap house here."

"What are you talking about?" Lowy asked, her face creased with worry.

"There's no way this was the first time!" Fleet said. "Does she not give a shit about her?"

Lowy frowned, trying to make sense of his words. "Is this about Jill? What happened to her? Talk to me!"

Fleet only continued his accusations, lost in his own emotions. "And you, you just sit up in that office and pretend like you don't know what goes on here. You know damn well what people do behind these doors. You give them access to do whatever fucked-up shit they want, then look the other way and wash your hands of it all. You're either complicit or ignorant of the truth, Lowy. And if it's the latter, you don't have that excuse anymore. Would this make your parents proud, huh? What you've turned their 'dream' into? Figure your shit out!"

Tears welled in her eyes before he even finished his tirade. "That's not fair..." she choked out before her voice gave way.

Fleet put a palm to his head and stared at the ground as he waited for his anger to subside, if only a little. "I can't... I can't think straight right now. Just leave me alone for a while."

Fleet hurried off, a sudden pang of guilt stabbing him in the chest. He made a beeline for his door and slammed it behind him. He sat down on the bed and massaged his temples, only now realizing that his hands were shaking.

"Not again..."

Fleet flexed in and out of fists, hoping that it would somehow help him regain composure. When it failed, he fell back on the mattress, closed his eyes, and took several deep breaths. He tried to wipe his mind of everything that had happened, but found it no easy feat.

Jill, those weird EMTs, that dude who showed up—all a waste of time. As much as he wanted to understand, to make some sense of it, the whole thing was pointless.

"It's not my problem."

He needed to get away from it all, even if just for a little while. Fleet locked the door to his room and went straight to his truck; perhaps a quick jaunt would do him some good. He plugged his phone into the cigarette lighter and started the vehicle.

Fleet drove in the opposite direction of the town with nothing but the sound of the engine to keep him company. He should check in with Curtis, though he debated if he needed to fill him in on what had transpired. In an act of synchronicity, the sudden jingle of Curtis' ringtone erupted from his phone as it flicked back to life. He tilted the screen toward him, surprised to see that he had driven far enough away to get one bar of signal.

Fleet's first instinct was to tell Curtis everything, but he stopped himself before clicking the answer button. There was no way in hell he could tell him about this. Even if he believed it was for the right reasons, it would mean admitting that he had fucked up once again—a huge one this time. Blaming your moral compass for the cataclysmic collapse of society seemed like a rather poor excuse, all things considered.

He had to let it go.

Fleet needed a few seconds to calm himself in hopes Curtis wouldn't pick up on anything from how he sounded. After one last deep exhale, he clicked the answer button.

"Whatcha got?"

"You need to come to the school now!" Curtis' frantic voice sounded on the line.

Fleet's heart rate spiked again at his words, and after having just calmed down, the sudden resurgence made him light-headed. "Are you serious?"

"Yes, I'm fucking serious!" Curtis echoed back. "Get down here!"

Fleet slammed on the brakes. "On my way."

The last thing he heard as his phone died was Curtis' mumbled admittance.

"You were right."

CHAPTER FOURTEEN

SAY CHEESE

FLEET SLAMMED THE CAR door and sprinted toward the side of the school where Curtis was waving him over. "What is it? What'd you find?" Fleet asked before he even came to a complete stop.

"Back here," Curtis responded as he motioned for Fleet to follow.

Curtis jogged around to the back of the building with Fleet in tow. In the bright daylight, it was much easier to see how dilapidated the old school building was; somehow, it felt more imposing now than it had shrouded in darkness.

Curtis slowed as he reached their destination. He then pointed to a cluster of unwieldy shrubbery. "Right over there."

Fleet gave him one last nervous glance and walked to where Curtis had indicated. At first, all he could discern were the unkempt shrubs, but as he drew closer, he could see what had put Curtis on edge.

Hidden away in between two overgrown bushes was a set of doors leading down into the basement. The wood was moldy and warped from the moisture and constant shade as a consequence of its seclusion. It stuck out to him that the grass near the entrance was matted and worn, showing the dirt beneath as if it had been trafficked often by heavy feet.

"What's down there?" Fleet inquired, turning back toward Curtis to find him maintaining a healthy distance.

"Fuck if I know!" Curtis responded, unwilling to get any closer.

"You didn't check it out?"

"Hell no! This isn't my fuckin' job!" he whisper-yelled at Fleet.

"Then why are you here?"

Curtis didn't respond to that. Fleet gave him a moment to speak up, but decided there were more important things to worry about.

"What makes you think this is something?" Fleet asked.

Curtis answered that just fine. "Because I opened the door." He took a few more steps back. "The second I did, it was 'that time' all over again."

At the mention of 'that time,' Fleet furrowed his brow, gazing at the cellar door with fearful reverence. Curtis had to be wrong about this. Even if Fleet had picked up on something earlier, he hadn't considered that it could be on the same level as 'that time.'

Fleet crept forward and grabbed the metal door handle. He hung there for several seconds, savoring the cold steel in his palm. His pinky finger twitched, a nervous tic he couldn't control; one that only seemed to manifest itself before a fight—or a bloodbath. Every fiber of his being was telling him to flee, and he hated to admit just how much the urge appealed to him.

But he couldn't run. Not if...

He took one final deep breath and yanked the door open, throwing it into the nearby bush.

The smell of rotting flesh assaulted Fleet, clinging to him as it latched on deep within his sinuses. He lost his footing and dropped to the ground as he battled his gag reflex. On one knee, he coughed in wet spurts, but nothing came of it besides globs of spit.

After regaining his senses, he gave Curtis a mortified look. Curtis returned one of his own, having experienced the same thing earlier.

Fleet sat there stunned, trying to keep the memories of 'that time' from overwhelming him—a portent of the horrors that awaited below.

Curtis came over and grabbed Fleet's shoulder to give him a quick shake. "I already called for backup. We just have to hold tight for a little and everything will be fine," he assured Fleet, despite the tremble in his voice.

His words shook Fleet from his momentary stupor. "Why aren't they here now? I told you to bring them with you."

Curtis couldn't hide his guilt. "Truth is, I didn't expect to find anything here, so I never bothered to call them."

"The fuck, Scriptor!" Fleet shot up and shoved him. "What is going on with you?"

"I'm sorry, but it is what it is, all right? Just tell me what your orders are, and I'll make it happen."

Putting his feelings aside, Fleet twisted his neck until it made an audible pop. "Fine. But we're gonna talk about this later."

He took a step back into the open, giving the building a quick once over as he formulated a plan. "The place is pretty big, but it looks like all the action is going to be down in the basement; not that it means that's where the fighting will be contained. The woods could be a problem, though. It's a safe zone if they can make it through us."

Fleet began dotting his fingers in the air, mentally calculating. He was replaying 'that time' over again in his mind, scrutinizing the successes and failures they had met that day. But most importantly, he was trying to work out how 'She' would do it.

"Fifteen," he concluded. "If we can get that many spread out here, we should be able to cover even the worst-case scenario."

Curtis gritted his teeth and winced. "I can get you two."

Fleet turned and stared Curtis down. "Two?"

Curtis nodded.

"Are you fucking kidding me!" Fleet shouted before overcompensating himself to a whisper, forgetting that whatever was down there might hear him. "Why can you only get two?"

"Your boss took them all!"

"What do you mean she took them all?"

"She has a positive on some Tryst," Curtis explained in defense. "She's been working on it for months and now she's ready to crack down. How was anyone supposed to know it would turn out like this? Our job was only to gather preliminary info. You can't compare what we're doing to putting an end to a fucking 'buffet'!"

Fleet cringed back at the word 'buffet.' It was a crass term used to cover murders where multiple people were devoured in a small geographical area. They were difficult to identify because the bodies are wholly consumed, leaving only trace evidence behind. It required a lot of detective work and data aggregation to pinpoint who or where the responsible parties might be, making them one of the more difficult cases to solve.

"Shit!" Fleet cursed aloud, realizing the merit of the argument. "Can you borrow some from her?"

Curtis shook his head. "Even if I could, she's like five states away. It would take forever for them to even get here."

Fleet cursed again. "What about the two we have coming?"

"About two hours."

Fleet looked defeated as he gazed down into the empty cellar. "I guess it's just you and me, then."

Fleet reached behind him and pulled a handgun that he had shoved into the waistline of his pants. He cocked the pistol in one swift motion and held it aloft, taking a bead on a tree far in the distance.

Curtis couldn't believe what he was hearing. "What? No way! No way, man. We have to wait for backup."

Fleet dropped the gun to his side. "You said it yourself, right? This is a bit too reminiscent of 'that time.' If that's the case, then there's a chance someone is still alive down there!"

"You got lucky last time and you know it!" Curtis exclaimed, getting heated. "You have to wait!"

"I'm the Servunday. I make the decisions," Fleet countered with authority.

Curtis tried to look defiant, but there was no hiding the worry that creased his brow. He wasn't trying to be insubordinate; he was just concerned for his friend and long-time partner—and Fleet knew that.

"This isn't some suicide mission, Scriptor," Fleet said, taking on a calmer tone. "I'm only going down there to look for survivors. If I find anyone, I'll grab them and get the hell out of there. I have no plans to engage unless I have no other choice."

Curtis frowned and let out a defeated sigh. "Alright, but be careful."

Fleet gave him a comforting nod before turning back to the cellar door. "See you in a few."

Fleet set his jaw and took a few steps inward, but he stopped at the precipice of darkness to pat at his thigh.

"You don't happen to have a flashlight, do you?"

─━████████████████████━─

Fleet kept his eyes front and center as he methodically made his way forward until he reached a point where the light faltered, falling victim to the void. He took a deep breath and cleared his mind so that his other senses would take over.

The basement was warm and humid; when coupled with the lack of light, it felt as if the darkness was wrapping itself around him, hoping to rob him of his very breath. He stood motionless, trying not to let the smell get the better of him as he listened. He heard nothing save for the buzzing of a lone fly that would come and go around his head like a carousel horse.

Fleet took the phone from his pocket and pointed it forward, resting the hand that held his firearm over it for stability. The flashlight function kicked in, and though weak, he could at least see enough to make progress. He continued his slow march inward until a peculiar sound made him stop. He waited, wondering if the noise would manifest itself again.

After a moment, he took another step, and there it was again.

Whatever it may be, it was close.

While he couldn't quite place it, he was at least observant enough this time to form a comparison: it sounded similar to someone trying to unravel a roll of plastic wrap. He moved forward and heard it play once more. It was only then that he realized it was playing in tune with each step he took.

He pointed his meager light down at his feet.

Blood.

Streaked all over the concrete was a coagulated carpet of blood slapped on the floor like wet paint; it was still fresh enough to stick to the bottom of his shoes. His pinky tapped against the cold metal of his gun as he panned his phone forward to see that it only grew thicker the deeper it traveled inward.

Not much farther in, the trail of blood snaked to the right, leading underneath a door. He pulled into the wall and pressed his back up against it. That horrible smell seemed to be concentrated in this area.

Fleet reached over to turn the knob. With a small click, the door unhinged. Using the tips of his fingers, he pushed the door inward until it tapped against something metallic, followed by a loud chorus of buzzing.

Fleet took one last deep breath, lowered himself, and lunged through the doorway with his gun drawn. A swathe of flies burst out at him as if they were riding a wave made of that horrid stench. Fleet took their meager assault straight to the face, never budging—'She' would have been proud to see that.

As the insects dissipated, he saw tentacles reaching down from the emptiness above like some Lovecraftian horror come to life. Upon further inspection, he realized the tendrils were actually rows and rows of sticky fly traps, most of which were so full they could no longer hold any more of their crunchy husks.

Keeping his head low to avoid getting stuck, he advanced and came upon the principal cause of the stench that filled the space. Just behind the door was a large metallic drum where all the flies were congregating. All down the side, a viscous goop clung in dark strands like thinning hair to the chipped blue sheen.

Fleet held his breath and got close enough to shine his light on the barrel's contents. What he found was a thick blackened soup that seemed to be...moving? He had to study it up close to realize what was causing the morbid illusion: thousands of maggots swarming underneath the surface of the congealed slop.

As Fleet turned away in disgust, he soon discovered that Satan's porridge was far from the worst treasure stored in this place.

"What the fuck?"

Along the walls were shelves upon shelves full of taxidermy animals: opossums, squirrels, deer, and numerous others, all misshapen beyond recognition. These abominations were either the work of an amateur or someone with a twisted sense of humor—perhaps both.

Their skins were set on bases that did not fit; some were stretched so tight that they tore and others so loose they hung like fresh pizza dough. The animal's faces sat off center with their teeth askew, poking out through their fur like yellow boils. Their limbs were crooked and mangled, bent at unnatural angles to fit their poorly planned dioramas.

One that Fleet found particularly disturbing involved an opossum boxing—or maybe dancing—with a brown fox. Though they faced each other in fisticuffs, their heads were turned outward toward the viewer. Their mismatched glass marble eyes sat crammed in their dusty sockets, reflecting the light from his phone back at him. It was almost as if they were studying his reaction. He felt their gaze boring straight into him, as if pleading to end their misery; a dire warning that not even death is escape from pain.

In this menagerie of the living dead, there were no humans.

Fleet slammed the door, his chest heaving from his heavy breathing. He was no stranger to gore and violence, but something about that room had profoundly disturbed him.

He took a few deep breaths to calm himself and turned his phone light ahead of him in the corridor. Beyond, he could see that it opened up into a larger area, though his light source was too weak to show him any farther.

He stopped at the opening to the room and scanned over it with his phone. Various support beams blocked his vision, casting ominous shadows that seemed to follow him as he shifted the light.

Near the wall was a hook that hung from the ceiling by a thick steel chain, plastered with blood and bits of hair. Underneath it sat a medium-sized blue bucket that was overflowing with something disturbing; the buzzing flies around it gave Fleet the impression that this contained the same 'material' that was in the large drum from earlier.

The blood seemed most concentrated here, and dark-red footprints led out that faded the farther away they got, as if left by a vanishing specter. Even more disturbing was that the prints showed the perpetrator was barefoot as they enacted their butchery.

Nearby were old folding tables and chairs that someone had turned into a makeshift workstation for whatever sick ritual they were concocting. A couple of kerosene lanterns were spread out among the debris; a necessity for a place that no longer received electricity. Various tools were set upon the table's surface that had been used for tasks beyond their intended purpose—this went double for the gore-encrusted teaspoon. If he didn't know better, he could have easily confused the whole place for some sort of medieval torture chamber.

Something struck him as odd as he made his way farther in: despite all the blood and gore, there was one small area that remained untainted. In the far corner, someone had draped a white sheet over one shelf. There was no grime or dirt, and try as the flies might, they could not penetrate the linen barrier.

Fleet crept toward the shelf and grabbed a corner of the sheet. He exhaled one last deep breath as he tried to prepare himself for what he prayed would be the last exhibit he would have to endure in this peculiar museum of horror. With a quick inhale, he yanked the cover down and stepped back to shine his light on what lay beneath.

<hr />

It had been almost fifteen minutes since Fleet had begun his excursion into the bowels of the old school. Outside, Curtis was pacing at the corner of the building to keep tabs on the cellar and the parking lot. Periodically, he thought he heard some random sound escape from the basement, but it was never anything that he could make out.

He had begun debating himself to stave off his anxiety.

Fuck, what am I doing? Why did I even agree to come here? I should have just lied and said I checked the damn place out.

He stopped and slapped himself in the face for thinking that.

No! If I hadn't shown up, we would have never found it, and who knows what might have happened. This is my fault for not taking this seriously. I should have believed him from the start, and now he's down there with no backup. That's my boy. My best friend. Godfather to my children—if my wife had let me. I can't just leave him down there like that.

His thoughts changed as he relented to the reality of his situation.

That's why I can't go down there: I have a family! Plus, I have no real combat training. If I went down there, I'd only get in the way. That's the deal: he goes in, does his thing, and I support him. But I didn't support him. I didn't even bring a goddamn flashlight!

Curtis heard a muffled shuffling sound that soon graduated into a rush of rapid footsteps that echoed from the dank cellar.

Fleet's frantic call echoed throughout the basement. "Scriptor! Get over here, quick!"

Curtis gave one last glance to the empty parking lot and cursed before dashing back to the cellar entrance. He ground to a halt just short of the stairs and yelled into the abyss. "You all right?"

There was no response; even the sound of footsteps had stopped, forcing Curtis into an uncomfortable malaise. He called out once more to no avail as he pulled his pistol from its side holster.

Against every decree from his own sense of self-preservation, Curtis took one trembling step into the ground. He made it down four treads before he realized he was holding his breath. He stopped and lowered his weapon, inhaling like he was about to swim underwater to the deep end of a pool.

As he did, there was a screech from the void, and something sailed at him from the darkness. Curtis let out a high-pitched scream as he fired off a round into the wall, sending up a puff of shattered concrete.

The UFO hit him square in the chest with a wet thud. He fell onto his back and kicked his way out of the hole, rolling on the ground and slapping at himself like he was on fire.

With both arms pressed against his chest, Curtis stopped out of sheer dread he was making his injury worse. He lay there bug-eyed, afraid that even the slightest shift of his hands would lead to something vital leaking through the gaping hole in his chest.

Then he saw a head pop from the earth as it crested the opening of the cellar. It was Fleet—and he was laughing his ass off.

"Oh shit, dude. I didn't expect all that," Fleet choked out through his laughter. "You okay?"

"W-what?" Curtis whimpered back at him.

Fleet emerged from the opening, carrying Curtis' dropped pistol in one hand and something round in his other.

Curtis forced himself to his knees, hands still glued to his body, as Fleet tossed the unknown object onto the ground in front of him. The thing was wrapped in a cloth that had come unfurled when it landed, exposing some sort of off-white ball. A portion of it was flat where it had smacked Curtis in the chest.

Curtis stared down at it. "What is that?"

"Cheese," Fleet said, nudging it with his foot.

Releasing his death grip, the confused Curtis looked up at him and then down at his chest; nothing fell out, but there was a large wet spot on his shirt.

He continued to chuckle as he sat down next to Curtis in the grass. "Turns out it might not have been exactly what we thought it was," Fleet admitted.

Still overcome by the cheesy assault, Curtis laid back and propped himself up with his elbows as he listened to Fleet's explanation.

"So, from what I can tell, there's nothing down there—at least nothing Tryst related. Looks like someone is using this place as some kind of, I don't know, workshop or something. They've been hunting game illegally and bringing them here to clean 'em, dress 'em, and...some other shit I'd prefer to never think about again."

Fleet made a big deal of it as he shivered in disgust.

"Was he having sex with them?" Curtis asked, his muddled brain filling in the gaps for 'other shit.'

Fleet crinkled his nose at him. "Why would you even ask that? But I mean, yeah, probably."

Curtis blinked several times. "What about the cheese?"

Fleet shrugged. "I guess he could be fuckin' the cheese, too. I didn't see any holes in the ones I looked at, but that doesn't—"

Curtis interrupted him. "No, I mean, why was it even down there to begin with?"

"Maybe whoever it is thinks this is a good place to age it," Fleet guessed, reaching over to poke at the ball. "But it's still kinda mushy, like it was just put down there. Hell, based on what I saw, we might have only missed the cheese-man by a few hours, if that."

"Good thing we didn't run into anyone," Curtis said, shaken by the thought. "A person crazy enough to do all this probably wouldn't have an issue blowing your head off if you snuck up on them."

"You got a point," Fleet agreed. He then cocked his head and started rubbing his upper lip with his thumb. "But now that you say that, I don't remember seeing any weapons. No guns, bows, traps—nothing. Some of those weird tools could be dangerous, but they would be worthless for hunting."

"Unless they're catching them bare-handed, they've got something," Curtis reasoned.

Fleet flicked away his thumb. "But I didn't even see a box of ammo or a spent shell casing in the whole place."

Curtis flipped up a hand. "Because they're smart. They know not to leave something behind that might incriminate them and blow their little operation here."

"Not smart enough to clean up their bloody footprints," Fleet muttered from the side of his mouth.

Curtis sat up to point at Fleet. "As I've told you before, it doesn't matter. None of this does. If what you said is true, there are no Tryst here. We're done."

Fleet exhaled, giving the building one last once-over. "I was wrong, but I won't say this was the wrong thing to do. Though you gotta admit, it had you going there for a minute."

"Yeah, it did." Curtis looked into that dark cellar. "I just figured you were having a little freak-out, but now I see why you thought this might be something. Should have trusted you from the beginning and treated my assignment like a professional. Instead, I showed up and acted like a goddamn amateur—didn't even bother to bring a decent flashlight."

Curtis grabbed his gun that Fleet had set down between them.

"At least I brought a weapon, even if I was more worried about snakes than Tryst."

"Then I guess we're both jackasses," Fleet said with a laugh.

They sat in silence until Curtis yanked up a handful of grass and threw it in Fleet's face. "You scared the piss out of me, you fuckin' asshole!"

Fleet grinned at his own mischief. "I know."

"I could have shot you!"

"And I'd have deserved it."

Curtis shut his eyes and lay down on his back, letting out a deep sigh before pondering aloud, "Someone turned this place into their own personal atelier of horrors, and we miraculously stumbled upon it during a Tryst investigation. What are the odds of that shit?"

"The hell's an 'at-lair'?" Fleet asked.

"It's...don't worry about it." Curtis got back on topic. "Now besides the cheese ball you stole, I assume we don't need to do any cleanup?"

"Nah." Fleet picked up said cheese ball and tossed it back into the cellar. "What are they going to do? Call the police? Let's just bail on this whole thing."

"Agreed," Curtis said. "Just gotta update our backup on the situation and we're golden."

"What are you going to tell them? I know I started this wild-goose chase, but we're both going to look like idiots when they hear what happened."

"No, we won't," Curtis contested. "We did exactly what we should have done: identified a possible threat and called in support. We have nothing to be ashamed of."

"Well, maybe not about this, at least..." Fleet got to his feet and wiped the dirt from his backside. "Whelp, as head of the investigation, I officially declare that this case is unrelated to Tryst."

Curtis exhaled, eyes still shut. "Glad to hear it. When we heading out?"

"First thing tomorrow."

Curtis opened his eyes. "Why not now?"

Fleet groaned. "I'm hungry, I'm tired, and I've still got my stuff at the motel."

"Just leave it and let's go now. We'll get you new stuff."

"If you want to buy me a new 'Tayumore,' be my guest," Fleet said with a laugh. "You can just skip Christmas for the next hundred years or so. I'm sure the kids will forgive you...eventually." Curtis groaned at the mention of the 'Tayumore,' so Fleet added, "My, uhh, car is back there too."

Curtis wrinkled his nose. "What car? I thought you drove—" The expression left him as he realized what Fleet meant. "Ahhh. Yeah, we can't leave that behind."

Fleet nodded in affirmation. "Lowy also has my license. I know 'Frederick' is only an alias, but I've gotten pretty attached to it at this point. Really don't want to get used to going by a different name because I left a picture of myself behind somewhere."

"I get it," Curtis empathized. "Hard to just throw that away over something so trivial."

"Yep. But first things first." Fleet pointed over his shoulder with a thumb. "There's this hole-in-the-wall restaurant back in town I wanted to try out. Lowy said it was a local favorite."

Curtis tilted his head back and narrowed his eyes. "How much time did you spend with this girl?"

"Enough to know she deserves an apology," Fleet said, offering Curtis his hand. "Now get your ass up and let's grab some food."

"Sounds good," Curtis agreed as he was pulled to his feet. "But only if they serve something without cheese."

Chapter Fifteen
APOLOGY

FLEET STOOD ALONE BY the screen door to the front office, a soggy brown bag in hand, trying to formulate what he was going to say to Lowy. He had been dropped off after the pair grabbed food at the local greasy spoon Lowy raved about the other day. Curtis had taken his meal to go, saying he had to attend to some business. Fleet had decided against joining him, realizing that he wanted to clear the air with Lowy before he left the next day.

Lowy was sitting exactly as she had been the first time Fleet met her, all her senses trained on the phone in her hand. He couldn't help but notice that she looked sullen and hoped that she was just reading a depressing article.

Fleet grumbled as he fought against that stubborn door before making it to the front desk. And just as before, she failed to notice him.

Not wanting a repeat of their initial meeting, Fleet opened the brown bag and placed it on the desk. It only took a few seconds before Lowy's nose wiggled, having caught a whiff of the overpowering aroma. She gave a start when she noticed him there, but at least there was no head trauma involved this time.

"Fleet! Hey!" She took out her earbuds and gave an exalted inhale. "You went to Tray's?"

"I did. How can you tell?"

Lowy poked the soggy sack. "Just based off how thoroughly the grease has soaked through the bag."

Fleet smiled at her. "I didn't know what you liked, so I got two of everything."

"Thank you, but you didn't have to do that."

"Yeah, I kinda did. I said some stuff to you that was uncalled for. That whole debacle earlier put me in a weird place, and I lashed out at you. You're a great person, and I know you're doing the best you can."

As he continued, Lowy grabbed a handful of fries from the bag.

"I just wanted to say I'm sorry, and that I'm glad you think the fries are more important than my heartfelt apology."

"They just smelled so good! My mouth was watering the whole time you were talking."

"Then you forgive me?"

"Of course," Lowy mumbled through a mouthful of fries.

"Well, that was easy." Fleet chuckled as he snagged a few fries for himself. "I'm glad you're not upset. I felt like shit about it all day."

"Mmm-unn!" Lowy shook her head and held up a finger as she finished swallowing. "No! Take it back!"

"What?"

"Your apology; I give it back!"

"Do what now?"

"I rebuke you! I, um, retract my apology acceptance, leaving your apology in a sorrowful limbo of rejection."

Fleet stared at her for a moment and then studied the fries in his hand before dropping them in the bag. "You can have the fries back."

"No, Fleet, that's not... What I mean is..." Lowy started to pick at her nails. "If you want to make it up to me, then you should..."

Fleet furrowed his brow, prompting Lowy to cover her face with both hands. The words she spoke came out almost whisper-quiet.

"You should take me out for drinks."

With face still concealed, she explained herself.

"Truth is, I was upset at you...then at me. Some of the stuff you said hit a little close to home, and I know I've got some things I need to think about, but I don't care about that right now. It's selfish, especially with everything going on. I know that but..."

She dropped her hands and looked up at him.

"More than anything, I don't want this to be our last memory together."

How did she know he was leaving? No, that was a stupid question. This was a motel. Its entire purpose was to give people a moment of respite as they were passing through. No one was ever supposed to stay here for long. It would be hard to make friends or build any meaningful relationships with the temporary tenants. But she must have some sort of life away from this place; Denvis was proof of that.

So why did this mean so much to her?

He decided to turn her down and to do it as callously as possible. Teach her now that it was best to avoid strangers—a valuable life lesson. It would keep her safe from junkies like Dash, douchebags like Oreen, killers like...

"Lowy, I don't..."

She smiled, her eyes pleading for him to accept.

"...think that will be a problem."

What harm could it do? He had proved beyond any doubt that there were no Tryst in the area; that made the mission a success! This was a celebration, a firm pat on the back for a job well done. It sounded like Curtis would be held up for the rest of the day anyway, so what was he supposed to do with his free time? Just sit alone in his room all night? Might as well have a few drinks.

And if this was the only way to make it up to Lowy, then what choice did he have?

Lowy's mood did a quick one-eighty. "Awesome, that's...that's awesome!"

"Sure is. When do you want to head out?"

Lowy stood up and made for the back door, unable to contain her excitement. "Give me about an hour to get ready, okay?"

"Works for me," Fleet agreed.

Just as the door closed behind her, she shouted back, "This'll be great, I promise!"

Fleet overcame his mild concern that Lowy had left the front office unattended and headed back to his room. He plugged in his phone to charge before hopping in the shower; he hadn't realized how much he needed one.

That wretched stink from the cellar still clung to him like a wet fur coat. He had been lucky that the greasy power of Tray's had overcome his own putrid aroma during his meeting with Lowy. Despite the difficulties afforded him by the clogged shower head, he left his bath feeling calm and relaxed, as if all his worries had been carried off with the water down the drain.

Lowy was right. This would be great.

An extra set of clothes followed by a quick check of his now charged phone and he was out the door. Outside, he saw Lowy standing by her car, waving him over.

He waved back at her. "You look like you're ready to go."

She was wearing the same outfit she had worn the night before with some slight alterations, but this time she had on her glasses. "Are you saying you're not?"

"Oh, I'm ready to tear it up."

Fleet took his place in the passenger seat. "Where are we headed?"

"It's a bar owned by an old family friend that I haven't been to in forever." Lowy got in and shut the door behind her. "This will be the first time I've been able to drink there—you know, legally."

Fleet cocked an eyebrow. "Whoa, didn't realize you were such a wild child. Perhaps I underestimated you."

Lowy gave him a half-smile and winked as she inserted the key into the ignition. As she started the car, the rear passenger door opened, and someone slid into the middle of the back seat. Surprised, Fleet turned to see the new arrival.

Oreen had a wicked grin on his face.

"I forgot to tell you," Lowy said, complicit but frustrated. "I invited Oreen to come along."

Oreen leaned forward and situated his head between the two of them. "I saw her all dolled up—she looks amazing, don't you think?—and knew that something fun was about to happen. Hope you don't mind me tagging along."

"The more the merrier," Fleet quipped, trying to sound sincere, all the while preparing himself for an evening of verbal abuse.

Lowy drew her lips to a line as she put the car in reverse. "Yay."

The conversation from then on was bogarted by Oreen, especially if Fleet ever had some sort of input.

At around the halfway point, Fleet realized something. He side-eyed Oreen, whose head was still annoyingly close to them both. "You missed out on some crazy shit earlier. Where were you all day?"

Even if he thought Oreen was an asshole, he didn't think he was stupid. During that whole ambulance ordeal, having someone with a level head—or at least somebody who wasn't batshit insane—might have been beneficial.

"I heard about it from Lowy. That poor girl," Oreen said. "But I can't say I'm surprised, considering who she associates with."

Lowy perked up as she remembered something. "I forgot to tell you. Uncle Denvis called me shortly after and told me Jill was in a stable condition. He also said that he might press charges against Dash."

Oreen clicked his tongue. "It's for the best, I think. For both their sakes—and yours too, Lowy. You were getting a bit too close to that woman."

"She's my friend. I just—"

Oreen interrupted her with an authoritative guffaw. "A friend? You don't even have her number, and I know I've seen her with a phone before. What kind of friend is that? Not like us. I had yours the first day we met because I care about you."

Oreen tilted his head toward Fleet.

"Does he have your number?"

Fleet wasn't certain whether Oreen had asked that to find out the truth of it, or if he had just said it to slander him.

"No, she doesn't," Fleet answered for her. "But what we do have is—"

Oreen broke in to halt his rebuttal. "Anyway, didn't you want to know what I was doing earlier today?"

"Not really," Fleet admitted. "I was just being polite."

"If you must know, BJ and I went antiquing."

"Wait, for real?" Fleet asked with a frown, his curiosity getting the better of him.

"That's right. I enjoy going so that I can find racist figurines and knickknacks that I then photograph and post on social media to shame the owners. I have quite the following," Oreen boasted.

"Any luck?" Lowy asked, clearly worried about the answer.

"I thought this place would be a gold mine, but I didn't find anything at all. I was rather disappointed—but in a good way."

"Of course you didn't! This is a good town, with good people," Lowy added with a hint of pride.

"We all need our hobbies," Fleet said, turning away from Oreen to study the road. "So BJ didn't want to come?"

Fleet couldn't help but ask about him; he preferred BJ much, much more than Oreen. He also thought seeing the big guy with a few drinks in him could be a laugh riot. Not to mention he would also be the one you want in your corner in case a drunken brawl broke out.

Not that Fleet had any intention of causing a commotion, of course.

"It's not his scene," Oreen explained. "I love the man, but he's seriously lacking in social graces. And you think he's quiet now? Get a few beers in him and he turns into a wax sculpture. Try to strike up a conversation and he'll put you to sleep faster than a tea party with Bill Cosby."

Fleet choked, surprised by the off-color joke as Oreen finished up.

"BJ will be fine without me for a little while."

"Lucky bastard," Fleet grumbled, eliciting a glare from Oreen. "And by that, I mean how lucky he is to have you."

Oreen turned back to Lowy. "How much longer? I've become burdened with the present company." He then whispered to her, "I'm not talking about you, though. You're perfect."

"I will turn this car around right now if you two don't cut it out," Lowy threatened.

"Please no," Fleet begged her. "I've never needed a drink more in my life."

"We're home!" Lowy shouted, her excitement rising as she pulled into the gravel parking lot.

"Are you sure this is the right place?" Oreen asked with a pinch of confusion and a mound of concern.

Lowy had taken them to a bar just outside of downtown. The ramshackle building looked as though it was abandoned; however, the lights from inside and the smattering of cars in the dirt parking lot suggested otherwise. Oreen got out of the car and stood by the door, giving the building a mortified scan.

"Lowy, am I going to die in there?" he asked in all seriousness.

"Possibly," she joked. "I know how it looks, but I promise that everyone here is super friendly."

This did not seem to assuage Oreen's fears as he considered getting back into the car.

"You can go back if you want," she offered. "Fleet and I can stay here and get a cab home."

"Are you kidding? This is my kind of place!" Oreen shouted to hide his trepidation as he slammed the car door shut.

The three of them made their way to the front door, avoiding the gentleman passed out on the walkway. They stopped at the entrance to inspect the sign that hung above them.

"Classy Bar," Fleet read aloud. "That's not me being sarcastic; that is its literal name."

"Curses!" Oreen—well—cursed. "And here I am, bereft of both my top hat and walking cane. I will be a laughingstock among the other socialites."

Not to be outdone, Fleet added, "This will be the last time I take recommendations from my addle-brained butler. Jeeves is going to get quite the verbal thrashing when I return to the mansion."

"Cretins!" Lowy interrupted in a snobbish tone as she pretended to clean an invisible monocle before putting it over her eye. "You plebeians wouldn't know class if the hounds were to drag it braying from your musty foxholes. Just follow my lead and do try to maintain a certain level of civility. We are in the company of aristocrats; you shall behave yourself in kind."

The two 'uncivilized cretins' looked at one another with a smirk.

Fleet raised his hands in forfeiture. "I think she's got us beat, man."

Oreen wiped away an imaginary tear. "I've never been so proud."

Fleet then gave a gratuitous bow as he opened the door and motioned them in. "After you."

Oreen returned the bow and shuffled in.

Lowy grinned as she walked past Fleet into the building. She had just seen a glimmer of what a cordial relationship could be between Oreen and Fleet, and she liked it. If she played her cards right, maybe she could temper the animosity between them and foster a friendship. With her mind set and thoughts of the future pushed aside, Lowy couldn't help but think that this might be a good night after all.

CHAPTER SIXTEEN

KEEP IT CLASSY

THE THREE OF THEM made it inside, where they basked in the neon glow of a humming beer advertisement. Lowy walked straight to the bar, waving at the bartender, who then returned one in kind accompanied by a high-pitched squeal.

Fleet sat on the nearest wobbly floor-mounted bar stool, struggling to steady himself as it shifted under his weight. Oreen opted to stand, unable to find a seat that did not disgust him.

"Lowy! Is that you? It's been forever since I've seen you!" the bartender called to her.

"I know!" Lowy met the grizzled old woman halfway over the bar to share a hug. "It's been far too long, Viv!"

Viv gave her the stink eye. "Yes it has, girl! You haven't been to church in ages. You haven't updated your Facebook so I can spy on you. But worst of all, you never came by on your twenty-first to let me get you loaded!"

Lowy winced at her onslaught. "I'm sorry. Work has been so crazy and I—"

Viv waved a hand at her. "All is forgiven. Besides, if anything noteworthy woulda happened to ya, I'm sure Big D would have told me about it."

"Denvis still comes here that often?" Lowy asked, masking her disappointment.

"Like clockwork," Viv confirmed with a nod. "You're a little early, but if you stay long enough, I bet you'll run into him."

Fleet cursed through clenched teeth. Why hadn't he thought about that? There was an excellent chance this would go south if they ran into each other. Oh well, too late now. He just needed to persuade Lowy to leave before Denvis arrived and everything would be fine.

The two of them continued their one-sided conversion, completely oblivious to Fleet and Oreen. After several minutes of this, Viv stepped back from the bar and turned sideways. "Lowy, watch this!"

Viv leaned backward until her upper body was almost vertical to the ground.

Lowy gasped like she had just witnessed a miracle. "Your back! It's all better!"

Viv righted herself and did some side stretches. "You know it, girl. I think I could start dancing again!"

Oreen perked up a bit. "Oh, that's wonderful! Did you do ballet?"

Viv had a laugh at that. "I did. Took lessons—and I mean a *lot* of lessons—but ended up doing a different type of dancing. You know, the kind that has less 'swans' and more 'beavers.'"

"Oh lord." Oreen groaned as he put his head in his hands, realizing what a terrible mistake he'd made in coming along.

Before Viv could catch Oreen's reaction, Lowy spoke up to divert her attention. "Did you get surgery?"

"Nope." Viv pushed in on her lower back. "I've ascended! Been seeing one of them natural doctors that don't use pills and knives. It's changed my life. Watch this here."

Viv bent forward, reaching downward until she touched her toes. Just as Viv extended herself fully, she released a squeaky toot and shot back up.

"Whoops, stepped on a frog."

Oreen shuddered, eyes rolling back into his head. Fleet had to cover his mouth to keep from laughing, but Lowy didn't hold hers back.

"Glad to see you haven't changed," Lowy said.

Viv persisted in her conviction about this new homeopathic practitioner. "The things he's done to me—girl, I can't even begin. It's. Done. Wonders."

"I can tell!" Lowy complimented. "It's like you've lost ten years. It's amazing, Viv!"

"And that ain't all!" Viv chirped.

She slapped her elbow. "Fixed my joint pain."

Flicked her nose. "Cleaned out my sinuses."

Patted her head. "Cleared up my scalp, and best of all..."

She slapped herself on the butt. "Got my plumbing flowing again. Watched MacGyver last night, and I got so soaked that I drowned all my crabs!"

Viv finished her spiel by smacking her hand against the bar and letting out a raspy cackle.

Lowy covered her face. "Oh my God, Viv!"

"I like her," Fleet said, nudging Lowy with his elbow.

"I think it's time for ol' Viv to get back on the horse, Lowy," Viv said with a laugh before she leaned in and gave Lowy's forearm a squeeze. "Or maybe it's time for that ol' horse to get back on me." Viv let out another cackle before releasing her.

"Stop that," Lowy chided. "What would your husband say if he heard you talk like that?"

Viv huffed with a smirk. "Nothing now," she said before turning her attention to Fleet and Oreen. "And speaking of extra-marital affairs, who are these two fine young gentlemen you brought here tonight?"

Yeah, Fleet knew how to deal with her type. He grabbed Viv's hand from the counter and brought it up to his face. "My name is Fredrick." He finished with a gentle kiss on the top of her hand. "And Miss Viv, I must say, after meeting you, it's obvious where you got the name for this fine establishment."

Viv fanned her face. "Oooo, girl! Tell me you don't have dibs on this one."

Lowy blushed as she stuttered, "N-No! We're not—"

"Then fuckin' dibs!" Viv shouted, not even waiting for Lowy's response.

She gave Fleet an exaggerated wink and blew him a wet kiss. Fleet caught her kiss in midair and then made an exaggerated show of him sliding his hand down the front of his pants. Viv let out another cackle as she slapped the table, thoroughly enjoying the exchange.

She then turned her attention to Oreen and extended her hand, expecting the same treatment she got from Fleet.

"Oreen," he stated, while pushing her hand away with the back of his own. "Your bar has a very...'unique' atmosphere, but I've been wondering about the name. Is it supposed to be ironic? Because if not, it seems a bit of a misnomer."

Viv put her hands on her hips. "You're gonna misnomer my foot in your ass if you aren't careful."

"That doesn't make any sense," Oreen contested.

Lowy grabbed Oreen's hand and gave it a hard squeeze where Viv couldn't see. This prompted Oreen to give a smile too strained for its own good, along with a stilted apology. "Just kidding! Pleasure to meet you."

With a raspy scoff, Viv turned back to Lowy. "One-out-a-two ain't bad. So, what can I get you folk?"

Oreen spoke first, reaching up a hand. "Do you have any ciders?"

Viv shot him a wink. "One cider, coming up."

She grabbed a large mug and stuck it under the tap, switching it on with expert precision. She stopped it before the head overflowed and slammed the mug down in front of Oreen without spilling a single drop.

Oreen raised his chin in thanks and took the glass in both hands, giving it a careful sip. He balked and set the glass down. "This isn't a cider."

Viv smacked herself on the forehead. "I forgot the most important part!" She then grabbed a whole orange and plopped it into his beer, which sloshed over the counter and onto Oreen's legs. "There's your cider, boy."

Oreen pursed his lips, holding his hands prone to his shoulders. "Ciders are actually made with—Owww!"

Lowy had pinched his side this time, hoping to show that this was not a fight he was going to win.

With a victorious 'Hmmph,' Viv addressed Fleet. "What about you, sexy?"

"Whatever's cold and on tap," Fleet said, unable to hide his satisfaction at how Oreen had been shot down.

With a flirtatious wink, Viv repeated the process from earlier, this time minus the orange. Fleet nodded his thanks and took a long swig, finishing with a contented exhale. "Not sure what it is, Viv. I can get this anywhere, but something about a beer straight from the tap, served by a pretty lady... It just tastes so much damn better."

Viv let out another one of her patented cackles. "You sure know how to turn on an old lady's faucet, don't ya? You let me know when you want to upgrade from that beer—the hard stuff's on me."

Not missing a beat, Fleet quipped, "Careful, Viv. Give me too much of that and the hard stuff's going to be *in* you."

Viv stared at him and bit her lip. "Thank God I've got flood insurance."

"Viv!" Lowy shouted, unable to endure the exchange any longer. She then poked Fleet in the ribs. "And stop encouraging her!"

Fleet shrugged and spun around to rest his elbow on the bar top as he took in the full majesty of 'Classy Bar.'

The joint seemed to be shooting for a rustic feel, but whether that was intentional or a byproduct from its many years of mistreatment was unknown. The walls were littered with different keepsakes: faded pictures of wildlife and people from times gone by, rusty metal advertisements for products that no longer existed, and stuffed deer heads that judged the patrons silently from above. He noticed that the entrance eschewed the overall motif, its wall covered in license plates collected from all over.

An old jukebox sat in the corner that someone had set to "Free Bird" on repeat. A well-used dartboard hung up on a section of the wall that seemed ready to collapse from the many holes that perforated it.

In the middle of the open area sat two well-used pool tables, their felt covered with so many stains and tears that one could almost confuse it for a topographic map. Two men stood immersed in their game of billiards, ignoring the fact that each shot bounced two or three times as it skipped to the pocket.

Fleet squinted at one of the men playing; he'd seen that guy somewhere before. He snapped his fingers when he remembered the name Gary. That was the dude that had fallen out of the window at the motel while they were roasting marshmallows. Fleet bet the fella would be heartbroken when he hears what had become of poor Dash.

Poor Dash...

Nah, fuck her.

Poor Jill...

Fleet took another long swig from his glass and continued to scan the bar.

At one end of the room was a collection of tables, spaced just far enough apart for a few chairs. Several people were seated there, having what looked like a heated conversation—except for one who was unabashedly staring at him.

"Not this asshole," Fleet cursed under his breath.

Peter. That's what Lowy had called him.

What the hell was up with that guy? First there was the milkshake, and then he pops up during the whole ambulance thing, somehow making the situation even more nonsensical than it already was. Fleet had been too distraught to press the man on anything earlier, but now his mind was clear, which led him to a singular conclusion.

It's not my problem.

At least that's what he told himself, but he couldn't even adhere to his own declaration. Something deep inside him was screaming, drowning out his rational mind like a whisper in a hurricane. It was as if the man's very visage foretold some impending doom, and Fleet was the only one who could see it.

Fleet locked eyes with him, but only for a split second.

Peter shot him a placid grin.

Fleet turned back around to face Viv, unable to tell if the moisture on his hands was condensation from the glass or his own sweat. Fleet downed the rest of the beer and wiped his chin. "I'll take another."

Before he had even finished asking, a Rum and Coke clacked down on the wood, accompanied by a wink from Viv. He didn't object, instead forgoing the straw and drinking from the glass itself. Still sensing the man's eyes boring into his back, Fleet looked around for something to calm his shaky nerves.

The wall behind Viv was decorated with a rather overwhelming selection of spirits: whiskey, gin, vodka, scotch—she had it all. Above the liquor, wrapped in white Christmas lights, was a large metal propeller blade of unknown origin; its prominent place signified it as the crown jewel of the bar's collection of gewgaws.

"Say, Viv. What's the deal with that thing up there?" Fleet asked as he motioned toward it with his drink.

Before Viv could answer, a large man—in height almost as much as width—sat on the stool next to Fleet, pushing Oreen away from the group. The man's muscular upper body sat atop a hefty beer gut covered by oil-stained overalls.

Viv poured a beer for the intruder as he explained on her behalf. "The old owner of the bar used to be a pilot back in World War Two. He flew the same plane through over twenty missions and took down over a hundred Nazi planes. On his last flight, he got shot down and lived but got hurt somethin' fierce. They discharged him with honors and he kept that there blade as good luck. Isn't that right, Viv?"

"Sure is, Big Earl," Viv responded.

She then turned to Fleet and shook her head as Big Earl downed his drink. Leaning over the counter, she whispered into Fleet's ear, "I got that thing at a garage sale. I told him that story as a joke. But he loves regaling it to folk so much that I just let him have it."

Fleet nodded in comprehension, then extended a hand to the gentleman next to him. "Well, thanks for the story...Big Earl, was it?"

"Sure thing," Big Earl responded through labored breaths. "And call me Earl. Biggun if you're feelin' friendly."

The man took Fleet's hand in greeting, eclipsing it with his own monstrous paw. It crossed Fleet that this guy could give even BJ a run for his money.

The handshake stopped, locking Fleet's arm in place as Earl looked over Fleet's head at Lowy. "Lil' Buck, is that you?"

The man leaped from his seat and ran to Lowy, embracing her in a deep hug before she could protest.

"It's good to see you, Earl," Lowy sputtered in a labored voice.

Earl released her, stepped back, and gave a broad smile. "It's been so long! How's life treatin' ya?"

"It's been good. Just staying busy," she answered. "But look at you! You look amazing! You've lost so much weight!"

Earl blushed and waved off her compliment. "As usual, you're too darn sweet." He jiggled his belly with both hands. "I still got a good ways to go, but I feel like a new man."

"Well, I'm proud of you!" Lowy replied with a big smile, causing Earl to once again turn bright red.

"Viv, Buck and my new friend's next drink is on me. You too, mister," Earl said, nodding to Oreen.

Oreen pointed to himself, genuinely surprised by Earl's act of generosity.

Earl pulled out his wallet with a grunt and slapped it down on the table. The billfold was made of deer hide—or was it rabbit? No, it was some sort of amalgamation of several different animals. The stitching was uneven and the proportions were off, which caused his money and cards to stick out at an odd angle.

The wallet reminded Fleet of something. "Say, Biggun. Did you make that billfold?"

Earl looked down at him. "I sure did! Do you like it?"

"I think it's cool as hell," Fleet said, rubbing the wallet with his finger. "You work with hides and stuff often? Any taxidermy?"

"Sure do. Getting pretty good at it, if I do say so myself," Earl boasted.

"That's great, man." Fleet locked eyes with Earl. "Do you hunt the animals yourself?"

Earl fidgeted as he averted his eyes from Fleet. "Yeah, uh, I sure do. Get them from hunting while they are in season. Which is when you're supposed to."

Perhaps it was the alcohol, but Fleet couldn't help pushing a little further for that last bit of confirmation. "Earl, do you like cheese?"

Earl's face lit up in response to Fleet's inquiry.

"Fuckin'..." Earl then began a series of irrelevant hand gestures in the air before slapping Fleet on the shoulders. "...love cheese! I even started making my own stuff! How did you know?"

Because I found your sloppy cheese wheels in that damn charcuterie horror shack, that's why!

Fleet grinned. "Let's just say that I have an eye for good taste."

"No kidding?" Earl gushed, undaunted by the odd turn in conversation. "What's your favorite kind of cheese?"

"I'm quite 'partial to provolone,'" Fleet responded, taking great pride in his unsolicited bon mot. Damn, the booze was hitting him harder than he thought.

Earl bellowed out a deep guffaw, entertained by Fleet's meager attempt at wordplay.

"Yeah and I'm, uhhh..." Earl took a moment to think. "I'm a 'fanatic for feta'!"

Lowy wasted little time as she chimed in with, "I'm a 'groupie for gouda'!"

Then all three of them turned their attention to Oreen and waited in silence as he took a sip from his 'cider,' anticipating what he might add. He coughed when he realized they were trying to pressure him into their progression of pitifully pathetic paronomasias.

"I'm lactose intolerant," Oreen finally added.

"Goddamn it, Oreen! Really?" Fleet shouted with feigned animosity. "We had a beautiful thing going here, and you ruined it!"

"It's okay. Not everyone is good at cheese," Earl covered for him, as if that statement somehow made any sense. He had not picked up on the fact that Fleet wasn't really angry.

"You're right, Biggun," Fleet said. "Not everyone can have a sophisticated palate—and sense of humor—like the three of us."

"You're all lame as shit," Viv interrupted from behind the bar. "Drink this, you cheesy muthafuckers."

Viv had lined up four shot glasses filled with whiskey. With muted thanks, each of them took one and held it aloft. They brought their glasses together, then downed their shots. Lowy struggled with hers a bit, requiring two tries to finish the whole thing. Even Earl looked shaken after that one.

"Damn, Viv. That shit is potent!" Fleet coughed as he wiped some excess liquid from his mouth.

"There's more where that came from." Viv gave him another one of her flirtatious winks. "You're not getting too drunk, are you?"

"No way. But if you catch me talking in accents, it's time to cut me off," Fleet admitted.

Viv loaded the four of them with more shots, sneaking in stronger and stronger spirits as they progressed. After the last one, it looked like Earl was ready to tap out when he laid down some cash.

But instead of leaving, Earl walked over to Fleet and started fishing in his homemade wallet. "I got something for ya."

Fleet looked up at him, the last shot still tingling his throat. "Was that?"

Earl handed him a card that had been creased and worn down by friction. In a tacky bubble font above a rather voluptuous pig mascot was the name 'BB's Butt Hutt.' Perforations lined the top and bottom of the card in the shape of hearts that filled squares numbered from one to ten.

"It's a punch card for a free meal at the best damn barbeque place I've ever been to," Earl informed him. "Since you're a 'man of taste,' I know you'll like it as much as me. Make sure you get burnt ends with a side of mac and cheese—it will change your life."

Based on the address, this place was five states over; it would take forever to get there! It wasn't likely that he'd be going that way anytime soon, but he didn't want to be rude.

"Wow, Biggun. I appreciate that," Fleet said, then he held the card back up to him. "But are you sure? I mean, you worked pretty hard to earn this."

Earl pushed it away. "Naw. I've got three of the damn things filled up as is. Take it."

Fleet made sure Earl saw him tuck the gift into his own wallet. "When I'm chowing down, I'll think of you."

Seems like a nice guy, Fleet thought as he turned back to the bar. *Weird-ass hobby, but a nice guy.*

Then it hit him: that odd tingle his body would produce whenever he got to the breaking point, almost always ensuring he would be spending a night by the toilet.

Fleet rubbed his forehead and groaned. "I might need to stop."

"You should," Lowy agreed. "Viv has a reputation for getting newbies wasted. She thinks it's funny, so don't feel pressured to drink if you don't want to."

"Yall's a bunch a bitches," Oreen chirped from the sidelines. He squeezed his way in between Fleet and Lowy, somehow pushing Earl out of the way. "I can drink anyone here under the table."

To Fleet's right, someone new answered Oreen's challenge. "I shall take that bet."

Fleet turned to catch Peter settling himself on the stool next to him. Fleet's muscles tensed involuntarily, as if he was preparing for an imminent attack.

Peter held up a finger. "Vivian, if you please."

Viv set to work without a word.

Peter watched the entire process in silence, that accursed smile plastered on his face. Fleet studied him for reasons he couldn't process, waiting for the man's next move.

Once everyone had their beer, Peter turned to them and held his drink aloft. "What should we dedicate this to?"

Lowy thought she had the answer. "How about new friends?"

"No," Peter disagreed. "To synchronicity."

Rather confused, Lowy returned the gesture, but with far less exuberance than Oreen. As there was no drink for him, Earl gave an awkward quarter bow and took off without saying goodbye. Fleet slid his glass in closer, giving only the slightest nod.

They all imbibed, some with more enthusiasm than others. After they were done, no one attempted to follow up, so the party descended into an awkward quiet.

Peter took a sip of his beer, watching Fleet as Lowy fumbled with her words for something to say. Before she could formulate a proper icebreaker, Peter turned and leaned toward Fleet, stopping inches from his face.

Fleet recoiled on instinct, bumping into Lowy and pressing against her shoulder. All he could do was return the man's gaze. It was like he had been shackled to the stool with his eyelids taped open, forced to watch some inexplicable horror play out in front of him. It was only now that Fleet discovered the source of his incomparable dread.

It was the man's eyes.

Something about those piercing gray irises kissed with the smallest trim of blue around the pupil resonated in his very soul like nails against a chalkboard.

But why? What was this horrible foreboding? He couldn't understand how, but deep down he knew the cure for this anxiety: all he had to do was drive his thumbs into this man's eye sockets until he felt the soft tickle of brain.

"You truly do not remember me, do you?" Peter asked with a hint of disappointment, rousing him from his stupor.

Fleet realized he had been shaking when Lowy put a hand on his shoulder out of concern. He glanced at her before shoving his thumbs into his pockets.

Fleet cleared his throat and said, "No, I remember you. I never thanked you for the milkshake, did I?"

"You did not."

"Well, thanks then. But just so you know, I'm not into you."

Peter laughed into his drink. "Is that so? How disappointing."

"Yep. Now if you don't mind, I'm trying to enjoy a night out with my friends here." Fleet turned back toward the counter and placed both hands around his mug to punctuate the fact the conversation was over.

"Come now, son. Why be such a wet blanket?" Peter leaned back and looked at the others. "Are you lot in the same mind as this one?"

"Not at all!" Oreen shouted. "The more the merrier! Isn't that what you said earlier?" He clapped Fleet on the shoulder hard enough to spill some of his own drink.

Peter gave Oreen a nod. "A fellow reveler. We shall have a grand time yet!"

Fleet remained facing forward. Those inflamed emotions had faded somewhat, but he was afraid they would resurface if he gave the man any more time. Fleet thought it best to ignore him; maybe he would get bored and walk away.

Peter looked back at Oreen and Lowy once more. "Is he always such a sourpuss?"

"Like a tabby in a lemon tree," Oreen confirmed.

"Well then, how about a drinking game? It might even get this one to open a bit," Peter said before waving to Viv. "Something harder this time, my dear."

In the blink of an eye, Viv had four shot glasses of tequila lined up on the table. Fleet did not acknowledge his glass as he continued to stare straight ahead at the wall.

"This will be a simple game—a classic, tried and true," Peter began as he slid his shot glass toward himself. "Simply ask a question, and if the answer is yes, take the shot." Without taking his eyes from Fleet, Peter called out, "Harlow, would you honor us?"

"Um, okay." Lowy passed her glass between her hands as she looked around the bar, nervous to have been put on the spot. Her eyes aligned on the propeller above. "Have you ever been on an airplane before?"

Peter downed his drink as Oreen scoffed and took his shot with a grimace.

"That's a lame question," Oreen complained.

"You can do better?" Lowy shot back.

"Duhhh." Oreen grabbed the shot Viv had poured to replace his empty one. "Okay. Okay. Okay." He gave a close-mouthed burp. "Haaaaave you ever pleasured yourself to a shampoo commercial?"

Oreen took the shot right after finishing his sentence.

Lowy started to drink, but she stopped short and set it back down. "Does it have to be a commercial about shampoo *specifically*?"

"Let's take it to the judge's table." Oreen turned his torso and threw a limp hand up to his ear as if he were straining to hear a response. He snapped back around and confirmed in slurred words, "I'll allow it."

"That's not... Whatever..." Lowy kicked back the shot and made a face so sour it looked as though she may vomit.

Throughout the entire game, Fleet had maintained his protest, not once looking away from his dedicated spot on the wall.

Peter took his shot and crossed his legs, giving Fleet a smile. "How chaste this one. Commendable."

"I don't think he's playing," Lowy said.

"Of course he is—whether he knows it or not," Peter corrected, tilting his head and giving Fleet another of those placid smiles. "He appears mute for the moment, so I will take his turn."

Peter put both elbows on the counter as if lost in thought. He then side-eyed the group and asked his question.

"Are you a good person?"

"The fuckin' best, bitch." Oreen took his shot without missing a beat.

Lowy was caught off guard by the question, but brought the shot glass to her lips—and hesitated. She set it back down and ran her thumb over the rim.

"Drink, Beck!" Oreen shouted, taking the glass and forcing it to her mouth.

Lowy swallowed the shot to the same accompanying reaction she had with the last one. Peter did not drink, his eyes firmly trained on Fleet.

"Well, well, well," Oreen mocked in a haughty voice. "Look who didn't drink, Mr. Dry-lipssss. I knew I was right about you, and you know it." He gave this condemnation even as he fell forward onto Fleet, nearly knocking him from the stool.

"Stop it," Lowy defended. "He's just not playing."

Peter seemed enthralled by Fleet's response, or lack thereof. With a smirk, Peter abandoned his watch and asked aloud, "Young lady, why did you falter?"

Lowy leaned back for a better view of Peter. "What do you mean?"

He pointed a finger at her. "You had doubts you were a good person. Why? What wicked deeds have you done? What heinous transgressions have you committed to make you believe that? Lies? Theft? Murder, perhaps?"

"No, nothing like that!" she responded.

"Then why?" Peter's voice was growing stronger, more intense.

"I mean..." Lowy stammered, trying to align her thought process. "Who am I to say I'm a good person, you know?"

Peter clapped his hands together in a burst of energy. "Exactly! You do not believe you are good because you have not earned the moniker from those you believe can award it. After all, there is no greater fool than the one who proclaims himself a wise man."

Lowy looked about, off-put by Peter's sudden change in temperament. "Yeah, I guess so."

Peter put his hands on his knees as he continued. "Then who decides how you live? What standards must you adhere to in order to affirm your 'goodness,' and why have you failed them? Is it your religion? Yes, that must be it. With your little paltry sins, you have broken their sacred laws, and it makes you question yourself."

Lowy turned away from him, but Peter was not deterred.

"Have you done no charity, no alms for the poor? Have you forgotten to say your prayers, or neglected to bring new sheep into the flock? Do you touch yourself at night in sinful ways? Is there a surge of guilt after the climax, knowing that God condemns your heathen impulses?"

Lowy looked down into her unfinished beer, rubbing the handle.

Peter leaned back with a smile. "You have been shaped by this need to attain the 'divine goodness' crafted by someone else. You let those you believe righteous dictate your actions to the point you cannot fathom any other way to live. They use it to control you. To further their own ends. Consider this..."

Peter pointed at her again, this time with quiet affirmation as he professed.

"What do you call a man who kills, rapes, destroys? A murderer, a villain, a **monster**. But what do you call this same man when he has the backing of a nation? A soldier, a patriot, a **hero**. Reject them, child. Control from within means control from without. Observe your friend."

Peter grabbed his beer and raised a toast to Oreen. "He took his libation, no qualms or doubts. This man knows what he is. He lives by his own merits and therefore has no question for what he is."

Oreen gave a crooked nod and mumbled something unintelligible, causing Peter to laugh.

"But this one..." Peter took a deep swallow from his beer and put a hand on Fleet's shoulder. "Tell me, son. Do you know what you are?"

Fleet's grip on the glass tightened when Peter grabbed him, but he maintained his silence even though his skin wanted to tear itself from the bone to avoid his touch.

Lowy shot from her seat and shouted, "He's a good person!" She stumbled and had to sit back down now that her advanced inebriation had manifested.

Peter leaned back, taking another long sip of his beer as he nodded in agreement. "You are absolutely correct, if not a tad misinformed. After all, it is not your doctrine he lives by."

Peter locked him with a knowing gaze, one that made Fleet feel as if all the organs in his body had shifted in an attempt to further themselves from his sight.

Peter smiled as if he could sense Fleet's unease. "He disagrees with you, child. He wants to say it, to shout it from the highest mountain. Proclaim his villainy for the world to condemn. But he has been misled, and I believe it my duty to rectify."

Peter leaned in again and whispered directly at Fleet.

"You are a 'good man.' I know this to be true. Yet you strive beyond such a simple exaltation. They call you 'upstanding' to the point you would give your own life were it deemed for the greater good. So 'benevolent' you would slay every person in this pub should you believe it a necessity. So 'righteous' that should it further the cause..."

Peter turned his head to the side.

"...that you would even sacrifice your first-born child."

Fleet's nostrils flared as his grip tightened, sending a hairline fracture up through the glass.

Peter grabbed him by the nape of his neck, causing a surge of pain to shoot through his spine. "That means it is only appropriate..."

He took the shot glass and brought it to Fleet's mouth with a maniacal smirk.

"...that you drink."

Fleet's mug shattered under his intense grip, leaving him holding a fraction of the handle as alcohol and glass swept over the bar. He swung his arm backward, aiming the jagged shard for Peter's throat. His attack was stopped short by Oreen, who had stumbled in between the two of them, forcing Fleet to turn his wrist at the last moment to avoid jamming the glass into his chest.

"You really want to make this guy drink? Ask him if he's hung like a Tic-Tac," Oreen joked, unable to finish before bursting out in laughter.

Fleet shoved Oreen aside with a curse to regain his line of sight with Peter, intending to finish what he started.

To Fleet, the next few seconds were almost in slow-motion. He had it all: a makeshift weapon, the intent to kill, the element of surprise—but he got no reaction from Peter. The man showed no signs of worry, no fear of what was about to happen.

Instead, all those emotions bloomed within Fleet himself. But he wasn't to be deterred. Something deep inside told him this had to happen; it gave him strength tinged with a hint of madness.

The glass soared at Peter's throat, aimed perfectly at his carotid artery. Fleet could feel it before it even happened—the spongy collision followed by that warm arterial spray.

Peter grinned at him as the glass was jerked away at the last second and sent spiraling into the air.

Oreen had slammed his fist into the bridge of Fleet's nose, upending him backward onto the floor. As soon as he could struggle up to his feet, Fleet tackled Oreen with all the force he could muster. This threw both of them back into the center of the room, where everyone gathered around them in a circle. From the sidelines, Lowy yelled and tried to dissuade them, but the mob pushed her aside.

What followed next was a graceful ballet of punches, kicks, and parries as Fleet and Oreen locked in combat—at least that's how it felt to them in their drunken stupor. To everyone else, their fight resembled a struggle between two in-bred ducks fighting over a saltine cracker. Every punch was wildly off the mark, kicks ended with the aggressor falling on his butt, and every parry looked more like they had just walked into a spider web.

Still in his seat, Peter's chuckle at their antics soon evolved into full-blown maniacal laughter to the point tears rolled down his cheeks. The mob soon joined in as they cheered and cajoled the two combatants before them. The "epic" melee lasted but a few minutes before it came to a stop when Fleet threw a punch that sent him crashing into the jukebox with enough force to crack the glass cover.

"That's enough!" someone shouted.

Fleet's feet were kicked out from under him, delivering him face first into the unforgiving concrete. Someone contorted his arms behind him, and he felt cold steel dig into his wrists.

Not long after, he was greeted by Oreen's smooshed face on the ground next to his own. Fleet strained his neck upward to see his assailant and discovered that it was Denvis who had broken up their fight.

"Wat's all this then, Guvnuh?" Fleet asked in a sloppy British accent as a bit of drool slid from his mouth.

"Shut up!" Denvis commanded as he pulled the two men to their feet amidst a chorus of boos.

"Denvis! Wait!" Lowy shouted at him as she pushed her way through the crowd.

"Can you drive?" Denvis responded, preempting whatever she was about to say.

Lowy shook her head.

"Wait here," Denvis growled at her.

He pulled Fleet in close.

"You should have listened to me when you had the chance."

Chapter Seventeen

MAUDLIN

THE LOUD CLANKING OF the metal door made Fleet stand to attention. Oreen had suffered a similar fate, occupying the cell adjacent to his own. The two of them filled the only units in the building, which sat in a small open area connected to the main office of the sheriff's station.

In between their enclosures stood Denvis with his arms folded, an expression of pure vitriol splashed across his grizzled mug. They waited, expecting some harsh opprobrium that never came. Instead, Denvis swiveled his gaze betwixt his prisoners to build some tension and set the mood.

As the sheriff opened his mouth to commence the verbal lashing, a loud screech emitted from his fist, causing him to jump as Oreen's phone fell from his hand and clattered to the floor.

"Lowy is texting me!" Oreen shouted, looking at his phone by the sheriff's feet. "She must be so worried!"

Fleet wrinkled his nose. "Why is that your ringtone for her?"

"I will not be judged on taste by someone who looks like they congealed on a hot sidewalk from a pile of used diapers."

Fleet slapped both hands on his chest. "You wanna go there, buddy? You wanna do this?"

"What is wrong with you two?" Denvis interrupted, sounding like a concerned father disciplining his children; and like stubborn kids, they only shrugged defiantly back at him.

"I thought I told the both of you already to get the hell out of my town. And what happens?" Denvis pointed at Oreen. "This little shit brings his dumbass back and starts a fight with this dumbass over here."

"I have a name, you know," Oreen said.

"I know your fucking name!" Denvis pulled out Oreen's wallet that he had confiscated. "Oreen Anderos Rothstein."

Before he could finish, Oreen held up a hand to shush him. "Stop! That's my civilian name. You need to use my prison name while I'm in here."

Denvis stared at him, coupled with an annoyed snarl.

With a straight face, Oreen enlightened him. "They call me 'Hemorrhage' in the pen."

"Hemorrhage?" Denvis questioned, taking the bait.

"Because if you mess with me, you're gonna bleed." Oreen finished by dragging his thumb across his throat.

"If he gets one, then I get one too," Fleet chimed in.

Denvis turned his menacing gaze toward Fleet.

Fleet added some bass to his voice and opened his eyes wide. "They call me...'Skee-ball.'"

"Why do they call you that?" Oreen asked in his gruff voice.

"Because I like playin' skee-ball." Fleet finished by making a slow underhand motion.

"You're a fucking moron," Denvis spat.

"Careful there, Big D," Oreen intervened, using Lowy's pet name for the sheriff. "He's a dangerous man. Mess with him and he'll put his balls all overffkk..." Oreen trailed off into a bout of laughter, unable to finish his nonsensical threat.

Denvis pulled the nightstick from his belt and slammed it into the bar next to Oreen's head, forcing him to fall backward. It did nothing to cease the chuckles.

"Hey, Oreen! I mean, I mean, Hemorrhage," Fleet called out. "You notice how almost everyone around here has 'Big' something as their nickname? There's that guy Earl, and like...more."

Oreen continued his fit, but he did nod his head in agreement.

"What's up with that?" Fleet continued. "Is that like a, like a title you have to earn? Like 'doctor' or 'esquire.'"

Oreen found room to breathe, though he had to talk through his laughter. "Yeah, they have to get a good score on the M-Fats and then pass the candy bar!"

"Aww, man. You shouldn't, you shouldn't make fun of people's weight," Fleet admonished.

"I don't give a shit," Oreen retaliated, wiping tears from his eyes. "Have you seen my husband? I like 'em big."

Fleet grabbed the bars and squeezed his face through as much as he could. "I know what you're thinking, Big D, but don't do it. He's married. Don't be a home wrecker."

Denvis swung his club one more time, barely missing the tip of Fleet's nose as he jumped back. "You both can fuckin' rot in here."

Denvis turned around and shut off the lights before slamming the station door behind him. The two of them stood in the darkness, snickering at each other until their eyes adjusted to what meager light was left over.

Fleet spoke up as he leaned against the bars of Oreen's cage. "To be honest, this was one of my better nights out."

"Hey, how about you shut up?" Oreen said as he plopped down on the lonely cot in the corner of his cell.

"The hell, man? We had such a good...like...back and forth going. What happened to that?"

"I carried that whole routine, and you damn well know it. Now be quiet." Oreen turned over on his side. "I think my toilet is overflowing, and I find the sound of gurgling poop-water more tolerable than your voice."

Perhaps it was because Fleet was still rather tipsy, but that last jab was a smidge too far.

"You're kind of an asshole, you know that?" Fleet said as he pushed himself off the iron bars. "And like a petty, bitchy asshole. I haven't had to deal with shit like this since middle school."

"I'm sorry you had to suffer like that throughout your whole middle school career. It must have been a tough eight years for you."

Taking a moment to calm himself, Fleet returned, "I'm trying to figure out why the hell you hate my guts so much. You've been on my ass since the second we met for no damn reason. I ain't trying to be your best friend or some shit, but I deserve an explanation!"

Oreen spread the meager threadbare sheet on his body. "I don't owe you a fucking thing. Goodnight!"

He punctuated the 'goodnight' in such a way to show he wished to no longer be bothered.

Fleet stood there, swaying from the lingering effects of the alcohol. The events of the evening seemed to be a blur now, but there was one thing that happened recently enough that it was still fresh in his mind.

"Why did you come back?"

Oreen did not answer.

Fleet grabbed hold of the bars and kicked one several times to make sure that Oreen couldn't ignore him. "That's what Big D said, right? You were here. You left. Then you came back. Why?"

Oreen maintained his cold shoulder, so Fleet continued.

"I mean, I get finding the place thanks to dumb luck. That's how I got here," Fleet lied to strengthen his argument. "But that also means you've already been here once, and from my experience, that's more than enough reason to never come back."

Oreen stirred.

"Oh, honey!" Fleet broke out in a cartoonish reproduction of BJ's voice. "What was your favorite thing we did this year?"

He then changed to a more high-pitched tone to represent Oreen.

"Well, my sweet, if I had to pick but one, it would without a doubt be that marvelous little B and B where we both contracted hepatitis. Every time I smell mildew, I can't help but recall those happy times. Oh, sweetie, let's go back right now. Maybe tetanus is still on the menu!"

"You wouldn't understand," Oreen grumbled as Fleet finished.

"Try me. What do ya got to lose?" Fleet challenged. "Like someone wise once said: 'There is no greater burden than an untold story.'"

Oreen sat up, somewhat impressed by Fleet's quotation. "That was deep. Who said it?"

"Umm, pretty sure it was the Nature Boy, Ric Flair," Fleet responded with mild confidence.

"I'm going to assume that's wrong, but I don't know enough to call you on it."

Oreen pulled the blanket tighter around his shoulders. He sat in silence for a time, but soon talked without further provocation.

"It was her, okay? I came back for her."

Fleet crinkled his nose in thought and said the first thing that came to mind. "You came back for Lowy?"

Oreen nodded, dragging his face across the pillow.

"Weird," Fleet remarked as he rubbed his temple.

With what seemed like a complete non sequitur, Oreen said, "I came on my honeymoon."

Fleet looked at him as if he were speaking a different language. "The fuck? You need to fire your travel agent, dude."

"Like you said earlier, I got here through dumb luck." Oreen switched sides so that he was now facing Fleet's cell. "We were passing through to our actual destination when we got a flat tire. We pulled into the nearest place we could find, which happened to be the *illustrious* Rose Hill Motel."

"Lowy said that was a problem earlier, but I still don't get—" Fleet fell silent when he heard the muffled sobs.

Oreen clutched the blanket to his chin as tears streamed across his face. "The way she talked, her mannerisms, her attitude—it was her. But I know it wasn't. Not really. I'm not a fool. But still...it was her. She had been waiting for me all alone there. I had a second chance. I could make it up to her. I could protect her this time. I could—"

Fleet stared in confusion at the formless lump in the darkness. "What are you talking about?"

"I killed her!" Oreen cried out. "It's all my fault! I'm sorry! I'm so sorry, Beck!"

Oreen was gone, now lost in uncontrollable wailing. Fleet backed away until he ran into the cot. He sat down, afraid to say anything further, though curiosity clawed at him like a wild animal trying to escape its cage.

Several minutes passed before Oreen regained some semblance of composure. He righted himself on the bed, using the sheets to wipe his face.

Fleet could no longer contain himself. "Who is Beck?"

He saw Oreen jolt and feared he had started the man into another round of hysterics, but Oreen shook it off and replied, "It's short for Rebecca. She was my sister."

Fleet lowered his head. "I'm sorry."

"Clearly, I've handled it well," Oreen joked, rubbing a palm over his eyes. "But if you knew her, you wouldn't blame me. Not one bit. She was smart, funny, sweet, caring, strong. She's the type of person who made the world a better place by simply existing."

"She sounds pretty amazing."

Oreen seemed to perk up as he reminisced, glad to have someone listening to his fond memories of her. "Oh, absolutely. She graduated top of her class, and she was homecoming queen, too. Literally started a volunteer organization that worked with abused animals in our town. That didn't hurt when it came time to go to college, and she got a full ride.

Like seriously? How smart do you even have to be to get that? She could also pitch at like a hundred miles an hour. Did I mention that? That she played softball. Not professional or anything, but still."

Fleet found himself grinning as he listened to Oreen brag on and on about his sister. Not once did he interrupt Oreen's stream of accolades, which lasted for well over five minutes. It wasn't like he had anything better to do, and he also enjoyed seeing a different side of the man he'd not long before viewed with contempt.

Besides, it was clear that Oreen needed this.

Oreen had his hands on his knees now, showing no signs of ceasing his regaling. "You know, if it wasn't for her, I don't think BJ and I would be together right now. I was so afraid to tell my parents that I was dating someone so much older than me—and a man—so I talked to her first. She was so supportive because she knew how happy he made me. She even set up the dinner date and went along when I introduced him to my parents. To this day, I think that if she hadn't been wearing them down behind the scenes, they would have disowned me."

Oreen's expression softened, the exuberance draining away.

"So when she introduced me to 'him,' I wanted to return the favor."

Oreen fell back onto the cot and orated with his hands.

"He was suave, wealthy, handsome, educated—perfect on paper. I should have loved him, but there was something odd about this guy. He was... I don't know. He just felt *off*. But all she would do was talk and talk about how great he was and what a good fit they were and how much she loved him. What else was I supposed to do? All I wanted was for her to be happy, and if this was the guy to do it, then of course I would support her."

Oreen's arms went slack above his head, the last of his energy spent.

"She moved in with him, and we saw less and less of her. She stopped updating her social media, and rarely did she take a call. If she did, it was either 'I'm fine' or 'don't worry.' But my parents did. They worried a lot. But I stepped in. I told them she was happy. She was discovering herself and needed some time. She'd be back before we knew it. I might even become an uncle. 'Uncle O.' I'd have been the coolest uncle."

Oreen fell silent, gritting his teeth as he prepared himself for the conclusion. He blinked back tears as anger welled in his voice, but he continued on as if this were some form of self-punishment.

"Then one day, after not hearing from her for several months straight, I got a call from an unknown number. It was a hospital. They had my sister. The fucker had dropped her on their doorstep like some piece of meat and just left her there all alone!"

Oreen punched the metal bar to his side.

"The doctor asked me if this was my sister, but it wasn't. No way. My sister was beautiful. This poor, ragged woman lying there was nothing like her. Those sunken cheeks. The blisters all over her face. All those bruises. Those empty, lifeless eyes..."

Oreen grit his teeth, spittle shooting between them as he shouted, "That's not my Beck! That's not my Beck! That's not my Beck! That's not my Beck!" Oreen punched the bar at every mention of his sister's name.

Finally, he stopped and brought his bloody and shaking hand to his forehead.

"But it was. It was my Rebecca."

Fleet was sitting forward, staring at the ground with both elbows on his knees and hands clasped under his nose. His heart was bursting for Oreen, but what could he do? He should say *something*. Something profound to help alleviate at least a modicum of the man's suffering.

"Shit."

"Yeah. Shit," Oreen agreed, rubbing his knuckles. "This was over a year ago, but it's still eating at me. I've been depressed, and it hasn't gotten much better. Being the sweetheart he is, my husband planned a vacation for us—called it our 'second honeymoon.' He said it would do me some good to just get away from it all. I knew I couldn't go on like that much longer, so I caved. Then one flat tire later, there she was."

Oreen sat back up and looked at the ceiling.

"I know it sounds stupid—and I know my grief-addled brain is mostly to blame—but she reminded me so much of Beck. Not her looks, but her energy, her demeanor, her sweetness. It was almost like I was with my sister again."

Oreen brought his knees to his chest and rested his chin on them.

"We talked all night until the morning. The next day, I talked BJ into letting us stay an extra night, even though it messed up his itinerary. Then we stayed another, and another, and another. Soon, we'd used up all our vacation. My God, the money we wasted on those reservations."

Oreen chuckled to himself.

"I hadn't felt that good in a long time. But of course, we had to leave. We couldn't stay there forever. But before I left, I told her to call me if she ever needed anything. Even after I was gone, not a day went by where we didn't talk or text at least once."

He pointed at Fleet, his injured hand still trembling.

"Then a few days ago, I received a frantic call from Lowy. That was when she found the hand. I said that if she didn't feel safe, she could come stay with me for a while. She refused, of course, saying that she couldn't leave that fleabag motel. Instead, BJ and I packed our bags and drove all the way out here that very night."

"Helluva story," Fleet muttered, his curiosity slated.

"But as to why I've been such a bitch to you, I..." Oreen trailed off as if the words were burning his throat.

Fleet didn't need to hear it. He had already figured out the truth during Oreen's heart-wrenching tale. Instead, Fleet answered for him, hoping that it might be some small mercy to Oreen's conscience.

"It's because I reminded you of 'him.'"

Oreen lowered his head as if the floor was the only proper audience for his admission. "You were there with Lowy, and she was so giddy and excited. All I could see was that man. That same piece of shit that ruined my sister's life, and here he was, back to do it again. But not this time. I knew better. I could save her. I could save my—"

Oreen stopped mid-sentence, bringing both fists to his forehead as he cursed his own foolishness.

"Fuck me! Not only am I a shitty brother, but I'm a shitty friend, too. I only ever talked to Lowy because she reminded me of my sister. It's like I was using her. Would I have done any of this if it wasn't for that? She deserves so much better. So much better than me."

Fleet's empathy peaked, and it carried him off the bed and onto his feet. There may be little value in it, but he could at least offer some advice.

"You know what you've done. That puts you in a good place. It means you can do something about it," Fleet reasoned, pacing his cell. "Personally, what I think you should do to be a better friend is tell Lowy the same thing you told me. Maybe don't drink before you do it, though."

"What if she hates me? What if she doesn't forgive me? What if she tells me I'm a...I'm a horrible, rotten troll that should go live under a bridge and eat stray billy goats?"

Fleet scratched his head. "Dude, this is Lowy we're talking about. Granted, you know her better than me, but do you honestly think she would say anything like that?"

Oreen wiped some snot from his nose. "No."

"Exactly. Just tell her how you feel. If anything, she'll love you all the more for it."

"You might be right," Oreen admitted.

"Bitch, I'm always right."

Fleet flopped down onto his cot. He had sobered up some during Oreen's emotional revelation, but not enough to keep the room from spinning.

Oreen did likewise, pulling the covers over his face to muffle his words. "I'm sorry for how I've been acting."

"No worries." Fleet waved off the apology with a grunt, his arm falling limp over the side of the cot. "Night night, Hemorrhage."

"Goodnight, Skee-ball."

Chapter Eighteen

FAILING GRADE

"Good morning, gentlemen." Denvis greeted his detainees as he slammed the front door to wake them.

Oreen groaned as he rubbed his temples in a futile attempt to drive away a headache. Fleet fared a little better, or at least he was able to muster a response.

"Mornin' sheriff. I hope you slept well," he responded, accompanied by a thick morning burp.

Denvis ignored him and pulled up a stool in front of their cells.

Getting straight to business, he said, "I spoke with Viv this morning. Turns out she won't be pressing charges for the damages you two caused."

Fleet smiled with relief. "See there? I knew Viv wouldn't hang us out to dry."

"There's still the case of everything else: drunken disorderly, assault, public urination—"

"I don't remember that one," Fleet interrupted.

"I do." The sheriff raised his lip in disgust. "But the point is, I can keep this up all day. There's more and more shit to charge you with if that's what you want."

From the tone of his voice, Fleet could tell Denvis was after something. "I think you know that is not what we want," he replied, struggling to his feet.

"Then here's my offer." Denvis leaned forward. "Both of you get out of this town. Now."

Fleet gave the man two thumbs-up. "Deal."

Denvis looked to Oreen, who had righted himself to give the sheriff a tepid nod of agreement. Denvis kicked his stool back and inserted a large metal key into Fleet's lock, but did not turn it.

"One other thing," he said. "Neither of you will contact Harlow ever again. No calls. No texts. Nothing. Is that understood?"

"No!" Oreen yelled, grabbing the bars. "I won't agree to that!"

With a huff, Denvis took out the key and inserted it into the lock on Oreen's cell. "Resisting arrest, huh? Guess I have no choice."

Realizing what the sheriff meant, Fleet spoke up. "Whoa, Whoa. Hey, man. We get it. Once we get our shit packed, we'll be out of here, okay? We'll never bother either of you again." Fleet gave Oreen a look that pleaded for him to play along.

"Yes. Understood," Oreen complied, backing down from the situation at Fleet's behest.

The sheriff gave them a shared nod. "I'm glad we see eye to eye."

Denvis unlocked their cells and shuffled the two of them outside. At the corner of the street, BJ was leaning against his car, patiently waiting for his husband. Oreen ran up and gave him an enormous hug as he apologized for making him worry.

"Hey, I think you're forgetting our stuff," Fleet complained as Denvis shut the door behind him.

A few moments later, Denvis reappeared from inside with his hands full of their confiscated items and offered them to Fleet. When he reached out to take them, Denvis showed no remorse as he dropped everything onto the pavement. Fleet winced when he heard one of phones crack.

As he backed into the building, Denvis gave them one last word of advice. "This is your last chance; I don't think I can get you anymore."

Fleet bent over to pick up the items. "We'll be tarred and feathered and run out of town on a rail. We got it. Have a nice day, sheriff."

Denvis huffed and slammed the door.

"Lowy sent these." BJ held out a small basket full of miniature blueberry muffins to the free men. "Said she was sorry she didn't come, but she thought you would only get in more trouble if she did."

"Aww, that's so sweet of her," Oreen cooed as he plucked one from the basket.

"Love me some muffins," Fleet proclaimed as he grabbed a handful and popped three of them in his mouth at once, just now realizing how hungry he was. He then used his other hand to give Oreen his phone and wallet.

"Fowwy, you sween boke," Fleet apologized through a mouthful of muffin.

"Thanks." Oreen turned on his phone and flicked through it to see if it was still functional. "Well, at least this will make a good story later down the road."

Fleet nodded and gave a thumbs-up as he struggled to chew through the wad of pastries.

BJ cocked his eyebrow, noticing the rather obvious change in their dynamic. "You two friends now?"

Fleet and Oreen looked at one another, then they both gave a hesitant shrug.

"I would say that we came to an understanding. How about that?" Oreen clarified as Fleet nodded in agreement.

"Cool beans," BJ replied.

Fleet choked down his food and asked BJ, "Do you mind if I catch a ride back with you guys?"

"I don't mind, but I ran into Curtis this morning and he asked me not to. Said he wanted to pick you up personally."

Fleet clenched his eyes shut and crinkled his nose. "Shit."

The devil must have been listening, because at that very moment a black SUV peeled around the corner and slammed to a halt just inches shy of Fleet's foot. Curtis stepped out of the vehicle and walked up to Fleet, stopping just short of touching noses. Without warning, Curtis threw out his arms, causing Fleet to recoil backward in surprise.

"Bro!" Curtis yelled with a smile. "I brought you breakfast!"

In one of his hands, he held a large brown sack with the bottom soaked in grease. As Fleet made to inquire about the sack, Curtis wrapped him in a bear hug until he was struggling to breathe. He only released his grip when Fleet tapped him on the back, unable to endure it any longer.

Curtis held up the bag and shook it. "Sausage and egg biscuits. Breakfast of champions."

"Mmmmm..." Fleet patted his belly, but his expression couldn't hide how nervous he felt.

A maniacal grin creased Curtis' face as he reached in and put Fleet in a playful headlock. "You're welcome, little brother!"

"You two have a weird dynamic," Oreen said before the awkwardness of the situation overtook him. "So, uh, I think we are going to go on and head back."

"Sounds good!" Curtis responded. "Don't wait up. We're going to take the long way back."

Fleet glanced up at Oreen and BJ with an expression of frantic concern, begging them not to go.

"Will do. Bye!" Oreen waved as he made his way over to their SUV.

They sped off, leaving Fleet alone with his passive aggressor.

Curtis shoved the bag into Fleet's chest and then held the passenger door open for him. Fleet accepted the invitation like a man walking to the gallows. Curtis' toothy smile shifted into a more palatable grin as they drove in silence.

"So..." Fleet began, no longer able to bear it.

"So..." Curtis repeated, his friendly grin now a manic smirk.

Fleet waited a moment before continuing. "How ya doing?"

"Fantastic! How are *you* doing?" Curtis thundered back, his volume rising.

"I'm...good."

"Goooooood..."

Fleet stared forward, trying to ignore the situation; perhaps inaction was the best option here. However, the pangs of hunger were gnawing at his gut. Fleet reached for the sack of food as if trying not to wake a sleeping rattlesnake. He opened the brown bag, wincing at every crinkle and snap it made in fear it would set Curtis off.

He unwrapped one of the warm savory biscuits from its paper enclosure and took a deep bite, but stopped short before he took the next. He glanced over at Curtis like a child caught stealing from the cookie jar.

"Did you get any jelly?"

"Jelly?" Curtis echoed. "Jelly? Jelly!"

Curtis' words were garbled as he punched the steering wheel over and over in a fit. He then reached over and smacked the top half of the biscuit out of Fleet's hand, causing the patty to slap against the window and leave a greasy trail of residue as it slid down. He then grabbed Fleet's wrist and shook it violently until chunks of biscuit flew around like debris in a hurricane. To finish, he took what remained in Fleet's hand and slammed it onto the dashboard with one last outburst of discontent.

Fleet sat there covered in crumbs, but once again his self-control failed him. "Is that a 'no' on the jelly?"

"Fuck your jelly!" Curtis shouted back. "This is not about the jelly! This is about your dumbass shit with a fucking... God damn it!" Curtis gave his steering wheel a few final blows to let out his excess anger, sending the car swerving over the lanes.

"Look, I know I screwed up. It was a lapse in judgment, and I am sorry for that," Fleet apologized.

"You think it's that simple?" Curtis asked, his teeth clenched.

He pulled over to the side of the road so that he could give Fleet his full attention and ensure that his words found their mark.

"You failed."

Fleet couldn't quite process what he was saying. "Failed what?"

"This! You failed *this*! Everything. Holy shit!" Curtis slammed the back of his head against the headrest over and over.

Fleet put up a hand between them. "I'm still not following here."

Curtis folded in his lips and gave Fleet a disappointed shrug. "This was a test, Hangman. All of this. I know you think this is your first official case as a Servunday on your own. But it isn't. 'She' didn't believe you could handle it. But I went to bat for you. I put myself on the line because my dumbass believed in you."

Fleet reached out, catching the patty before it fell from the window onto the dashboard. "How is this a test?"

Curtis snapped his fingers so Fleet would look at him. "Because there was never anything here. You've got the fighting down, but we wanted to know if you possessed the comprehension, the logic needed to become a Servunday."

Once Curtis' words registered, Fleet had to say it out loud. "You knew there were no Tryst here."

"That is correct." Curtis leaned back against the door and tried to calm himself as he explained. "Maybe it will help if I give you the grading scale for your 'test.' We'll go with a basic A-to-F format to make it simple. In order for you to have made an 'A' on this assignment, you should have never come here. That's it."

"Never come? You're the one who told me to come in the first place!"

"No, I didn't," Curtis contested. "I gave you all the facts and asked you what you wanted to do. You decided on your own to come here because you couldn't figure out the truth."

Curtis grabbed his right wrist and shook it at Fleet.

"Remember the damn hand? The forensics said that it had been sawed off. Why the fuck would a monster with ungodly strength need to use a saw? Why would that same monster leave any physical evidence at all when it can just eat the whole damn body? It wouldn't. You should have seen that and questioned why this was even coming across your desk! We have a whole analytics team for shit like that!"

"That's exactly what I'm saying!" Fleet shouted, inadvertently pointing at Curtis with the limp patty in his hand. "If they sent it up to me, why shouldn't I believe it was credible?"

"It doesn't matter!" Curtis shot back. "You're at the top now. It's your job to make the call. That's why 'She' let it get to you. To see if you acted with authority and either shot it down or asked someone for help or clarification. You could have come to me. I wouldn't have told you the answer, but I sure as hell would have hinted at it like I have been the whole fucking time I've been here."

Fleet turned back toward the window, only now understanding why Curtis had been acting so strange. "Then I guess I didn't get a good grade, huh?"

"Well, let's finish out the scale and see where you stand." Curtis tilted his head and drew his lips to a line. "So 'B' to 'C' range would be you coming down here and investigating, which you did, but eventually calling it quits, which you didn't. A 'D' would be using unnecessary manpower to scour an area completely unrelated to the case."

"Big talk coming from the man too scared to go into the basement."

Curtis side-eyed him but continued. "An 'F' would be getting shit-faced at a bar while on duty."

"Now that's not my fault. See, there was this guy and—"

"I don't fucking care." Curtis cut him off. "You shouldn't have been there at all, or was there another lead you were chasing at the bottom of a bottle?"

Fleet pursed his lips. "So I got an 'F.'"

Curtis laughed derisively as he shook his head in disappointment. "No, no. Hell no. When they tried to grade your test, they slid it through the Scantron machine and it burst into flames. Those flames spread and took out an entire city block, including a children's hospital and a petting zoo. And quite frankly, I believe I am being generous with describing how bad you did."

"I think you're overreacting a bit."

"Am I? Am I, though?"

"Is this about me getting arrested? It's not great, but we have fake identities in the system for this exact purpose," Fleet reasoned.

"That is true," Curtis admitted. "But once again, you haven't thought this through."

"Is that right? Then please, by all means," Fleet said, encouraging him to explain.

Curtis took a deep breath. "You got in a drunken fight in a public place. What's the first thing people do when they see that? Why, they whip out their phones so they can post it online for some worthless internet points. It goes viral. Some guy you haven't seen since kindergarten or some shit watches it. He goes 'Hey, I know him! He's supposed to be dead!' Questions start getting asked. Then, through some fine sleuthing, someone discovers that there are monsters walking among them. Now the whole fucking world is thrown into chaos because you couldn't control yourself. But no, you're right. There's no issue here. My bad."

Fleet gritted his teeth as the weight of Curtis' words set in. "I fucked up, didn't I?"

"Yes, you did. Now I have to stick a team on scouring social media to make sure no videos get out. The only way this could be worse is—" Curtis turned to Fleet and grabbed his shoulder, genuine mortification on his face. "You didn't fuck that girl, did you?"

Fleet's eyes somehow grew wider than they already were. "Lowy? No way! Scriptor, I swear to God we didn't!"

Curtis was so relieved he collapsed over the steering wheel. "Holy fuck, I almost shat myself."

The two of them fell silent. Fleet sat there dejected with his head down, crushed under the gravity of his own failure as Curtis looked out the window.

Without looking up, Fleet asked, "Is 'Vuota' going to kill me?"

"Nah, too easy," Curtis mumbled into his crossed arms. "But I bet it's gonna be a long-ass time before you're allowed on your own again."

Fleet leaned against the door and propped his chin on his knuckles. "Well, if there's one thing I've got, it's time."

"True that," Curtis agreed.

Fleet leaned back in his seat and exhaled in defeat. "Let's go back to the motel."

Curtis peeked over his shoulder at him but didn't say a word.

"I've got to pack up. After that, we're out of here, man. I'm calling it: this is the end."

"You swear?" Curtis asked, his voice filled with hope.

"Yeah."

Fleet took a bite of the smashed sausage patty as Curtis put the car in drive and pulled back onto the road.

CHAPTER NINETEEN

SO CLOSE

FLEET STEPPED OUT OF Curtis' SUV and into the sunlight, shielding his eyes. This was the last time he would ever see this place. It was a good thing; no one wants to revisit the site of one of their most embarrassing defeats. The sooner he could bid this motel goodbye, the better.

And yet he felt this strange nostalgic heartache as he scanned the motel grounds. He thought of all the people he'd met, all the crazy things he'd done—it had been quite the trip. He hadn't imagined that his investigation would grant him so many unique experiences, both good and bad.

It was just...funny.

Nothing more. Nothing less. He wondered if Lowy and the others would see it that way, too.

He didn't relish saying goodbye to them. In fact, he had thought about bailing on it all to save himself the emotions and avoid the awkward sadness of an official resignation. But he couldn't bring himself to do it. He just couldn't.

Fleet leaned down and spoke through the open window. "Hey, I need you to go up to the office and distract them for a bit, at least until I get 'Spooter.'"

Curtis' shoulders drooped. "I can't believe you brought it with you."

"Of course I did. Remember, I thought this was a legit incident, and I treated it as such," Fleet replied.

"I'll give you that one," Curtis said, getting out of the car. He then started his jog up to the main office, turning back once to usher Fleet on to his task. "Get moving!"

Fleet waved at him and walked up to his room as he fished in his pocket for the key. Just as he was about to unlock the door, Fleet noticed some movement from the corner of his eye. He turned and saw that someone had emerged from Dash's room farther down. They were wearing an oversized t-shirt and holding a calico cat cross-armed against their chest.

"Jill!" Fleet couldn't help but smile with relief. "Hey, kid. Glad you're okay."

She returned a genuine but waning smile, giving him a warm feeling of accomplishment that offset his current despondence.

"You know, I'm not supposed to be talking to you," he said. "You're putting me in a very dangerous position."

She smiled again and shook her head.

"I can't tell if you don't care, or you actually want to see Dash kick my...butt." Fleet censored himself as he crossed his arms.

Jill continued to smile as the cat fidgeted in her hold.

"Jill, I'm heading out...for good," Fleet admitted with a deep sigh. "And it would mean a lot to me if you promise... Would promise me that..." Fleet paused as he tried to come up with a good way to say it. "If you promised you won't do anything that will leave little Patchy all sad and alone."

Jill looked down and touched her nose to Patchy's forehead, causing the cat's ears to lie flat and its tail to swish about. She then looked back up at him and gave a small nod.

Fleet smiled. It felt good to have confirmation, even if there was no assurance she would hold true to her word.

This was all he could do.

"Thanks, kid. Take care of yourself." Fleet bid farewell as he turned back toward his door.

Before he even inserted the key, Jill had walked over to him. He froze in anticipation, like one would do when trying to get a skittish animal to come out of their hiding place. To Fleet's surprise, she extended her arms and lifted Patchy up into his face.

Fleet laughed, not realizing he had been holding his breath. He pet Patchy, watching as the cat's face became an oxymoron crafted from some odd mixture of enjoyment and intolerance.

He grinned and leaned his head so he could see Jill behind the cat. "What do you know? I guess he likes me after all..."

Fleet's last words drifted off. He stopped petting Patchy and left his hand awkwardly on the cat's head as he stared down at Jill. He tried to speak, but the words caught in his throat; only a few odd syllables made it past his lips.

Once the cat growled at him in annoyance, he backed away from Jill, giving her a crooked smile and a limp wave. With no words to accompany his departure, he rushed back toward the main office where Curtis was waiting. Jill watched him go, once again holding Patchy to her chest as Fleet picked up speed.

He flung the screen door open, causing it to slam against the wall. Lowy, Oreen, BJ, and Curtis all started in their own unique way thanks to his clamorous entrance. Fleet looked at them with wide eyes, struggling to think of something to say.

Thankfully, Lowy spoke up, disappointment clouding her face. "Is it true that you're leaving?"

"Where the hell did you hear that?" Fleet responded, blinking his eyes back to normal size.

Lowy's despondence warped into confusion. "Curtis said so. And Oreen told me you both had to leave because Denvis threatened you and said that—"

Fleet waved her off, his movement frantic and speech quick. "Nah, nah, nah, I'm not going anywhere, but I need to borrow my brother real quick. Curtis, if you would?"

Fleet motioned him to the door but didn't wait for a response before leaving himself. The expression on Curtis' face had grown sour as the conversation went on, but once beckoned, he complied by giving everyone his best forced smile before walking outside.

"How much longer do you think you're going to stay?" Lowy called after them.

"Could be weeks!" Fleet shouted back once they were out of sight.

"If he's staying, then so am I!" Oreen stated in defiance.

BJ shrugged in approval, resigned to his fate; he knew it was best to just go with the flow.

Oreen looked over at Lowy to see her beaming like she had just discovered *Jurassic Park* was a real place.

"You could at least pretend not to be so excited about him," he said.

"I'm smiling for both of you," she responded, bouncing on the balls of her feet.

"Awww," Oreen cooed, putting a hand over his heart.

Outside, Fleet had guided Curtis off to some distant corner of the parking lot where they would not be overheard. As they talked, Fleet scanned the area to make sure no one had followed.

"What the fuck was that about?" Curtis yelled, holding up his hands.

"It's her," Fleet whispered under his breath.

"Her? Her who? What are you talking about?"

"It's the kid. It's Jill. She's the one!" Fleet explained, not realizing that his volume was increasing.

The more baffled Curtis became, the angrier he got. "The one what!"

Fleet shushed him even though their voices were on the same level. He then held out his arm and tapped the inside of his elbow. "They're gone! The bruises are fucking gone!"

"What are you even on about, man?"

Fleet remembered he had omitted the part about him finding Jill overdosed in the room. It was time to elaborate, but he decided it was best to leave out that he called 911.

"I found her overdosed on something yesterday that used a needle. It looked like someone had tried to take off her forearm with an ice pick. I see her today and there's nothing: no puncture marks, no bruising, not even a goddamn Band-Aid. There's no way it should have healed that fast if she were a regular person!"

"You found a...!" Curtis took a moment to rub his forehead as he tried to make sense of the situation. "Putting aside the fact you kept this from me, maybe she's wearing makeup to cover it?"

"I checked all through their place and I didn't see any makeup like that. It was only the black stuff. The, uh, eyeliner!" Fleet countered. "She's a junkie, Scriptor! You know as well as I do that there have been cases where a Tryst has killed their dealer or someone else to feed an addiction. I think that is exactly what's happening here!"

"She's too young, Hangman! She couldn't do that even if she wanted to!"

This made Fleet falter, though his conviction did not waver. "You don't know that for sure. She could be an early bloomer or something."

"Didn't we *just* go through this shit!" Curtis began to shout but lowered his voice. "You have no proof!"

"I just gave you my fucking proof!"

"I'm done." Curtis threw up his hands as he pretended to walk off, but he wasn't finished yet. "You've gone batshit crazy. Is it the stress? Too much pressure? It's fine. It really is. I can take care of you, but you have to end this, all right? It. Has. To. Stop."

"It will stop. I promise it will," Fleet assured him. "Right after we interrogate Jill."

Curtis froze in shock at the words Fleet had spoken. "Please, man, please don't do this," he begged, clasping his hands together. "If you do, there's no going back."

"No shit, that's the point."

Curtis clenched his fists in anger. "Regardless of the truth, once she's in, she's in for life. You understand that?"

"Explain to me how that's a bad thing? Even if I'm wrong, if she comes back with us, we can take care of her. We have programs and shit to get her the help she needs instead of just leaving the poor girl here to rot herself away from the inside."

Curtis stared at him with a frown framed by pity. "What's the truth here, Hangman?"

"The truth is, she's Tryst. I know it for a fucking fact." Fleet started to pace. "But based on her age, she shouldn't be able to transform. Which means she's probably not the killer. It could be Dash. But she isn't Tryst. But if she's not Tryst, why is she with Jill? And how are they even connected to the sawed-off hand? There's just too much I can't fucking understand!"

Curtis shook his head as he watched Fleet's conspiratorial rant, unable to bring himself to interrupt.

"Hey, what happened to those guys you brought down? The ones that we ended up not needing."

Curtis scratched his shoulder with a sigh. "They're on standby." He then narrowed his eyes in suspicion. "Wait, you're not—"

Fleet cut him off. "Good. Call them up."

Curtis turned his back on him. "No. I will not let you do this."

Fleet took on an authoritative tone. "Scriptor, this is an order from your Servunday. It is absolute." He then relaxed. "That means you won't take any heat if shit hits the fan. You have my word."

Curtis glared at him and spit on the ground. Despite his open defiance, he had the countenance of a pleading man, one who wanted more than anything to dissuade his best friend from opening his wrist and jumping into shark-infested waters.

Fleet's commanding voice returned as he said, "Call in the reserves. Now."

"Yes, sir," Curtis responded, giving him a formal nod, though his tone expressed his anger at the situation.

"Good." Fleet planted a fist into his open palm to psych himself up. "Okay, here's the plan."

Chapter Twenty

EXPOSURE

-He said they're sitting down to eat-

The text Curtis was reading was in reference to Lowy, Oreen, and BJ; the group had left earlier in the day to get food. Fleet had gotten one of Curtis' subordinates to tail the trio and relay their whereabouts back to him to avoid any unnecessary complications. While Fleet and Curtis received an invitation to join them, they both passed on it with Fleet using the excuse that he needed some extra sleep after last night.

Dash had been missing since yesterday. Her unheralded return could spell disaster in more ways than one, but Fleet had gone on with the plan despite Curtis' disapproval.

The best thing to do would be to get Jill back to headquarters and interrogate her there, but current circumstances made that very difficult. It would be easy to grab her and make a run for it—if she couldn't transform, that is.

While the risk of her having that ability was low, it wasn't sitting comfortably at zero, which is what protocol demanded. They lacked the equipment or medical knowledge to keep her sedated for such a long trip, and having her go berserk and transforming while they were on the road would be an unrecoverable error of catastrophic proportions.

They would have to make do with something closer.

Fleet took a deep breath and looked down at the small cylindrical tube in his hand that resembled a miniature EpiPen. Curtis had told him the best place to stick her was in the neck, but the serum would work regardless of where it was injected. As long as he administered it near a vein, she would be out in a second.

Fleet had suggested using the serum on her whenever she woke during the ride, but Curtis had vetoed the idea. Apparently, it was easy to overdose on it if administered repeatedly in a short period.

Jill didn't deserve to go through that again.

Everything about this felt wrong, but there was nothing else for it. He rubbed his thumb along the tube one last time and slid the syringe into his pocket, paranoid that he was going to prick himself.

After a deep breath, he stepped from the center walkway into the backyard to find Jill sitting in the same spot she had taken during the bonfire, staring into the fire pit despite an absence of flame. He waved a salutation, claiming the same seat he had taken that day as well. She did not return this greeting, but she did at least give him one of her wistful smiles.

He found himself at a lack of words or even possible actions on how to proceed. Instead, he joined her in contemplating the mystery of the barren fire pit. The charred remains within had long fizzled and burned out, leaving behind only an empty hole filled with unwanted soot.

Fleet jumped when Patchy came over and rubbed up against his leg. In the cat's mouth, she held something long and brown that twitched about frantically.

"See what he's got here?" Fleet said, pointing down at the cat.

Jill leaned over a bit to get a better view as he continued.

"It's a tail. Sometimes when a lizard is threatened or attacked, it will drop its tail off to distract the predator so they can get away, and it looks like it worked on Patchy here. Pretty cool, huh?"

He momentarily forgot the gravity of the situation, finding himself proud of the little factoid he had just shared. Jill got off her seat and walked over to get a better view of what Patchy was parading about.

Fleet slid a hand into his pocket.

As she crouched down to squint at the tail, he grabbed her arm and tugged her toward him, jamming the syringe into her neck. He then stood up and wrapped his hand over her mouth to muffle her screams as the drug went to work. Unfortunately for Fleet, she still had enough strength left to swing her heel backward and catch him hard in the groin. He choked out a small scream of his own as Jill wriggled free and darted off.

She only made it a few yards before her knees buckled and she fell to the ground. A few more seconds of her clutching at the dirt to drag herself away and she was out.

Fleet held his crotch and hobbled toward her as he muttered, "A second, my ass."

Trying his best to ignore the pain, he hefted Jill's unconscious body onto his shoulder and tore off down the path of broken trees he had discovered on his first day at the motel. He emerged near the crime scene to find a windowless black van awaiting his arrival.

Curtis jumped out of the back and shouted, "Hurry your ass up!"

Fleet climbed in and gently placed her limp body onto a blue gurney. The innards of the van resembled what would happen if an ambulance and a SWAT vehicle had angry sex behind a gas station. There were various containers of fluids and medical supplies interspersed with an assortment of guns and explosives. There were also snacks.

Curtis closed the doors as he shouted to someone in the driver's seat, and they took off at a brisk but sensible speed.

Fleet looked to the front as he grabbed a bag of potato chips from a tote bag. "Who's driving this thing?"

"That's Sea," Curtis replied. "Java is out checking on your folks. I told him to pack it in and meet us at the school."

The man known as 'Sea' gave them a small wave from the front without turning around.

"Java and Sea?" Fleet said. "Interesting code names."

"Yeah, 'code' names. Get it?" Curtis laughed, unable to hide a hint of pride.

The joke flew over his head, but Fleet nodded in agreement.

Curtis seemed bemused by Fleet's apathy as he turned his attention to Jill. "I've never been a part of anything like this before. I hope you know what you're doing."

Fleet opened his bag of salty chips with a pop. "I guess we'll find out."

Curtis sighed and pulled out his phone to shoot off a quick text. "By the way, there's body armor along with the other shit you wanted in the cabinet."

Fleet checked where Curtis had indicated and pulled out the 'armor.' It was the typical plated body suit that they all wore on dangerous missions. The plates were held together by an elastic material that could grow and shrink as needed; a one-size-fits-all for both human and Tryst forms—though more for Tryst.

He hated this type. Ignoring the fact it was easier to transport, Curtis must have brought this model along just to spite him.

It was broken into two separate pieces: one for the pelvis and one for the torso. Its primary purpose was to shield your vulnerable bits, such as your organs and groin, while not hindering overall movement, speed, and precision. It was irrational, but with the midriff, arms, and legs exposed, he always felt this version of the armor looked like a tactical bikini.

The juvenile truth of the matter was he liked how cool he looked in full regalia.

Fleet put on the armor over his clothes after realizing that he wasn't wearing the proper attire. It's prudent to wear baggy things, or at least something a good size or two higher than normal, whenever you are going to conceal the armor underneath.

He hoped he wouldn't need the protection, but it was better to be safe than sorry.

The 'other shit' was nothing special: a basic handgun with a full clip, and a fanny pack with 'provisions.' Fleet stuck the gun in the waist of his pants; it was a snug fit thanks to the armor pressing against it. He wrapped the fanny pack around him with a click, giving Curtis the middle finger when he caught him rolling his eyes.

"Still can't believe you insist on carrying grenades around like that. You look like a goober," Curtis criticized.

"A deadly goober," Fleet corrected. "And just so you know, this isn't a fanny pack. It's a 'tactical satchel.' Besides, it's less intimidating or conspicuous than having them strapped around my torso like Rambo."

"I don't know, man," Curtis said, not holding back the truth. "It feels super creepy. I'm a part of this, and even I think I'm about to get molested. Please tell me you don't have candy in there, too?"

"They're cheese crackers, and they're for me!" Fleet countered, shifting the bag away from Curtis.

Fleet finished adjusting himself to find the best level of comfort and sat back in repose, unable to enjoy his own levity as he contemplated what he was about to do. They continued on in silence, save for the crunch of chips as Fleet ate his way through two more bags.

He could tell they had arrived based on the vehicle's vibrations when it hit that old gravel road. Sea brought the van to a stop and joined them in the back. He offered to help move Jill, but Fleet waved him off, instead taking her into his arms.

Fleet hopped from the back, feeling a slight chill as he gazed on that abandoned school building once more. He made his way to the gymnasium to find that someone had sheared the padlock with bolt cutters to avoid jumping in and out through the windows.

"I'm going to rig this door once you go in," Curtis warned as he strode up behind him. "That means you don't let that girl try to make a break for it. Tackle her ass if you have to."

"Was it necessary to stage the whole place? It feels like overkill."

Curtis shrugged as he opened the door for him. "If we're going to do it, we might as well do it right. Besides, it'll be good practice for them."

Fleet furrowed his brow. "Practice?"

"Hurry up. We need to get this done as soon as possible," Curtis warned, dodging the question. He walked behind Fleet, ushering him into the building with Sea following after.

The inside of the gymnasium was just as Fleet had remembered; even the basketball he and Lowy had played with still sat on the floor where they left it. At the other exit to the gym was a man standing with a pump-action shotgun cradled in his arms; it had to be Curtis' other operative, Java.

He gave the man a nod and received one in kind, but Fleet didn't pursue any further introduction. Though he wished for more bodies, Curtis had handpicked these two; he knew he could trust them.

Fleet waded through the detritus to the middle of the gym, where he laid Jill on the glass table with as much caution as he would an infant child. This would be the best place to question her; it was easy to watch and equidistant from any escape points.

Curtis reached in his pocket and tossed Fleet a syringe similar to the one he had used earlier. "We don't have time for her to wake up on her own. Just poke her with that and let's get this over with."

"That's a bit callous, don't you think?"

Curtis shifted his weight and slid his hands into his pockets. "This coming from the man who upended the poor girl's whole life. Just do it before shit somehow gets worse than it already is."

Fleet bobbed the little needle up and down in his hands a few times, psyching himself up for what was to come. "Okay, here we go. On guard, everyone. Just in case."

Curtis threw his head back and rolled his eyes—a common theme at this point—as Fleet walked over to Jill's prone body. He stuck the needle in her neck and then backed away.

Jill stirred as Fleet made sure she did not roll off the table. Her eyelids fluttered open as she escaped from her forced slumber, still woozy from the drugs.

"Jill? Hey. It's me, your buddy. Feeling okay?" Fleet asked in a soothing and calm voice.

Jill sat up and glanced around the gymnasium, overcome by the unfamiliar surroundings. She began to hyperventilate as she pulled her knees into her chest, tears forming in her eyes.

"Shh, shh. Calm down. Everything is all right. I promise," Fleet whispered to placate her.

His words did little good as she scrambled away from him and onto the floor. She pulled herself underneath the table and curled around its metal leg.

Fleet had to squat down to get on her level. "We're not going to hurt you. I give you my word. I just need to ask you some questions. That's it."

Her breathing seemed to lighten, though her demeanor remained unaltered.

"Jill, I know what you are. There's no need to hide it." Fleet patted himself on the chest. "You're one of us. That means we're 'family.'"

This seemed to calm her down a little, so Fleet pushed onward.

"And as family, I only want the best for you. But first, you need to tell me the truth." Fleet took a deep breath as he studied her face. "Jill, have you ever hurt anyone?"

Jill shook her head, wiping her nose on her knees at the same time.

"Not at the motel, or anywhere else?"

Jill only continued to shake her head.

"I want to believe you, I really do. That's why I'm going to ask you another question: Jill, have you ever hurt yourself before?"

Jill stopped shaking her head. Instead, she buried her face in her legs and began to sob as she nodded.

Fleet could feel his heart breaking as he said, "Jill, I know you have a problem; that's how I figured out you're like me. It's why I know I can help you."

She peeked up at him, her falling tears obscured by her knees. While her tremors had not ceased, they had at least receded; Fleet hoped this was a good sign.

"Please, Jill, let me help you." Fleet reached out to her underneath the table, which caused Jill to shriek and shift away. She was now bawling and unresponsive to any of Fleet's coaxing.

"This is just sad," Curtis muttered.

Fleet turned around to curse at him but relented, realizing that he did not want Jill to see any sign of hostility regardless of the recipient. Instead, Fleet waved him off before taking a moment to compose himself.

"Jill, if you don't want to talk right now, that's okay. We can talk later once I get you home. But you're going to—"

Jill froze. She looked up at Fleet with bloodshot eyes. "H-Home…"

Feeling like he had made a breakthrough, Fleet's enthusiasm grew. "Yes! That's right! Once this is all over, I promise to take you home!"

Jill let out an earsplitting shriek and dashed out from underneath the table. She sprinted to the corner of the gym that housed all the large debris and clawed her way into a small opening underneath the pile like a rabbit escaping into a dense thicket.

Fleet gave chase, but he lost sight of her underneath the rubbish. He got down on all fours to see underneath the mountain of mats and furniture as he called out her name. When she did not respond, he leaned back and cursed up at the ceiling.

"Just call it, Hangman," Curtis advised as he came up on Fleet.

"We just…we just need to get her out of there. Let her cool off and we can try again." Fleet said, trying to rationalize despite his panic. "She doesn't believe that I'm Tryst, too. If I can prove that to her—"

"She's not Tryst!" Curtis yelled.

"I'm telling you, she is!"

Curtis was at the end of his rope. "Guess what? At this point, it doesn't even matter anymore! You exposed her to us, and now we can't let her leave! You stole this kid's life away because you think 'saving' her will make up for the past! It won't, Hangman! It won't because she is not—"

Fleet shot to his feet and shoved a hand over Curtis' mouth to silence him. Curtis batted his arm away and threw a punch at Fleet's jaw. However, he stopped shy of his chin when he saw the perplexed expression on Fleet's face.

Out of the corner of his eye, Fleet had seen some kind of movement, almost as if the mound of debris were breathing. Curtis made to speak, but Fleet shushed him again. He craned his head forward, now able to hear something familiar: the horrible, sickening sounds that always accompanied—

Fleet looked over at Curtis, his wide eyes filled with terror, and muttered only one word.

"Run."

CHAPTER TWENTY-ONE

FIGHT OR FLIGHT

JILL EXPLODED FROM UNDERNEATH the heavy mats and furniture, sending splintered desks and tables clattering against the walls and ceiling. Before he could react, Fleet found himself dangling, held aloft by Jill's vascular hand wrapped around his throat.

The young girl that didn't even come up to Fleet's chest now towered over him. Her fur was completely gray except for a solid white diamond that stood prominently in the middle of her sternum. Her mouth was pulled back along her snout, revealing a wall of razor-sharp teeth all bared at the man flailing about in her grasp.

She was of the lupine family of Tryst, just like the rest of them; a werewolf was the easiest way to describe it. But as she was now, she lived up to the more common moniker: a monster.

Jill held Fleet straight out in front of her as if he were nothing more than an empty plastic bag. He punched and kicked whatever he could reach, but she did not loosen her grip in the slightest.

Curtis had fallen backward in shock but was now shouting orders at Sea and Java. "Hurry and turn! We can't let her out of here!"

Fleet's wide eyes pleaded with the beast before him, and what he saw gave him pause. Despite her toothy snarl and menacing glare, he caught a hint of fear behind her gruesome expression that mirrored his own.

With her ungodly strength, she could have killed him already if she wanted to. Even now, with just a flick of her thumb, she could pop his head back and gnaw on his vertebrae like a human Pez dispenser.

But she didn't.

Being choked to death wasn't much better, but it stood to reason that she didn't want to kill him. If he could just talk with her, maybe he could find some way to deescalate the situation.

'I know you don't want to do this!' is what he attempted to say, but all that would come out of his mouth was spittle and gasps. He was going to pass out soon if she didn't loosen her grip. She was scared for her life, but giving up his own out of pity would do neither of them any good.

He apologized to her in his head for what he was about to do.

Fleet reached behind him and grabbed the pistol from his waist. He shoved the muzzle into the crux of Jill's arm and fired, sending bursts of flesh and blood flying from her elbow. It took the whole clip before she let go and sent him crumbling to the floor, gasping for breath. Before Fleet's feet had even touched the ground, the gunshot wounds in her arm had seared shut and she was on the run.

The front entrance was blocked by Sea, who had already shifted into his own bestial form. Java, who had yet to finish transforming, guarded the hallway exit. The man was still on his knees, screaming from the unfathomable pain of the process.

Jill knew which way had better odds.

She ran headlong at Java with blinding speed and tackled him through the doorway into the corridor. They hit a tripwire which triggered the claymore mine that had been set for just this possibility. A concussive blast sent them both crashing through the wall and into a classroom. Jill was spared a direct hit thanks to Java's body absorbing most of the explosion.

Java writhed on the floor as the wounds from his charred flesh healed; the damage would have been much worse had he not been wearing his armor. Jill shook off the impact and darted for the window but stopped short when she noticed something along the trim: it was another explosive trap. She turned back toward the entrance hole instead, but the injured Java lashed out in desperation and grabbed her foot, causing her to trip and fall.

With a demonic cry of desperation, Jill flipped over, interlocked her fingers, and slammed her balled-up fists down onto his head over and over and over again. With each impact, blood squirted from Java's muzzle and ears like an organic industrial sprinkler. It wasn't long before he blacked out and Jill wriggled free.

Meanwhile, Fleet had regained his breath. With a burst of energy, he ran toward the hallway, sliding under a table and grabbing the shotgun Java had dropped before his transformation.

"Jill! Stop!" he shouted as he dashed after her. "Don't—"

His words were lost as the explosion-weakened floor of the hall collapsed underneath him. The wind was knocked out of his already struggling lungs when his chest slammed against the precipice of the hole, leaving him dangling from the side as the shotgun slid across the tile out of his reach. Ahead of him, he saw Jill shoot out of the classroom and make a break for the exit at the far end of the building.

"She can't escape!" he yelled in anguish while attempting to pull himself up.

Behind him, Fleet heard thunderous footsteps approaching at great speed. Supporting himself with only one arm, Fleet reached into his 'tactical satchel' and fished out a grenade. Using his teeth, he pulled out the pin and flung the explosive upward.

"Scriptor!"

In unspoken accordance, Curtis flew over the hole, snatched the live grenade out of the air, and flung it down the hall all in one swift motion. It took off like a bullet as it whizzed along, finding its mark when it struck Jill on the side of her head.

Jill glanced over in time to see it hovering mere inches from her face as it exploded. The blast pushed her headfirst into the wall as her momentum sent her spinning across the floor toward the end of the corridor, taking a row of lockers down with her.

She screeched in pain as she clutched her head, writhing in agony. The entire side of her face was gone; all that remained were tiny strips of flesh that slapped about over blackened teeth and bone as she rolled on the ground. Her brains would have been shredded as well if not for her nigh impervious skull.

"How is she still moving?" Fleet yelled, dumbfounded by her perseverance.

Curtis lifted him out of the hole with one hand, at which point Fleet exclaimed another question.

"Why the hell are you naked?"

On any dangerous mission, the special body armor is mandatory, but Curtis had foregone it this time. Fleet had just assumed he was concealing his armor underneath his clothing, but here he was, rocking his lupine birthday suit.

Without protection, he could see Curtis' complete fur palette: chestnut brown with small specks of white that resembled constellations of stars all over his body, except for the tip of his tail where it was solid black.

But the man's full pattern wasn't the only thing Fleet could see...

Curtis cupped his genitals with long fingers, taking special care not to poke himself with his claws. Forgetting his inability to talk, he attempted to say something in his defense, but all that came out were a few low growls.

"She's making a break for it!" Fleet shouted, dismissing Curtis' gaff when he saw Jill stumbling for the exit.

The wounds she had sustained had almost completely healed already. She was regaining her vision as a milky eye pushed its way back into the socket like a mushroom poking through the soil.

Jill grabbed an errant brick from the floor and hurled it at the exit, triggering an explosion that sent one of the double doors flying off its hinges.

Fleet couldn't believe what he was seeing. How did she know to do that? Had she picked up on the situation that quickly, or had she somehow seen this all before?

Curtis was on her, his rapid lunges closing the gap. He stopped Jill short of the exit by wrapping her in a headlock and lifting her off the ground. He then fell onto the floor so he could wrap her up with his legs and complete the hold.

Even though Tryst are near invulnerable to any physical affliction in their beast form, they still had the basic need for oxygen. If Curtis choked her out, they could restrain her before she woke back up. This was the perfect way to end it.

But before he could lock in the hold, Jill contorted her body enough to reach behind her back and take hold of his...unit. Curtis' eyes bulged out of their sockets when he realized what was about to happen.

With a sharp twist, Jill dug her nails into his groin and squeezed, ripping his bits to shreds like fruit in a blender.

Curtis unleashed a high-pitched wail and dropped Jill to grab himself. She rolled over onto her knees and jammed her claws deep into his throat. With one quick swipe, she flung a handful of his esophagus against the lockers. Curtis clutched at his neck, inducing a momentary mental breakdown when his fingers ran across his exposed spine.

His wounds would heal, but for the time being, he was running out of oxygen. He choked on his own blood as it filled his lungs, all the while trying to decide which of the injuries she had given him was the worst.

Jill kicked away from Curtis and rammed herself through the remaining exit door to freedom. Before she even took a breath of fresh air, Sea emptied her lungs with an unexpected running tackle from the front, picking her up on his shoulder and sprinting back into the hallway.

After getting over the initial surprise, Jill reacted by shoving her hand into his mouth. She then sunk her claws into the inside of his cheek and yanked with everything she had. His skin peeled down the side of his face and didn't fray off until it tapered at his abdomen.

Sea fell forward as Jill dropped the blanket of flesh on the ground with a slosh. The momentum sent her flying straight toward Fleet, forcing him to sidestep into a classroom as Jill tumbled into the open hole and down to the basement below.

Fleet recovered the shotgun he had dropped and bent over the opening to shout into the darkness. "Jill! You have to stop this!"

———————————————

In the basement, tremors were racking Jill's massive body as she took in this strange shift in scenery. She let out a bestial, mournful scream that echoed off the brick walls and throughout the school.

The hooks, the blood, the rotten scent of death...she was back there again. Jill's psyche could not comprehend that this was not the same nightmare she had escaped.

Her ferocity, her strength, her will—they were forgotten. It all meant nothing inside these walls.

She crawled, tail between her legs and tears pooling at the end of her snout, beckoning upward toward the last vestige of light that shone above—not out of reverence, but sheer unbridled terror.

Was this all part of the game? Had this entire charade been concocted to remind her she was still just a plaything? Where was her hero now? Was the one who had saved her another accomplice sent to trick her into believing she was free, only to snatch it away in a sadistic show of whimsy?

This was the cruelest one yet. So elaborate. So convoluted.

It fit. It fit all too well. Why would it be anything else? It was all she had ever known. It was all she would ever know.

She had fought for so long, but time can grind down even the strongest soul.

Please! Please, no more...please...

No more. No more. No more.

nomore nomore nomore

nomorenomorenomorenomorenomorenomorenomorenomorenomore

Jill curled into a ball and wept. The monster was gone. What lay on the cold floor now was a pitiable creature, cursing the fact she had clung so tightly to what humanity she had left.

It would be so much easier to just let go.

From above, Fleet heard her sobs, spurring him into action regardless of the danger.

"I'm coming down!" he yelled at her crumpled form. "And I'm not bringing my weapon! It's just me!"

She did not grasp his words; they were lost on her along with all semblance of reason or understanding. She had surrendered herself to the void, a premature offering to whatever deity would provide succor and end the pain.

Yet still, something ached within her. Though she tried to suppress it with all her might, her most basic instinct was screaming, rippling through every fiber of her being...

It was the will to live.

She looked down at her trembling, blood-soaked hands and had a sudden epiphany. Game or not, this was the furthest she had ever gotten, and regardless of what happened, she wasn't going back—even if it meant her end.

Freedom or Death.

There is nothing else.

Jill dragged her fingers across the floor, leaving streaks of blood matted in the dust. She pushed herself to her feet to glare at the horrible instruments that surrounded her. There was no more fear. Resignation to the end had given her the strength to throw everything she had into one last fight.

All she had to do now...was get through them.

Fleet dropped his shotgun and braced himself to jump down, but he stopped as something stirred from below. The sound started as a small cry that continued to grow like an oncoming train. It evolved into a guttural roar that shook the very foundation, causing dust and debris to rain down from the ceiling.

Jill tensed every muscle in her body and used her powerful legs to shoot upward with no regard for what was above. She burst through the floor like a geyser close behind Fleet, sending splinters and tile into the air.

Fleet's blood evaporated as he turned around to face Jill. Her eyes no longer possessed the fear he had noticed earlier—they now held only rage.

Jill bared her teeth and locked into position, ready to strike. At this distance, it would only take a brief twist of her arm to tear Fleet in two. With no way to defend himself, all he could do was accept his fate and pray that it would be a painless death.

Jill tightened her muscles as she lifted her hand up toward the ceiling.

Vertical or horizontal? Fleet pondered in those few moments. *If I was a betting man, I would put my money on vertical. She might even surprise me and go diagonally. But I guess it's not much of a surprise if I've already counted it as a possibility. In any case, it's the dealer's choice.*

Fleet closed his eyes, ready for the end.

He heard a wet squelch and felt hot blood spray across his face. The warm sensation of the droplets lingered, which is odd considering he was dead and all. Fleet dared to open one eye and found Jill's hand hovering above his forehead.

Called it, he thought.

Jill's attention had been stolen by the metal pipe sticking from her shoulder. Down the hallway, Curtis stood with his arm still outstretched from the projectile he had let fly.

Even at this distance, Fleet could tell his partner was struggling. The fur on his chest and groin were matted with gore, and his neck wound had yet to fully heal. Every labored breath he took sent a small spurt of blood from the tiny hole in his throat.

Curtis was in a sorry state, but he wasn't about to let his friend die.

Jill looked at him over her injured shoulder, and Curtis met her glare by motioning his fingers, taunting her over for a fight. Jill accepted the invitation by sprinting at him with full force and tackling him to the ground. Curtis covered his face with his arms as Jill tore into him with a swift flurry of slashes from her claws. Every swipe of her hand added a new splash of blood to the wall until the entire area around them was a collage of crimson.

Hoping the pain might hamper her assault, Curtis reached out and twisted the pipe in her shoulder. It broke free, taking a hunk of meat with it. Unfortunately, his attack did not register with Jill—her tunnel vision saw only red.

Curtis' defense waned as his eyes glossed over. Whether it was from the pain or lack of energy, he was losing consciousness. If he dropped his guard, it would mean his death.

Fleet grabbed the shotgun from the floor and tore off after them. He jumped up onto Jill's broad back with one foot on her and one on the ground. He then jammed the shotgun between her shoulder blades and pulled the trigger, which fired a blast that sprayed him with a wet mixture of blood and fur.

Some pellets from the shot ricocheted back into his leg. He shook off the pain, but so did Jill; she didn't even flinch as she continued to tear into Curtis.

How is she still going? She's just a kid. She should have collapsed long ago from the pain alone! Fleet thought as he pumped the shotgun, expelling a smoking shell.

He fired again and again and again in rapid succession, each time damaging himself and sending sprays of bodily fluid up into his face. He tasted her blood through his gritted teeth as he continued the assault.

Finally, Jill had enough.

She turned and elbowed Fleet in the side. Even that glancing blow was enough to break his ribs and send him skidding across the floor and into the stairwell. He clutched at his side as Jill got off Curtis and made her way toward him.

Fleet kicked backward as she drew near, fear making him forget to grab the shotgun at his feet. Jill pulled her arm back for the killing blow, but she stopped short, her gaze now focused past him down the hall.

Java had come to his senses and emerged from the classroom, though he had to support himself against the wall as he walked. Sea had healed as well, more overtaken by the shock of having to look at a soggy carpet of his own flesh than the actual physical damage.

Realizing she was once again outnumbered, Jill turned and sprinted for the exit.

"Stop her!" Fleet shouted as a tiny trickle of blood streaked down the side of his mouth.

Sea and Java did their best to chase after her, but their injuries had taken a toll.

Fleet cursed as he struggled to his feet. *If we lose sight of her, it's all over!*

He looked up at the stairwell and decided the roof would be the best vantage point. Despite the sharp pain in his side and leg, he managed to climb all the way to the top, shotgun in hand. Finding it locked, he kicked down the door and fell over in anguish before running to the edge of the building.

The roof was littered with old industrial air conditioning units, forcing him to weave in between them in order to get a good view. In the distance, he saw Jill making a beeline for the woods, though not as fast as he had expected; it appeared her wounds were catching up to her as well.

"Jill! Stop!" Fleet shouted in vain as she vanished from sight.

He saw the trees rustle and shake as her large body forced its way through the dense foliage. In desperation, Fleet blurted out the first thing that came to his mind.

"What about Dash!"

The rustling in the woods halted. He couldn't believe that actually worked.

Fleet looked over the edge to find Sea and Java hobbling out onto the lawn. He snapped his fingers to get their attention and then motioned for each of them to go a separate way into the forest. If they used the abandoned cars for cover, he might be able to distract her long enough for them to trap her in a pincer formation.

"We know what you are, and we know she's connected to you!" Fleet shouted. "Do you think we can just let her go? If you run, the next thing we are going to do is go after her!"

Fleet gasped as Jill appeared at the edge of the woods to glare at him. She had narrowly missed Sea and Java, both of whom had now disappeared into the thicket.

Fleet pointed down and was about to continue his threats when Jill burst off at full speed toward the building. About halfway there, she vaulted off a van with enough force to shatter the windows and take her all the way to the second floor. Her claws dug into the brick as she collided with the building, giving her a handhold as she climbed up to him.

Fleet jolted away from the edge and took cover behind an air conditioning unit. He waited with his shotgun at the ready for when she poked her head over the clearing. After her rampage, it was better not to take any chances; Curtis couldn't save him this time.

Wait, how many shots had he fired already? Not that it mattered. Jill had shrugged off every blast he had put into her; a couple more wouldn't make a difference, but it could be a deterrent if she came at him.

The smart thing to do was shift and make it monster versus monster. He had the training. He had the experience. He would win.

But if he did that...

"Jill! There's still time! I can save you!"

The roof nearly caved in under the weighted silence.

Where the hell did she go? She was right there!

As if in response to his internal question, Fleet heard the sound of shifting gravel. He spun around and pointed his shotgun at the empty air. It was quiet again, but he didn't notice over his own desperate panting.

"I never wanted it to go down this way," Fleet said, checking around another corner of the units. "All I ask is that you talk with me, and I promise no harm...no further harm will come to you or Dash."

Once again, he thought he heard the soft crunch of gravel. He froze, but when the sound did not repeat, he continued to pace between the units, trying to find some way to appeal to her.

"You know, you're pretty good. You took down three of my guys. Not bad for a kid. If you come back with us, I might be able to get you a job. How's that sound? No more having to stay at shitty motels. You can live the good life. That goes for you and Dash. We can all—"

Behind him, he heard the groan of metal being twisted and torn apart. Fleet turned to find one of the units rising into the air above the others, lifted by Jill like it was nothing more than an aluminum trash can. Seeing no other option, Fleet fired a shot at her exposed leg, but the explosion of flesh did not deter her in the slightest.

With a horrible yell, Jill launched the unit at him with all the strength she had left. Fleet cursed and dove behind the nearest air conditioner for safety. He made it just in time to avoid her throw, but it did little good. Her projectile collided with his cover, causing it to slam into his body like a freight train.

Fleet was sent careening over the side that connected to the gymnasium. He crashed through the glass skylight and landed square across the glass table where the failed interrogation had begun. The table shattered, splitting the metal frame in two from the impact of his body, followed moments later by a deluge of glass raining down on him from above.

Fleet mouthed a soundless scream as the air rushed from his lungs, his body convulsing from the pain. He gasped for breath, but he did not have any time to regain his composure. Above him, he saw Jill's frame silhouetted against the blue sky. She had jumped off the roof with the full intent of ending him once and for all.

Fleet's body went numb with fear as she soared down at him; it was like being able to see the bullet that was careening straight for your face. Perhaps out of desperation or instinct, Fleet found the strength to roll out of the way. As he did, he kicked the jagged metal frame and set its razor-sharp edge pointing toward the ceiling.

Jill landed inches from his head, splintering the wooden floor. Fleet covered his face and cowered, awaiting the final blow. He didn't look up until he heard what sounded like someone emptying a gallon of milk onto the floor.

He then realized the sound belonged to the blood pouring from Jill's mouth.

She had been impaled on the impromptu spike Fleet had created. The makeshift spear had pierced her inner thigh, scrambled her guts, punctured her lungs, and finished by poking through the side of her face, lodging itself between her upper and lower jaw.

Fleet gawked in disbelief as he attempted to process what had transpired. Through sheer luck, the spike had missed her bones and only perforated her organs, locking her in place through a combination of internal damage and unfathomable torture as her body healed around the foreign object.

Seeing her in this immobile state made his mind flash back to those horrible taxidermy displays in the basement.

Still in their lupine form, Sea and Java came running down the hall and faltered, completely in awe at what they were seeing.

Fleet turned to them and shouted, "Get something for her pain! Now!"

Java took flight and burst through the lock on the front door, jumping to evade the trip wire on the still active claymore. Sea came over and kneeled next to Fleet to check on his injuries. Fleet hacked up a clot of blood and used Sea's knee as a crutch while he struggled to his feet.

In front of him, Jill's eyes were vacant as she stared off in the only direction her posture would allow. Her legs had collapsed underneath her, forcing her massive head down to chest level. Fleet could only tell she was alive thanks to the deep gurgle that echoed from her throat every time she tried to breathe.

Fleet hobbled over and held out trembling hands toward Jill's disfigured frame as he repeated, "No. No. No." His fingers hovered just over her face and his eyes lined with water like a child who had broken their mother's favorite vase.

Fleet wrapped his hands around the tip of the spike piercing through her face and whispered, "It's okay. I'm here. You're going to be fine. I promise. I promise."

Against all logic, Fleet tried to pull the spike upward, slicing his palms open as they slipped on the blood-soaked metal. Each time he failed, he tried again; every attempt became more desperate until the pink of bone peeked through his wounds. His blood flowed down onto Jill's face, branching between her teeth and joining the downpour that was still draining from her maw.

Sea watched the pathetic scene with his mouth drawn to a line and ears folded against his head, but they shot up when he noticed the finger on Jill's right hand twitch near Fleet's side. She moved once more, but this time Jill balled the hand into a fist before it fell limp.

Without shouting a warning, Sea wrapped his hand around the back of Fleet's neck and jerked him away from her body. With the last of her strength, Jill took one final swipe at Fleet's midsection with her right arm.

He fell into Sea's chest, his eyes wide with shock as his brain snapped back to reality. Fleet grabbed at his stomach, expecting to feel his innards pouring out. His breath returned in quick gasps when he realized all his organs were where they should be.

But in that same motion, he realized that something was missing.

Her hand trembling under its weight, Jill shifted her eyes to inspect the pack that clung to her claw. She coughed when she caught a glimpse of the bag's contents through a hole she had torn open. Her labored breathing intensified as she slid her thumb inside it.

"Don't do it!" Fleet yelled.

With a flick of her claw, she sent a grenade pin flying.

Before Fleet could shout another warning, Sea enveloped him in his arms and jumped back to press them both into a corner to brace against the incoming explosion. They hadn't gotten nearly enough distance from her. Even with her injuries, the mere flick of her wrist could put the explosives directly underneath them.

Sea bent his whole body around Fleet and turned his back toward her in hopes that he could shield his Servunday from the worst of it. They cowered there together in a ball, each second feeling like an eternity.

Why hasn't she thrown yet? Fleet wondered. *Is she trying to catch us off guard? If she doesn't get rid of them soon, they will—*

Observing through a gap under Sea's arm, Fleet watched as tears streamed from Jill's eyes and mixed with the blood that had pooled in her lower jaw. Even though her mouth was locked open, it was still easy to read the expression of despair that blanketed her face.

Fleet screamed in panic as he was overcome by a horrible realization.

"Stop!" he shouted, his eyes watering with desperation as he tried to wrest himself from Sea's protective embrace. "Don't do it!"

Jill jammed the pack into her mouth, using her long fingers to push it deep into her throat.

"No!"

Jill exploded into a temporal mist of red, showering chunks of meat and hair across the gymnasium. Fleet dug his nails into his scalp as he felt bits of her rain down gently upon him like he had shaken a tree after a rainstorm.

After checking over his shoulder to make sure the danger had passed, Sea released his grip on Fleet, allowing him to fall to his knees. Fleet grit his teeth and put his forehead to the floor. It took him several deep breaths before he could sit up and observe what his carelessness had wrought.

The upper half of Jill's body had almost completely evaporated; only remnants of her spine and rib cage remained. Bits of flesh were peeling from the walls and ceiling, making moist splats that patterned the uneasy silence. The explosion had blown away all the detritus from around her, leaving her corpse in an empty carmine circle bathed by light from the broken sunroof.

Fleet's mouth moved, but no words came out.

Behind him, Sea had reverted to human form, his armor now sagging off his much smaller frame.

"You did it, sir," he congratulated, putting a hand on Fleet's shoulder. "Mission accomplished."

Fleet turned around to face him. "I did it?"

"Yes, sir."

"I did it," Fleet echoed with a deranged laugh. "Mission accomplished! Thank God!"

Fleet fumbled his way over to an old file cabinet and picked up a wooden chair.

"Thank! Fucking! God!"

With each word he spoke, he slammed the chair against the metal with what remained of his strength. When he had no more words, he continued to swing until there was nothing left in his hands but splintered wood. He let the fragments fall to the floor, his battered fists no longer able to hold them.

Fleet looked at his blood-soaked hands and then back at Jill's body.

"I did it."

CHAPTER TWENTY-TWO

ROADKILL

"The hell happened in here?" a voice from behind asked.

Fleet turned to see Curtis leaning against the entry to the hallway in his birthday suit. Shortly after, he collapsed to his knees, and Fleet limped over to check on him.

Curtis' body had shifted back to human form to conserve what little energy he had left. But other than being drenched in sweat and a little dirty, he looked perfectly fine. All his wounds had healed like they had never even happened.

"How's your dick doing?" Fleet asked with all due sympathy.

"Hanging in there." Curtis shuddered. "But that one's going to stick with me for a while. How you doing?"

That had to be a rhetorical question. Fleet was covered in blood, a combination of his own and Jill's. His body was perforated with cuts, and almost all of his ribs were broken. He winced in pain at every breath, and his knees buckled with every step. Basically, he looked like he had fallen into a meat grinder, made it out alive somehow, slipped on a strip of bacon, and fallen in again.

"Fantastic," Fleet said with a mock thumbs-up.

He extended a hand to help, regretting the offer when pain surged through his entire body as Curtis pulled himself up.

Fleet saw him looking at what was left of Jill and answered his unasked question.

"She did it to herself."

Curtis didn't respond to that, instead deciding it was best to get on with business. "Yeah, we're gonna have to burn this place to the ground," he reasoned after a quick survey. "There's no way we can clean all this up. Easier just to erase all the evidence."

Curtis covered himself with an old clipboard and trudged toward the exit as Sea came over to proffer him a shoulder to lean on.

"Why are you naked?" Fleet asked, his eyes still focused on Jill's remains.

"I just shifted back," Curtis responded without looking at him.

"You're not wearing your armor."

"No, I'm not," Curtis admitted before giving Sea a nod, sending him off.

"Why?"

Curtis inhaled before turning to Fleet, readying himself.

Fleet pointed toward the exit where Sea had gone and asked, "What are those guys supposed to be? They went down after one shot! There is no way they are combat-ready!"

Fleet yanked shards of glass from his body, showing them to Curtis before throwing them away as he hobbled toward his partner.

"Before I was even allowed in the field, I was set on fire three times a day, every fucking day, for a month! Your boy there passed out after having his skin ripped off! That's a goddamn paper cut! Hell, the other one could barely handle the transformation, much less put up a decent fight! They should have been nowhere near this!"

"They're not at your level, Hangman! Neither am I! No one is!" Curtis shouted in his defense.

"It's not about that! This is about the fact that once again, you didn't believe me. You couldn't even be bothered to put on your fucking armor! Came in here all high and mighty, putting in the least effort possible because you just *knew* I was wrong. Look where that got us!"

He pointed to Jill's body, his voice tainted by anger and sadness.

"She's fucking dead!"

Fleet pushed Curtis hard, causing him to fall into a file cabinet. He did not fight back, the truth of Fleet's words cutting into him.

"I'm sorry, man," Curtis apologized, unable to meet Fleet's gaze. "You're right. I fucked up."

Curtis' apology brought him no solace. "You didn't believe me...and now she's gone..." Fleet choked out the words as he backed away until he hit an overturned desk that became an impromptu seat.

"It wasn't supposed to be like this," Curtis lamented, pushing himself off the cabinet. "But I know... I know this is all my fault."

Before Fleet admonished Curtis further, he gave himself a mental lashing to reel it in. *Shut the fuck up and calm down. This isn't helping anything. What's done is done. Remember your training and focus.*

"No. No, it isn't." Fleet let out a sigh that transitioned into a wet cough. "She tried to escape. She wanted to kill us. There were things we should have done better, but there was no other way this could have gone."

Fleet lowered his head and let out another deep sigh as he pinched the bridge of his nose.

Curtis limped forward and put his free hand on Fleet's shoulder. "Would it make you happy if I dropped my clipboard?" he asked, motioning down to the thin slab of wood that protected his decency.

"Sure." Fleet snickered. "It always cheers me up knowing how much bigger my package is than yours."

"I think you might have gotten some brain damage in that fight, my man," Curtis countered with a laugh.

Sea pulled up at the tail end of the conservation with a change of clothes. Curtis accepted them and dressed himself as he struggled through his fatigue.

Once he was finished, Fleet gave him a gentle punch on the arm and said, "Dick jokes aside, you sure got a set on you, standing up to her like that. You saved my life back there."

Curtis gave Fleet a friendly tap of his own. "Don't mention it. I know you'd do the same for me."

"While we're on the subject... You guys, come here!" Fleet shouted to grab the attention of Curtis' men.

Java was still in his bestial form, using his strength to move the larger chunks of Jill back to her remains in the center. His ears perked up at the call and he rushed to join them. Sea was already in attendance, but he moved to take a more formal position in front of Fleet.

The two men stood side by side with hands clasped behind their backs. The juxtaposition of a normal human against that of the lupine Tryst truly exhibited the beast's impressive scale; this only further proved what a fool's errand it had been for Fleet to take Jill on as he had.

But this wasn't the time for regret or the congress of hindsight.

He had a job to do.

Fleet addressed them, motioning toward each one as he said their names. "Java. Sea."

"Sir, I'm Sea and he's Java," Sea corrected.

Fleet cleared his throat. "Of course." To make sure that he got his point across, Fleet took up a stance similar to theirs. "I wanted to say that I'm aware neither of you have combat experience—and it showed."

Both of the men deflated at his words; Java's tail even curled between his legs. However, their demeanor shifted as Fleet continued his speech.

"But for agents with no intensive combat training, you put your lives on the line today and fought with everything you had. Courage like that is not something that can be taught, and I am glad that you were by my side today. You have both earned my respect and my gratitude. It would be an honor to work with you again in the future."

Sea fought with all his might to keep a smile from showing, failing miserably as one sprouted from ear to ear. And though he raised his muzzle higher, Java's face remained emotionless—however, he had to grab his tail to keep it from wagging.

"Look at you, Hangman." Curtis gave a sniffle and wiped away an imaginary tear. "You've grown up so much."

"Whatever," Fleet said, dropping the formality. "Let's get everything ready and get the hell out of here."

Java and Sea gave them both a quick salute before heading out to the van, with Curtis and Fleet following at a much slower pace.

"What are you going to do with her body?" Fleet asked once he believed the others were out of earshot.

"We'll take back the bigger parts, but the rest of her is going up in flames. We can't leave any evidence."

"Sure." Fleet stopped short of the exit, prompting Curtis to do the same. "Aren't you going to ask?"

"Ask what?"

"Why I didn't turn."

Curtis shook his head, unsure of whether this was a rhetorical question. "I assume it's because you wouldn't be able to talk."

Fleet did not answer, his silence showing he wanted Curtis to justify this line of reasoning.

Curtis made to put his hands in his pockets but missed, not quite used to his new pants. "It's normally one warning and the gloves come off. But the whole time we were engaged, you kept trying to reason with her regardless of how bad things got. That's the only thing I can think of."

Fleet looked out the exit, staring at the point where the gravel road disappeared behind the trees. "And why did I do that?"

Curtis' countenance shifted to one of profound pity. "I think..."

Fleet turned toward him, a hopeful expression on his face.

Curtis lowered his head to study the concrete outside the door's threshold. "There are some monsters even a Servunday can't kill."

He gave Fleet a half-smile and then carefully stepped over the explosive tripwire without saying another word.

◄━▌▌▌▌▌▌▌▌▌▌▌▌▌▌▌▌▌▌▌▌▌▌▌━►

The entire ordeal had taken over an hour and a half, but the secluded location of the school had been far enough removed that no one had come by despite the calamity. It was decided that Curtis and Fleet would keep up appearances by returning to the motel, their cover being that they had gone to get food to help Fleet with his hangover.

Sea and Java would stay behind, waiting several hours before setting the school ablaze with an incendiary device to give Fleet and Curtis a valid alibi. The fire itself would be centralized at the school as it contained the damning evidence, but spontaneous combustion was hard to justify without questions being asked.

In a preliminary search, Java had discovered that there was a large tank next to the church that still had some propane in it. They were going to use that as a catalyst, leaving people to believe it had somehow blown and caught the school on fire as well. From there, people will either blame it on faulty hardware from lack of maintenance or drunk teenagers taking potshots at the tank. C-4 was planted outside the church and connected to a remote detonation switch. All his subordinates had to do now was wait until Curtis gave the order.

After the plan had been finalized, Fleet healed his wounds with a quick shift and put on the new set of clothes given to him by Sea. The only unknown now was whether they would beat Lowy and company back to the motel.

Fleet sat in the passenger seat of the black van, rubbing his forehead to massage away his fatigue. He whispered 'mission accomplished' to himself like a mantra. When he had first said it, the words tasted like ash in his mouth, but the more he repeated it, the more he came to believe it.

The end result had not been optimal, but they had fought hard, taken down a rogue Tryst, and suffered no casualties. From the standpoint of a Servunday, this was an objective success. When he reported on this, he was likely to get an accommodation, or maybe even—

Fleet swung his palm into Curtis' chest and yelled, "Stop!"

Curtis slammed on the brakes, letting out a curse as he did so. "What the hell, man!"

Instead of responding, Fleet pushed open the door and walked to the side of the road. Curtis exited the car and followed behind him in bewilderment. Fleet pointed at something, and Curtis pulled in next to him to see what had him so transfixed. A few yards down the road was a furry lump lying motionless on the ground.

"I think it's a cat," Curtis said after a few seconds of study. "Roadkill now, though."

Fleet recognized that fur pattern even at a distance.

It was Patchy.

"That's what you wanted me to stop for? I almost ran off the damn road. We can't afford to get careless now," Curtis admonished.

Fleet continued to stare at the motionless cat, almost as if he were hoping for it to spring back to life.

"It's not like you killed it," Curtis said, sensing something was off. "The thing was dead long before you got here."

Fleet spoke as if he was coming out of a daze. "Go on ahead. I'll be there soon."

Curtis put a hand on Fleet's shoulder and squeezed. "I know we just been through some shit, but it's going to look real weird if they're back at the motel and you come walking up alone. Whatever this is, you need to drop it. Okay?"

Fleet didn't respond, his eyes still focused on the carcass. Curtis wanted to protest further, but the look on Fleet's face told him it wouldn't make a difference.

"Alright. It's your call," Curtis relented. "Just don't take too long."

Fleet waited until Curtis got in the car and drove past him. Once satisfied Curtis was out of sight, he walked up to the cat and took a knee to put his hand on Patchy's tiny chest. There was a slight warmth, meaning she had been alive until recently; it almost felt like she was just lying down for a nap, tired from her arduous journey.

"You came such a long way…" Fleet whispered, his lower lip trembling.

Why was Patchy so far out here? Had it come looking for…

Fleet stroked her fur, still just as soft as it had ever been. With each pass of his hand, a deep sadness welled up within, as if he were wiping away the last vestiges of her soul. He fought the tears, but soon they filled his eyes and blurred the body at his fingertips.

"I'm sorry... I'm so sorry..."

Alone, he wept over the tiny, innocent creature.

Chapter Twenty-Three

MARSHMALLOWS

"Sorry if you get indigestion later," Lowy apologized as she closed the door to Oreen's car.

BJ gave a small grunt as he ducked out of the cab. "Anything to sample the local cuisine."

"I don't think Tater Tots and fried Oreos count as local cuisine," Oreen said as he shut the door behind him.

"Agree to disagree," BJ countered as he rubbed his belly.

Lowy glanced over at Fleet's truck. "I hope he's feeling better."

She was disappointed that Fleet had not joined them, but she understood why. The combination of a hangover with the lack of sleep he had gotten while in jail would be more than enough to put any person out. The same could not be said of Oreen, who had woken her up from a nap craving something sweet.

To her chagrin, Oreen had refused to talk about what happened between the two of them in prison, so she concocted some embarrassing fantasies over lunch to get him to correct her with the truth. He fell for none of it, of course, though BJ had taken a lively interest in her imaginative scenarios.

"I'll go see how he's doing," Lowy said to remedy her own question.

"Lowy!" Oreen called in exasperation. "We've been over this. You know he's not going to be here much longer."

"I know. But there's no reason I can't enjoy his company while he's here. Same goes for the two of you, right?" Oreen tightened his lips in defeat as Lowy gave him a tilt of her head and a saccharine smile. She only made it a few steps before she turned back around. "Can I ask you guys something?"

Oreen waved his consent as BJ reclined against the car.

Lowy picked at her nails. "Do you think Fleet is a good person?"

There was a lot going on in that strange conversation from last night, but there had never been a straight answer to that odd man's question. She was drunk at the time, but she had championed his moral fortitude even though he had ignored her. It had weighed on her ever since.

Oreen thought on her question. "I can't tell you if he's a good person. But I don't think he's a *bad* person."

It wasn't the answer she was looking for, but his response made her feel much lighter.

Lowy waved to them with a smile and made for Fleet's room.

If I dread what the future holds, I'm just going to ruin the present. They're all going to leave one day, but we can at least make some memories before that time comes.

The revelation had come to her last night in that "heightened" state of being achieved after too much drink. This one was a bit of an outlier as her thoughts during this time typically involved horrible business ideas or scathing comebacks against her high school bullies. But unlike her normal epiphanies, this one had stuck with her after she sobered up.

She kept replaying the night's events in her head, at least as far as her alcohol-addled mind had recorded. Safe in the knowledge that everyone had made it out unscathed, she found herself laughing about the entire ordeal all throughout the day. While it had been one of the weirder things she had ever experienced, she realized it was a moment in time that she would never forget.

All her current friends would leave one day, but the memories they made together gave her something to hold on to. It was the same with her parents: they were gone now, but the happy times lived on inside her, popping up whenever she needed them.

To her, those memories were priceless—but there was always room for more.

She skipped in moderation, happy that she had reached some form of catharsis about her temporary relationships; that's why she wasn't going to let Fleet waste any more time all by himself.

Before she reached his room, Dash rounded the corner of the building and ran up to her. "Have you seen Jill?"

"No, I haven't," Lowy responded, startled by her sudden appearance. "She was here when I left, though. You can ask Fleet or Curtis about it. They might know."

The sour expression Dash made at the mention of Fleet's name told her that was a bad idea.

"How long has she been gone?" Lowy asked.

Dash's tone became more frantic as she talked. "I'm not sure. I got back a minute ago and she wasn't here. She's always here. I looked all over the motel and in both our rooms. This isn't like her."

"She's probably just off somewhere playing with the cat." Her theory did little to calm Dash, so she suggested, "Come with me and we can ask Fleet together. He should be in his room."

Though she was hesitant, Dash agreed to the plan.

Lowy knocked on Fleet's door as Dash wrung her hands beside her. There was no answer. She knocked louder and called out his name.

This time, they heard a muffled yell from behind the door. "I'm coming! Give me a second!"

A few moments later, the door swung open, and a shirtless Fleet greeted them. He gave a loud yawn and scratched his chest with one hand while rubbing his puffy, red eyes with the other.

"What's up?" he asked, unable to hide his shock that Dash was there.

Lowy wanted to answer, but she was frozen. Seeing Fleet's muscular torso in the flesh had caught her off guard, making her draw out the first syllable of a sentence she failed to start.

Dash pushed Lowy aside. "You seen Jill?"

"Can't say I have. Last I saw, she was headed to the hospital." Fleet looked her in the eye when he said this, as if he were tying to make a point. "Kind of surprised you care enough to look for her."

Dash got in his face, forcing him to back away in defense.

Broken from her trance, Lowy stepped between them and tried to deflate the tension. "She's out of the hospital, but now we can't find her. She's not in her room, and Dash has already checked the rest of the motel."

"Her room? I thought she lived with you," Fleet said, nodding toward Dash.

"She's there a lot, but she has her own room in the top right of building two," Lowy informed him.

"That's none of your business!" Dash shouted as she shoved Lowy out of the way once more to address him. "If you know something, you better fucking tell me."

Fleet grabbed Lowy by the shoulders and pulled her in front of Dash again to prevent further encroachment. "Hey, I haven't seen her once. I've been laid up here most of the day trying to sleep off this hangover. The only time I left the room was when me and Curtis went to get something to eat. If anything, I bet she took off to get away from you before she died in this shithole."

Fleet winced, realizing he had inadvertently glanced Lowy's motel with his barb at Dash. But Lowy didn't even hear what he said—she was in her own world.

Lowy's hands hovered around his waist, wanting desperately to engage in an embrace but too nervous to follow through. He had pulled her in rather close when he used her as a meat-shield, almost to the point of a one-sided hug; it was no wonder she misread his intent.

"Earth to Lowy," he said, shaking her from her reverie.

"Oh! I was just...umm..." Lowy flushed when she realized what she had been doing and lowered her head in embarrassment. She stopped talking as her eyes squinted down at something. "Did you get new shoes?"

Fleet let out a modest 'uhh' as he stared down at his own feet for several seconds, though Lowy chalked his slow response up to sleep deprivation.

As he faltered, a wailing klaxon offered him a reprieve.

"Is that a siren?" Lowy wondered aloud.

She soon had affirmation as a firetruck zoomed past them on the road. A few seconds later, Oreen came running up to them with BJ in tow.

"There's a fire!" Oreen shouted.

"Where?" Lowy asked, growing concerned.

Oreen pointed in the direction the firetruck had gone. "Not sure, but you can see smoke coming from somewhere that way."

Lowy took off toward the road, followed by everyone else. Over the trees in the distance, they witnessed smoke billowing up into the sky.

"That looks like it's coming from the old school," Lowy said, her brow creased with worry.

"Lowy, I need to borrow your car!" Dash blurted out, eyes wide with fear.

"My car is still at the bar. But why do you need it?"

"She might be down there. I have to go check. Someone, please!" Dash pleaded, her eyes filling with tears of desperation.

"Are you crazy? This could be a forest fire!" Oreen shouted, his voice tinged with panic. "We need to evacuate!"

"I don't give a shit what you do! I'm going!" Dash yelled back.

Lowy stepped in to rationalize the situation for him. "Oreen, we can't find Jill anywhere. You've got to admit, the timing is pretty odd with the fire and her disappearance. If by some chance she is down there and she gets hurt, I will never forgive myself."

At her words, Fleet lowered his head and turned away from the group.

"Thank you," Dash said, wiping her eyes.

"She's right. I'll come and help as best I can," Fleet added.

Dash gave him a half smile. Though she clearly didn't trust him yet, she was grateful for the help.

"Fine!" Oreen cried out in defeat. "We can all fit in my car, so come on."

BJ nodded, knowing this was the right thing to do.

"I need to go fill in Curtis about all this. You guys head out. I'll meet you down there," Fleet explained before racing back to his room.

The rest of them filed into Oreen's SUV, with Dash and Lowy sitting in the back. Lowy frowned as she watched Dash lock her fingers in worry and plead with Oreen to hurry up.

She scooted in closer and put an arm over Dash's shoulder to comfort her.

"Don't worry. I'm sure Jill is just fine."

"What are you doing?" Curtis asked with mild contempt, annoyed that Fleet had woken him from a deep slumber with his knocking.

"Just listen. I'm leaving with everyone, and I need you to check out the top right room on the second floor of your building. It was the kid's place, so there may be something in there."

"The kid?" Curtis mumbled, still trying to wake up.

"The kid! Jill! The one we just—" Fleet stopped short and bit his lip. "Take care of it. I'm trusting you."

Fleet left without a parting word and ran out to his truck. The others had already left, but he sped down the road with reckless abandon until he caught up with them. They all made their way down the long driveway and into the gravel parking lot to discover they weren't the only ones who had come to investigate.

The area had been cordoned off by yellow tape and lined by a large group of onlookers staring slack-jawed at the intense flames. Dash jumped from the car after they arrived and was running through the crowd, asking people if they had seen Jill. The rest of them followed suit to find a good place to watch the fire.

They don't play around, Fleet thought to himself as he admired Sea and Java's handiwork. There was no source of water to attack the blaze with, so the firefighters were doing their best on damage control to keep it from spreading.

Among the crowd, Fleet spotted Lowy off on her own. "Should have brought some marshmallows," he joked as he pulled up next to her.

To his chagrin, his dad joke didn't even get a titter. Lowy stood stiff with her lips stretched across her teeth, her hands clasped underneath her chin, and an expression of sorrow on her face.

"Sorry. I shouldn't have made light of it. I know this place holds some fond memories for you," he apologized.

Lowy turned to him with a wistful smile, the flames' reflection dancing in her glasses. "It's weird. This place has been here my whole life, and I've never even given it a second thought since I left until we came out here the other day. But it feels like I've lost something important. There's no reason I should feel like this, but I just…"

Sensing her feelings, Fleet moved his arm behind her where it hovered awkwardly inches from her back. It felt wrong to console her for the actions he had taken, so he let his arm fall back to his side as he joined her in watching the roaring fire.

Soon after, BJ wandered up next to him, chewing on a stick of beef jerky as he studied the blaze. Fleet looked up at the burly man, and their eyes met. Fleet gave him an awkward smile, which led to BJ pointing toward the fire and quipping, "Did anyone bring the marshmallows?"

Fleet laughed and nodded as he wagged his thumb between the two of them. "You and me, man. You and me."

Not far away, Fleet caught sight of Dash interrogating people in a futile attempt to find Jill. Fleet excused himself and etched closer to better hear what she was saying. While he wasn't able to pick up specifics thanks to the roar of the fire, there was something that caught him as odd: everyone seemed to be acquainted with her, some even calling her by name.

One man Dash addressed had a very different response from everyone else. When confronted by her, he smiled and slid his arms around her waist before patting her on the rear. Dash returned the greeting by head-butting him in the face. The man crumpled as he nursed his newfound bloody nose. Without·breaking stride, Dash returned to questioning everyone in the immediate area.

Fleet grimaced at the thought of what she would do to him if she knew the truth.

As he watched her, the silhouette of a familiar figure came into view against the flames, causing Fleet to curse. As Denvis turned his head Fleet's way, he ducked behind a gaggle of onlookers to avoid detection—just a bit too late.

"What the fuck did I tell you!" Denvis shouted, startling several people.

Fleet froze in place, hunched over with his lips stretched almost back to his ears. He heard Denvis' heavy footsteps approaching him—and continue on past. Fleet looked over his shoulder to see the true source of the sheriff's ire: Oreen.

Denvis cursed and berated the man, causing a swell of bystanders whose passion for the fire had waned. However, Denvis made the mistake of advancing too close, thus prompting BJ to step forward. The sheriff was not a small man, but even he seemed doubtful as he stared up at BJ's warning gaze.

Denvis leaned to address Oreen on the other side of BJ. "I won't be held responsible for what happens from here on."

Oreen wore a smug expression as he moved his hand from behind BJ's back to expose a fist with an extended middle finger. The surrounding crowd gave a juvenile whoop as Denvis shook with rage.

Before he could act on his anger, BJ spoke up to end the madness. "Yes, sheriff. Sorry for the trouble. We'll be leaving now."

Oreen gave his husband a look of indignation, but BJ shot him a look of his own that told him now was not the time.

During the commotion, Lowy had walked up beside them. With a roll of her eyes, she asked, "Again? Can't you guys just get along?"

Oreen grabbed Lowy's hand, giving it a quick squeeze. "Looks like we're leaving. See you back at the motel."

Lowy nodded and waved the couple off. Still in a huff, Denvis stomped after them to ensure that they stayed true to their word. Fleet straightened back up and breathed a sigh of relief as the crowd resumed watching the fire.

"That school has been here for so many years," muttered an older lady off to Fleet's side. Even though she directed her words at no one, they were clearly meant for him. "It's a shame to see it go in such a way, but it certainly is magnificent."

Not sure what to say, Fleet nodded in accompaniment to a reasonable 'mmm-hmm.' He was now stuck in that awkward place where one is unsure whether they should make the effort to keep the conversation alive, or let it die a slow and floundering death; his social graces forced him to choose the former.

"At least the church is all right."

Wait. The church *is* all right. But it shouldn't be. It should have been nothing but a crater from the explosion. Had Curtis decided against it for some reason? And if so, why wasn't he informed?

Whatever.

In the grand scheme of things, it didn't matter. All they needed was to eliminate the evidence of what had happened in that school; everything else was simply Curtis being a perfectionist and leaving no loose ends. Their fabricated story may have changed, but the main objective had been achieved based on the intensity of those flames.

The church was of no consequence.

"Yes! The church!" the lady shouted with a rapturous sway. "Truly, it is a sign that we tread the righteous path!"

The woman then proceeded to lick her palm, point up into the darkening sky, draw a circle in the air as she blew a raspberry, and then finish by slapping herself square in the forehead.

Fleet watched in stunned silence as the woman then bowed her head in a silent prayer. All around him, he heard the sound of *pbbbfft* and then a loud slap as others mirrored her actions.

Fleet backed away as his eyes darted among the members of the crowd. *That's...odd*, he thought. *Must be a local thing.*

He didn't even realize that Lowy was standing behind him until he backed into her.

"Have you seen Dash?" she asked.

"Yeah, she's here somewhere," Fleet stammered before asking his own question. "Do you know what this is all about?"

Fleet mimicked the woman's actions from earlier with great embarrassment, faltering a bit when he had to make the noise with his mouth. Not long after, the familiar chorus rang out as random people in the crowd joined in, followed by the slap as they hit their foreheads in unison.

Lowy burst out laughing. "How did you get everyone to do that?"

She blew a raspberry of her own, which prompted another round from the crowd. Lowy doubled over in laughter; at least this nonsense had lightened her spirits a bit.

"I think I'm gonna pee!" she squealed.

Fleet found her glee rather contagious, though he did a good job of holding it back. She did it again for kicks, which caused her laughter to intensify into a coughing fit.

"Okay. Okay. Calm down or you're gonna choke," Fleet warned, stifling a chuckle.

He then saw Dash still going through the crowd and waved to get her attention. With hopes of good news, Dash came running over to them.

"Anything?" She gave Lowy a sour look once she noticed her laughing. "What's so damn funny?"

"Nothing. Sorry." Lowy straightened herself up as she conquered her giggles. "Dash, we're heading back. Oreen got kicked out by Denvis, and I'm sure Jill can't be here. We've looked everywhere we can."

She omitted the one place they couldn't check, aware of how dire the implications would be—but unaware of how correct she was.

"That's fine." Dash frowned and turned away from her. "I'm going to stay here. There's a few more people I need to talk to."

Before Lowy could protest, Dash dipped out of sight.

"I really don't want to leave her like this," Lowy said, picking at her nails.

"She can take care of herself," Fleet assured her, remembering the head-butt he witnessed earlier. "Let's go. I'm sure Oreen is waiting for you."

As they walked away, Fleet turned and scanned the crowd. He recognized a few faces he had seen at either the bar or the restaurant, but everyone else was a stranger. The one person he was looking for was nowhere to be found.

He found himself relieved that Peter guy was absent. The last thing he needed was another fight in public, especially after getting chewed out by Curtis earlier. Still, that anger from last night came bubbling back up. Even just thinking about that asshole pissed him off. He needed something to calm his nerves.

Fleet called out Lowy's name to get her attention. When she turned around, Fleet blew one last raspberry to send them out in style.

Chapter Twenty-Four

ISOLATION

"Shouldn't they already be here?" Lowy wondered aloud, noting the absence of Oreen and BJ's car. "They left well before we did."

"They might have gone out for food or something," Fleet responded. "Or maybe they took your uncle's threat to heart and skipped out."

She stifled a laugh. "Come on. Do you really think they would be driven out of town by a measly little threat of violence?"

As she spoke, Fleet glanced over to Jill's room. There was no light on, but he caught the slightest twinge of movement behind the curtains.

Shit! I thought we were going to be gone longer than that, Fleet thought. *Hopefully she doesn't...*

Without warning, Lowy started walking toward the building. He knew immediately what her plan was: she was going to check and see if Jill had returned in their absence.

He needed to distract her.

"Hey, Lowy. How about you give me my license back?" Fleet said, mentally praising himself for getting the money from Curtis earlier. "I finally got some cash."

"Oh...um, sure, we can do that," Lowy said. "Do you need it right now?"

Fleet shrugged. "No time like the present. We should have done this before we went out for drinks. If Viv had cared, I wouldn't have been able to get anything. Probably wouldn't have ended up in jail either, but whatever."

Lowy gave a sad nod of acknowledgement before turning toward the front office.

"Let me get my wallet out of the car and I'll meet you there," Fleet said as he backed up towards his truck.

With that, Fleet ran back to his vehicle and flung open the door. He made a show of leaning in and fiddling with the center console, where he just so happened to *accidentally* hit his shoulder against the horn.

Fleet looked through the windshield toward the apartment, catching a brief glimpse of Curtis' face as he peeked through the curtains. Fleet sent him a quick 'hurry' in sign language before exiting the cab, hoping Curtis got the message. He then locked the door behind him and went to join Lowy.

Once they were both inside the main office, she walked behind the counter and pulled out a lockbox that she never bothered to lock. Fleet took out three hundred dollars and placed it on the countertop.

Lowy stared at the bills before holding out the license once she fished it out. "Does this mean you'll be leaving soon?"

Realizing that was the logical conclusion, Fleet assuaged her fears. "No, I'm not leaving yet. That's just all the money I have on me right now, and I figured you weren't going to give my license back for only one night's rent."

"Technically, you did only spend one night here. Besides, that's way too much."

Fleet waved it off. "Then consider it a tip for your outstanding service as a tour guide for this lovely little hamlet."

The smile came back to her face as she fiddled with the rim of her glasses. "I guess I can't turn that down then, can I?"

"You deserve it," Fleet said, giving her a genuine smile that seemed to make her fidget even more.

Lowy was enjoying herself. She had been hoping for a similar interaction the night she had asked him out for drinks; it was supposed to be an excellent time to flirt with him, or at least attempt to. Now here he was, taking the reins, far removed from any social pretext.

It felt good.

Even if it went nowhere, at least for now, it felt good.

But why stop at this? There was no reason to let it peak at mere flirtations. She just had to step up, make the first move, and tell him what she wanted.

"Fleet, do you think... Would you like to..."

A sinkhole of guilt opened in her stomach. Here she was trying to score while poor Jill was missing. What kind of friend did that make her?

A shitty one.

A real shitty one.

She had to keep up the search for Jill's sake, even if it cost her this brief moment in time. Making sure her friend was all right was far more important than anything else.

"I'm worried about Jill." Lowy turned away from Fleet and grabbed a key from the wall. "I need to go check and see if she's back."

As she was about to break the threshold of the counter, Fleet moved to the side of it, blocking her exit. "Lowy, wait!"

Startled, Lowy dropped the key as she walked into him. In that instance, they stared into one another's eyes, her mind racing with possibilities.

Fleet put his hands on her shoulders. "Lowy, I need to ask you something."

In an instant, Lowy's mind was clear. No responsibilities. No impending dread about the choice she was making. No unnecessary need to justify herself to her own encumbered ego. No guilt mongering herself into questioning her own desires.

This was for her.

This was what she wanted.

She slid her hands up Fleet's side and pulled herself in closer. Lowy's heart throbbed in her throat as the last vestige of air escaped her lungs through trembling lips. She closed her eyes and leaned forward. All trepidation evaporated as she waited for him to join her.

Fleet leaned in and asked his question.

"Why are you here?"

Lowy opened her eyes, blinked, and then responded, "Why am I here?"

"Yes, exactly!" Fleet blurted out.

Lowy took a step back, putting a hand to her beating heart. "I'm here because I want to be."

"Are you sure?" Fleet probed.

Lowy backed off farther as she tried to account for the sudden change in atmosphere. "What are you trying to say?"

Fleet took a few steps away from her, holding out his arms. "You're a people person. Out here, you're isolated away in the middle of nowhere, far away from everyone else. You host random campfire s'more parties and latch onto literal strangers like me and Oreen because you are so desperate for human interaction. Shit, Lowy, it sounds weird to say, but I feel like I'm one of your best friends. That's not right."

"I thought..." Lowy took a couple more steps back and folded her arms. "I didn't realize I was such a burden to you."

Fleet clenched his fists and groaned. "That's not what I'm saying! I think you're awesome. You're a literal joy to be around. That's the problem. You should have people falling all over each other to hang out with you. But that's not happening, and it's because of this motel."

Lowy tucked her arms in like a straight-jacket. "What you don't get is just how important my job is. It might not be glamorous, but I provide a valuable service to the community, and everyone respects the hard work I do."

Fleet pursed his lips and nodded at her. "Is that right? Well, let's see how much your loyal patrons respect you, shall we?" Fleet grabbed the guest book from the table and flipped through it until he found a good page. "Tell me, how familiar are you with a Mr. 'Lester'?"

Lowy tried to recall. She had an excellent memory, but she couldn't remember anyone who came in with that name.

As she stumbled over her thoughts, Fleet spoke up. "Don't remember? Maybe the first name will help. It's 'Moe.' What an unfortunate combination. Parents really dropped the ball on that one."

He gave her a moment to put it together before continuing his tirade in a condescending tone.

"Here's another: the prestigious 'Dick Tickler.' Next to him we have 'Tally Wacker.' I bet they would make a cute couple. And of course, who can forget 'Harry Wreckdum.'"

Fleet didn't have to scroll far to find another batch, ignoring the growing frown on Lowy's face.

"Over here, this guy wrote 'Raise Hell, Praise Dale.' That's not even a name, and they misspelled both 'raise' and 'praise' somehow. Oh, but here's my favorite."

Fleet flipped the book toward Lowy and pointed at a scribble about halfway down the page.

"This guy drew what I assume is a carrot going into a butt; it's even got stink lines and everything. If you saw this, there's no way you could have believed this was someone's name."

"I thought it was cursive," Lowy admitted, sulking.

Fleet slammed the book shut and threw it back on the table. "That's what you're staying for? People who don't even respect you enough to give you their real names? If this doesn't bother you, that's fine, but you cannot use 'community' as a reason to stay here."

Lowy's eyebrows furrowed as she looked down at the floor, her anger mounting with each word Fleet spoke.

"Lowy, you are the living embodiment of wasted potential, and you know it. You can't tell me you don't fantasize about bailing on this place. It's like you already checked out long ago, but you're afraid to leave. I mean, look around. This motel is falling apart. Half the stuff here doesn't even work because you do no maintenance or upkeep at all. You want this place to go under, but you won't admit it to yourself."

Lowy balled her fists as the blood ran to her face. "That's not true!" she said through gritted teeth. "My parents put everything into this motel! It's their legacy, and they left it to me! I won't betray their trust and just abandon it!"

"Did they tell you that?" Fleet asked in an accusatory tone. "Was their dying wish that you manage this place regardless of what it does to you? That you forsake everything else so long as this shitty patchwork of wood and concrete remains standing? Do you think they were that selfish?"

Lowy's emotions overpowered her as tears of rage formed in the corners of her eyes. "You don't get it! You're here for a few days and suddenly you've figured out my entire life? You sound just like Oreen! It's not your place to sit there and judge me!"

"No, *you* don't get it!" Fleet countered with vehemence. "It's you, Lowy. You are their legacy. The way you speak of them, it's clear how much they loved you. Trust me on this. They would want you to be happy, and if you can look deep down and say that staying here would do that, that's great. I can't tell you how to live, but as your friend, I want you...to live a good life."

Lowy tried to counter, but she couldn't; her words were caught up somewhere in between her conflicting emotions. This was the second time now that Fleet had pulled the rug from under her. She wanted to curse at him, punch him in the face, tell him to get the fuck out of her life. But she also wanted to forget it all happened. Just erase the last few minutes from existence and return to that one wonderful moment when she believed there could be something more.

In the end, she settled for staring down at the floor and mumbling, "It's none of your business."

Fleet lowered his head as she walked out the front door and headed back to her mobile home without another word.

CHAPTER TWENTY-FIVE

JIZZ MATH

FLEET OPENED THE DOOR to Jill's room without knocking and gingerly closed it behind him to avoid making a sound. A small LED lantern sat in the center of the room, acting as a meager light source to avoid drawing attention.

Java was poking around the walls and gave a small nod as he entered. Curtis stood near the bathroom lost in thought as he tapped his thumb against his nose.

"This is her room," Fleet mumbled to himself.

Jill's sheets had been stripped from the bed and balled up in the corner like an oversized rat's nest; it seemed she had been more comfortable holed away there than on the bed. Fleet's heart sank when he saw the empty can of orange soda sitting on the floor next to her spot.

"What did you find?" he asked to get Curtis' attention.

Curtis grabbed the lantern and pushed open the door to the bathroom. "Tell me what you see."

Fleet walked into the bathroom and swiveled about, trying to figure out what Curtis meant. The layout was the same as the other bathrooms he had been in. There was a metal sink, a plastic shower curtain, a clean toilet...

"Clean toilet?" Fleet blurted as soon as he noticed.

The porcelain toilet was in immaculate condition; no grunge running down the side or rust on the bolts. Something was off. He walked over and lifted the lid to find that the inside was as pristine as the outside.

He then went over to the bathtub and pulled back the curtain. No grime or mildew to be seen. It was as if someone had polished the thing to a fine finish.

"Looks like you caught on. But you haven't seen the real deal yet." Curtis held up something that was long and cylindrical. "Black light. Check this out."

Curtis turned off the lantern and flicked on his black light, causing the bathroom to burst alight in an eerie, pale glow.

"Holy shit..." Fleet trailed off, enamored by the spectacle before him. It almost looked like some sort of dark magic as Curtis waved the light about, making the area luminesce.

"I noticed how clean the bathroom was compared to mine," Curtis said. "The owner isn't cleaning them, which means it had to be a guest. And the only reason someone would do that is if they had something to hide."

Curtis walked around the bathroom to cover more area with the light.

"Took a chance, put down some luminol, and the whole place lit up. It literally covers the entire floor wall to wall. The worst of it is in the bathtub."

Curtis shone the light on the bathtub, which caused the entire thing to burst to life like a neon sign.

"That's a lot of semen," Fleet joked nervously as he backed into the bedroom.

"Doubtful," Java said from behind them as he moved in closer. "The median volume per ejaculate is around three milliliters. Assuming it would take approximately 1.5 gallons to cover this floor when distributed equally, and that each involved had a similar release—which is nigh impossible—it would take one thousand eight hundred and ninety-three participants over the course of an extended period to accomplish what you suggest."

The two stared at Java with a lukewarm mixture of confusion and disgust.

Fleet closed his eyes and rubbed his forehead. "You choose now to finally speak to me, and the first thing that comes out of your mouth is a load of jizz math? Scriptor, the fuck are you teaching these guys?"

Curtis put up his hands in defense. "Whatever they want to do in their personal time is their own business."

"I won't apologize for being right," Java grumbled.

"Nor should you," Fleet agreed to end the conversation. He then squatted to examine the floor and rubbed his hand along the tile. "What are the odds someone could survive something like this?"

"I'm not a doctor, but I'm going to go out on a limb and assume 'not good.'" Curtis waited a moment before continuing. "I guess we found where our severed hand came from. You were right...again."

Fleet didn't acknowledge the praise. "But it doesn't make any sense. If she killed someone here, why leave a hand by the road?"

"You're asking for reason out of someone who was mentally unstable," Curtis responded, trying not to remember the trauma she had dealt him.

Fleet winced at the 'was' in Curtis' statement, but he did not lose focus. He rubbed his upper lip as he tried to envision what might have led to this, mumbling under his breath as his eyes darted about like a madman trying to decipher some ancient script.

Suddenly, Fleet's jaw dropped and his eyes widened as all the pieces miraculously came together in his head. Without standing, Fleet bobbed his hand as he explained aloud, his face framed by the unsettling glow of the luminol. "The only way I can see this making sense is if something started here, but did not *end* here. My money is on an argument about drugs. The corpse is a dealer and won't give Jill anything because she can't pay for it. Jill loses control because of her addiction and kills the victim."

"What about the hand?" Curtis interjected.

Fleet stood up and paced as he imparted his theory. "Hear me out: I think it was Dash."

Curtis raised an eyebrow, prompting Fleet to continue.

"I'm not sure what their relationship is, but I do know Dash is very protective of her. I bet after Jill killed the victim, she freaked. She gets Dash because she can't bring herself to 'take care' of the body. Dash decides the best way to get rid of it is to cut it up and dispose of it out in the woods. That would explain why something sharp was used on the hand instead of it being ripped off."

Fleet walked to the bathroom window and pulled back the curtain to peek through.

"That means somewhere out there are the dealer's decomposing remains that no one ever found. Then a wild animal sniffed out the corpse and carried the hand to the road before dropping it when it got scared by a car! And that's where Lowy found it!"

When he finished, Fleet clapped his hands together to signify the conclusion of his argument.

Curtis fell silent as he pondered the theory.

"Well?" Fleet asked in anticipation.

Curtis nodded. "You've been right about everything thus far."

Fleet groaned and threw his head back. "I don't need you blowing smoke up my ass right now. Tell me what you really think."

"Honestly, I think that's as likely a scenario as any other I can come up with based on what we have right now. Of course, that is barring the theory where a thousand plus dudes all came in here and wanked it simultaneously." Curtis elevated his voice at the end to make sure that Java would hear.

Java harrumphed in return.

Fleet rubbed the back of his neck with a sigh. "I feel like I'm on the right track, but there's still a lot we're missing. All we really know is that this is confirmed Tryst activity, and that Dash is definitely involved somehow. Scriptor, I assume you won't have any complaints when I tell you we need to bring her in."

"No, but I do have one question." Curtis tapped the black light into his open palm, making the room dance with light. "You said that Dash was involved...but that she isn't Tryst. But if anything, all this points to her being one, right? Why are you so certain she isn't?"

"Because of her injury," Fleet stated matter-of-factly.

Curtis cocked his head back. "Injury?"

Fleet sounded a bit disappointed in Curtis as he continued. "Come on. There's no way you didn't notice that bloody bandage she's had on her finger."

"Oh yeah. I forgot all about that."

"She got that cut doing some dumb shit the first night I got here. It was a deep one, but if she was Tryst, it should have healed by now."

"That's true," Curtis agreed. "Even healing at base speed, any kind of basic flesh wound should have closed up in that amount of time."

Fleet put out his hands in a thankful gesture to Curtis' consensus.

However, his mood floundered when Curtis provided an alternative. "Unless she was doing it herself."

"Do what now?" Fleet asked as he leaned in.

"If you saw her get cut, the only way to cover it up would be to redo it every so often. If she was walking around all healed the next morning, it wouldn't go unnoticed."

He was right.

Fleet backed against the doorway as something dawned on him. Earlier, when he had been rummaging through her room, he had come across a knife sitting on her sink. Could she have been using it to...

Fleet turned away from the bathroom. "We have to find her! Right now!"

"Sure," Curtis agreed. "But we have no idea where she is."

"Then make it your priority!" Fleet stepped toward him as panic rose within. "In her current mental state, we don't know what she'll do. And if she is Tryst, and she figures out what happened to Jill, she'll make what we did at the school look like reruns of Family Matters."

Curtis nodded, his voice cracking once he grasped the seriousness of the situation. "Then what's the plan?"

"Try the school first. It was the last place I saw her, so maybe she's still running around down there. She won't go too far if she thinks Jill is still in the area."

"What do we do when we find her?"

Fleet threw up his hands. "Hit her with a fucking cinder block and throw her in the trunk for all I care. But we have to contain her at all costs, understand?"

"Whatever it takes," Curtis said before heading to the door. "Come on, let's go!"

In response, Java made his way to the exit without a word.

Fleet took out his phone, his sudden panic making him forget there was no service out here. "Hold up!" he called out, catching Curtis just as he broke the threshold. Fleet grit his teeth and held out a hand. "Give me the phone. I'm going to call 'Her.'"

Curtis reached into his pocket and pulled out a bulky satellite phone with a fat antenna. Despite it being his idea, Fleet took the phone from him like it was a loaded gun in a game of Russian roulette—and there was only one chamber left.

"Good luck, Hangman." Curtis gave Fleet a resigned slap on the shoulder before vacating the room.

Fleet scrolled through the short list of contacts until he reached the one he was looking for. He flinched as his finger trembled over the screen, just above the name. He took several deep breaths, like he was about to dive to the bottom of the ocean, and then pressed down. The phone rang as a name appeared on the screen.

-Violet Jessop-

CHAPTER TWENTY-SIX

DISCOVERY

WHO THE HELL DOES he think he is? Lowy raged as she choked the life from her body pillow. *He waltzes up in here and tells me how to live my life! He acts like he's got me all figured out!*

"That pretentious douche!"

Lowy suplexed her body pillow onto the bed and took a moment to relieve some stress by shouting into it. Feeling a bit silly, she wrapped her legs around the pillow and pulled it in close.

So why does his opinion matter to me so much?

Her phone vibrated on the table next to her bed, and she kicked the pillow away to see who had messaged her. Lowy slumped when she saw the message on her phone: it was a notification stating that her battery was at ten percent.

Lowy clicked on her messages and scrolled through them. Every single one she had received over the past three months was either from Oreen or a bill payment notification. She then opened her contacts and scrolled through the rather sizable list of people—people she hadn't spoken to in years. They were all former high school and college friends who had long since moved on to better things.

"Whatever," Lowy mumbled as she tossed the phone behind her.

All she needed was something to clear her mind. She glanced at her computer and found the usual compulsion to check social media had dissipated, leaving her with a hollow feeling. She turned her attention to the other end of the trailer, where an open door gave her a clear view of her bathroom. It needed a good scrubbing, but she wasn't in the mood for manual labor. She then looked at the drawer where her 'little friend' resided, but even that seemed like a waste of time and energy. Instead, she rolled on her back, staring up at the dingy tint of the ceiling.

"I am happy, right?" she wondered aloud.

For once, there was no one around to convince. No one to placate by parroting out the same basic assurance. No need for false pretense to assuage the concern of another. She was free of that here. Yet even in solitude, the question still lingered, far away from the fortitude born of another's doubt.

The only person she needed to convince now—was herself.

Tears soaked her sheets as she sobbed. She buried her face in the pillow, wishing for it to hide her from reality as it had done for the monsters under her bed so long ago. But it offered no solace this time—the truth was far more cruel than any monster could ever be.

She turned her head to breathe and found herself focusing on the picture sitting atop her dresser. Even with blurred vision, the image was clear in her mind thanks to the many nights she lay awake staring at it.

It was her as a child, held aloft by her father with her mother standing beside them. The young Lowy had a beaming smile brought on from a fit of laughter as she playfully struggled to free herself from her father's grip, her mother of no help as she tickled her daughter's sides.

"Is he right?" Lowy choked out the words. "All you ever wanted was for me to be happy, and I couldn't even do that."

Guilt now joined her other emotions, their combined weight pushing her down into a cold, dark hole. She slid over to grab her phone and picked the most recently dialed number. Lowy hung up before the first ring had even finished.

I can't talk to him right now sounding like this! What if Oreen is out living it up with BJ on a date night or something? He doesn't deserve to be burdened like that. Though I bet he would love to know he was right. But then who can I talk to? I really need someone.

Lowy sat up in bed, running the pillow across her face to mop up her runny nose. She bent the pillow in half, making sure the snot was on the inside crease, and then clutched it close as she attempted to calm herself.

As much as I love Denvis, this is way out of his league. He's got the emotional range of a moldy bath mat. Dash might understand where I'm coming from, but I have no way of getting hold of her. Not that she doesn't have enough on her mind without having to worry about me. I could always talk to—

"No!" she shouted. "He's the reason I'm in here boogering up my favorite pillow! Asshole!"

With an angry grunt, she flung said pillow away from her toward the bathroom. It unfurled just as it passed through the door frame, knocking her toothbrush into the toilet before tenderly dipping itself over the rim to join it in a nice soak.

She watched the scene unfold, letting it all sink in. Once satisfied it couldn't get any worse, she took a deep breath through her clogged nose and released a primal screech. It felt good, much better than crying. She did it one more time for the hell of it.

That's it! I don't need someone to talk to. I need someone to fucking scream at!

"And I know just the person!" Lowy exclaimed as she shot up and kicked open the trailer door.

She stomped all the way down to Fleet's room with a righteous fury burning in her heart. Unfortunately, as she noticed the light on in his window, she realized that her bravado had waned somewhat on the trip over.

She was not to be daunted, however. Though despite her earlier intent, instead of pounding on his door and demanding an audience, she tapped it with her knuckle and called out to him politely.

"Fleet, can we talk?"

She received no response.

The light's on. He has to be in there. Is he ignoring me on purpose? Did I make him mad when I blew up at him earlier? Maybe I should apologize. Wait, no! That isn't how this is going down! I came here to make him apologize to me, and I'm not leaving until I get one!

"Don't ignore me! We need to talk about this!"

She jiggled the door handle and pushed inward, not expecting anything to come of it. To her surprise, the door swung open, and she found herself faced with an empty room. She felt an odd mixture of disappointment and relief at his absence, but it did nothing to deter her from the primary goal.

"That's fine. I can wait," she said aloud as she sat down on the bed.

Several minutes passed with no sign of Fleet. Boredom took hold as she kicked her feet over the side of the bed, grimacing each time a puff of dust spewed from the old mattress. She took out her phone to check the time.

"Where is he?"

As if to answer her query, the sound of two car doors slamming shut caught her attention. She jumped up and ran over to the window in time to see Curtis' vehicle driving away.

I guess he went with Curtis to get some food. They could have asked if I wanted to go along. Or at least offered to pick me up something.

Lowy pressed her forehead against the glass.

Looks like Fleet's doing just fine after our argument. I wonder if he's even a little sorry.

That all-too-familiar sensation of inescapable loneliness rushed back in full force. It felt as if she were wearing a ball and chain as she walked back and flopped face-first onto the bed. Worried she might have missed it, she pulled out her phone to see if Oreen had returned her call.

He had not.

She sighed as she slipped the phone into her pocket. "Guess I'll go back."

Lowy started to get up, but something caught her eye on the nightstand. She crawled over to it and examined the odd arrangement of faint footprints that littered its surface.

"What was he doing?" she questioned with a tilt of her head, grateful for the rather mundane bit of detective work to take her mind off the current situation.

She lifted one foot up and placed it on top of the nightstand as she pantomimed tying her shoe. The flat surface was at a good shoe-tying level, so it kind of made sense. However, it only explained away a few of the footprints.

She went to each available side and repeated the process, this time standing up to lean on her propped knee. This worked as well if you gave it a decent margin for error. But there was one set of prints that left her stumped: the ones that looked as if they had come straight out of the wallpaper.

No matter how she rationalized it, it would have been impossible to make those footprints if the nightstand was flush against the wall. She checked the floor and noticed that there were several indentions in the carpet from where the nightstand had stood undisturbed for so many years.

He had to have moved this. But why?

Lowy looked up at the ceiling, remembering the time she had to get on the nightstand to crush a cockroach overhead with her shoe. She discarded the thought when she didn't see any errant roach legs or insect residue dangling above.

She swung the nightstand out of place with a grunt to give herself enough room to match her foot to the mystery print. It worked that way, but moving the nightstand seemed unnecessary if all you were doing was tying your shoe. Lowy looked up straight ahead, but the only thing she saw was the air vent.

"Wait a minute," Lowy mumbled as she walked toward the wall.

On the metal trim, particularly around the screws, it looked like the dust had been wiped away. To further drive the point home, she noticed individual fingerprints on the corners.

Lowy pushed the nightstand up to the wall, fueled onward by a sudden rush of excitement. She hopped up and squinted into the vent like a kid searching for buried treasure.

"There's something in there!"

She took a step backward in shock, narrowly avoiding a tumble as she decided how to proceed.

Fleet put it in there for a reason. It's none of my business. He came here expecting a certain level of privacy, and as the one in charge, it is my duty to see that he gets it.

Lowy stepped down, but she stopped as one foot hit the floor.

However, as the owner of this establishment, it is also my duty to make sure that the other guests are safe. He's created a fire hazard or something by blocking this vent. The whole place could go up in flames! I have to think of the greater good! I won't have their blood on my hands!

Lowy hopped back up and clawed at the screws with great fervor. They came undone with relative ease, kind of like someone had rushed the installation.

She froze as the last screw fell onto the nightstand. She held the grate in place, her hands now trembling as she took one last moment to consider what she had done.

I'll just have a quick peek before he gets back. He'll never even notice. Holy shit, I'm really doing this!

Even though she said quick, it was anything but as she let the grate slide down the wall. Inside, she could make out the top of the black canvas bag that was stored within. Her eyes widened as she reached in, her fingers just centimeters from the—

"Lowy?"

Lowy yelped as she lost balance, caught off guard by the sudden exclamation. She cracked her ass on the corner of the nightstand before upending onto the floor with a dull thud. The grate slid down the wall and bounced off her makeshift stool with an echoing crash. Lowy looked up through her legs to find Dash staring down at her with a quizzical sneer.

"What are you doing?" Dash asked.

"I'm doing fine, thanks," Lowy grunted as she flopped onto her side. "Didn't hurt at all."

A sharp pain spread up her spine where it met with a sickening thought. Lowy pulled out her phone to see a shard of glass fall from her cracked screen.

"I just got this phone," Lowy whimpered as she struggled to her feet. "You couldn't have knocked?"

"Even if I had, feels like you would have ended up the same way."

"Well, yeah. I guess," Lowy admitted before changing the subject. "How did you get back?"

"I got someone to drop me off," Dash stated in a flat tone, her attention now focused on Lowy's handiwork. Dash pointed up at the open vent. "What's that?"

Lowy blurted out a quick excuse. "Nothing! I was just doing some maintenance, that's all."

Dash stepped over Lowy and hopped up on the nightstand. She examined the bag before grabbing the sides and giving it a tug that brought it halfway out of its confinement. Another solid yank sent it bouncing onto the bed. The mattress collapsed inward as the frame threatened to shatter under the bag's weight.

"What are you doing? He could show up any second!" Lowy said, looking toward the entrance. "We have to put it back!"

Dash paid no heed as she unzipped the bag. She had the focus of a surgeon as she unfurled the edges to expose the bag's contents. Lowy leaned over to get a better angle. Despite her protests, she could not contain her curiosity.

Inside the bag was a large black case with two locks on the front. On the top was an emblem of a stylized wolf head that appeared to have a noose around its neck.

"What do you suppose is in the case?" Lowy pondered, running her finger over the elaborate crest.

"Where is he?" Dash said, her eyes glued to the emblem.

Lowy was so focused on the case that it took a moment to register what Dash had said. "You mean Fleet?"

"Where is he!" Dash yelled, her bottom jaw trembling.

The force of her demand made Lowy take a step back. "I-I saw him leave a while ago. He and Curtis went out somewhere. Why do you—"

As if expecting her question, Dash spoke in a low and menacing growl as rage flashed in her eyes.

"I'm going to kill him!"

"What has he done now?" a voice asked from the other end of the line, skipping the greeting—she was not in a good mood.

Fleet was bouncing his foot as he prepared his introduction. He had come up with several before she picked up, but he was struggling to determine which one to use. She was big on decorum—as long as he stayed professional, she would at least hear him out.

"Howdy."

He winced the second it came out of his mouth.

There was a tense silence before Violet said, "Hangman, I told you not to call me."

"I know, I know. And I'm sorry about this, but the situation down here has changed. Something's come up, and I need your help."

"I do not care," she retorted, sounding rather perturbed.

"What if I had been compromised?"

"Were you?" she asked, her voice rising.

"No! No! I was just saying, is all." Fleet backed away from the hypothetical. "But it's almost as bad. I've come across—"

Violet cut him off. "Then I defer you back to my previous statement: I. Do. Not. Care."

"But you don't have all the details. There's a lot going on here that—"

"I am on a critical mission," Violet interrupted again, "and I will not be called away to hold your hand like some whimpering child."

"I get that, but—"

"Let me tell you a story," Violet prefaced, breaking off on a tangent. "There was once an eager wolf pup who set out on a mission of discovery. Though the pup understood it to be one dangerous and fraught with peril, it accepted the honor with great pride. With a hardened heart and tempered will, the pup thrust itself into the fold with unmatched fervor, eager to see it done."

"Hey, that's one cool pup," Fleet interjected. "But back to what I was saying—"

"Don't interrupt!" she scolded before returning to the story. "But in truth, the pup was not up to the task. It could not handle the pressure and succumbed to their own craven impulses. The pup curled into a ball and soiled itself from the pure indignity of defeat, all the while begging for their mother like the pathetic little whelp it was."

"Wow," Fleet said after several seconds of dead air. "How embarrassing that must have been for you, but thanks for opening up to me like that."

"Wait, what do you think is happening here?" she asked.

"You're trying to make me feel better by telling me about the time you pooped yourself on your first mission," Fleet reasoned, aware of who the actual subject was.

"The story is not about me, you fucking moron," Violet yelled, loud enough that Fleet had to move the phone away from his ear. "I do not poop! A proper lady never does that!"

"How foolish of me. I forgot basic biology does not apply to such cultured women." Though he said it in jest, he assumed she was probably telling the truth.

There was a silence on the other end of the line, one that made Fleet feel like the entire room had filled with gas and his mouth was a match.

"You infuriate me like no other," Violet finally said, taking down the proverbial 'no smoking' sign.

"That was not my intent," Fleet apologized.

This was only half a lie. He had not wanted to start the conversation like this, but he had fallen back into his old ways.

She was his boss, or at least she had been. They were of the same rank now that he had graduated to full-fledged Servunday. But after all this time, he struggled to think of Violet as anything but his mentor—his cruel, sadistic mentor.

She had trained him for years, put him through horrible torture and unspeakable situations, all for the sake of preparing him for times like these. She had destroyed and rebuilt him from the ground up, though she did seem rather disappointed that his old personality had stayed intact instead of transitioning into the calm and collected demeanor that the position demanded.

It was why he would often mess with her. Despite the consequences, whenever he broke her iron mask with his nonsense, it made him think as though he had achieved some level of equality with her, brief though it may be.

The truth was, he knew she was leagues above him in strength, experience, and intelligence; he would never be able to catch up with her. People in the organization worshiped her as a goddess for all those qualities, though many feared her for the same reasons—perhaps the more rational choice.

"I am going to finish my story," Violet continued. "Be quiet and pay close attention to see if you can pick out the underlying theme."

Fleet nodded, forgetting that she couldn't see him.

"And so, the young pup—which is you—failed at his mission. In turn, the wolf who allowed the pup to go off on his own looked like a blathering twat in front of her superiors, damaging her credibility far beyond repair. The pissed-off wolf—which if you have not caught on, is me—took her unbridled rage out upon the pup for his incompetence."

Fleet shivered at the implication, too afraid to interrupt her.

"The moral of this story is simple: deal with it. You are a Servunday now. This is your job. Stumble if you must, but make sure you fall forward. Fall backward, and rest assured, I will be there holding the dagger that goes into your back—then I will eat your face."

The urge to say something else snarky welled up within him, but the fear of how she might react pushed it right the hell back down.

He wanted to at least plead his case one last time, but he was cut off by the chime that signaled she had hung up. Fleet stared at the screen before letting fly a loud expletive. He sat down hard on the mattress and buried his face in his hands, rubbing his palms into his eyes.

She's right. I can't rely on her forever. But why did my first mission have to be the one that blew up to shit fuckin' hell?

Fleet slammed his fist down on the bed and cursed his luck before making his way outside in hopes the fresh air would help calm him down. He closed his eyes and leaned against the railing as he took a long, exaggerated breath.

A loud clatter rang out, causing him to jerk his head in the general direction of the sound. He leaned over the rail and noticed that the door to his room was ajar.

"Did I leave that open?"

He made his way down the steps and over to the other building, stopping short of his room when he heard Lowy's voice. He put his back to the brick and tried to think of a few excuses as to why he was running around so late at night.

A second voice chimed in. He crept closer to the door, trying to remain as silent as possible. The words soon became audible, and he overheard Lowy say something that made his blood run cold.

"What do you suppose is in the case?"

Fleet could have bitten down on his heart as far as it had jumped up in his throat. It had to be his 'Tayumore' she was referring to. The metallic clang made sense if he framed it as her dropping the grate while rooting through the vent.

Fleet cursed under his breath, his brain frantically trying to formulate a plausible excuse for that as well. It was impossible for her to get into the case, but it would still come off as an oddity for it to be hidden in the vent.

However, his mind went blank when he heard shouting and recognized the other person as Dash. She couldn't have picked a worse time to show up, especially with Lowy around. If Dash was still unstable—and based on that outburst, she was—Lowy could be in grave danger.

He gave a mental 'fuck it' and stepped to the door wearing his best shocked expression. The number one way to avoid suspicion is to go on the offensive—just like Violet had taught him.

"What are you guys doing in here?" Fleet shouted at them. "And why are you going through my stuff?"

Lowy was caught like a deer in headlights as she yammered her apology with little pause between words. "I-I'm so sorry. I came in to talk to you about what happened earlier and I noticed the footprints and then I opened the vent but I wasn't going to look but I did and then Dash came and she—"

"I don't want to hear it!" Fleet exclaimed as he stormed into the room. "You think you can—"

Dash interrupted his scolding by vaulting over the bed and slamming both her feet into his chest like a javelin. Fleet sailed back into the window, shattering the glass before he slumped to the ground. Ignoring Lowy's screams of protest, Dash got up and shot a knee directly into his heart, sending a shockwave of pain throughout his chest.

Fleet's mouth dribbled blood as he put up his arms in defense while Dash kicked at his head and screeched 'where is she' with each blow. After the fourth kick, Fleet caught her foot and twisted her ankle so that she fell facedown onto the floor. He yanked her upward by the leg and pressed his foot on the back of her neck, keeping the ankle lock tight.

"Stop this right now!" Lowy demanded, fighting past the obvious undertone of fear in her voice.

"She started it!" Fleet retorted.

Dash clawed at his leg like a wild animal caught in a trap. "I'll fucking kill you!"

"Good luck with that," Fleet said as he twisted even harder, causing her to scream out in pain. "Now, how about you calm down before I snap your ankle?"

As if in response, Fleet heard the unmistakable sound of tearing flesh and cracking bone. Large nails penetrated the sole of Dash's shoe as Fleet struggled to keep his grip. She pushed upward, lifting him off the floor as he clung to her foot.

Dash yanked herself free and delivered a mule kick that sent Fleet flying backward with enough force to crack the wall studs. He coughed up blood and wrapped his arms against his already injured chest, somehow staying on his feet.

There was no other choice. If he didn't fight Dash on equal ground, he was going to die. In contrast to Jill, he held no pretense that she wanted anything besides his head.

He glanced over at Lowy and found her frozen in place, stupefied by the sight before her. He pleaded with her as he committed to the transformation.

"Lowy, get out of here! Now!"

Chapter Twenty-Seven
VERSUS

To Fleet, saying things like 'rending flesh' and 'snapping bone,' though disturbing as they may be, always paled in comparison when it came to the actual transformation itself. Then again, there really weren't any better descriptors for when your body was reassembling itself into some nightmarish creature.

Hair pricks its way through the skin like needles to cover the body in a thick fur. The mouth elongates into a muzzle as teeth sharpen into fangs. The spine extends, piercing the flesh to form the base of a tail as the bones lengthen and stretch to create a foundation for the new body. Organs expand to meet the demand of the growing frame, often causing them to burst before they heal into their proper place.

The entire ordeal can take up to three minutes for a normal Tryst, but Fleet can finish the entire thing in less than thirty seconds. He had blacked out countless times when Violet had first started with him. But after her intense training, he was now at the point where he withstood the process, even excelled at it, although the whole thing was still pure, unadulterated agony.

In fact, the process is so painful that the average Tryst has never transformed in their entire life without the help of drugs and painkillers. Hell, it had taken Fleet years of physical and mental torture to get to where he was now. That's why whenever he found himself up against one that can shift at his level, he knew he was in for a hell of a fight.

Fleet braced himself as his body outgrew his clothes, sending the tatters curling to the floor. Thankfully, he had been wearing his baggier pants, so at least his privates remained tucked away; he didn't want to endure the same trauma Curtis had in the fight with Jill.

Fleet looked up to see Dash towering over him, her head almost scraping the ceiling. Her fur was a deep gray, almost to the point of being blue. She was covered in random clusters of white: the tips of her ears, a vertical line between her eyes leading up into matching hair (some of the dyed bits still showed through) and a large diamond in the center of her sternum.

She had started her transformation before him, but Fleet had never expected her to finish so quickly. This placed him at a considerable disadvantage for the next few seconds.

Dash planted her foot and came at him with a balled fist. Fleet covered his face, misjudging her intent as she stooped down and caught him hard in the gut, following through to send him pancaking against the ceiling. As he fell back down, Dash caught him with a round-house kick that sent him sailing.

Fleet crashed through not only the wall of his room, but the next one as well. He was only able to stop himself by stabbing his claws into the ground on a lucky bounce. He got back to his feet, placed a thumb over one nostril, and blasted out a clot of blood.

Fleet stared her down through the cavernous holes he had made and held out his hand, gesturing with his fingers for her to attack.

Dash swayed as she walked into the room between them, her eyes locked on his. When she reached the center, Fleet pounced forward and threw a punch down at her from the air, shattering the concrete floor under the shaggy carpeting. Dash dodged his telegraphed blow, shifting her weight back into a counterattack.

She faltered as Fleet twisted into a handstand, spreading his legs out as he twirled around like the blades of a helicopter. A heel caught Dash in the side, sending her reeling into the wall. Before she reacted, Fleet put down his foot, kicked off the ground, and slammed his fist hard into her snout. His follow through sent his entire arm through the wall, accompanied by Dash's upper body.

"What now!" he shouted, overcome by the natural thrill as he yanked his fist free and shook off the debris. Of course, his elation only came out as an indistinguishable growl.

Dash flipped over the foot of the bed in the adjoining room by grabbing the mattress with her claws, sparing her a trip into the brick wall behind her. After coughing up a deluge of blood, she looked around and realized that she had been knocked into apartment 104—her room. Ignoring Fleet, she clawed at her disgusting mattress, filling the air with bits of fluff.

Fleet watched her frantic actions with a snarl. *The hell is she doing? If she's trying to distract me, I guess it's working.*

He wasted no more time and leaped through what was left of the wall separating them. As he landed on the mattress, he felt an excruciating pain as something cut down into his forearm, deep enough to hit bone. He slapped it away only for another one to slice into the side of his neck. Fleet let out a gurgled scream as Dash yanked something out with a wet slosh, sending a swath of blood across the room.

He hopped away and pressed his back to the far wall as he covered the gaping neck wound with his hand. His jaw dropped when he saw what she had attacked him with.

In each of her hands, Dash held a silver hatchet with a flared head and a metallic loop that came out of the handle. Though they looked normal in her hands, the hatchets were three times the size of a typical axe.

Those are Tayumore! How does she have a fucking Tayumore?

Dash saw the panic and confusion in Fleet's eyes as he stared at her weapons. A maniacal, toothy grin spread across her face as she slotted a finger in the loop of each hatchet. She spun them around, building speed until they were whirring like buzz saws. The wind she was creating was even strong enough to knock over the lamp and push around all the garbage that littered the room.

She advanced on him with that same methodical, undulating walk. Fleet backed away in response until he hit the corner of the room, his eyes darting back and forth between the spinning blades.

With nowhere else to go, Fleet went on the attack.

He leaped forward, but before he even got near, Dash had sliced him deep across the chest. He made to grab her hand, but instead found the other hatchet buried deep in his scapula. Mere seconds had passed since his attack, but Dash had wounded him no less than twelve times with her armament.

Fleet backed up again out of pure desperation. Though the cuts had already healed, the front of his body and face were covered in a blanket of solid, dark crimson. He had lost a ton of blood; lose too much and he may start to lose consciousness. It was an effective tactic on her part.

His eyes darted about, but there was nowhere for him to run without being ripped to shreds. He could break down the wall to get some distance, but she would tear him apart as he tried to escape. The only way out was to catch her off guard, but he wasn't going to get away unscathed.

Fleet feinted to the right, but instead of following through, he kicked off the wall and lunged right into Dash's blades. One lodged itself deep into his armpit, the other into his shoulder, but it was enough to stop the spinning. Fleet wrapped Dash in a crushing bear hug, constricting one of her arms down at her side and the other bent up near her head.

He then clamped his jaws down across her face. Attempting to crush her skull was pointless, like trying to crush a diamond with another diamond, but if he could blind her, it may give him the upper hand.

She cried out in pain as blood squirted from her eyes, which spurred him to bite down even harder. Fleet closed his legs to keep Dash from kneeing him in the groin, but pinned as she was, there was no real means for reprisal.

Her lungs deflated with each squeal of anguish, allowing Fleet to tighten his grip even further. If this kept up, he could end it right here by making her pass out.

The pain in his shoulder subsided as Dash yanked the hatchet from it with a spout of blood. He did not relent, knowing full well that she could not swing it down with any force with her arm pinned the way it was.

To his surprise, instead of trying to slash at him, Dash flipped the hatchet back and aimed the handle at his face. Fleet looked wide-eyed at the weapon's ferrule as his confusion hardened into dire concern.

Dash's thumb pressed down with a click, causing a controlled explosion to erupt into Fleet's face. He released his grip as he staggered back, clutching at his bleeding, empty eye sockets.

Dash wasted no time, her hatchets finding purchase with every swing at his defenseless body while she screamed in uncontrollable rage. Fleet bent down into a defensive position, trying to avoid as much damage to his vital areas as possible. It wasn't long before the entire wall behind him became a splattered canvas of gore that would have given Jackson Pollock a run for his money.

Fleet threw out a desperate uppercut, knowing full well that it would miss. He whiffed the hit, then crossed his arms across his face to protect his head. Dash took advantage, planting her hatchets deep into Fleet's ribs, one on each side of his body.

A toothy grin sprouted on his muzzle.

He brought his elbows down hard at his sides, pushing the hatchets deeper into his body as he fought back against the excruciating pain. Bellowing a primal yell, Fleet stepped forward and used all his strength to stab upward into Dash's stomach.

His hand found only air, sending a massive burst of wind that made the curtains dance. She should have been standing right there trying to pry out her weapons, frozen in awe of his suicidal technique.

This was not the case.

The second Dash saw he had dropped his guard, she anticipated his next move. She then stepped out of range to set her feet and take her sweet time charging a devastating haymaker.

Fuck me.

Dash's punch rocketed into Fleet's sternum like a cannonball, cracking his bones—not an easy feat. A massive burst of blood shot from his mouth as he crashed through the brick wall behind him, over the center walkway, and through another brick wall into the adjacent building.

Fleet skidded to a stop against the inside drywall, clutching at his chest. Even though it was agony, he got to his knees and coughed enough to clear his airways, soaking the shag in red.

His eyes had regenerated, but his vision was limited and blurry; all he could see was a blob creeping toward him. Dash's last assault had done immense damage, and if he was going to survive, he needed to get some breathing room.

Out of desperation, he tensed his muscles and leaped straight upward. He crashed through the ceiling not once, but twice, before erupting into the cool night air.

Fleet tripped and fell on his stomach as he landed on the roof, his entire upper body now throbbing from the successive impacts. He propped himself up and looked around, realizing that his damaged vision was even worse out here in the dark.

Was she coming for him? Of course she was. But how was she going to get to him? Coming up through the opening he made or making her own would put her at a disadvantage since he already had the high ground—she was smart enough to know that.

Memories of the fight with Jill flooded his brain, creating a scenario where he saw Dash zipping up the building to finish him. He peeked over the edge of the roof, but no amount of squinting enabled him to make out the ground below.

If he couldn't see, perhaps he could hear—those ears had to be good for something. Fleet became a statue as he moderated his breathing to prevent interference.

After a few seconds of calibration, he could hear...everything! This was amazing! He had always kind of shirked his training in that area, figuring it was more of a party trick than anything—but holy shit, was he wrong! The fidelity was truly astounding. It was almost like having eyes was a hindrance.

He could almost taste the splashing water as it poured from broken pipes. He visualized the exact shape of every brick that fell from the crumbling walls as they clattered to the ground. He found himself crouched next to a snake as it scurried through the grass, frightened away by—

Footsteps! Fleet's ears perked up. *I was right! She's trying to come around the side of the building instead of coming from below. She thinks she can get the jump on me.*

The footsteps came to a halt at the building's base. Fleet lowered his head and waited for any sound that might show she had started to climb. His ears twitched when he heard the scraping as her nails cut into the brick.

There you are!

Fleet yelled in accompaniment to a devastating punch timed perfectly with the sound as it burst over the ledge. His fist connected with a loud clang, sending the assailant flying back down into the dirt like a bullet.

Fleet flipped his hand over to check his bloody knuckles.

That wasn't—

Before he even finished his thought, Dash tackled him from behind, putting him in a headlock as they both tumbled over the side. She then reached back with her free hand to clamp down on his foot. Dash kicked off the siding and used that momentum to send them both spinning end over end until they came crashing down hard into the ground.

Once Fleet felt Dash's weight slide off his back, he braced himself for another assault that never came. Instead, he heard her walking away with no more urgency than someone off to check the mailbox.

When he opened his eyes to look around, the first thing he saw was a set of feet dangling in the air close to his head with the heels facing toward him. He blinked several times, hoping that this was just some sort of visual distortion from his damaged eyes. Then, in abject horror, he reached out to touch a toe, slowly coming to terms that these feet were his own.

He was bent like a misshapen oval from the impact, and his legs now curved above him like a scorpion's stinger. It was the kind of pose you would see from a contortionist at the circus, not from the guy who got kicked out of yoga class for laughing when the old lady next to him blasted one during downward dog.

As his shaking fingers poked at his toes, he noticed something in the distance. Framed between his feet, Fleet saw a sizeable chunk of rusted metal implanted deep in the ground.

That's Lowy's fire pit! She threw it up the wall to distract me while she came up from behind! She's one step ahead every fucking time!

Fleet pushed up on his hands, trying to flip over, but jolted back down when a frightening realization overcame him.

She broke my spine! I can't feel anything below my waist!

That's why she was so nonchalant: she knew exactly what she had done to him.

In what can only be described as a surreal experience, Fleet put his palms under the soles of his feet and pushed upward. They flew back over his head and his legs fell down behind him as his spine made a series of sickening cracks and pops.

I have no idea how long this will take to heal, but I'm a sitting duck like this! I have to get out of here before she gets back!

He crawled forward in a rush, digging his claws into the earth to pull himself along. He didn't make it far before a hatchet sliced into the ground right at the tip of his nose with a deep *shunk*.

Dash walked over to him, taking dark delight in the twitching grimace of fear on Fleet's face. He flinched away as she squatted down next to him, prompting Dash to snap her fingers until Fleet looked up at her hands.

-Tell me where she is-

She knows sign language! Fleet thought after her inaudible demand. *Who the fuck is this woman!*

Fleet propped himself up on an elbow and put out a trembling hand. Dash leaned forward, ready to read his answer. He made a circle with his hand, put it over the tip of his muzzle, and blew a bloody snot rocket into her face.

Dash didn't even blink as the disgusting wad of red mucus slapped right between her eyes and ran down the side of her mouth. Fleet smiled at her and extended his middle finger as the blob plopped down from her chin.

Dash's response was to yank her hatchet from the ground and swing it up in an arc at his face. The bit landed hard enough in Fleet's neck and chest to send him back to a standing vertical position in defiance of gravity. She left the weapon embedded as she spun around and slammed her heel into the butt of the axe head during that brief moment Fleet was upright. He crashed through the brick wall behind him and into a bathroom door, which acted as a makeshift sled that carried him into the center of the apartment.

Fleet's screams sent up a sanguine geyser from his mouth as he clutched at the hatchet lodged inside him. Dash's kick had shattered his ribs, allowing the blade to slice down into his lungs. The wound would heal, but it wouldn't do so properly until the foreign body was removed. If he didn't extract it soon, he might very well drown to death in his own blood.

Fleet sandwiched the hatchet with his hands and pushed upward with everything he had. He only made a bit of leeway before Dash's foot came down on him, forcing the blade deeper into his body.

Fleet's ululation was cut short as Dash grabbed him by the head and lifted him to meet her gaze. She gripped the handle and unsheathed the hatchet from his chest with a wave of blood before she slammed it into the floor. Fleet coughed as air rushed into his lungs, giving Dash the perfect opportunity to spit directly into the back of his throat—a bit of retaliation for earlier.

As he hung there, Fleet perceived a welcome sensation: a gentle friction on his toes as they brushed over the carpet.

All right, I should be able to use my legs again. That's good! But I've lost too much blood, spent too much energy. Not sure how long I can stay conscious. There's got to be some way to break her guard and end this quick!

Dash dug her claws deep into Fleet's scalp to make sure she had his unwavering attention. She brought her free hand up to his face and spelled it out for him letter by letter.

-J-

-I-

-L-

-L-

With a shuddering hand, Fleet brought a fist up to his neck and let it rest there. Dash's steely gaze latched onto it with anticipation as she waited for his response. Once he had her complete focus, he extended a thumb—and dragged it across his throat.

Dash's pupils dilated as she took in Fleet's confession. A vicious snarl spread up her face, creating a stark dichotomy when met with the tears falling from her eyes. She unleashed a baleful scream and cocked her arm back in preparation to land the killing blow.

And there it was: the opening he had been waiting for.

Fleet jammed his hand into her throat deep enough to slot his fingers around her spine.

Dash released her grip on Fleet's head as she fell to her knees, struggling to breathe. Fleet swayed on his wobbly legs as he supported Dash's head in his hand, blood hemorrhaging from her neck.

Fleet raised a fist, hoping to land a blow strong enough to put her out of commission. However, before he could commit, Dash stood back up and shot her hand at his face. He caught her wrist just before she made contact, the razor-sharp nail of her middle finger vibrating millimeters from his eye.

Fleet then felt something hard strike into his skull. What was left of his blood ran cold when he realized what happened: Dash had grabbed her weapon when she took a knee and was now jamming the ferrule of the hatchet deep into his ear canal.

Fleet was all too aware of how much danger he was in from the previous encounter with her Tayumore. Even if the explosion didn't shatter his skull, the force would still be enough to turn his brain into an unpalatable, waxy pudding.

She smiled at him, letting her tears flow down over her teeth. Her reaction was strange, but understandable. Dash was about to achieve the purest form of vengeance there was. Who could blame her for enjoying this blip of happiness before reality came crashing back down? He certainly couldn't.

Fleet closed his eyes.

It was over.

She had won.

Soon, all his pain would be gone. No more guilt. No more suffering.

It felt...nice.

A voice broke through the serenity of his mind. *Your suffering might end, but what about everyone else? This isn't about you! Now fight, you fucking piece of shit coward! Fight!*

Fleet opened his eyes.

He refused to leave this mortal coil just yet. Not when there were people he wanted to protect. Not when there were innocent lives on the line. Not when his own vengeance remained unfulfilled.

Not fucking yet!

His defiance of the grim reaper's call brought about one last desperate grasp at victory.

Fleet bared his teeth and jerked Dash's hand forward, puncturing two of her claws deep into his eye socket with a sickly squirt of ocular fluid. The grimace of surprise on her face proved she had not seen that one coming, which was just enough to keep her from pressing the trigger.

He knew this was the only chance he was going to get—better not waste it.

Fleet threw himself backward, forcing Dash to lose her balance as she tumbled forward on top of him. He yanked his hand from her throat just before hitting the floor, tearing the flesh anew that had healed around it. He then planted the gore-soaked hand on the carpet and pushed his entire body skyward in one last powerful kick.

His foot cracked under Dash's jaw, causing her to bite off the tip of her tongue as she shot straight up and crashed through the ceiling, sending plaster and dust down like a contained blizzard.

Fleet twisted back onto his feet, ready for her next move, but there was no counterattack. Dash was lodged up to her shoulders in the ceiling, clawing at it from below as she tried to escape. Fleet jumped forward and rammed a fist deep into her gut, sending her body swaying back and forth like a sandbag.

Holy shit, she's stuck!

When Dash pierced the ceiling, she broke a pipe and now the serrated tip was stabbing into the neck wound Fleet had inflicted moments ago. Her flesh had healed around the foreign object, locking her in place.

This was his chance to end it.

Fleet flexed, locking his legs and clenching his fists as he focused himself with a crescendoing growl to concentrate the last of his energy. Accompanied by a powerful yell, he then rained lightning-fast blows deep into her defenseless body like a hailstorm.

Blood poured down from the hole in the ceiling, soaking the front of her and splattering the walls and curtains with each shot. Dash tried to block with her arms and legs, but it was ineffective against Fleet's precision machine-gun strikes. His entire body burned from the exertion, but he refused to let up in fear she would once again find some way to turn the tables if given the opportunity.

Fleet's continued barrage broke down her body, shattering her bones to the point it felt like he was pummeling a spongy sack of grain. Before long, her appendages fell limp as they flailed about under his relentless assault.

It was time to finish it.

Fleet hopped back and bellowed a roar that shook the building like a localized earthquake. He then kicked off the floor and slammed his fist into the diamond on her sternum like a concentrated freight train.

Her limp body shot through two walls and another made of brick before she reached the center walkway. She ended her flight by crashing into the defunct soda machine with a resounding bang, cratering the wall behind it. Dash stayed lodged in the machine, eyes rolled back into her head as blood seeped from every orifice.

The ceiling fell on top of him after that final blow, but Fleet didn't even blink; not once did he take his last good eye away from her. He focused, trying to hear her breath, but all he got was the hiss of soda cans as their sugary contents sprayed out as a gentle mist.

Fleet stepped forward but was slowed by a sudden wave of lightheadedness as the world bent and shifted around him. He made it to the adjacent room before the last of his strength evaporated.

He had spent everything in that fight. Never in his life had he faced an opponent like her, and he knew damn well that luck was the only reason he had made it out alive.

But a victory is a victory, regardless of how it was achieved.

Time to make it official.

He stood upright on crimson legs, held out a trembling hand, and pointed two fingers at Dash. He let out a labored howl of proclamation, the meaning of which was relegated to his mind.

Fiat Justitia.

Fleet then fell forward into a pile of debris where darkness overtook him.

Chapter Twenty-Eight

PROMISE

A FAMILIAR VOICE STARTLED Fleet from his involuntary slumber. "You starting to wake up?"

"Scriptor?" Fleet said, his head still swimming.

"Yeah, it's me. Glad to see you're not dead."

Fleet blinked his working eye as he tried to get his bearings. From the looks of it, he was in one of the beds at the motel. The room was in pristine condition; somehow it had escaped the ravages of the intense battle.

There was a needle in his arm that connected to an IV hung from a nail on the wall. Fleet tried to sit up, but a wave of nausea brought him back down.

"Whoa, take it easy." Curtis put a hand on his shoulder. "You still need to rest."

Fleet noticed the morning light illuminating the curtains. "How long have I been out?"

"Close to six hours."

Fleet touched his injured eye and winced from the pain.

"You look like shit," Curtis said, pulling no punches.

Fleet chuckled. "You should see the other guy."

"Oh. Oh, I did. She was knocking on death's door when we found her. You destroyed her skeletal system to where it was impossible for her to revert. I gave her to Java so he can take her for treatment. If we're lucky, she'll live long enough for us to get some answers out of her."

When reminded of Dash, Fleet asked, "What about the diamond on her chest? Jill had the exact same thing. That has to be their crest. Can we trace it back to anyone?"

"In theory." Curtis leaned back on the nightstand he was using as a seat and rubbed his chin. "But I've never seen that one before. I'll have to do a little research to see what I can find."

His own ignorance was no surprise, but Fleet found it odd that Curtis couldn't place it. All known crests were meticulously cataloged, their origins and the accomplishments of their families archived along with them. Still, it was unfair to hope Curtis would have them all memorized. It would be like asking someone to remember all the names in a phonebook.

Fleet left that concern to ebb when something more pressing forced its way into his brain. "Scriptor, why did she have a Tayumore?" he asked, rubbing his chest where Dash had struck him with her hatchet.

Curtis shrugged and shook his head. "No idea."

Memories of the blade slicing through his flesh played in Fleet's mind. "The craftman-ship was impeccable. It's one of ours, and not some shitty back-alley weld. It even has a trick in it where an explosion comes out of the handle."

"Yeah, you won't find those at any ol' flea market," Curtis agreed, tapping his forehead. "But I bet the knife guy would bust a nut if he got hold of one."

Fleet did not laugh at his joke, instead focusing on the events preceding their fight. "Dash figured out what I was the second she saw my weapon's case. She isn't just some random apparition. She has ties back to us."

"She found your weapon? Why didn't you hide it better? If you did, maybe you could have avoided all...this," Curtis chided as he swept his hands over Fleet.

Fleet balked at the accusation. "Hey, I did a great job hiding it! It's just that Lowy—" Fleet's eye shot wide as he shouted, "Lowy! I lost track of her when we started fighting! Is she all right?"

"She's fine," Curtis assured him. "But she locked herself in your crapper and won't come out."

Fleet sighed with relief, but then groaned afterward. "Damn, I guess this is a 'breach.' She saw Dash and me turn."

"We'll deal with that later. First, I think you should go down and try to coax her from the bathroom. I haven't had any luck, but hopefully she'll listen to you."

Fleet coughed, still trying to shake the exhaustion. "I'll get right on it. Just need to catch my breath for a sec."

Curtis pointed to a large mixing bowl sitting on the nightstand next to him. "Here, eat this. You need some calories to get your energy back."

Fleet tipped the bowl in his direction and caught a view of the unholy goulash within. "What the hell is this?"

"It's all the stuff I scavenged from the kitchen: shrimp, peanut butter, regular butter, potato chips, bacon grease, old Chinese food, super old Mexican food, cat food, guacamole, and about five off-brand snack cakes called 'Twonkers.'"

Fleet grimaced. "Did you have to mix them all together?"

"Nope."

Fleet gave the bowl one last apprehensive glare before swiveling off the bed. "Sorry, man. Right now, Lowy is my primary concern. I have to make sure she's okay."

"I understand," Curtis conceded as he picked up the bowl and kneaded the contents with his hand. "Plus, it will give this some time to mush up a bit more."

Fleet gagged before heading outside. Despite his torpor, he made his way down to his room to find Sea standing guard at the door. As he saw Fleet approach, Sea nodded and cordially stepped aside. Fleet waved to him but ignored the invite, choosing instead to walk through the large hole in the building's side.

After he stepped through, Fleet whistled as he surveyed the damage. In the heat of things, it had never crossed his mind just how destructive his battle had been.

Dash's room was splattered in blood to the point it looked almost comical. Even now, bits of debris still fell from the ceiling and slapped into the puddles of water created by leaking pipes. Behind him, he saw straight through into the other building. It was a miracle that both structures were still standing.

How am I going to break this to her? She loved this place so much, and I completely destroyed it.

His thoughts were interrupted by a terrible realization. He hobbled through the holes in Dash's wall to his own room, tripping several times. He made a beeline to the nightstand and flipped it onto its side to see under it. The panic built as he ran to the dresser and swept his hand over the surface.

"Looking for this?" Curtis said as he came in through the proper entrance. He tossed something at Fleet, which he caught out of the air.

Fleet flipped his hand over and sighed in relief when he saw the little red car resting in his palm. He clutched it in his fist and brought it to his forehead. "Holy shit, thank you."

"No problem," Curtis said, then pointed to the bathroom. "But let's not forget why you're down here."

Fleet surveyed the room one last time before giving Curtis a small nod of understanding. Holding the car close to his chest, Fleet limped over to the door and gave it a gentle knock.

"Lowy, you in there?" There was no response, so he knocked again. "It's me, Fleet. Can you come out so we can talk?"

Inside the bathroom, Lowy shivered as she huddled in the metal bathtub with the shower curtains enclosed around her like a dingy force field. "Go away!"

Even though her voice had volume, it was impossible to hide the trepidation that permeated her words.

Fleet put his forearm on the door and rested his head on it. "You need to come out, Lowy."

"No, I don't!"

"I want it to be crystal clear when I say that this is not a threat: you don't have a choice in the matter. You've seen something you weren't supposed to see. We need to sit down and discuss this so you can better process what's happened, and what will need to be done from here."

"You're not coming in!" Lowy shouted back in defiance.

"Lowy, I destroyed half of your motel like it was a gingerbread house. What makes you think some shitty slice of plywood will keep me out if I wanted in there?"

Fleet leaned against the wall as he waited for her response.

In a low, quivering voice, she responded, "Are you going to kill me?"

Fleet placed his hand on the door as he pleaded with her. "No! Lowy, I swear to God that I won't hurt you. No one is going to hurt you. Believe me, I am doing this for your own good. I just need you to trust me on this."

"Trust you?" She scoffed at the audacity. "Why the hell should I trust you?"

"Because...because it's me..." Fleet said, his voice trailing off. Even he couldn't think of a good reason for her to believe him.

"But who *are* you?" Lowy asked, her voice cracking. "To me, you're just some guy that showed up here out of nowhere, lied to my face, seduced me, and then upended my entire life!"

Curtis wrinkled his nose and mouthed the word 'seduced.' Fleet's only response was a dramatic shrug before leaning back against the door.

"So if you want my trust," Lowy continued, "the best thing for you to do is to sit your ass outside that door and tell me what the fuck is going on!"

"I understand how you feel. I do," Fleet empathized. "And I promise that I'll tell you everything. But I haven't lied to you. I've only kept certain things from you for your own protection."

Lowy choked on her own forced laughter. "Is that right? You've never lied to me? Okay, then give me the truth. Is Fredrick Ferdinand Fleet really your name?"

Fleet rubbed his throat as he answered. "No, it's not. It's a code name."

"Is Curtis your actual brother?"

"No. He's my handler. But I *think* of him as my brother."

Curtis made a soft 'aww' as he patted his fist twice over his heart and pointed at Fleet.

Lowy jumped to the next question. "Do you have sweaty feet?"

"Where the hell did that even come from?" Fleet shouted in embarrassment, causing Curtis to double over in a fit of laughter.

Undeterred, Lowy continued on. "Are you traveling the country on a journey of self-discovery?"

"Lowy, you heard what you just said, right?" Fleet said, unable to hide the condescension in his voice. "To be fair, I'm a little surprised you even believed that in the first place."

"You're right!" Lowy agreed, her tone heavy with sarcasm. "This is obviously all my fault for thinking you were a decent person. This is all just what a stupid, gullible idiot like me deserves."

That one hit him pretty hard. "Lowy, that's not what I meant."

"Well, that's how it sure feels! This is all some big joke, and I'm the punchline! Laugh it up, you guys!"

"You know, I'm kind of impressed," Fleet admitted with a chortle. "You're focusing on the part where I lied to you and not so much on the fact that I'm a monster."

"Because I can't even process that right now!" Lowy yelled at him, pulling back the shower curtain. "Lies are something I can wrap my head around. Government conspiracies—or whatever the hell you guys are—not a huge stretch, either. But monsters? I feel like I'm going crazy! Like I'm losing my mind, and I'm so...I'm so fucking scared."

Muffled sobs echoed off the bathroom tile, making the sounds of her sadness sting him even worse. Fleet put his back to the door and slid down into a seated position, wincing from bursts of pain every couple of inches.

"I'm sorry. It was never supposed to go like this." He hoped she heard his apology through her sobs. "What can I do to make this right?"

Lowy had no response for this, and he didn't blame her. He had destroyed everything she had ever known in an instant. He would never be able to make up for what he had done. But if he could get her to calm down, help her understand...

Fleet felt a sensation in his hand as he subconsciously squeezed his tiny car. He looked down at it, rubbing his thumb across the toy car the way he always did. He then placed it under the door and flicked it backward into the bathroom.

The tiny car serpentined, rattling for a few feet before coming to an abrupt halt. Cautiously, Lowy peeked out of the tub to see what had intruded on her domain.

"You're wrong," Fleet said, taking the sudden silence as evidence that he had gotten her attention. "Not everything I told you was a lie. Remember when I said I was your friend? That was the truth. And it's why this is hurting me so much."

Hearing no reply, he continued.

"Remember when you asked me about the car? I said it was special to me. That wasn't a lie, either. That little red car is the most precious thing I own. It's all I've got left of..."

Fleet wiped a tear from the corner of his eye.

"It's important to me, but so are you. That's why I want you to look after it for me. I'm trusting you with it because that is my promise that no matter what happens, I'm going to protect you, and I don't want it back until you believe I've kept my word and earned your trust."

Curtis stared down at a spot on the carpet and bit his lip. A small sniffle echoed from outside the front door where Sea stood guard. Everything was silent for a time except for the sounds of the building crumbling around them.

Fleet suddenly fell backward, the weight of his upper body pulling him into the bathroom. He hit the back of his head on the tile with a mild thud and looked up to find Lowy staring down at him, her hand still on the doorknob.

"I'm ready to talk now," Lowy said with forced confidence.

Despite the pain, Fleet gave her the biggest smile. "Sure thing."

Lowy bent over him when she noticed his injuries. "You look like shit."

Fleet chuckled and held up a hand, which Lowy accepted without hesitation. With a gentle tug, she helped him to his feet.

"Can we do this around the fire pit?" she asked. "It always helps me relax."

Fleet winced at her request. "Yeah, about that..."

CHAPTER TWENTY-NINE

TRYST

"You did this?" Lowy exclaimed, taken aback by the mound of twisted metal that had once been her fire pit.

"Yep. Punched the shit out of it," Fleet confirmed. "On accident, though."

"You did this with only your fist?"

"Yes, keeping in line with the definition of 'punch,' it did involve my fist," Fleet affirmed. He walked over and placed a foot on the metallic hunk. "You know, I've always wondered about that."

Curtis and Lowy gave Fleet their attention, encouraging him to continue.

"If my hands were on my feet, would it be called kicking or punching if I hit something with them?"

Lowy gave Fleet a blank stare, but Curtis took it seriously, mulling it over before he said, "I suppose it depends if the foot is a necessity."

"Right. So, can a footless man kick a ball?" Fleet asked.

"He could with a prosthetic foot."

"Now we're back at square one since he has a foot again, unless instead of prosthetic feet, they were prosthetic hands. What then?"

"This hypothetical guy has four hands but no feet."

"Correct. His punching power is effectively doubled at the loss of his ability to kick."

"How the hell would he even be able to kick anything?"

"Exactly."

"No, like how can he even hit anything with the prosthetic hands? He couldn't even stand up."

"It's called a handstand for a reason."

Before Curtis countered, Lowy clenched her fists and let out an exasperated scream. "Do you have any idea how hard it was for me to step out of that fucking bathroom? I am scared for my life, but I found the courage to hear you out because you promised you would explain everything to me. Now, the only thing on your mind is whether a man can kick a ball with his stumps!"

"Well, that's the question," Fleet responded after a moment of timid reflection as he wiggled two fingers upside down. "I mean, sure he could hit the ball if you dangled him or something—but kick? Come on."

"It's too open-ended." Curtis crossed his arms. "You can get kicked out of a place, right? There is no physical act involving the feet. We need a more precise definition of—"

Lowy let out another deafening scream, forcing both Fleet and Curtis to take a defensive step back.

Fleet put up his hands to both show remorse and calm her nerves. "I'm sorry! I'm sorry! You're right. I mean, this has never happened to me before, and I have no idea how to proceed from here. I'm just talking out my ass in hopes my partner here will step in to take point on this one."

"Like hell I am!" Curtis deflected his plea for help. "I was just going along because I knew what you were trying to do. This is your case. If there's something you can't answer, I'll step up. Otherwise, this is all you."

Fleet took a deep breath to prepare himself. "Where should we start?"

"How about with what you guys are?" Lowy interjected.

"Good a place as any." Fleet waved a finger between Curtis and himself. "We are 'Tryst.'"

Lowy stared at him, expecting further explanation, but when none came, she decided it was best for her to lead the conversation from here on. "Okay, so you are Tryst. Is that code for werewolf or something? Because what I saw before I ducked into the bathroom sure looked like werewolves."

"Kinda, but not really." Fleet propped an elbow in his hand and scratched at his lip as he tried to explain. "There are other types of Tryst based on different creatures, and unless you see their animal form, you will never know what they are. Calling every Tryst you meet a werewolf is very insensitive, or so I'm told."

Fleet rolled his fingers in the air as he thought up an example.

"Think of it in terms of your everyday average person. We have all types of people on earth, but in the end, everyone is still a human being. It's the same way for us: wolves, foxes, bears—all Tryst. But our organization deals primarily with wolves, since that is what we are."

"What if something happens with Tryst that is not related to werewolves? Then who handles it?"

"We collaborate sometimes, but for the most part, everyone sticks to their own kind," Fleet elaborated. "The majority of Tryst in North America and Europe are lupines, so we don't cross paths a lot with other types."

"That means it's kind of a geographic thing," Lowy speculated. "Everyone from America is a wolf, and if I went to China, everyone there would be a panda. Actually, that sounds kind of racist, and if it is, I'm really sorry!"

"That's not... I mean, maybe?" Fleet fumbled through his words. "Look, it doesn't work like that. Each 'breed' of Tryst is its own strain, like a virus. If I infected—sorry—*gifted* you with the virus, then you would be a wolf. If a bear gifted you, you would be a bear. Nationality and race have nothing to do with it. Some types may be more concentrated in a certain area because that is where the strain originated or expanded, but that's it."

"You say it's like a virus. Is that how you two turned into werewolves? One of them bit you or something?"

Curtis decided it was his time to speak up. "It can happen that way, but it isn't necessarily the case. I married into it and got a blood transfusion in a formal ceremony. But my two subordinates were born as Tryst. They've never known life as anything else."

Lowy found Curtis' sudden interjection rather strange, especially when he glanced over at Fleet beforehand, but she decided not to push it.

"This is crazy," she said, picking at her nails. There were a thousand questions in her mind, and finding just one to focus on was proving difficult. "I can't believe you've been able to keep this all a secret. Does the government not know anything about you guys? It sounds like you've been around for a while, and I would think they'd have caught on at some point."

"Well, you're not wrong," Curtis said, with a tilt of his head. "But think about it: how long have stories of werewolves and other cryptids been around? All those old wives' tales have a bit of truth to them, even if they tend to stretch that truth a lot. It's just that we've gotten a lot better at hiding ourselves over the years."

His words piqued Lowy's curiosity. "Does that mean you *are* weak to silver bullets, or is that made up?"

"A complete fabrication. There's an old story—or I guess a joke—about that, but we'll save it for a more opportune time."

"What about normal bullets?"

"Not completely worthless, but close to it. They have about the same effect as you standing ten feet away and throwing pushpins at someone. You might get lucky and hit them in the eye or something, but it only serves to piss 'em off."

Lowy found it hard to believe Curtis when she looked at Fleet. He was in such terrible shape, it looked like a stiff breeze might take him out, much less a bullet.

At Lowy's silence, Curtis addressed her other concern. "As far as the government goes: of course they're aware we exist. In fact, they're partially the reason we're here. We take the lead on Tryst related incidents and tell them to back off when appropriate. But in certain cases, they ask for us when something shows up and they have suspicions that Tryst may be involved."

Lowy stopped picking at her thumb to voice a sudden epiphany. "The hand!"

"Very good!" Curtis gave her a congratulatory gesture before continuing. "We have access to vast stores of data and reports. We study everything to discern patterns that may indicate a rogue entity is on the loose. This typically correlates with a rash of disappearances or a string of brutal murders. At which point, we get called in to investigate to determine if there is an actual threat or if it's just a morbid coincidence."

"There's only the two of you?" Lowy asked. "No offence, but that doesn't seem like enough."

"We're not the only ones, if that's what you mean. It's just that this mission was deemed low priority at the start, so there was no need to waste the manpower on it. But it also helps that we have one of the best right here," Curtis boasted, nodding toward Fleet with a smile. "I mean shit, this guy took out two Tryst pretty much on his own."

"Two Tryst?" Lowy's eyes went wide as her words rushed out in a panic. "Dash! That's right, she's one! But if there's another, then... Jill? Is it her? It has to be, right? What happened to them?"

Curtis was struck by her quick logic, though now his voice took on a more serious tone. "Dash is in custody as we investigate her involvement in the murder. Jill..." He trailed off for a second. "...took her own life when we attempted to question her."

"Oh my God..." Lowy whimpered as she fell to her knees in shock.

Fleet looked to the ground as Curtis continued. "You have to understand that none of this is your fault, Lowy. You couldn't have known."

Seeing her continued distress, Fleet spoke up. "He's right. We can't even tell if someone is Tryst by looking at them. The only way to know—short of visual confirmation in beast mode—is to dissect their brain like a rabid animal. Good luck getting someone to volunteer for that, right?"

Fleet gave a chuckle that Lowy did not return. She was running her hands through her hair and muttering to herself.

He bent over and placed a hand on her shoulder. "Lowy, I need you to hang in there, all right?"

Lowy shook her head and looked up at him. "This is all so—" She let out a small yelp and fell backward at what she saw: a line of reddish puss that had oozed from Fleet's injured eye.

"What?" He rubbed a thumb across his cheek, smearing the bile over his nose. "Is there something on my face?"

"That's gross, man," Curtis admonished.

Fleet wiped the tainted hand on his pants. "What the hell do you want me to do about it?"

Curtis glanced at Lowy and then suggested, "How about you shift?"

"Right now?" Fleet put a hand to his head. "Not sure if I can handle it after all that. And look at her. Do you really think she's ready?"

"I promise I am!" Lowy stated with a hint of bravado as she got to her feet. "I'm tired of being in the dark about all this!" She then put up a hand to block Fleet's leaky eye from view.

"Of course, I have no say in the matter. Like I haven't suffered enough today," Fleet complained to himself.

"Quit your bitching and get it over with," Curtis chided as he dialed a number on his phone.

Fleet sighed as he double-checked the elasticity of his pants. He then took off the pullover he had been given and threw it onto Curtis' head as he chatted on the phone.

He exhaled and gave Lowy a nod. "Try not to freak out."

She returned the nod, even though she knew he was asking the impossible.

Lowy covered her open mouth as she watched Fleet begin to convulse. As his body grew and reformed, she covered her ears to shield herself from the stomach-churning sounds emanating from underneath his skin. Lowy watched until his teeth pierced through the front of his face, at which point she balled up on the ground and shut her eyes in fright.

The sounds stopped.

Lowy cautiously opened her eyes to peer up at the monster towering over her. It was just standing there, its mouth curled into a devilish grin so that all its razor-sharp teeth were on full display.

The monster's fur was almost completely white except for a few spots of pure black that stood out in contrast. The markings overlapped both its eyes, making it seem like it was wearing professionally applied eyeliner. Around the neck was a thick line that encircled the entire throat like a permanent collar or choker. The ends of the mouth were lined as well, making the maw seem larger than it was. The tips of its ears looked as though someone had dipped them in ink, which had then bled downward from the apex before stopping at the base of its skull. Save for those markings, the entirety of the monster's front torso remained a pristine, blank canvas.

Realizing she was not getting the full picture, the monster held out its arms and made a show of turning around. On the back, there were incongruent swathes of black on each shoulder blade that conjoined above its lumbar to form a sort of 'Y' shape. The bottom point of the letter continued down to surround the base of its snow-white tail.

The beast peeked over its shoulder at Lowy before turning back around. It extended an arm toward her. Lowy recoiled out of instinct, but the hand stopped short, hovering in front of her. The beast wiggled its fingers, that shit-eating grin still on its face.

Lowy felt her fear evaporate. Though she did not recognize this imposing monster, she knew it was Fleet looking down at her.

She could see it in his eyes.

With a hint of caution, she gripped his hand and held on as he gently lifted her to her feet. When upright, instead of letting go, Lowy ran her fingers across the inside of Fleet's palm. She splayed out her hand in the middle of his and marveled at the sheer difference in size. Realizing how long she had lingered on the touch, she yanked back her hand in embarrassment.

Fleet gave her another toothy grin and began moving his hands about in strange patterns.

Curtis gave a small snort of laughter and translated for Lowy's sake. "He said, 'You know what they say about guys with big hands?'"

"Well, that's definitely you in there." Lowy smiled. "Was that sign language just now?"

"Sure was," Curtis confirmed. "In that form, most of us don't have the ability to talk, so it's mandatory that everyone learns sign language so we can still communicate."

"I see." Lowy crossed her arms. "I guess you didn't learn it because of your deaf grandmother."

Fleet looked away and lowered his ears.

"Wow, that's not a bad excuse to be honest," Curtis said, giving Fleet a nod. "But what would be even better is if you had never let it slip to begin with. Then you wouldn't have had to make up an excuse at all."

Fleet recoiled as he tried his best to seem remorseful, but Curtis wouldn't have it. "Shut up. I know damn well you were show-boating."

Lowy gasped and pointed to something behind Curtis. "Who's that?"

Curtis turned to find that Sea had joined them. He had Dash's hefty hatchet slung over his shoulder while also carrying the green bowl filled with Curtis' concoction in the other arm. The way Sea carried himself showed how much of a struggle it was to manage both items.

Curtis gave an inadequate introduction. "Oh, that's Sea. He's cool."

With a grunt, Sea dropped the hatchet onto the ground, almost slicing his leg open in the process. He then placed the bowl next to it and twisted his body to stretch out his back.

"Appreciate it," Curtis said before pointing back at the motel. "But there were two hatchets."

Sea gave a loud groan and headed back to the building.

"What is that?" Lowy asked, her interest in the newcomer overtaken by the enormous weapon.

"That is a hatchet, but to be more formal, that is called a 'Tayumore,'" Curtis explained, once again acting as if it were some mundane fact. "Go on, try to pick it up."

Curtis motioned her over toward it. Lowy was reluctant at first, but curiosity got the better of her and she walked up to the weapon. With a nod of affirmation from Fleet, Lowy wrapped both hands around the handle. Despite using all her strength, she was only able to turn it on its edge.

Lowy conceded defeat and let the weapon slap back down. "This is insane. Why would you even make something like this?"

"Pretty heavy, right? Don't feel bad. None of us can do anything with it." Curtis held up a finger. "In human form, that is. But after we shift..."

As Lowy backed away from the weapon, Curtis motioned over to Fleet. In response, Fleet cracked his knuckles, walked over to the hatchet, and picked it up as if it were no heavier than a pinwheel.

Fleet flipped it over twice, inspecting the weapon that had nearly taken his life. He then threw it behind his back, caught it in his opposite hand, and spun it on his finger in an impressive feat of showmanship that he'd copied from Dash—it was harder than it looked.

"I couldn't even..." Lowy's words faded into amazement.

"That's what a Tayumore is," Curtis said, answering her unasked question. "It's a custom weapon designed only for use by Tryst. Each one is uniquely forged to play to its user's strengths. They're invaluable in our line of work, but a pain in the ass to transport—not to mention hide."

"A Tayumore," Lowy whispered to herself. "Is that what was inside that black case I found?"

"Sure was," Curtis confirmed. "Though you should have never found it in the first place. This is also ignoring the fact that he never even used the damn thing in either fight."

Fleet ignored him as he continued spinning the hatchet.

"But Dash knew! She knew exactly what was in there the second she saw it!" Lowy shouted. "That's why she flipped and attacked Fleet!"

"You're right," Curtis once again agreed. "Pretty much every Tryst knows about us. Some even think of us as the boogeyman."

"Boogeyman?"

"Let's just say that the thought of us visiting them in the night is more than enough to keep most Tryst in line."

Lowy swallowed hard at the implication. "That's what you do? Keep other Tryst in line?"

Curtis tilted his head and clicked his tongue. "That's more of a byproduct of what we do. Let me explain a little more in depth."

He pointed a thumb at himself.

"To start, you can call me a 'Wayman.' I provide support and guidance, but the basic function of my job is to follow this guy around and clean up whatever mess he makes." Curtis indicated Fleet with a wag of his finger.

Lowy gasped. "Then the fire at the school! That was you?"

Curtis was once again impressed by her sudden deduction. "Damn. Pretty quick on the uptake, aren't ya? Yeah, that was us. When it gets real messy like that, fire is the best way to destroy the evidence."

Lowy made a soft 'oh' of comprehension; she didn't need to ask why they burned down the building. The fire lined up a little too well with Jill's disappearance, and trying to rationalize the 'messy' part made her ill.

Lowy mouthed all the new words she had learned before eyeing the large hatchet. "The axe. I mean, the Tayumore. Is that one yours, Curtis?"

"Hell no, it's not mine!" Curtis laughed back. "Tayumore are only given to Servunday. I stay as far away from violence as I can. While I have some training since it's mandatory to do any type of fieldwork, I am not big on fighting—or pain." Curtis swept a hand over his crotch as he finished his explanation.

"Servunday?" Lowy asked as she turned to give Fleet another solid once-over. "Is that you?"

Fleet gave her a grin as he dangled the hatchet by its loop on his pinky. He then flicked the head, causing the weapon to emit a soft metallic hum.

"Yep, and I hate to say it, but that also means he's my boss," Curtis responded for Fleet. "Beyond that, all you need to understand is that if you hear a Servunday come calling for you, shitting your pants may be the appropriate response."

Lowy looked apprehensive in response to Curtis' explanation. "Does that mean you guys are killers?"

Curtis sliced his hands through the air. "Not even close. Nine times out of ten, we do absolutely nothing and walk away because it doesn't involve us. The other times, the guilty party usually gives up without a fight."

Curtis' pitch rose as he spoke, taking obvious pride in the subject.

"Being called 'killers' is just the reputation we've gotten because no one ever hears about the good stuff we do. Our primary job is to keep people safe. Always. If a Tryst has broken the law, we give them every chance to turn themselves in. It's only when they refuse that we have to get violent, or more specifically, *he* has to get violent."

Fleet gave Curtis a small bow of recognition. As he straightened himself back up, Fleet flicked the hatchet upward, caught it, and sent it buzzing end over end into the woods. It collided with a tree, sending out an explosion of splinters and sap as the Tayumore sliced through it like drywall. His pitch razed two full-grown conifers before lodging deep into a third.

As the trees cracked and fell, Fleet put his hands on his hips with a huff, clearly disappointed with the 'meager' amount of damage he had done. Curtis golf-clapped from behind, though he muttered 'show-off' under his breath.

Lowy's mouth fell agape long enough for a bug to fly in, bounce about her teeth, and vacate before she even noticed. She had seen the destruction done to her motel, but witnessing that power with her own eyes was surreal.

Curtis stepped forward and pointed at the fallen trees. "That's why they call us. You could send an entire SWAT team after a Tryst and they'd all be whipped into a creamy paste in less than a minute. Instead, we put ourselves in the line of danger to save people's lives, and they have the audacity to call us killers behind our backs. I take great pride in what we do, and it really—"

Curtis stopped when he noticed Fleet was holding out his hand flat and lowering it in a gesture that meant he needed to tone it down.

"I'm sorry, Curtis," Lowy apologized, thinking his anger was directed at her. "I didn't really mean it when I called you that."

"No worries. But based on all you've seen, I can't blame you if you did feel that way." Curtis let out a labored sigh. "Sometimes it just kind of sucks, you know?"

Feeling a change of subject was in order, Lowy pointed out the other unexplained object Sea had brought. "So, umm, what's that supposed to be? It looks a bit...well..." Lowy leaned over for a better view into the bowl, afraid to get any closer than necessary.

"Oh, that's his breakfast: 'Ad-Hoc Ambrosia,' I call it. It's all the shit you can find mixed together to get as many calories as possible." Curtis sent Fleet a devilish smirk. "Being in that form burns an insane amount of energy, and considering that ass-whoopin' he received, he went through his reserves pretty damn quick. The man was in such dire straits that he passed out from the strain, so his body naturally reverted itself back to conserve his strength and keep him alive. He's running on fumes right now, but he's at least gotten enough energy back to shift and finish healing. See his eye?"

Her initial shock was so great that Lowy didn't even notice it had been healed. To drive the point home, Fleet spread his eyelids with two fingers and rolled his newly formed eyeball around in its socket.

"When he turns back this time, the eye will stay that way, good as new," Curtis finished.

Fleet nodded emphatically in agreement and tried to sign something, annoyed that despite being the primary subject, he was being left out of the conversation.

Curtis ignored him and continued while Fleet sulked. "Even when we aren't turned, we still have an increased healing factor. His eye would have healed in a few days, or I guess a week, since it's a more complicated organ. But in this form, it heals in seconds. On average, we need about two to three thousand extra calories a day to keep up with it. If you happen to turn for an extended amount, I'd say at least triple that—the more the better. Speaking of calories..."

Curtis ran off and returned holding two cans of soda he retrieved from the broken machine.

"Forgot the broth."

He cracked them both open and poured each into the green bowl, causing the contents to hiss and foam like the concoction of some mad scientist. He picked up his creation and sloshed it around, making sure everything was nice and mixed.

"Eat up, big guy!"

Fleet grabbed his head, stretching his face back as he made a soft whine of trepidation.

As Curtis walked by, Lowy got a good view of the bowl's contents and gagged. "Is that the shrimp from my freezer? That's been in there for as long as I can remember. Do you really expect him to eat that?"

"You bet I do." Curtis lifted the bowl up to him. "If he doesn't, he's going to pass out. Worst case: he might die. There's a shit-ton of calories in this slurry, and he needs all of it if he wants to live." Curtis spat out his last words through gritted teeth, showing Fleet he meant business.

Lowy knew Curtis was right. It was as if she could literally see the life draining away from Fleet the longer their conversation went on.

Fleet crossed his arms and frowned at Curtis' unpalatable mixture, akin to a child refusing to eat his vegetables.

"Come on, it's not that bad," Lowy added, spurred on by Curtis' warning. "I bet if you eat it fast, you won't even taste it."

At her words, Fleet swirled a pinky around in the "ambrosia" and pulled out a shrimp on his nail, presenting it to her. Despite the canid face, his countenance was one that taunted 'you first.'

Lowy plucked the shrimp, causing a vestigial lump of cream to fall from Fleet's outstretched finger as she brought it to her mouth and placed it between her lips. She sucked it in and made a contemptuous 'mmmm' sound while she rubbed her belly. This lasted two seconds before she wretched and ejected the shrimp from her mouth—along with some other stomach contents.

"Yeah, not sure why you did that," Curtis said. "This has been sitting out for a good while, so I'm sure it's gone bad—err, badder. Probably should have stopped you, but I kinda wanted to see if you'd go through with it."

Lowy gave a wan smile and spat on the ground.

Curtis frowned at the expelled shrimp, now covered in grass and saliva. "No reason to waste this." He picked it up and plopped it back into the bowl.

Lowy and Fleet both gagged again.

"If he eats that, won't he get sick like I did?" Lowy asked.

Curtis walked forward and forced the bowl into Fleet's hands. "Nah, he'll be fine. In that form, it will only take a few minutes to digest everything—and I mean *everything*. Nothing will go to waste. He won't even have to shit later. All he's got to do is suppress his gag reflex and he's golden."

Fleet looked woozy as he stared down into the bowl, the smell of the concoction overpowering his delicate nose. He folded back his ears and feigned the sound of crying.

"Come on, you can do it!" Lowy encouraged. "Just don't think about it!"

After taking a deep breath, he cupped the bowl to his mouth and downed the mixture. Lowy watched in disgust; it was as if she could almost feel the sensation of those soggy chunks massaging his esophagus as they clawed their way down to his gullet.

Fleet dropped the bowl and stood with his eyes closed as he waited for the ambrosia to finish its journey. Curtis took a few steps back, and Lowy followed suit when she realized the possible danger. The two of them watched him in anticipation until Fleet's head bobbed forward in brief intervals, accompanied by a disturbing *gurk* sound.

"No! Don't you fucking do it! You keep that shit down or you'll be eating it off the ground!" Curtis threatened.

Fleet clamped both hands around his muzzle as a milky-looking runoff seeped from the corner of his mouth. Several tense seconds passed before Fleet released his grip and gave everyone a tepid thumbs-up to a collective sigh of relief.

"You'll be feeling better in no time, my man," Curtis congratulated. "Now, go grab that axe you hurled into the woods before you turn back."

Fleet nodded and made for the trees as he clutched at his stomach.

As he trudged off, Lowy took the opportunity to ask Curtis a crucial question that had been bothering her—one she didn't want Fleet to hear.

She held up the little toy for him to see. "Curtis, what he said earlier about this car—"

He put up a hand to cut her off. "I've got nothing to tell you."

Lowy nodded and turned away as if she had just done something wrong. "I'm sorry, I shouldn't have asked."

Curtis sighed, feeling the need to explain himself. "Lowy, the way I came into this world was of my own volition. Hangman—I mean Fleet—never had a choice in the matter. Maybe one day he'll fill you in, but as his friend, that's all I'm willing to say."

Lowy nodded again, this time with a mingling of understanding and concern. His words had only instilled more questions in her mind, but the implications of the answers she crafted for them left her with a deep sadness.

Catching her in thought, Fleet dropped the retrieved hatchet at their feet.

Perhaps out of reflex, Lowy cooed, "Good boy!" She then put a hand over her mouth and gasped. "Is that offensive to you guys?"

Curtis quelled his laughter long enough to give her an incredulous smile. "You kidding? Who doesn't want to be a good boy?"

Fleet gave her a broad grin as he bounced on the balls of his feet and wagged his tail in delight. Lowy laughed at the playful display he put on for her benefit, happy to have her friend back.

Chapter Thirty

PILLOW TALK

Lowy had watched with rapt attention as Fleet shifted back into his human form. She found his transition from a werewolf to a normal person just as enthralling as the other way around. The wounds on his body had now healed, but the events of the past day left him drained and lethargic.

After Sea rejoined the group, all four of them stood in the pathway between the two buildings and surveyed the damage. Lowy looked around dumbfounded as her mind tried to decipher what manner of carnage must have taken place to cause this. Fleet only yawned as he cracked open a soda he had nicked from the rubble.

"I'm sorry to tell you this," Curtis began, apprehension on his face, "but I don't think we can save your motel. There's just no good way to spin it. Even if I said it was a foundation issue, I can't explain away all this structural damage. And that's not even accounting for the fuck-ton of blood and hair all over the place."

"That's all right," Lowy replied in a distant voice as she continued to observe.

Fleet and Curtis exchanged a look before sharing one with Sea, who grinned, just happy to be included.

Curtis signed something to his two compatriots.

-I think she's in shock-

Fleet nodded as he chugged the rest of his soda and threw the can on the ground. "Lowy, we're going to pay for everything. You'll have a brand-new motel built with only the finest wood and shit to replace this one, which is basically just moldy drywall held together by a sticky paste of farts and sadness...and asbestos. Pretty sure that's asbestos over there." Fleet spat as if some had gotten in his mouth.

"He's right," Curtis agreed. "We have the funds to do it. This place will be a thousand times better than it ever was."

"No thanks." Lowy declined the offer in that same vacant voice.

"Do what?" Fleet and Curtis said in tandem.

Lowy walked deeper into the breezeway. "I spent my entire life here and made some wonderful memories that I will cherish forever."

She held out her hand as she envisioned a younger version of herself using the soda machine as cover during a game of tag with her parents. The image faded away as they caught her in a fit of laughter, revealing the current state of her blood-soaked hiding spot.

"It's all I've ever really known, and now it's gone. Seeing my home like this, I should be more...sad? Or angry?"

Her outstretched arm fell to her side.

"But I'm not."

She picked up a small piece of brick and rolled it over her fingers.

"I'm actually kind of relieved. I'd often dream about what my life would be like if I just dropped everything and ran, but I was never brave enough to do it—guilt or fear always kept me bolted to this place. It's why I got so defensive when you called me out on it. I didn't want to admit how right you were."

She looked over at Fleet with a half-smile.

"My parents would never have wanted me to keep living a life that I hate. And while you didn't mean to, you gave me a chance to start over, to try for something different—something better."

Lowy tossed the brick back into a pile of rubble.

"I'm not going to waste this chance."

"Hear that, my man?" Fleet poked Curtis in the ribs. "I'm right again. Sounds like somebody's on a roll, eh?"

Curtis gave a dry 'mmm-hmm' to match the droll expression on his face before he changed focus back to Lowy. "So, what's your plan?"

Lowy didn't have to think for long. "I believe the first thing I'm going to do is pocket those 'funds' you were talking about, Curtis."

Curtis nodded with a grin. "I think we can work that out. I'll even throw in some extra 'hush money' on top."

"Deal," Lowy agreed. "What about insurance? Should I try to collect from them, too?"

"It'd be strange if you didn't," Curtis reasoned. "People would start asking questions if you walked away from this without trying. We don't want that."

"That's going to be quite the windfall there," Fleet said, followed by a small whistle. "Your new life is already off to a pretty good start, I'd say. Tell us, now that you can do literally anything your heart desires, what's next?"

Lowy put her hands behind her back and looked at her feet as she kicked at some debris. "About that... I was wondering if you guys would take me on."

They both gaped at her before Curtis decided he should be the voice of reason. "Lowy, you've seen what we do. I can't in good conscience—"

Lowy interrupted him, a hint of desperation in her voice. "I don't have to do what you guys do. There's no way a large organization can be all about violence and gore, right? I could be a personal assistant or something, like that guy from earlier who brought the bowl of crap for Fleet to eat."

Sea raised a finger to correct her, but Fleet interjected before he made his case. "She's right. There are tons of jobs that don't require her to be put in danger: financial, logistics, medical. She can pick any career she wants. And it's not like we haven't taken on non-Tryst before for certain jobs."

The cadence of Fleet's voice rose along with his enthusiasm for the idea.

"Plus, it'll be easier to keep an eye on her to make sure she doesn't blab about all this. I mean, it works out pretty damn well if you think about it!"

The two of them stared at Curtis in anticipation as they waited for his response.

"Why the hell are you looking to me for approval?" Curtis said. "You have more authority than I do, remember?"

"Yeah, but let's be honest here." Fleet shrugged and shook his head. "This stuff is way over my head. The inner machinations of Trystdom are still a mystery to me. Besides, if something goes wrong, then I can always blame you for it."

"Thanks," Curtis groaned.

"I'm kidding," Fleet assured him. "I'll back whatever you decide, and if it goes south, I'll take the fall. No worries. Just help us out here."

Curtis gave Lowy a studying glare. "Lowy, if you do this, you're going to have to abandon everything you've ever known. That includes friends, family, and property. And once you leave, under no circumstance can you ever come back. Are you willing to do that?"

His warning had little effect on her decision. "There are some people I would like to say goodbye to, but other than that, my mind is set."

Lowy and Fleet watched Curtis with bated breath as he rubbed his chin and contemplated their suggestion. He then looked toward the pathway's ceiling and theorized in a subdued voice, "Yeah, I guess that could work."

His words were met with a resounding cheer, but he cut them off with a slash of his hand. "But no fieldwork. And you can't pick what job you want. They're not going to let you be a doctor just because you think it'd be cool."

"I'll take it!" Lowy jumped with glee. "I don't mind working my way up if I have to."

"That's good, because you very well might," Curtis mumbled under his breath. "I can't make any promises, but I'll pull some strings and see what I can do."

"Thank you so much, Curtis!" Lowy squealed, unable to contain herself as she gave him an appreciative hug.

"Yeah, yeah," Curtis grumbled with a reserved smile before backing out of her embrace. "Anyway, now that we've settled that, let's move onto the next issue."

He motioned Sea over toward him and pointed at the large hole in the wall.

"We're going with fire again, but I need it to be intense enough that it knocks down these damaged brick walls; those are going to raise the most questions. Use some small explosives if you have to. That drink machine could be an issue as well."

The two of them got to work establishing the best plan of action to cover all the angles. Lowy and Fleet moved out of their way so as not to be a burden.

"They're in the zone now," Fleet said with admiration.

"Yeah, they sure are serious about this," Lowy agreed.

"Best in the business, no doubt about it."

Out of nowhere, Fleet put his hand on Lowy's shoulder and pulled her in close to whisper in her ear. "Speaking of the best, I think the way you've handled all this is freakin' amazing. This might not mean much coming from me, but I wanted you to know I'm proud of you, Buck."

Lowy flushed with a smile. "Thanks. It means more than you think."

Fleet gave her a satisfied grin before playfully pushing her away. "Your new life starts now. You ready for this?"

"How about we say it starts tomorrow? Starting over while my motel is still standing seems wrong," Lowy admitted. "Just doesn't feel as cathartic as I'd hoped, you know?"

"It's your call. Now, if you don't mind, I'm going to find a bed and spend the next seventy-two hours of my life passed the fuck out."

"Where you planning to crash?" Curtis asked, grabbing him by the arm as he tried to leave. "It better not be here, because we're hoping to torch this place before the sun comes back up."

"At this point, I don't care. I'm so damn tired I could curl up on the pavement and sleep like a log," Fleet said, his eyelids drooping.

Lowy's hand shot up. "He can sleep with me!"

The two of them turned to her wide-eyed, causing her to wave her hands in embarrassment. "What I mean is you can lie down in my trailer. I have some blankets and an extra pillow you can use."

"Sounds great," Fleet agreed, happy at the promise of some rest.

Curtis nodded his consent. "Yeah, get some sleep. You've earned it."

Fleet waited for Lowy to catch up, but before leaving, he had one last question for his partner. "What about you guys? You've been dealing with this shit even longer than I have."

Curtis shook his head, almost as much to disagree as it was to shake away the fatigue. "We rest when the job's done. You've done your part. Leave the rest to us."

"That sounded pretty badass," Fleet said with a grin. "When we're done, drinks are on me. That goes for Java and Sea too."

Curtis nodded, then set back to work.

Lowy poked Fleet in the arm and motioned for him to follow her. As they made their way down the trail, Lowy had to slow down to match Fleet's pace as he trudged along in silence. She knew he was tired, but she couldn't help herself, and before long, the exhilaration of her new circumstance was too much to bear.

She pulled ahead so she could walk backward and address him formally, proud to show off her newfound knowledge. "And another case closed by the Servunday Fredrick F. Fleet: master werewolf hunter and defender of the innocent."

Fleet stopped and gave a wan smile, struggling to maintain his balance. "First off, you're giving me a bit too much credit. I'm more like a detective or something."

This somehow made Lowy even more excited. "You're like a werewolf Hercule Poirot!"

Fleet squinted one eye at her. "Who?"

"Jane Marple?"

"That's a girl's name."

"Okay, ummm... Walker, Texas Ranger?"

"Now you're talking. But you could have said Sherlock Holmes and I would have gotten it. I'm not completely bereft of culture."

Lowy giggled at his response, but his answer wasn't enough to slate her curiosity. "What was the second thing?"

"Second thing?"

"Ya know, when you start a sentence with 'first off' that means there is something that follows. What were you going to say?"

Fleet rubbed his face to put his weary mind back on track. He then held up a finger with a sudden pop of realization. "Oh yeah! Second, in no way is this case closed."

"Really? It seems pretty closed to me."

Fleet began his shuffle once again as he explained, somehow moving even slower than before, as if the words were draining him. "All we did was eliminate an immediate threat—there's still a lot up in the air that we need to figure out."

"Like what?"

Fleet threw up a hand. "We still don't have any real ties to the hand you found, and if it involved Dash and Jill, what was their motive? Speaking of, we're still in the dark about their relationship even though they have the same 'crest.'"

Lowy stopped short when she heard this new term. "Crest?"

"Guess we forgot to tell you about that." Fleet took a moment to catch his breath. "Basically, every Tryst has a specific mark on them that designates their bloodline. You're either born with it, or you get it from the Tryst that turned you."

Fleet rubbed a finger across his throat.

"Did you notice that long strip of black around my neck? That's my crest."

He then reached back and pinched the tip of an imaginary tail.

"If you saw Curtis in wolf form, the tip of his tail is solid black, like it was dipped in a barrel of oil. Everyone who shares the Scriptor bloodline will have that same mark on their tail, even though their overall fur color and body structure may be totally different."

Lowy nodded, taking in his words as he explained.

"That's how we know Dash and Jill were of the same line. They both had the same crest: a white diamond about right here."

Fleet formed a diamond with his fingers and put it to his chest.

"The issue right now is that it's one I've never seen before. Crests aren't my area, but Curtis hasn't seen it either and he's the expert on all that."

Lowy tapped her fingers together as she compiled the information in her mind. "If I have this right, then that means they share the same bloodline, but you don't know if they are siblings or just got infected by the same Tryst."

"Bingo," Fleet said, impressed with how quickly she was catching on. "Dash could even be Jill's mother for all we know. We'll have to do a DNA test to find out if they are related by blood or bite."

Lowy nodded, taking it all in. She didn't even realize they had made it to her place until she backed into her garden fence. Fleet was already opening the screen door, eager to get off his feet.

Lowy stopped at the bottom step and asked, "What are you?" Fleet turned around, prompting her to clarify. "Your bloodline, I mean. You told me Curtis is 'Scriptor,' but you haven't told me yours."

Fleet stroked his neck with his free hand.

"I'm a 'Hangman.'"

He then opened the door and stepped inside.

"Hangman," Lowy quoted to herself, letting the word linger in her mind.

"Uh, Lowy?" Fleet called from inside.

Before she could muster a response, she was struck by a horrible realization.

Fleet peeked his head back through the doorway. "Why is there a pillow in the toilet?"

Lowy just stared at him, mouth agape.

Fleet nodded and made a gesture of understanding. "Say no more. Nothing to be ashamed of. Had the same issue after eating twelve roast beef sandwiches from Arby's once. Sometimes you just got to grab onto something tight and ride it out."

Lowy's body temperature rose so high it could have turned the dirt beneath her feet into solid glass. "That is not what happened!"

She rushed inside to find Fleet dropping the toilet pillow on the floor with a wet slap. She grimaced as he collapsed onto it with a loud squelch, sending water streaming from the bottom.

"I can get you a different pillow!" Lowy shouted with disgust.

Fleet yawned as he replied, "This is fine. Don't worry about me."

Lowy gave an exasperated sigh and pulled a blanket from the drawer, draping it across his body. Fleet gave a thankful grunt as she stepped over him and into her bed.

She hadn't realized how tired she was until her head hit the pillow. This had to be one of the most taxing days of her life, both physically and emotionally—and yet she was still too excited to sleep.

"Fleet, can I ask you something?"

A disapproving moan wafted up from below.

She leaned over the bed to look down at him. "This will be the last thing, I swear."

Fleet's arm shot up to point a crooked finger at her. "Then you promise you'll let me sleep?"

"Yes, I give you my solemn vow."

Fleet's arm dropped back down to the floor with a smack. "What is it?"

"Why Tryst?" she asked, causing Fleet to grunt up at her in confusion, unsure of the question. "You call yourselves 'Tryst' to represent all were-animals, creatures...whatever. Why not were-folk or wolf-kin or something?"

"This is what you wanted to ask me?" Fleet sighed and spoke without opening his eyes. "Remember how ancient gods had a tendency to turn into animals and come down to earth for a quickie? Zeus being a prime example. I believe the thought process is that we are the creation—or consequence—of those 'trysts.'"

Lowy blurted the first example that came to her mind. "Like Hercules?"

"Sure, why not."

Lowy scrunched her face as she looked down at him. "You call yourself Tryst because you think you're descended from gods? Seems a tad pretentious, don't you think?"

"Hey, I didn't come up with it. In fact, I think it's pretty damn stupid, myself. But as self-aggrandizing and overall idiotic as it sounds, it's the only explanation we've got. Now go to bed!"

Fleet then faked a snore that quickly turned into a deep slumber.

Lowy flipped back onto her bed and poured over Fleet's audacious explanation.

Gods? Come on. There's no way. Like I'm really going to believe I'm sleeping with a god. NEXT TO! Next to a god. Something like that is impossible—just like all the other things I've seen today are impossible.

Lowy clenched her jaw and picked at her nails.

Being able to turn into a giant monster is impossible. Or healing your wounds in seconds is impossible. Or tearing through brick and metal like they were tissue paper is impossible.

Lowy turned onto her side.

What have I gotten myself into?

She let her eyes drift around the room, a view she had seen time and time again. But now, something was different. Instead of those feelings of loneliness it normally brought her, she now felt an odd sense of nostalgia. She looked over at the picture of that happy family as a smile crossed her lips.

"I can't wait to find out."

"Damn it, woman! You said you would let me sleep!" Fleet called up from the floor.

"I am, you grump!"

Lowy reached over and poked him in the ribs, causing him to retaliate by swinging his arm up and whacking the bed frame with his wrist. He gave a pitiful whine and wrapped the body pillow around his head in defeat.

Lowy laughed and brought the covers back around her as she tried to fall asleep. However, she still could not curtail her excitement, and it took another hour before she was able to nod off.

CHAPTER THIRTY-ONE

ORANGE SODA

A VIOLENT HUMMING FORCED Lowy to jolt from her restless sleep. A small pulse of light from the table next to her bed showed a text message had arrived. Half-awake, she reached over Fleet's prone body and pulled her phone close, the screen momentarily blinding her. She put on her glasses to see the message was from Oreen.

I forgot all about them! What am I going to do if they're on their way here? I'm supposed to be keeping all this a secret, right? What if they find Curtis and that other guy burning down my building?

Lowy flicked open the message, her mind racing to decide the best course of action. Her nose scrunched up as she mouthed the words of his message.

-Come down 2 Classy Bar-

Why would he be going there? I figured that would be the last place he would want to visit after what happened.

As if predicting her very thoughts, another notification buzzed to life on her phone.

-Swung by to say sorry Viv says no heart feelings fells bad we didn't have good time wants to give free drinks!-

The end of the message was punctuated by several smiling emojis and one of a beer.

Since when did he start using emojis? He must be drunk already.

She checked the time on her phone to find it was a little past noon. Had Viv ever opened the bar this early before, or had Lowy never known the hours to begin with?

She sent a message back asking where they had been. It took several minutes before she received a response.

-Lol just hurry tell you when you get here and brick him with you-

Him? Does he mean Fleet? I guess they really did get closer in jail.

She reached down and shook Fleet's shoulder. Taking his groan as a sign that he was cognizant, she said, "I just got a text from Oreen."

Fleet waved her off, but then bolted up right after. "Shit! Where are they?"

"He says that they are at Classy Bar."

"Seriously?"

Lowy shrugged. "Says he went back to apologize, and now he wants us to join them down there."

Fleet grunted as he used her bedpost like a crutch to pull himself up. "Well, at least that means they're not on the way here. That's the last thing we need right now." He then pointed at her phone in confusion. "Wait, you have service out here?"

"I have satellite internet in my trailer, so I get mine through Wi-Fi," she explained.

"That works. Scriptor has a satellite phone, so I should be able to reach him if you give me your password." Fleet patted at his sides in a mild panic. "Shit, that's right. I bet my phone got destroyed in the fight. Guess we'll just tell him in person."

Fleet was already out the door before he even finished talking. As Lowy stood up to follow, she felt something hard press against her thigh. She looked to where she had been sitting and saw the little red car that Fleet had given her.

It seemed disrespectful to just toss it somewhere, so she scanned around to find the best place for it. But the longer she searched, the farther away Fleet got, so she tucked it in her pocket and ran out the door after him.

The two jogged until they reached the central passageway where they had last seen Curtis.

"Scriptor! You here!" Fleet called out.

From the opening in the brick wall, something soared out toward Fleet's head. He grabbed the flung object out of the air and flipped it over in his hands to discover he was holding the shattered remains of his phone.

"Don't lose that," Curtis warned, emerging from the same opening.

Fleet threw the phone back at him. "Then don't give it to me. You know damn well I'll lose it."

Curtis caught it and called out to his subordinate. "Sea, take care of this."

Sea popped out from the hole in the opposite building and held out his hands. Curtis sent the phone spiraling only for it to slap against the wall.

Seizing the opportunity, Fleet quipped, "Talk about a blocked call, am I right?"

His words were ignored by all as Sea retrieved the phone and shuffled back inside to resume his duties.

"That was a good one." Fleet spat on the ground. "You guys suck."

"What are you doing here?" Curtis asked to fill the awkward void. "I figured you would both still be asleep."

"Oreen texted us," Lowy explained, holding up her phone. "He says they're at the bar and wants Fleet and me to join him. What should we do?"

"I had wondered what happened to those two. We lucked out that they didn't turn up earlier." Curtis rubbed his chin in thought. "This could work, actually. Two birds with one stone, even. We're almost ready to start here, so you guys can go down there and keep them busy. It'll also give you an alibi for the arson."

"Speaking of that, what about all their stuff?" Lowy asked.

"There's no other way," Curtis lamented. "From an outside perspective, it would be suspicious if you move all their things out right before a fire starts. Don't worry, I'm sure there's nothing they can't replace."

Lowy was still apprehensive about it, but what else could they do?

"Okay, once you get there, stay as long as you can or until someone tells you the place is on fire," Curtis instructed. "At which point, you come back, act surprised, and wait for the cavalry."

Even though Curtis made it sound so simple, Lowy found herself overwhelmed by the whole thing.

Fleet waved a hand over his face when he noticed her dour expression. "Lowy, you can't go looking like this. It needs to seem like everything is normal."

Lowy patted her cheeks and took a deep breath. "No, I'm ready. Act natural. That's not so hard."

"There you go! You got this!" Fleet's rumbling stomach interrupted his motivational chants. "Do you know if they serve food at the bar?"

"Not to my knowledge," Lowy answered. "But I bet we can talk Oreen and BJ into going to the diner afterward."

"Okay, time's a wastin'!" Fleet said, excited at the prospect of more waffles.

"Do I have time to do my makeup or brush my teeth?" Lowy asked as she followed Fleet to his truck.

"You look great, considering everything that's happened," Fleet complimented. "Now breathe in my face, and I'll tell you if your breath stinks."

Curtis watched as they walked away, the two of them leaning together to administer the breath test on each other. All he could do was grin and shake his head.

—◄|||||||||||||||||||||||||||►—

Half an hour had passed since the duo left, leaving Curtis and Sea to prep the motel. They were making good progress by all accounts, but the work was taxing him more so than normal following his brawl with Jill. Though after what had happened in the old school, Curtis was happy to get back to his normal duties instead of fighting for his life.

As Curtis tended to the drink machine, he felt a soft vibration in his pocket and pulled out his blocky phone. "Hey, what's her status?"

Java answered right away, skipping all formalities. "The rogue Tryst is alive, but just barely. She's in a medically induced coma because she can't turn back into human form with those injuries. The doctor said he will have to reconstruct her entire skeletal system, and even then, it isn't looking good for her."

"After what I saw, I'm not surprised."

"Yes, he equated her condition to 'a sack full of water balloons and broken glass,'" Java quoted.

"That's pretty damn gruesome." Curtis stuck out his tongue with a grimace. "But if anyone can keep her alive, it'll be him. Anything else to report? What about the blood samples we got from the bathroom?"

"I'm waiting on the results as we speak."

"Good. Keep me updated."

Curtis made to end the call, but stopped when he realized Java was still talking. "Wait, sir. While I have you, I wanted to take this opportunity to apologize for the slip-up at the church."

"Don't worry about it. In truth, that one's on me. I should have thought it through better. You had to abandon them, but the important thing now is that we get the explosives out of there as soon as possible."

"It's so odd," Java pondered aloud. "We were going to detonate after we were sure the blaze in the school had ignited. But not even five minutes in, people started showing up, and we couldn't do it without endangering them. Sea will retrieve the explosives later, so not to worry, but I can't understand how they got there so fast."

"Chalk it up to bad luck. Happens to the best of us," Curtis sympathized. "You can have everything planned out to the letter, and then out of nowhere, it can all go to shit over the simplest thing. What's important is how you adapt, and you guys did great."

"Thank you, sir," Java said, sounding relieved. "Between the words of praise from you and Servunday Hangman, I can feel myself bursting with pride. It is such an honor, and I hope to ride this high for—"

"Nobody likes a kiss-ass, Java."

"My apologies, sir."

"Anything else to report?"

"No, that is all I have for—wait a moment, sir. It looks like the lab has found something. If you will give me one second."

There was muffled talking over the receiver before Java came back on.

"The lab has some preliminary results regarding the samples we took from the young lady's bathroom. It seems they all came from the same source, meaning all that blood only belonged to a single individual."

Curtis nodded. "That makes sense."

"But there's something else, sir." Java paused as if he were struggling with the information. "They also noticed that the blood seems to match with the sample from her corpse as well."

Curtis stared down at his phone, his eyes blinking erratically. All that blood in Jill's bathroom had belonged to her? If it did, that means there had been no murder, which also meant that the hand had no connection to the bathroom, either.

All their theories had just gone to shit.

Curtis lifted the phone back to his ear as if it weighed a hundred pounds. "I need to reevaluate a few things. If anything new pops up, let me know."

As Java responded, Curtis ended the call and walked to the front of the building to look at Jill's room.

"What the hell happened up there?"

<hr>

"I'm back!" Dash shouted as she walked through the door with four shopping bags in her free hand. She sat them in the corner and rifled through their contents, looking for something specific.

Her eyes crossed over a bottle of whiskey, and she gave a small shudder. The last time she had whiskey, she got blackout drunk and ended up vomiting all over the place—even thinking of the smell made her nauseous. Still, she was going to need it very soon. To her, the alcohol seemed the least vile of the mandatory vices she had been assigned.

Finally, she found what she was searching for: a six-pack of orange soda.

"I got your favorite! But you can't drink all of them at once, okay?"

Her words evaporated into the shag carpet as she walked over to the bathroom. She put an ear to the door and smiled at the sound of running water.

"Good idea. A nice warm bath will do you wonders."

Dash kicked off her shoes before sitting down on the bed and slapped at the dust cloud that formed around her. This roach motel was awful. Everything about it was such a distant cry from what she was used to.

However, considering their circumstance, it certainly beat the alternative.

On the plus side, the owner seemed nice, if not a bit too saccharine for her own good. She'd been overjoyed when Dash informed her of their prolonged stay, making plans for them to hang out and have 'girl time.' Dash had agreed, not wanting to share her true feelings on the matter. Then again, maybe a little girl time would be good for 'Jill.'

Dash cringed a bit at the names she had concocted for them.

She spoke louder than normal to be heard over the running water. "Hey, I'm sorry if you don't like 'Jill.' I kind of panicked when she asked for your name. I figured she was in on it and wouldn't ask questions. But Jill is a cute name, right?"

She received no response.

"Well, at least your name isn't Dash. When she called me 'missus,' that was the first thing that popped into my head. I must have had food on the brain or something."

She laughed but did not receive one in kind, realizing after that Jill wouldn't get the reference. Dash bellowed a deep sigh and flopped back onto the bed, shutting her eyes to avoid the evocation of dust.

"Are you mad at me?" she asked.

Still, she did not receive a response.

"I know you wanted to share a room, which I would have loved. Honestly." Dash swallowed like she was shoving vomit back down her throat. "It's just that I'm going to have to do some things that I don't want you to be around. That's the only reason I got you a room so far away from mine, okay? When I'm in there with somebody, I need you to be in here. But any other time, we can be together, I promise."

All she heard was that same drone of water gushing from the faucet, and even it seemed to have grown quieter.

Dash's bottom lip trembled as she spoke in a broken voice. "I'm so sorry. I should have done something sooner, but I just didn't know..."

Tears rolled down her face, breaking through the dam made with her palms.

"I'll do whatever it takes; anything to keep you safe. All I want is for you to be happy. You deserve that more than anyone."

Despite her outpouring of emotion, Jill still did not respond.

Dash dried her eyes and stared up at the ceiling in a fugue. She was only brought out of her state by the jarring rhythm of water slapping against the floor.

"Are you swimming laps in there or something?" Dash joked, trying to lighten the mood. "Take it easy, would ya? You don't want to get us kicked out of here on the first day?"

The sound only continued to intensify.

Dash got up and knocked on the bathroom door. "Please talk to me."

She stopped when she felt a warm sensation on her toes. Water had flowed under the door and seeped its way into the carpet, turning it to a dark shade of brown. Dash squinted at the floor as she clenched her toes together, pushing the bathwater up between them. What dribbled across her foot had an odd discoloration to it, a sort of—

Dash shrieked and flung open the door, freezing in shock as she gazed over Jill's prone body surrounded by a sea of crimson. She leaped forward and fell into the bathtub as she grabbed for Jill, sending a deluge of tainted water over the sides that swept across the bathroom floor like a red tide.

With a surge of adrenaline, Dash ripped Jill from the tub and onto the floor. She propped Jill up between her legs and noticed the long vertical cut going down her right wrist. Dash clamped her hand down over the wound like a vise and raised both their arms over her head.

"Please, please..." Dash frantically repeated as she put her head to Jill's chest.

Her whole body shook as she tried to halt her rapid breaths to hear. Though faint, there was a weak heartbeat struggling within Jill's rib cage. Tears streamed down her face as Dash coughed in relief, wrapping her free arm around Jill to pull her in close.

"We're together now, and nothing is going to change that. I swear on my life, you'll never have to suffer again."

She nuzzled her face into Jill's neck.

"You're free now…"

Chapter Thirty-Two

GARBAGE

"That could be a problem," Curtis muttered to himself as he surveyed the old fire pit Fleet had punched.

The twisted mass of metal looked like some sort of deranged art piece. He peered closer and ran a finger over the imprint of Fleet's attack. Though no one would believe it, it was impossible to see anything else besides an enormous fist.

He kicked Fleet's metal punching bag. "You never make it easy for me, do ya, Hangman?" He turned around to address the figure moving behind the bathroom curtains. "Sea! We're going to take this with us!"

The figure vanished at his request, likely moving into the interior.

Curtis rubbed his eyes with a thumb and forefinger; the exhaustion had dried them out and left them red and irritable. He'd tried to sound cool earlier with the whole 'now it's our turn' thing, but in reality, he was just as tired as Fleet, if not more so. The fight with Jill had taken its toll. He wasn't trained for prolonged transformations like that, much less having to deal with the pain she'd inflicted on him.

"They gotta be there by now! We need to start this before too long!" he called out, forgetting that Sea was out of earshot. His subordinate had been in there for well over an hour by himself, putting the finishing touches on the ignition while Curtis combed the place on one last round of clean-up.

Curtis craned his neck, causing it to make a sharp pop before he bent over to pick up the can of soda he'd taken earlier. He cracked it open and let the foam settle before he took a long sip. In the absence of coffee, this would have to do.

I should offer one to Sea. He had a hell of a time earlier, and he's even less trained for this kind of stuff than I am. Fuck, they should have never even been there in the first place. It's my fault they had to go through that at all. Maybe I'll see if I can get everyone a pay raise or something.

After the gentle burn of the soda faded away, he pulled out his satellite phone and dialed Sea. It rang a few times before going to voicemail. Curtis let out an annoyed grunt and slid the phone back in his pocket. He turned his attention once again to the fire pit and gave it one last push with his foot to test how heavy it was.

"With two of us, we should be able to—"

He stopped mid-sentence when something caught his eye, hiding at the edge of the fire pit's shadow. Curtis chuckled once he got closer and saw what it was: the plastic bag full of 'evidence' that Fleet had told him about earlier.

"Garbage or not, I need to talk with that guy about how to properly catalog stuff."

Curtis chugged the rest of his soda and stomped the empty can flat before putting it in his pocket. He started toward the building to find Sea, but he only made it a few steps. A sudden thought began tugging at his collar, refusing to let him go farther.

He turned back around to study the plastic bag. "He's been right so far," he whispered to himself. "What's the harm in looking? Shouldn't leave it behind, anyway."

Curtis walked over and prodded the bag with his foot, causing the broken glass to clink as some garbage slid out onto the ground. It was as he assumed: all crap.

"You're just cleaning up the road, Hangman. Nothing wrong with a little public service, I suppose."

He gave the bag one last kick to empty the rest of the contents—and then froze.

A colorful picture that had been torn in half was sticking out from the sack, partially covered by the other refuse. Curtis put his foot over it as if he were about to step on a landmine and slid the piece of garbage closer to pick it up.

It was some sort of strange pattern printed on large card stock, though it had been ripped straight down the middle. Tiny bits of foil glinted at him as he flipped it over to see a hand-drawn picture of a man hanging by his ankle from a tree branch.

Bile gushed into Curtis' throat as he realized what it was: a tarot card of the hanged man torn in half. A powerful chill snaked down his arm to culminate in needles throughout the tips of his fingers that made it feel like the card was biting him.

"No way. There's no way. It has to be a coincidence."

Deep down, he knew better—he just didn't want to admit it.

Curtis turned and raced back up to the building as he shouted out Sea's name. He made it to the window he had seen the shadow in before and slapped his palm against it.

"Code white! Code white! I found his token! Drop everything and get in the car!"

A small shadow moved within the tiny sliver of light that shone from under the bathroom door, but there was no other reaction.

"Sea, goddamn it, come here!"

Deciding it would be more efficient, Curtis ran around the building to the room's entrance. He called out for Sea as he twisted the doorknob, only to find it was locked. He tried the next room, figuring that he had perhaps miscounted the rooms in his panic, but found that one to be locked as well.

Curtis beat on the original door in abject frustration. "Sea! Unlock the damn door!"

Realizing it was a waste of time, he started toward the center walkway, intending to bypass the entrance and take the large hole left from Fleet's fight. Before he got far, there came a solid click from the door he had checked prior.

"Sea? What the hell are you doing?"

Curtis stood there, staring at the entrance as he waited for Sea to emerge. After a few moments of inactivity, his impatience welled up once again. He stomped over and put his hand on the doorknob, ready to reprimand Sea for his inaction in a time of crisis.

"How did you not hear—"

Spread across the bed lay what must have been a human body, though it was impossible to tell anymore. It had been flayed apart into careless lumps, causing a powerful aroma of copper to emanate throughout the air. The organs had been festooned about the room, creating tendrils of blood that creeped down the walls before being soaked up by the thick carpet.

Curtis backed away, but fear had clamped down his body to where even basic movement had become a monumental effort.

"S-Sea. Is that you?" he stuttered.

As if to answer the question, the large body of a transformed Tryst slid into view from a blind spot beside the entrance. Curtis tripped and fell backward into the parking lot, unable to take his eyes off the monster before him.

The Tryst was so large that its head and shoulders were obfuscated behind the door frame. Its upper body was a coat of solid black that transitioned into brown around its torso. This dark fur made it hard to see that the entire front of its body was caked in blood and chunks of flesh. The feet were solid red, the natural white of them now dyed from the remains of its victim.

The Tryst bent down until its murderous gaze was locked upon Curtis as its tongue undulated around something clamped between its teeth. Curtis' eyes watered as he reached toward the oval object in its mouth. A wicked smile stretched up the beast's face as it shook with a sick pleasure from seeing his reaction.

"Sea?" Curtis called out, pure shock diluting the knowledge that he would not receive an answer.

Sea's face still held his last expression of terror as a mixture of drool and blood seeped out from around his severed head. The beast's eyes grew wide with delight as it chomped down, shredding the last thing that proved the rags of flesh in there were once his trusted subordinate and friend.

Curtis forgot everything.

No amount of training could have ever prepared him for a scenario as nightmarish as this. After an unceremonious start, Curtis ran, driven by a deep fear for his own life.

The monster wasted no time as it burst through the opening, taking the entire door frame with it. In the blink of an eye, it was in front of him, blocking the way to his vehicle and the road. Curtis did a one-eighty and sprinted back toward the building to cut through the center pathway. He hoped that perhaps if he got to the woods, he might lose it long enough to shift and make an escape. But as he streaked forward, a man stepped forward at the end to block his exit.

The stranger spoke, taking no urgency from the situation. "Code white? That is what you chose for me? Why not pick a more threatening color, or at least something fun, like chartreuse? Or have you been calling me that because of my complexion? If this is a race thing, I must say that I do not approve."

The man's glib words didn't slow Curtis in the least. Without even halting his sprint, Curtis grabbed a brick from a pile of debris and slammed it sideways into the man's temple. The stranger didn't even blink as he stood motionless against the impact.

Curtis screamed as the brick ricocheted from his hand, shredding the skin on his fingers and palm. He clutched his injury as he assessed the man for any damage he may have done. To his chagrin, only a small trickle of blood was now creeping down the side of the stranger's face.

From behind him, the beast let out a threatening roar and charged, driven by anger at seeing the man hurt. However, it ground to a halt when the stranger held up a hand, his eyes still locked on Curtis.

The man smiled as he wiped a thumb across the meager cut. "Not much for humor, are we, Scriptor? Though I must admit, mine can be a tad dry. Not for everyone, but did it really warrant the assault?"

Curtis' mouth fell open in shock when he realized that not only had the bleeding stopped almost instantaneously, but the wound had vanished as well.

"Shit," Curtis whispered in defeat as he backed into the wall and slid down onto his knees.

The man put his hand on the wall as he stood over him. "Salutations. You may call me Peter, though I surmise you already knew that. I shall excuse your rude introduction, considering the circumstances."

Curtis stared up at him and trembled. Even though there was a transformed Tryst only meters away that could tear him to shreds, he was far more afraid of the man addressing him in such a formal manner. He jerked backward as Peter kneeled to his level, unable to meet the gaze of those piercing gray eyes.

"You seem a bit out of sorts, so I will take the lead. How did I know your name? That information came from your subordinate—Sea, was it?" Peter giggled to himself. "A real chatterbox, that one, and ever so generous."

Peter held out a tiny black device with a clear plastic lid. Curtis recognized it as the remote detonator they had planned to use.

Peter tossed the item in the air and caught it. "Such a dangerous little trinket. A good thing I took it from him before he got hurt."

He followed his words with a knowing grin as a hint of rage flashed over Curtis' face.

Peter bowed in apology. "My condolences for the state you found him in. I charged my follower with the extraction of information, but she has a tendency to be...overzealous." He craned his head to look back at her. "But I would be ever so lost without her."

The beast swooned as she trailed her fingers sensually across the front of her body.

Peter gave her a quick smile before returning to Curtis. "This whole thing has turned into quite the fiasco." He held up his hands to accompany a shrug. "At least it has been entertaining."

The audacity of Peter's words helped Curtis muster the courage to speak, though it came out more of a stutter. "Why are you doing this?"

Peter leaned in and stuck a finger in Curtis' face. "Now. Is not. The time. For questions." At each pause, he poked Curtis in the forehead, causing him to flinch. "I detest repeating myself, so all I ask for is a modicum of patience until all relevant parties have gathered."

Curtis nodded in agreement.

Peter removed his finger. "Very good. However, I will curb your curiosity and let you in on one secret about myself."

He reached over and retrieved the same brick that Curtis had used in his futile attack.

"I have a bad habit of being rather petty."

The last thing Curtis saw before going unconscious was a flash of white as the brick slammed down across his head.

CHAPTER THIRTY-THREE

STRING THEORY

FLEET YAWNED AS HE covered his mouth with the back of his hand. "Why are there people here so early?"

It was only the beginning of afternoon and already the place was alive with the sound of clacking billiards and crackling music. They found an empty table in the corner away from everyone and sat down across from each other.

Lowy turned to scan the bar. "I don't see Viv anywhere, but Oreen said she was here. Maybe she's in the bathroom or something."

Fleet looked around the room, craning his neck from side to side. "Where the heck is that guy, anyway?"

Lowy's phone made a soft chirp. "Speak of the devil," she said as she clicked open the new message. "He says they are running a little late."

"Running late? What the hell? I thought they were already here."

Lowy scrolled back through her previous messages. "That's what I thought too. Maybe I misread?"

Fleet put his head in his hands and propped himself on the table. "Damn it, Oreen. I'm way too tired for this shit."

Lowy leaned forward over the table. "Someone's a little moody today, aye Fredrick Hangman?"

Fleet dropped his hands to frown at her. "It's Hangman." Lowy's confused look prompted him to explain. "If you have to call me that, you might as well do it right. Since it may come up anyway, I'll tell you the proper way to address a Tryst."

"If there's one thing I don't want to do, it's piss off a werewolf by committing a social gaffe." Lowy looked focused as she prepared to listen. "Okay, I'm ready."

Fleet gave a quick double-check to make sure no one was listening. "You only ever want to call someone by their full name if there is another Tryst in the room with the same crest. Example: if Curtis was with his wife, you would call him Scriptor Curtis because there is another Scriptor right there. If it was just me and Curtis, you would call him by his crest, so just Scriptor. Using the first name is something you can only do with close friends in private—I learned that the hard way."

"I think I get it." Lowy nodded as she played it out in her mind. "Since we're friends, I can call you Frederick or Fleet, but only around us. Otherwise, I call you Hangman in 'proper' company. And if there is another Hangman around, then it's Hangman Fleet."

"Correct," Fleet confirmed. "But you won't have to worry about that last one, so just stick with Hangman."

"Why wouldn't I use your full name?"

"You would only call me by both names if there was another Hangman in the room," Fleet reiterated, his voice taking a more serious tone. "And if that's ever the case, there's going to be blood. Being cordial would be the least of your concerns."

Lowy leaned back in her chair, pushed away by the gravitas of his words as the cryptic explanation Curtis had given earlier played in her mind. Both of them fell silent as Fleet reinstated his original posture.

All those worrisome questions Lowy had from last night came flooding back.

What happened to him? I want to know, but there's no way I can ask him that. Our relationship is too new. I don't want to push him away or make him upset by bringing up bad memories. I should start with something that he wouldn't be upset talking about. Something general. Very general.

"Fleet, how's your life going?"

He lifted his head and blinked at her. "What?"

"How's life? Well, outside of recent events, I guess."

Fleet leaned back in his chair. "Where'd that come from?"

Lowy shrugged and looked to the side. "I don't know. I mean, I'm going into all of this blind. I just figured knowing how it's working out for you might make me feel better. But it's a dumb question. Forget I asked."

"It's okay. I get where you're coming from," Fleet responded with a wan smile. "But that's a pretty broad question, so give me a second."

Fleet put his arms behind his head as he pondered her query. His eyes studied the blend of stains on the ceiling as he asked, "You ever heard of string theory?"

Lowy gave him an odd look. "Just from science fiction stuff. That's the theory that there are an infinite number of parallel universes or something. Like there's one where I'm a cowboy, or one where I'm an astronaut."

"Or one where you gave examples that didn't sound like someone asked a small child what they wanted to be when they grow up," Fleet chided.

Lowy blushed and pouted. "Whatever. They're still accurate, kind of. But what's this got to do with anything?"

Fleet gave a small huff of amusement. "Okay, so I don't want to be off-putting for your future plans, but take this how you will. To answer your question: I feel like I'm in the one universe where every other version of myself looks and says, 'At least I'm not that guy.'"

Lowy burst out laughing and waved a hand in apology. "I'm sorry. Your answer is super sad, but you framed it in such an interesting way."

Fleet shook off her apology with a chuckle. "It's all good."

His voice became a bit more reserved, but the smile stayed on his face. "It crosses my mind every once in a while. If that theory is true, then there's an infinite number of myself existing out there, and that means somewhere there is a version of me where everything in my life went exactly right. A version that wasn't shat on by the universe. As stupid as that sounds, it makes me feel kinda good."

Lowy gave him a tender smile. "No, I don't think that's stupid at all. In fact, I might steal that sentiment for myself."

"By all means." Fleet grinned. "Anytime you're down, just remember astronaut Buck up there floating around the cosmos, farting up that space suit like an intergalactic Dutch oven."

"Who needs space for that?" Lowy laughed. "Just wait until we get back in the car."

Fleet bent over with laughter as he wiped a tear from the corner of his eye. Lowy removed her glasses to wipe a few tears of her own. It was good to see him laughing again. It helped curtail her worries, but it also brought with it some *other* thoughts.

Don't think about the universe where we hooked up! Don't think about the universe where we hooked up! Don't think about the universe where we hooked up! Don't think about the universe where we hooked up!

Fleet exhaled to reset himself and asked, "What's up with that face? You look super focused all of a sudden."

"No, I was just thinking that...uhh..." Lowy racked her brain as she pushed those thoughts from her mind a little too late. "That there's a universe where you hooked up...hooked up with Dash."

She bit her lip. *Why did I say that!*

Her statement caused Fleet to guffaw as if it were the most ridiculous thing anyone had ever said. "Even with infinite probability, ain't no way that would happen."

Lowy tilted her head to the side. "Why?"

"Because it means I would have to answer to my superior," Fleet explained. "And there is no version of me that has balls that big."

"Why would you get in trouble for having sex?"

"Well, first off, it's just plain unprofessional," Fleet explained. "Second, doing the nasty with someone is a way to pass it on. Granted, I didn't know Dash was already Tryst at the time, but if I had sex with her and she was human, there's a chance she might have been infected. That's why sex between a Tryst and a normal person is strictly forbidden without direct supervision, which would totally kill the mood—unless you're into that, I guess."

Lowy's demeanor changed as something concerning overtook her.

"That last part was a joke," Fleet clarified. "The supervision part, not the forbidden part."

Lowy didn't even acknowledge his joke as she picked at her fingernails.

Fleet was intrigued by her lack of response. "What are you thinking now?"

She asked the question slowly, as if trying to validate her own thoughts. "Does it have to be *unprotected* sex?"

"Of course. Otherwise, it would just—" The weight of his own words pulled Fleet down so that he was hunched over the table, his eyes darting about with no actual point of interest. "Shit. Shit. Shit. I didn't... I haven't had time to..."

Fleet's voice trailed off, his focus now bouncing between the other occupants of the bar. The tension within Lowy grew from witnessing his obvious distress.

"Maybe Dash used protection?" she suggested.

Fleet's pinkie began to twitch as he spoke through his fingers. "Out of all that garbage in her room, the only things she ever cleaned up were the condoms? I was in there and I didn't see so much as a single wrapper among that filth!" Fleet had to catch himself before his voice escalated any higher. "I need you to look around this room and tell me if any of these people ever slept with her."

"I don't keep tabs on who all she bangs!" Lowy whisper-shouted as she surveyed the crowd. "But the guy working the bar is Gary. He's the one you saw that day around the fire who sped off after climbing out of Dash's window."

Without even bothering to verify, Fleet locked eyes with Lowy, a serious expression creasing his troubled face. "I need you to listen and do exactly as I say. Do you understand?"

Lowy was taken aback by his shift in tone; all she could do was return a pensive nod. Fleet pulled out his keys, clenching them tightly to avoid any attention-grabbing jingles. He then placed them in her hand, making sure she showed them the same respect.

"When we got here, I saw your car was blocked in, so I want you to go out and start my truck. Wait thirty seconds, and if I don't come out, you leave me and get as far away as you can. Got it?"

"Come on." Lowy laughed to cover her nervousness. "Don't you think you're overreacting a bit?"

"Doesn't matter. If I'm wrong, so what? If I'm right, this could... Just do as I say! Please!" Once again, Fleet had to calm himself before he got too heated.

"I can't!" Lowy said as she fumbled with her phone. "What about Oreen? I need to text him and see if he's okay! We can't leave him!"

"Do it in the truck!" Fleet whisper-yelled through gritted teeth.

Lowy had already sent the message before he finished his objection.

An obnoxious, high-pitched screech echoed throughout the bar. All other noise vanished as if that simple sound effect were a klaxon of war. Everyone turned to the bartender, who wore a compromising shit-the-bed expression.

"Well, guess the cat's out of the bag," Gary said.

"That's...Oreen's ringtone for me," Lowy said, furrowing her brow.

Fleet slammed his fist down hard on the table. "Go! Now!"

Lowy almost fell from the table at his sudden outburst, but it was enough to get her focused. She gave him one last glance before she scrambled for the door, threw it open, and disappeared outside. Before the door had even swung back, two men were already headed after her.

Fleet shot up and sprinted toward the entrance, slamming it closed before they reached it. The couple stopped short of him, both sharing a similar menacing look.

"Lock the door," the man to Fleet's right demanded.

Fleet turned back and nodded. "If you insist."

After he clicked the lock into place, Fleet was dragged away with excessive force by the two imposing figures and sat at a table in the center of the room.

The two burly men who had apprehended him now stood on either side as the rest of the patrons gathered around. Fleet scanned his captors, taking special care to get a proper headcount. He recognized one man as the guy that got his face caved in by Dash at the school, though he showed no cuts or bruises now.

The crowd parted when Gary came from behind the bar and slid into the semi-circle. He crossed his arms and smirked down at Fleet, savoring the moment.

As the silence forged on, Fleet tapped his fingers on his leg and leaned back with his other arm over the chair. It didn't seem like they were going to elucidate, so Fleet decided he would set the mood. "If I may be so bold, I would like to say something to the one guy wearing body spray: thank you for trying, but it's not doing a thing for the group. It just makes it smell like eight guys ate blue cheese and farted on a pinecone."

A fist came across Fleet's chin from his right, slamming his face into the other guard's side.

Car keys and chewing tobacco—nothing useful.

"Damn, Righty." Fleet spat as he pushed off the man, a small dribble of blood leaking from his mouth.

Gary nodded his head with an approving grin. "This is going to be a fun night, I can tell."

"I'm all about fun," Fleet groaned as he wiped his chin.

"Do you know why you're here?" Gary asked as he put a foot up on the table, perhaps trying to look imposing.

"Can't say I do," Fleet replied. "But I do know you're all Tryst, so I figure it's got something to do with that."

Gary frowned at him as he struggled to take his leg down. "Tryst? What the hell is that?"

"Monsters! Shapeshifters! Werewolves, you ignorant fuck!" he clarified after reviewing their blank expressions.

There was a rumble among his captors before their leader spoke up.

"We are no monsters, boy. We are the chosen ones. We have been blessed through the Lord's prophet as those whose ascension is imminent. We shall take—"

Fleet began rubbing his temples as he moaned. "It's some kind of goddamn cult. Because of course it is. That's fucking great."

Gary continued to proselytize to this non-believer. "I remember when I had doubts. That was before I felt it. Before he lay his gentle hand on my brow and blessed me with this gift—this power." Gary held up his hands, cherishing them as if they were the most beautiful things in the world. "But this level of being cannot be maintained without sacrifice. That's where you come in, Cupcake."

"'Cupcake'? Damn, I knew it!" Fleet shouted as he slapped the table. "I'm about to get 'frosted,' aren't I? I got uneasy when I saw all the boners pop up the second I sat down—well, all except for this guy."

Fleet turned to the man on his left and frowned up at him.

"What's wrong, Lefty? I'm not cute enough for you? No, that can't be it. Erectile dysfunction? Those trousers house a wet noodle, I bet. Nothing to be ashamed of; it happens to a lot of guys. Then again, I might be wrong."

Fleet pointed a finger towards the man's crotch.

"Maybe you *are* all boned up, but I can't see yours cause it's too small. Don't think of it as tiny, my friend. Think of it as cute, like a little hamster tail."

The man's fist slammed down on the top of Fleet's head, causing him to bite his tongue. Fleet had the taste of iron in his mouth as he rolled the blood around his cheeks before spitting on the floor.

That's not what I wanted, Lefty!

Violet had always told him how good he was at pushing people's buttons, saying how it was a fantastic means to catch people off guard. It was one of the few genuine compliments she had ever given him, and he had no intention of letting her praise go to waste.

Fleet threw his head back to glare up at his assailant in defiance. "If you put your dick in a headphone jack, would music come out your ears?"

This elicited a laugh from the group but sent another punch Fleet's way, this time connecting square in his jaw. Fleet was knocked out of his chair and onto Righty.

Bingo, Fleet thought as he brushed against something long and metallic pushing through the man's denim. As he was forced back onto the chair, Fleet slipped his hand into Righty's pocket and removed the item: a folding pocket knife. He slid it under his palm and kept it pressed against his leg.

Gary snapped his fingers to silence the group. "That's enough. We need him alive or we can't perform the rights."

Fleet rubbed his jaw as he addressed the leader. "Based on context clues, it seems like you are going to kill me. In that case, can't you at least offer a dead man one last drink?"

Gary considered it before responding, "I suppose it would be cruel to deny a man his dying wish." He nodded to one man who ran behind the counter and brought back a brown bottle.

"Couldn't spare the good stuff, huh?" Fleet bemoaned as he twisted off the cap.

He took a deep swallow before smacking his lips and letting out a strong *ahhh*. He repeated this process several more times just to annoy his captors.

To fill the time as Fleet imbibed, Gary said, "If it brings you peace, we have no intention of hurting Harlow. We knew her parents. Real good people. Think they would have fit right in. We'll give her the same chance."

"A weight has been lifted, good sir." Fleet gave a bemused smile, all the while thinking, *Lowy, you better have made it out of here.*

"But the others, not so much." Gary pulled Oreen's phone from his pocket and slid it across the table.

Fleet set down the bottle and picked up the phone. The thought gave him a sinking feeling, but he had to ask. "Where'd you get this?"

Without saying a word, Gary stood up and walked over to the bar. When he returned, he threw something down on the table with a clatter. "Same place I got this."

Fleet took the thin slab of aluminum and flipped it over in his hand to discover it was a license plate. Though the numbers didn't ring a bell, he recognized the pattern as the same one he had seen when tailing Oreen's vehicle.

"Why did you take their license plate?" Fleet asked, an impending sense of dread growing within him.

A sadistic grin spread across Gary's face. "Well, we got to have it for the wall."

Fleet mouthed the words back at him as he deciphered their meaning. He focused on the last word, which led his eyes to the wall behind Gary. Goosebumps permeated his skin as the slab of metal dropped from his fingers.

"There's no way."

He'd noticed it on his first visit to the bar: an entire section of brick by the entrance was full of license plates. From a glance, Fleet estimated there had to be over fifty plastered on there.

"That's right!" Gary confirmed, tapping himself on the nose. He pointed over his shoulder without even turning around. "Florida. Row three, column two. That one's mine."

His face softened, overcome by nostalgia.

"I let mine loose in the woods. Even let her have a solid head start. No matter how far away she got, I could still hear her struggling, crying. It was like she was calling to me."

Gary tilted his head back and closed his eyes.

"I was on her so quick. She didn't say a word in the end. Just sat quietly as I went to work. I took my time. Helped myself."

Gary lowered his head.

"But all the while, I kept wondering if this was wrong. I worried if it was all right to carry out my holy duty...and be this fucking rock hard at the same time!"

Gary burst into laughter, implying he had already concluded on the matter. The others joined in his amusement until he finally broke off, satisfied that his perverse point had been made.

"What about you boys?" he asked of the others.

Each of the men took a turn as they pointed out 'their' plate, some letting out a contented sigh as they swooned over their 'hunts.'

To Fleet, their words were nothing but white noise.

His nails dug into the table as he stared unblinking at their macabre display. Each slab of metal tacked onto that wall was a person—maybe even more than one. That gaudy mishmash of numbers and letters served as a callous epitaph for the innocent souls that had been lost here. So many people, so many families that would never see their loved ones again. Every second he looked at that wall brought an irrepressible rage that seethed within, coursing through his veins until he could no longer contain it.

Fleet kicked back his chair, stood up, and in a militaristic tone, he rendered his judgement. "I am a Servunday: seeker of truth, present to bear witness to your sins. Through this venerable servant's unwavering faith, I am given right! Their voice is my voice, their hand is my hand, their judgment is my judgment! It is with this blessing that I pass sentence, and my burden to deliver it."

The circle of men exchanged bewildered glances with one another as Fleet continued.

"The servant has seized upon verity and cast the verdict of guilty! Mercy is forfeit, your blood the final toll! Death be your recompense."

He gave a flourish of his hand and finished with, "Dare I proceed?"

The baffled group stared at him with shocked expressions. The silence was broken by a small chortle that soon grew into a chorus of guffaws.

Fleet made a perturbed grunt. "You stupid fucks. Real Tryst would have shit their pants when they heard that."

"That was an interesting bit of theater, I gotta say." Gary wiped away a tear. "But you'll have to forgive us for keeping our drawers clean."

"No worries." Fleet grabbed the bottle on the table and brought it to his mouth. "Still plenty of time for that."

He tipped the beer back one last time, his face going sour as the liquid touched his tongue. He turned it over and let the last dregs of foam clap to the floor. "I hate when it gets hot."

Without warning, Fleet slammed the bottle on the edge of the table, shattering the bottom half into pieces. In one quick motion, Fleet threw his arm back and jammed the broken neck of the bottle into Lefty's throat, leaving it buried deep in his flesh. He then turned and slammed his palm into the glass, pushing it hard enough that it entered the cavity of the man's esophagus. Lefty fell and clutched at his throat as he struggled to scratch out the shards of glass.

Recovering from his initial surprise, Righty threw a punch that never even got close to landing. Fleet had continued to turn after his last attack and led the momentum into a powerful kick to the back of Righty's leg. As he fell to one knee, Fleet yanked him backward by his collar and stabbed him in his throat with the stolen knife over and over and over.

The other men backed away in fear, deflated by the show of bloody force; one man even tripped over his own feet and fell on his ass. Fleet didn't halt his assault until Righty's body went limp and collapsed like a rag doll.

Fleet whipped the knife around to point at Gary, flinging a trail of blood over half the men. He concocted something clever to say, but once he saw their mortified expressions, he decided words were unnecessary.

Fleet's mouth curled into a deranged smile as a mirthful laugh echoed from his throat.

Not even the pungent odor of the pine body spray had the power to conceal the smell of urine and shit that flooded the room.

Lowy stumbled over the stoop and fell face-first into the gravel, sending her glasses clinking over the rocks. She gave a yelp and flipped on her back as the door slammed shut behind her. She stared up at the blurry entrance, waiting for someone to burst out, but all that followed was the soft clack of the lock.

She wiped the gravel from her throbbing hands before retrieving her glasses and running to Fleet's truck. After getting in the unlocked cab, she slammed the door shut, trying her best not to hyperventilate. She cradled her face in her shaking hands and choked out a sob, still at a loss for what was happening.

To help calm herself, she counted—it was what Fleet had asked her to do anyway, wasn't it?

"O-One. Two. Three." Her breathing stabilized somewhat. "Four. Five."

Before she got to six, there came a tap from the driver-side door that caused her to scream. Without thinking, she slammed her hand down on the lock before turning to see Big Earl standing outside.

"Lowy, what's wrong?" he asked in his baritone voice. "You look real shook up."

Lowy was apprehensive, but the expression of genuine empathy on his face made her question herself.

"What do you want?" she asked in a trembling voice.

Earl pointed to his ear. "I can barely hear you. Roll down the window."

Lowy responded by shaking her head.

Earl put a hand on the glass. "Lowy, whatever's got you, we can work it out."

She caught him glance at the open lock on the passenger side door, prompting her to shoot over and slam it down.

Earl groaned. "It's going to be a lot easier if you just come with me."

That was all she needed to hear. Lowy reached for the ignition, her fingers grazing the empty slot. She began to whimper as her heart dropped to her feet, through the floor mat, and onto the gravel.

Earl held up Fleet's keyring and jingled it. "Gonna be hard to do that without these."

In her haste to escape, she hadn't even realized that she dropped them.

"Please, just let me go," Lowy pleaded.

Earl shook his head. "I can't do that."

Lowy turned the manual crank to lower the window an inch. "You promise you're not going to hurt me?"

"I give you my honest to God word," Earl swore as he crossed his heart with a finger.

"Pinky promise?"

Big Earl smiled and tucked the keys into his palm as he extended a pinky. Lowy ground on the crank until the window had completely lowered before extending her pinky as well. Her hand was trembling as she locked her finger around his.

Earl smiled. "See? Nothing to worry—"

His coddling was interrupted by the awkward clack of his jaw as Lowy used her free hand to throw open the door, ramming the frame into his face. As he tumbled back, she deftly yanked the keys from his open hand and started the engine.

She put the truck in reverse and slammed on the gas—but not before a meaty hand grabbed onto the open window. Lowy screamed as the car shot backward, kicking up a storm of dust while Earl clung to the door. She turned the wheel in desperation, doing doughnuts to break Earl's grip. Despite his size, he was making leeway towards pulling himself up through the window.

There was a loud crash as Lowy rammed into another car, causing her head to whiplash. She switched into drive and hit the gas only a moment too late. Earl reached in and grabbed her by the neck, yanking hard to slam her head into the doorframe. She was so disoriented by the hit that her foot slid off the gas.

"You broke a pinky promise!" he yelled, incensed at her perceived betrayal.

Lowy was in a haze as she stared in the side-view mirror at Earl. His iron grip was crushing down on her head, choking her against the open window as he lifted himself up.

As her vision began to fade, one last plea crossed her mind.

Oreen, BJ, Fleet. Please be okay.

There was a loud bang, and the mirror Lowy watched was splattered by gore. Earl fell out of view, releasing his grip to let Lowy slump back in her seat.

"Lowy!" Denvis shouted as he ran up, noticing the dribble of blood seeping from her wound. "Shit! This is all my fault. I never should have let it get this far."

Lowy raised her head and winced as she poked the tender area. "Uncle Denvis? It's you, right?"

Denvis opened the door, catching Lowy before she fell outward. "Yeah, it's me. Shit, are you all right?"

"I'll be okay," she muttered, checking her hand for blood.

"Can you drive?"

"I think so. But—"

Before she could finish, Denvis threw a wad of keys into her lap. "The big one on there is to their cell. Drive down to the station and let your friends out, then get the hell away from this place."

"My friends?" Lowy poked at the mass of keys. "Denvis, please tell me what's going on!"

"There's no time!" Denvis shouted as he reloaded his revolver. "Just do as I say!"

"No!" Lowy yelled back, causing her head to throb with pain. "Not until—"

"If I don't go now, they're going to kill that boy!"

Lowy fell quiet when confronted by Denvis' pleading gaze; never in her life had she seen him like that. Though she was still frustrated, she nodded her complicity, which Denvis returned in kind.

"Good. Be safe, all right," he said, holding his weapon at the ready.

Denvis started for the building, but he didn't make it far before turning back. He leaned into the cab and wrapped Lowy in a tight hug.

"Love you, Buck."

With that, he took off, leaving Lowy speechless and alone. Her mind was in a stupor as she watched him kick in the door to the bar.

Despite everything else going on, her biggest fear was that she wouldn't get the chance to return his declaration.

Chapter Thirty-Four

SERVUNDAY

Fleet's eyes jumped from person to person as he assessed who was going to make the first move. Two of them were now immobilized, which left him with seven still standing. The assailants all glanced at each other, hoping someone else would take the reins.

"Guess it's on me," Fleet volunteered, making a show as he readied the knife to throw at the man nearest him.

His target crossed his arms over his face and throat in defense, forgetting to cover one other important area. Fleet leaped forward and kicked him hard in the crotch. As the man doubled over, Fleet jammed the knife in the nape of his neck and carved it around to his Adam's apple. A wave of blood hit the floor before his victim followed suit.

Realizing that they had underestimated their captive, the rest tried to converge on him at once. Fleet flung the knife at the nearest assailant, but it was so sticky with blood that it just slapped against his shoulder. Luckily, it was at least enough to make him recoil away with a squeal.

Fleet dodged a couple of punches, back stepping until he hit the pool table. He countered the next swing by grabbing the man's arm and twisting it behind his back, pinning him face-down against the felt. With his free hand, Fleet grabbed a billiard ball—the striped seven—and slammed it into his captive's head like he was planting a tent stake. Each sequential connection with the man's skull was accompanied by an escalating squish.

Fleet turned and threw the bloody ball at the attacker sneaking up from behind, hitting him on the bridge of the nose and sending him to the floor. Fleet grabbed another weapon—eight ball this time—and continued to bludgeon his captive until he was satisfied the man no longer posed a threat.

There was a painful crack against Fleet's back as a pool stick splintered across his spine, sending the upper half of the cue onto the table. Fleet let go of his hold and grabbed the broken end of the stick, brandishing it like a knife. The one who had hit him backed far away, aware of Fleet's intentions.

"Who the fuck is this guy?" the man next to Gary shouted. "You said this would be easy!"

"I know what I fucking said!" Gary shoved the man toward the front door. "Just go get the goddamn guns!"

The man obeyed and ran for the entrance. Just as he undid the lock, he was hurtled to the floor when the door slammed into his face.

Denvis stood in the opening, his gun drawn and pointed at the man he had knocked over. "Move or start trying to ascend and I swear to God that I will shoot you right in the fucking head!"

Fleet raised his hands, confused that everyone else in the room was doing the same. Seizing the opportunity, he vaulted backward over the pool table and took some meager shelter behind it.

"Not you, boy!" Denvis called out to him.

This prompted Fleet to poke his head out and shout, "Whose side are you on?"

"I'm on your side!" Denvis scanned the bodies on the ground. "I think."

"It was self-defense. These assholes were going to kill me, and apparently, I wouldn't be their first." Fleet pointed at the wall of license plates. "Are you in on this? Did you fuck Dash too?"

Denvis looked like he had been called out for adultery while taking his wedding vows. "How did you..."

"God damn it, Denvis!" Fleet cursed. "I appreciate the help. I truly do. But God damn it!"

Denvis crept forward in apprehension, still trying to figure out how to deal with the situation. The man farthest from them saw an opening and made for the door.

"He's getting away!" Fleet shouted.

Denvis already had his revolver trained on the escapee's back, but he did not fire. His hands shook as he watched the man run through the door unimpeded.

He cursed as Fleet called out his failure. "Why didn't you shoot?"

"I know these people! They're good people!" Denvis announced to everyone. "I can't just mow them down!"

Those remaining lowered their hands as Fleet ran over to Denvis, taking the long way to distance himself from his attackers.

Fleet held out his hand. "Give me the gun. I got no problem with it."

The crash of breaking glass caught everyone by surprise. A cinderblock had flown through one window, accompanied shortly after by the recent escapee feeding an automatic rifle through the opening. The man closest dove for it as Denvis fired at him, the bullet hitting the wall.

"Fuck me!" Fleet cursed as he sprinted toward the bar and hurtled himself over the counter.

He was joined by Denvis as a hail of shots erupted above. Glass and alcohol rained down on them as bullets shattered the bottles lined against the wall. The roar of the assault only grew louder as more guns were added to the chorus.

"I'm sorry you got involved!" Denvis shouted over the symphony of gunfire. "You shouldn't have to die like this!"

"You guys really *are* ignorant, huh?" Fleet marveled in disbelief as he reached for something he noticed under the counter: a double-barreled shotgun. Fleet cracked it open to see if it was loaded and snapped it shut. "Watch that side and make sure they don't try to sneak around."

During a brief ceasefire, Fleet tried to peek over the counter, which elicited another volley at his exposed head. He ducked back down just as a shot glass exploded near his face.

"They said that each of those license plates belonged to at least one of them," Fleet said without taking his eyes off his end. "Does that mean there are more killers out there?"

Denvis couldn't bring himself to look toward the wall.

"A lot more."

He then whipped over the bar to fire some suppression shots before returning to cover.

When the next wave of bullets started, there was a loud crack as the large propeller blade that hung above the bar broke free from the wall. It fell straight down, landing short of Fleet—Denvis was not so lucky. He yelped in pain as the heavy blade clanged down on his knee.

"Are you all right?" Fleet asked as he kicked the blade away.

"I'll live," Denvis responded, trying to hide his anguish.

"Wishful thinking," Fleet muttered. "Denvis, can you shift?"

"Shift?"

"Shift! Turn! Beast mode!" Fleet shouted. "You know, morph into a big fucking werewolf!"

Denvis nodded, causing shards of glass to fall from the brim of his hat. "I can ascend, but not without his 'blessing.' Even then, I still pass out for a while after."

"Ascend? Really?" Fleet scoffed at the term. "That's a new one."

"That's what he told us it was called."

Fleet wanted to follow up on this 'he,' but something was off—he had heard Denvis with a bit too much clarity just now.

Fleet poked his head over the counter and saw that all of them were now either writhing in agony or nearing the tail end of a shift. The bastards had been smart enough to stagger their transformations to keep them locked down behind the bar while they finished. Even a blast from his shotgun wouldn't stop them at this point, not to mention that he only had two shells.

Fleet threw the shotgun in Denvis' lap. "They're about to come at us full force."

"That's not good. Those guys are some of the best when it comes to ascending. They won't fall out like I would."

"Fire with fire, sheriff. Stay down here and let me show you how to really 'ascend.'"

Denvis watched in utter shock as Fleet endured the grueling transformation. "You're chosen, too?"

Fleet did not answer as he fought through the searing pain to grab the metal blade that had just assaulted Denvis from above. Once finished, Fleet took a momentary breather before standing up, propeller in hand. He pointed at Denvis as his way of saying 'stay down' before hopping over the counter.

There were four other Tryst left in the room. That number grew to five when another leaped through the broken window. Fleet had fought with only one Tryst yesterday, and it had nearly cost him his life.

This wasn't going to be easy.

But Fleet noticed the surprise on their faces; they hadn't expected to be fighting one of their own. However, it didn't last long. Fellow Tryst or not, they had the numbers, and they knew it. Fanning out in a bid for caution, they encroached on his position.

Fleet stuck the tip of his tongue from the front of his maw as he assessed the situation. *They're nowhere near the same level as Dash. I can tell by the way they move. Still, five is a lot. I'll start off by testing their constitution.*

Fleet sighed like a chainsaw as he licked the side of his face, reciting his personal mnemonic device for engaging the enemy in his mind.

Rabid Doorknobs Incubate Energetic Peanuts.

He was aware of how stupid it was, but that was the very reason he remembered it.

It broke down into:

Reason.

Declaration.

Intimidation.

Example.

Purge.

He had already run the gamut of what he could do as a human, but it might be worth another go in Tryst form now that his attackers were aware of what they faced.

Reasoning with them was out of the question if they were still coming at him after all the damage he had done. Plus, he highly doubted they knew enough sign language to communicate past a middle finger.

Declaration was pointless since he lacked the ability to speak in this form, not to mention sign language didn't really have the same impact as a grandiose speech. Besides, he had already tried his hand at it in human form and was met by a chorus of laughter.

Intimidation it is.

Fleet held out the propeller blade for his attackers to see. The other Tryst stared him down but halted their assault, memories of the impromptu weapons he had attacked them with still fresh in their minds. He then cocked his head and gave a derisive grin, making several of them glance around to see if their friends were as nervous as they were.

With their eyes on him, Fleet gripped the base of the blade and shoved it into the back corner of his mouth, biting into the 'hilt' like a piece of moist taffy. He pulled the blade through his maw from one side to the other between his teeth. Sparks shot from his muzzle, and smoke curled around his head as he sharpened the blade, using his own iron jaw as a makeshift grinder.

When he reached the tip, he jerked his head and yanked the blade from his mouth, tearing the flesh away from the side of his face. Fleet leaned his head to the side and ran his tongue along his teeth, sticking it out through the gash before the wound could heal.

Fleet studied his orally crafted weapon with a pursed mouth as he ran a thumb along the serrated edge. The metal ripped into him, leaving behind a substantial cut that faded in seconds. Two long puffs of smoke streamed from his nostrils like a menacing dragon as he turned a sadistic smile toward his prey.

Even with those monstrous forms, their fear was palpable. Two were backing away, but the others were frozen in place, their eyes wide with fright.

However, none of them gave the immediate impression they wanted to surrender—at least that's what Fleet told himself. In reality, it was just an excuse for what he was about to do. The truth of that wall still plagued him, and his rage was only exacerbated in beast form.

Their punishment would be just, this was beyond scrutiny, but admit it or not, all he wanted right now was for them to feel the same pain they had inflicted on so many others.

The thought made his smile grow even more deranged.

The Tryst closest to him had fallen onto its ass, its legs fumbling to escape as it tried to scoot backward. He couldn't tell which man this had been, but it didn't matter for what he had planned.

Sucks for you, but someone needs to be the example.

Fleet charged forward and slashed at the downed Tryst, taking off half of its neck. Before it healed, he kicked forward and jammed his foot into the wound, locking it underneath the Tryst's jaw. He then cut a backflip that severed the spine and sent its head spiraling into the ceiling with a wet smack, creating a crimson splash on impact. As it fell back down, Fleet stuck his blade in the back of the head and through the open mouth to hold it aloft for them to see.

The others screamed in abject horror at the macabre puppet he had created.

I hate to say it, but it works. All you have to do is break them mentally. They don't deserve it, but I might let them live if they surrender.

Fleet twisted the blade back as he viewed the impaled head face to face.

That was too easy. Their bones are so brittle compared to mine. It took nothing to pop his head off. They're new to this, but still better than most.

Done with it, Fleet flicked his blade and sent the head rolling across the floor, causing them all to recoil—except for one who started crying. He gave them a solid once-over now that they were no longer a threat. All of them were different colors and patterns save for one defining feature: the prominent white diamond that emblazoned their chest.

I was right. This is Dash's doing. She spread her disease, and it led to whatever the fuck is going on here. And this isn't even all of them. Fuck knows how many more there are out there. I need to end this now and call for backup. Vuota can't say no to this one.

Fleet tapped his makeshift sword on the floor to get their attention. When all eyes were on him, he held out his hand flat at eye level and lowered it, a sort of nonverbal instruction on how to surrender. The last four Tryst took note as they lay down on their stomachs, a couple even going the extra mile and putting hands behind their heads.

But they all stopped when an odd sound broke through the tense silence.

Instead of lying flat, one had taken to his knees and clasped his fingers together in prayer as he mumbled to himself. He then stopped, blew a raspberry through his sharp teeth, and smacked himself on the forehead. A chain began as those who had obeyed prior now rose one after another and repeated the incantation.

This time it was Fleet who was taken aback. He watched as the broken Tryst before him renewed their vigor all at once. Even the one who had cried now looked as if the only thing on his mind was blood.

Wait, I've seen that before! That same stupid thing!

Before he could ponder it further, all four were upon him. Fleet was forced to back step as he swung his sword at any appendage that got too close.

One broke through his guard and ripped a chunk of flesh from his chest, but Fleet countered with a slice that sent his attacker's severed arm spiraling into the air. He slashed the wounded Tryst's neck as it clutched its stump and grabbed its muzzle from underneath. With a yell, Fleet pushed the attacker's head backward and down with such ferocity that over a foot of its spine ripped from its body. The Tryst fell to its knees with head dangling against its back, caught in a hoodie of its own skin.

A Tryst tackled Fleet and was soon joined by another before he could wrench himself free. The couple pinned him back against the bar as Fleet swung his weapon about wildly, destroying a portion of the counter and cutting down two of the stools. Fleet had to drop his weapon from a combination of frustration and necessity.

The last free Tryst ran forward, his fangs bared as it made a swipe at Fleet's head. Before the hit made contact, there was a loud blast as its face exploded, sending it to the floor.

From behind the bar, Denvis switched targets, bringing the shotgun barrel to rest on the temple of the closest Tryst. The blast took the beast down as chunks of flesh sprayed in the air.

Fleet overpowered the last attacker by sticking his thumb in its eye—it was nice not to be on the receiving end this time. As the creature wailed with pain, Fleet tossed him over his hip and onto the ground where the jagged metal stand left by the stool jammed into its ear canal. The Tryst screamed as it struggled to push itself off the spike, unable to break away from Fleet's grip.

With his finger still lodged in its socket, Fleet pushed down with all his might, forcing the metal pole through the Tryst's skull. The monster sputtered blood from every orifice of its head as he pushed the beast's face to the floor, skewering the palm of his own hand in the process.

A pair of claws dug into Fleet's shoulder and yanked him backward, bringing with him the metal pipe still stuck through his hand as it snapped off at the base. Fleet dropped to his knees, sacrificing his flesh to those razor-like claws as he spun about and slapped the Tryst, stabbing that metal pole through its jaw. Several of its teeth were sent flying as the pipe perforated the opposite side of its face. Fleet grabbed the other end of the pipe and twisted it, snapping the Tryst's neck until its head made a complete one-eighty.

As his last attacker fell, Fleet collapsed over the bar to catch his breath.

Denvis backed away, still unsure of what he had been company to. "You okay, boy?"

Fleet panted from exhaustion, but his eyes drifted up to Denvis as he forced a meager thumbs-up. Before he finished his gesture, a pair of teeth sank down into his neck, sending a spray of blood over the sheriff.

Fleet cried out as he dug his claws into his attacker, trying anything to break the assault. The attacking Tryst wasn't even healed—its exploded eye looking like it belonged more to a fish than a beast—but it did nothing to deter its ferocity.

Denvis grabbed his revolver and jammed it square in the Tryst's eye socket and un-loaded three shots into its skull. Fleet wrestled the beast's jaws from his neck as it fell limp, taking a little extra time to stomp its head into a wet pulp before he collapsed next to it.

His once snow-white fur was now soaked red; nary a spot of him remained untaint-ed—by whose blood it was impossible to tell. Fleet clamped a hand over his throat as he waited for the wound to heal. It was taking much longer to mend than normal because of his compounded exhaustion from the recent fight with Dash.

No longer able to feel the warmth of blood flowing from his throat, he decided it was best to shift and conserve what energy he had left. The transformation back was no less painful than the initial shift, but at least he confirmed that all his injuries were now gone.

"Denvis!" Fleet called to him from the floor. "Give me your phone!"

Denvis was surprised by this sudden demand as he stared wide-eyed at Fleet splayed out amongst the large hairy corpses. "I-I left it in my squad car."

"I need to call for backup!" Fleet wheezed before coughing up some blood. "Any phone! Please!"

Denvis did a quick search behind the bar for an alternative, but all he found were the remains of a landline that had been destroyed in the firefight. "Let's get to the car and you can call on the drive out."

Denvis hobbled from cover over to Fleet, helping him up and supporting him with his shoulder.

As they trudged toward the exit, Denvis addressed the surrounding carnage in a somber tone. "They're all dead. People I grew up with. Went to church with. Saw them marry. Now they're just..."

"If it makes you feel better, there's a chance they might still live if help comes quick enough," Fleet rasped. He caught a glance of the headless Tryst on the floor. "Not him, though. Probably not those two guys, either. And maybe not... How about we get me to that phone?"

When they stepped through the busted door and out into the fresh air, there was a loud and prolonged series of *blats* as puffs of smoke erupted from the building walls. A white-hot pain burned in Fleet's side as he slipped to the ground, clutching his abdomen where blood surged from between his fingers. Denvis joined him soon after, clutching at a bullet wound in his thigh.

Earl stood before them, automatic rifle in hand and a hole in his cheek so large that his molars were visible. He made to say something, but the words came out as an inaudible garble.

With an annoyed grunt, he closed his hand over the hole and rasped, "Hank in fer, bubby. No dine. Nosh yek."

———————————————

"Oreen! BJ! Are you in here?" Lowy called out as she entered the station.

Oreen shot up from the bed and ran over to the bars. "Lowy? Lowy, I'm over here!" He gasped when he noticed Lowy's head wound. "Oh my God! Are you okay? What happened?"

BJ was splayed out on the bed, the springs struggling to support his weight. At Oreen's exclamation, he awoke from his nap, worry creasing his face when he saw her injury.

She ran up to the cell door and fumbled with the keyring Denvis had given her. "It's nothing."

"Don't you tell me it's nothing!" Oreen clapped back. "Was it Fleet? Did he do this to you?"

Lowy stopped fiddling with the keys when she heard Fleet's name. "Please be okay."

"Yeah, we're fine," Oreen replied, misunderstanding her concern. "But don't change the subject."

Lowy found the cell key after some trial and error, then set the two of them free. Oreen ran up and hugged her before pulling back to inspect her injury. BJ rolled from the cot with a grunt as the springs groaned with relief.

Lowy grabbed Oreen's hand and pulled him to the entrance. "Come on!"

When he did not comply fast enough, she dashed from the station, leaving the two with no choice but to follow.

"Wait, is that his?" Oreen asked when he joined her outside and saw her mode of transport. "Why do you have his truck?"

"Just get in, we'll talk on the way!" Lowy responded as she hopped behind the wheel.

Oreen threw up his hands, but did as instructed. BJ got in the cab after him, his wide frame forcing Oreen to scoot up next to Lowy.

"Okay, now you can talk," Oreen said. "Then tell me what happened to your head? Why do you have this car? Why did you have the keys to the cell? How did you know where we were?"

Lowy grimaced against his barrage of inquiries. How much should she tell him? Fleet and Curtis were trusting her to keep their secret, but that was under different circumstances. Perhaps it was best to subvert the conversation, at least for now.

"Denvis told me," she explained, shrouding a portion of the truth. "He gave me the keys and told me to come let you out."

"Don't you trust that fucking pig!" Oreen shouted.

His outburst reminded her of something. "What happened to you guys? Last I saw, Denvis chased you off at the school."

As if he had been rehearsing the entire tale, Oreen recounted the events that led up to his second incarceration in less than two days. "Oh my God, Lowy! I was sure I was going to die! You remember when the pig kicked us out of the school bonfire, right? Well, he watched us the whole time as we got in our car and left. Super creepy, but whatever."

Oreen held up his hands as if he were a director setting a scene.

"We headed back to the motel to wait it out, but then we see a car in the middle of the road with a young lady waving at us in distress. Of course, the good Samaritan over here just had to stop and help."

BJ nodded. "They got me good."

"It's okay. Your kind heart is one of the many things I love about you," Oreen cooed and gave BJ a soft pinch on the arm.

He returned his attention to Lowy and continued. "Anyway, they went all *The Hills Have Eyes* on us and started emerging from the woods. They held us up at gunpoint and forced us out of the car."

BJ nodded. "I was mortified."

Oreen gave BJ another gentle pinch. "Poor baby. Anyway, just as I was sure we were about to get 'Deliverenced,' your sheriff pulls up, blue lights all flashing. We're saved, right? Wrong. He pulls out his gun and throws us into his cruiser, saying that 'he needs us alive for the ritual' or some weird shit. Then he lets them take our car and our phones. They even threatened to kill BJ if I didn't give them my passcode. Next thing I know, I'm back in that damn cell."

"That explains the texts," Lowy remarked to herself.

"Speaking of phones, let me see yours," Oreen demanded, holding out his hand.

"W-why do you need my phone?" Lowy stuttered.

"To call nine-one-one, or the FBI, or the army—somebody!" Oreen shouted, appalled at Lowy's lack of urgency.

"You can't!" Lowy screamed, eliciting a small jump from Oreen.

"Why the hell not?"

"You...you just can't," she said, realizing how hard it was to justify.

If someone did come to help, it risks exposing Fleet, but is that worse than letting him die? Even if we did get someone here, what could they even do? They would get torn to shreds if what Curtis told me was true. Wait, that's it!

"We have to get Curtis!" Lowy shouted. "He's waiting back at the motel! He'll know what to do!"

Oreen somehow reached an even higher level of stupefaction. "Curtis? Why him?"

Unable to contain herself any longer, Lowy sank her nails into the steering wheel and spilled her guts with nary a pause between words. "Curtis and Fleet are in a secret society where everyone is a werewolf and now everyone else is a werewolf too and they're going to kill Fleet if we don't do something!"

BJ raised an eyebrow at her swift confession, while Oreen blinked like he had just heard the world's lamest dad joke.

"See, was that so hard?" Oreen said, his words dripping with sarcasm.

Lowy's eyes darted between the road and him. "You believe me?"

"Is that a rhetorical question?" Oreen put a hand on her shoulder. "Now, how about you pull over, okay? I don't think you should be driving in your condition."

"I know what you're thinking, and I don't have a concussion!" She softened her tone after an exasperated sigh. "All I'm asking is that you trust me. Please."

He made to protest but was swayed when he saw the pleading sincerity in Lowy's eyes. He then looked at BJ and received a shrug in response.

Oreen acquiesced with a huff. "All right, let's go back. But after that, I'm calling the shots."

Lowy exhaled in appreciation. "Thank you. You'll get answers later, I promise."

Oreen leaned against BJ, resigning himself to Lowy's temporary command. She turned her focus back to the road, but she couldn't control her worry. The more she thought about Fleet, the harder her foot pressed down on the pedal.

"Fleet, please hold on..."

Chapter Thirty-Five

ZEALOTS

"WAS THE SOCK NECESSARY?" maligned a familiar voice. "He will know where he is the moment it comes off. Earl, your thought process is a mystery even to me. Well, come on, let us not leave him waiting."

Fleet could tell that he was seated in a hardwood chair and that his wrists were bound in front of him with what must have been duct tape, but the rest of his body seemed to be free. However, with each testing movement he made, his gunshot wound burned in agony. His arm glanced over the injury and he realized duct tape had been wrapped around his waist to seal it off.

Fleet winced as the wool sock that served as a makeshift blindfold was yanked from his head.

Staring down at him was a familiar face sporting a placid grin. "How are you, son? In good spirits, I hope?"

They were in a large room with high ceilings and tall mullion windows to match. The carpet was some gaudy flavor of green that had long since begun to rot. Through a small crack in the window, Fleet saw the smoldering remains of the school, a telling sign of his confinement within the old church next door.

Though what stood out to him most were the symbols spray-painted across every inch of the dingy white walls—they were the same as the one he had found carved into that tree.

Before he could assess any further, his captor tapped his forehead as he scolded, "Listen. When. Father. Speaks!"

Fleet jerked his head away to avoid the final tap. "Who are you again?"

Though his memories of that night were still hazy, he recognized the man who had accosted him, who had toyed with him, who had made him want to kill.

Peter.

"Twice you wound me; a third and I fear I shall not recover," Peter lamented as he held a hand to his heart.

Behind him, there seemed to be a chorus of disapproving murmurs that erupted at his words. Fleet craned his head to see around Peter, his mouth falling agape. Behind the man were rows and rows of pews filled with people, all of whom were enamored by the spectacle presented before them.

Peter turned to look back at them. "I see you have noticed my congregation. Quite the pack I have amassed in this town."

"It's them." Fleet's pinky twitched. "They're the ones that…"

His words fell soft. In his mind, all Fleet visualized were images of that wall and all the wasted lives it represented. Now here the killers sat, smiles on their faces with hands stained by the blood of their nameless victims—but in truth, he did have one name.

"They're the ones that killed Eddy."

Peter squinted one eye at him. "Eddy?"

A shrill voice erupted from a pew in the front row. "Eddy, remember?" Viv shot to her feet, bursting with pride. "He was the out-of-towner that wore that stupid purple windbreaker. Told him I'd give him a handy if he went to the motel with me."

"That does spark something," Peter said, crossing his arms. "Edward was the very first one if memory serves. That was months ago. Goodness, how time flies."

"Ol' Viv never forgets," she boasted, her sick smile growing as she looked down at her hands. "Split him in two for our Lord. Then I ate him. Took in every last bit."

Her mad glare softened a bit as she remembered something.

"Couldn't digest the zipper, though. Really tore up my asshole on the way out."

"Thank you, Viv," Peter said with a cringe, holding up a hand to silence her. "The pinnacle of sophistication, that one. She was the first, however every person you see here has done their part to honor our Lord—except for one."

Peter raised a finger to point behind Fleet's left. Fleet turned and was greeted by a burning pain that burst from the wound in his side. He changed his tactic and used his feet to rotate his body to avoid disturbing his injury.

"Denvis! Are you all right?" Fleet shouted when he saw his fellow captive.

About fifteen feet away, the sheriff sat in a chair with his arms and legs bound, blood still oozing from his thigh. Denvis nodded like a man who had accepted his fate as he stood before the gallows.

Peter walked forward and blocked Fleet's line of view. "The sheriff committed a rather heinous act of blasphemy. Not only did he neglect his spiritual duties, he allowed not one, but *two* lambs to escape."

"Two lambs?" Fleet repeated before looking up at Peter. "He was supposed to kill Oreen and BJ."

"Just one, actually," Peter corrected. "But that is even worse. In letting them both go, not only did he reject ascension, but he also ripped it away from another!"

A chorus of boos and hisses erupted from the congregation; some even threw moldy hymnals and debris at the cowering Denvis.

"Yet, behold!" Peter bellowed, holding his hands aloft. "Our Lord, in his infinite forgiveness, has returned those lambs to us. Is this not a sign of his love and mercy? If you had any doubts, they have been crushed under the weight of his grace! Brothers and sisters, we are the chosen ones!"

The raucous crowd gave a collective *pbbbfft* before a collection of mistimed slaps as they hit their foreheads.

In that moment, Fleet could have sworn he heard Peter snort.

"Now it is our turn to show our love!" Peter continued to proselytize. "We have been given these three sinners, and it is our duty to condemn their heresy and end this affront to our Lord!"

Peter caught him mouthing the word 'three' and pointed over Fleet's shoulder to the right. Once again, Fleet forgot his situation and turned, causing himself to double over in pain. Peter sighed and rolled his eyes as he tipped Fleet's chair backward, dragging him along for several feet before dropping him down hard. With a flourish of his hand, Peter stepped aside to watch his reaction with a smile.

Fleet cursed in defeat when he saw Curtis bound and gagged with duct tape to his left. Now it was not only Fleet's life on the line, but those of Curtis and Denvis as well.

Wait a second! Fleet thought with a flicker of hope. *He said 'three.' Sea might still be out there. He could be going for help!*

Fleet tapped his foot to get Curtis' attention, then wrote the letter 'C' in the moldy carpet with his big toe. Curtis almost burst into tears as he shook his head in regret.

Fleet grit his teeth and looked down at the floor. He didn't need any further confirmation; Curtis' condition and overall despair told him everything: there was no help, no backup, no last-minute rescue.

They were all alone.

"Is this revenge?" Fleet asked, without looking at his captor.

Peter leaned in close. "Revenge?"

"For what we did to Dash and Jill?"

Peter crossed his arms and stood upright. "Dash and Jill?" he pondered to himself. He then broke into a quick laugh and waved his hand. "Oh, those two. No, this has nothing to do with them."

"Bullshit! I saw it on the Tryst I fought at the bar. Every one of them had Dash's crest. I'm not sure where it started, but I sure as hell know how it spread."

Fleet leaned back and spoke as loud as he was able.

"I'm here to tell you that you're not God's chosen—you're a disease! You can shift because you had sex with Dash! That's how you 'ascended,' even if you don't realize it! To the married women here: you got it from your husbands because they cheated on you!"

Peter looked aghast at Fleet's exclamation. "How dare you slander my congregation with your lies! I demand you promptly cease with these preposterous insinuations post-haste!"

The congregation shouted in agreement, but it was impossible to miss the crowd's shifty eyes. Calls for the blood of the deceivers followed not long after, an easy scapegoat for the guilty.

Peter lurched forward and clamped his hands around Fleet's face. "You spit in the face of the divine! I have been charged with delivering these people to their birthright! Your blasphemy is an affront that can only be repaid in blood!"

Fleet could only gape through scrunched eyelids at the twisted face before him. Is there anything to be done when confronted with such unrelenting madness? In the end, Fleet settled on the first desperate and idiotic thing that popped into his head.

He stuck out his tongue and blew a wet raspberry into Peter's face.

The congregation followed suit with a raspberry of their own and slapped their foreheads, an abridged form of the prayer he had witnessed at the school fire.

Peter's face softened as he let out an inadvertent snort. Catching on, Fleet blew another raspberry, which caused a repeat performance from the congregation. Peter's once fierce snarl had now shifted into a taut grin, tears forming in the corners of his eyes as he choked back laughter.

Fleet made to do it again, but Peter beat him to it. Unable to contain himself, Peter released his grip as he doubled over with laughter. Holding his sides, he did it once more, though he struggled to make the sound through his wheezing breaths.

"Wait, wait!" Peter choked, tears of laughter streaking down his red face. "This is only a taste. Watch. Watch." Peter turned to the congregation and held his arms wide. "I feel it! The Lord wishes to hear our praises. Let us perform our liturgy so that he may be slated!"

At his command, the entire congregation began a synchronous yet ill-composed dance routine. There were bits of river dance, pop-n-lock, and any assortment of inscrutable motions accompanied by shouts of vulgarity and gibberish.

In the midst of it all, Peter had taken to all fours, unable to control himself. He fell over onto his side, his laughter reaching a point where it only crept out as a wispy croak.

The hollers and off-kilter dancing of the congregation caused the foundation to shake as slabs of wood and molding fell from the ceiling, yet anyone hit by them did not falter as they maintained their nonsensical routine.

Their choreography lasted over three minutes—it would have been impressive if it wasn't so absurd. Their heavy breaths filled the building as they finished by slapping themselves on the forehead.

Peter choked back his laughter to speak. "I have wanted to show that to someone else for so long! And look! Look!" Peter rolled over onto his back and waved his arms around like a madman. "What is it! What do you see!"

Fleet assumed he meant the symbols emblazoned on the walls of the church. He craned his neck about, his mind unable to manifest a tangible guess.

Peter had crumpled up again, slapping the floor as he rocked back and forth. He choked out a few words that were muddied with laughter before he could say something meaningful. "It's our symbol, a manifestation of all we are! The Christians have their Cross, the Jewish their Star of David, and we have this!"

Peter's fits continued growing more fierce.

"O-okay?" Fleet stammered.

Peter rolled over and grabbed Fleet's ankle, shaking it as he laughed. "I told them it was the crater God lived in on the dark side of the moon! A stroke of brilliance if you consider the werewolf motif!" More uncontrollable laughter as he shook his head. "What is it! What does it look like!"

Fleet attempted to say something, but no words came out; the absurdity of the situation had washed him of all rational thought.

"Say it!" Peter demanded, his grip becoming so tight on Fleet's ankle that his bones cracked.

With a cry of desperation, Fleet said the first thing that came to his mind.

"It looks like a fucking butthole!"

Peter rolled around again as he nodded, tears of joy streaming down his face. "Yes! Yes! Exactly! Can you imagine it?"

Peter pushed himself up on his knees and prostrated himself before an imaginary god.

"You find yourself in your darkest hour, saying your prayers: *'Dear Lord, please hear the words of this wretched soul.'*"

He pantomimed along with his insane diatribe, making a shrill voice every time the imaginary believer talked to the Lord.

"The clouds part as a celestial beam of light shines down upon you. Here it is! Here is your Lord savior come to answer your prayers! Two pillowy mounds surge from the clouds cupped by firm hands!"

"What bounty is this that you present me, my Lord? Speak, so that I may understand!"

Peter's composure was crumbling, but he forged onward.

"You can taste his glory as the hands pull apart, slowly opening the gates to heaven. Angels descend from between the heavenly orbs, blowing trumpets of exaltation!"

He changed position and crouched down, holding up his hands in mock reverence.

"You have deemed me worthy to gaze upon thee! Speak, O Lord, speak!"

Peter jumped up, waving his arms about as if conjuring a storm.

"There is a flash of light as the hands finish their traversal, protracting the two glorious moons. You are blinded! But you press on, for you will not waste this gift! Your eyes adjust! Gaze forth at the wonder before you!"

Peter had to stop and wipe his nose.

"And there it is, the holy pie crust staring you down like a squinting cyclops, set above two juicy danglers swaying in the breeze! If you want him to hear, you need to speak into the mouthpiece! Look out, he's coming in for a kiss!"

Peter blew a raspberry and smacked himself on the forehead. The congregation followed suit, but with far less enthusiasm as they shared looks of abject confusion.

Fleet was shaking, not from fear of pain or death, but from his complete inability to comprehend what just happened. "Is this a joke?"

Peter pulled himself up with great strain and trained his puffy eyes on Fleet. "I agree. Seeing your own reflection is a hollow joke, but understanding it can be liberating. Being able to laugh at yourself is a gift few will ever enjoy. I wonder if you are the same?"

"You're fucking insane!" Fleet spat, clamping his duct-taped hands on his wound from the exertion.

His insult had no effect on Peter as he continued. "To answer your question: No. This is not a joke. This is an experiment—or perhaps an exercise, considering I already knew the outcome."

Fleet grit his teeth at him. "All those people? You killed them for an experiment?"

"Exercise, boy. Listen," Peter corrected, his laughter finally under control. "I knew the results before I began, but that is not to say I did not learn something along the way."

Peter paced about as he pontificated.

"I wanted to see how easy it was to have someone worship me. Give everything to me. Not some teenager with a barren mind, or some lost soul at the end of their rope. No. I needed those who once considered murder to be an abhorrent concept to now willfully take life at my behest."

"You manipulated these people," Fleet reasoned. "You tricked them into—"

"Tricked?" Peter interjected with a scowl. "A magician with their legerdemain is a trick. A mongrel balancing a treat on his snout..."

He flicked Fleet on the end of his nose.

"...is a trick."

Peter stopped and held out his hands like a maestro conducting his orchestra.

"But perhaps you are right. So, let me show you my favorite *trick*."

Peter called out the name without turning around.

"Earl!"

Behind him, Earl stood up and waited for his orders. Peter waved him over without a word, and Earl shuffled through the crowd in obedience to be at his side. Earl came up to Fleet and stood over him like he was a fresh kill, ready to be devoured.

Fleet braced himself for something horrible, aware of the irony that Earl's lack of skill in taxidermy would translate quite well into the field of torture. Instead, Peter cocked his head and narrowed his eyes at Earl's face.

As with Fleet's wound, Earl had used duct tape to cover the gaping hole in his cheek that Denvis had given him. With no warning, Peter ripped the duct tape off, causing Earl to seethe in pain.

Peter tossed away the bloody tape and snarled. "Earl, I am disappointed in you. If there is one thing our Lord hates, it is..." Peter increased the cadence of his last word as he turned toward the congregation with a flourish, prompting them to answer.

In unison, they all cried out the same response.

"DOUBT!"

"That is one, true, but it is not the worst thing, my children," Peter corrected in a tone reminiscent of a teacher scolding his class.

Everyone looked at someone else, confused that they had somehow given the wrong answer.

"Very good." Peter pretended to hear the correct response. "The answer is: asymmetry."

There was a mumbled consensus from the congregation despite the sudden—and ridiculous—change to their 'holy' doctrine. More than a few became self-conscious as they put their hands together to see if all their fingers were the same length.

"Good, you still have the gun," Peter said, looking at Denvis' confiscated revolver in Earl's pocket. "Earl, in order to assuage our Lord, what I need you to do is take that revolver—and even out your face."

Fleet let out a raspy guffaw. "Are you serious right now? Do you really think—"

Before Fleet could finish his criticism, Earl grabbed the pistol, stuck the barrel through the hole in his cheek, and pulled the trigger. There was a brief mist of blood as the bullet erupted from his face and hit the wall with a loud pat. Earl fell to his knees and covered his mouth as blood seeped in between his fingers from a flap of skin that drooped from his jaw.

All sound vanished save for Earl's screams of pain and Curtis' whimpering.

Peter cackled as he studied Fleet's mortified expression. "Quite the 'trick,' is it not?"

Fleet had no words. All he could do was watch Earl as he writhed in anguish.

Perturbed by his lack of response, Peter continued. "Not impressed? Understandable. However, I do believe it is premature to render judgment before you have seen the finale."

"Don't..." Fleet pleaded, his words falling short.

Peter kneeled and lifted Earl's head by the chin to stare into his tearful eyes. "Earl, you are my most loyal deacon and friend. I am sorry that I caused you such pain. I have only done this because I love you. And with that love, I bestow upon you the greatest honor of all: I want you to be the first. You will be there to greet us at the cusp of eternity with open arms."

"Don't listen to him!" Fleet screamed in between coughs. "He's a manipulative fucking liar!"

Peter picked the gun from the floor and put it back in Earl's hand.

"Biggun, come on. Think about this!" Fleet said, trying to get through to him. "Do you realize what he is asking you to do?"

Peter guided the pistol and positioned it so the tip of the barrel was underneath Earl's jaw. Peter released his grip and took a few steps back to gaze upon his trembling disciple.

Earl's forehead glistened with sweat that diluted the blood as it collected on his chin. He looked to Peter for consolation with wide, red-rimmed eyes. What felt like hours passed as the tension grew in anticipation of what would happen next.

Sensing Earl's hesitation, Fleet made one last attempt to dissuade him. "We can go to that place you told me about! Yeah, the best barbecue ever! Just thinking about it is making my mouth water! Come on, please! Earl, for God's sake, would you—"

It was in that moment that Fleet saw the determination on his face.

"No!"

Earl gritted his teeth and clenched his eyes shut as he pulled the trigger. There was a muted pop as the bullet tore through his flesh and into his brain. Earl's body collapsed to the ground as everyone in the audience gasped.

Peter clapped his hands. "Amazing. Truly amazing."

Soon, the entire congregation rose to their feet and applauded so loud that Fleet's screams were drowned out by the deafening roar. Peter turned to face the crowd and gave them a genial bow, akin to an actor at the end of a Broadway show.

"You fucking piece of shit!" Fleet spat with hatred through clenched teeth. "You sick fuck!" Fleet's insults only escalated as he threw every curse and combination thereof at Peter's back.

"Must you tarnish my prestige with such vulgarities?" Peter lamented. "All you have done is insult my character and method throughout the entire set. Is your vitriol simply the result of a bruised ego fraught with jealousy, or do you truly believe your own slander?"

Fleet snarled at the man. "Every damn word."

"Is that so? Then allow me a counterpoint." Peter stepped on Earl's lifeless body and swept a hand over the room. "Could a lying, callous, manipulative, egomaniacal, depraved, and greedy cretin such as myself become a leader of men?"

"Clearly," Fleet growled back.

In an instant, Peter grabbed Fleet by the neck and lifted him into the air. Fleet kicked at him as Peter barked in a maniacal and frenzied voice, "It's infuriating! Self-awareness is within your grasp, and yet you still cling to ignorance! Must everyone be so fucking blind?"

Fleet collapsed back into the chair as Peter released his grip. It was impossible to decide which hurt more: his bullet wound or his crushed throat.

Peter sighed as he buried his head in his hands. "How disappointing, but I should have expected nothing different."

After a deep breath, he dropped the cover on his face with the flick of his wrists.

"And thus, I have taken this as far as I care to go. However, there is one last thing that continues to irk me."

Peter pointed to Viv in the front row. "Viv, my sweet, would you please turn for me?"

Viv looked a bit confused but rotated in place as ordered, stepping softly as if she were afraid of doing it wrong.

Peter let out an exasperated groan and poked himself in the eye. "I brought this on myself." He then held out his hands in frustration. "No, damn it. I mean 'ascend,' Viv, 'ascend.' Just become a bloody monster for all sake."

With the clarification, Viv shifted into lupine form as the crowd backed away to give her room. While she turned, tears streamed from Curtis' eyes as he screamed into his duct tape once her fur pattern became visible: black head, brown torso, white feet.

Without provocation, Peter pontificated once more. "I had to build my congregation, but where to start? Violence and force were out of the question, of course. I needed them to trust me, after all. That was the whole point. I could not go around giving out blood transfusions, either. So, what options are left to me when you take those away?"

Peter smiled as he turned back to Fleet.

"Only the oldest and most primal motivator known to man..."

Peter finished as Viv completed her transformation. She struggled on her knees as she caught her breath, a clear sign she was unused to the strain. However, just being able to endure the entire process while conscious proved she far outclassed most Tryst.

Once she recovered, Viv stepped forward and bent over to put her massive head on Peter's shoulder, wrapping her arm around his body to rub his chest with her enormous hand.

"Viv was my very first," Peter said as he stroked her face. "Her infidelity came easy—perhaps too easy, really. I do not mind a woman making the first move, but my goodness."

Viv grinned as she let her tongue slide over her teeth and onto Peter's cheek.

"Then I waited. When she hit the initial stages of the acceptance, I would be the first one there, offering guidance, a helping hand, but most importantly, answers."

Looking at Viv, she lacked the white diamond like all the other Tryst Fleet had come across, meaning that she was no spawn of Dash's. This also confirmed that Peter was a Tryst of the lupine variety, same as him. Though he tried, Fleet was having a hard time picking out a possible crest on Viv that he could use to identify Peter.

Peter pat Viv on the hand to signal his release. "I pulled some nonsense from the air about my religion and ran with it. The whole thing is incredibly moronic, so I refuse to bore you with the details, but I am rather proud of the choreography you saw earlier."

Peter turned back and smiled at the congregation.

"Anyhow, it was easy to make her believe that schlock. Interesting how simple it is to fill a void with even the flimsiest glimmer of hope and semblance. But to be fair, it is not often you are confronted by something that simultaneously spits in the face of both science and religion."

Peter squatted next to Fleet as he continued.

"Now that she had the 'Fear of God' in her, it was time for a test run. That was when we met—Edward, was it?—and we performed our first 'sacrifice.' Everything went absolutely perfect. I could not have asked for a better result. I was so proud of her."

Viv squirmed in delight at Peter's compliment.

"Then she decided to kill her husband, which I was less than thrilled with."

Viv shrank like a scolded child as she dug her toe into the rug, drilling her nail into the floor.

Peter shrugged. "But she took care of the body, and nobody seemed to miss him. No harm done."

Viv put a hand on her chest and exhaled in relief.

Peter stood back up and began to pace. "Now, here is where I hit a spot of trouble. Turns out it was harder to seduce these people than I had anticipated. This was a very religious community, and the women tended to be loyal to their men, while the men looked unfavorably on sleeping with me—regardless of my good looks. I then set Viv about it, to no avail."

Peter leaned down and whispered, "In all honesty, she can be a bit...abrasive."

Viv made a mirthful chuckle as he coughed into his hand and righted himself.

"It was at this point that I decided perhaps it was best to cut my losses and move on. Then something serendipitous occurred."

He gave Fleet a crooked grin.

"That is when she showed up. Dash, I believe you called her."

"I knew she was involved in all this," Fleet wheezed.

Peter stuck up his nose and gave a half-shrug. "About as much as the sow is involved with the butcher. You see, she came to me seeking sanctuary for both herself and one other... What was her name again?"

Fleet said it aloud for him. "Jill..."

"That was it. So, being the tenable fellow that I am, I agreed to help—on one condition: she had to do something for me."

Peter took a furtive glance back at the congregation before giving Fleet a knowing smile.

"Beautiful girl that Dash. Even the most pious man would struggle against her wiles. Do you agree, sheriff?"

Denvis continued to stare down at his lap, the shame from Peter's rhetorical question lowering his head even further than it already was.

Peter returned to Fleet and rested his hand on the chair's back. "And so it spread. Many started with her before it traveled from person to person through one means or another. As they were 'reborn,' I was there. Those who listened to my gospel were welcomed into the flock, and those who did not became victims of their once trusted friends and neighbors. From there, they started picking off tourists and wanderers who drove through town to ensure that everyone got to taste at least one."

He gave Fleet a calculated grin.

"And none of it would have been possible without young Harlow."

Fleet's horrified expression gave Peter no end of amusement, but before Fleet could question him, Peter burst out in laughter.

"That face!" Peter doubled over, holding his sides as he waved away Fleet's notions. "No, no. Delightful as that twist would have been, she was only a means to an end, never the wiser. It was her mere existence that facilitated my experiment."

"She would never help you!"

"What did I just say?" Peter groaned, putting a hand to his face. "Why does no one ever listen?"

He walked forward and tapped Fleet on the forehead with enough force to send the chair onto its back legs, leading Peter to right it with his foot.

"Think about it. A livable structure, miles from civilization, devoid of cellular service—how could I ask for more?"

Fleet winced hard from the pain in his forehead but still asked, "You mean the motel?"

"Of course I mean the—" Peter brought a hand to his face again, digging nails into his forehead. He then moved his hands away from his body, like he was pushing out the negative emotions. "Yes, the motel. It would house my 'catalyst' and befit her a place to keep accordance with her ward while still fulfilling her duties to me. The desolate nature of the dwelling also served as an excellent place to procure the 'sacrifices.'"

Peter sifted through the debris on the floor until he retrieved a long metal nail.

"I would camouflage myself in the woods nearby and flatten a tire or two as some poor soul drove by."

To demonstrate, Peter flicked his wrist and sent the nail flying like a bullet at Fleet's feet. It struck the chair's leg, splintering it and sending him face-first to the floor. He lay there, staring into the carpet, paralyzed by what he had witnessed.

Peter could use his strength outside of the transformation. It was the ultimate pinnacle of control and mastery over the Tryst form. People with that ability were few and far between, so whenever someone of that level popped up, it was a huge deal.

Maybe that's what had set him off at the bar? Perhaps Fleet's subconscious had realized the danger this man posed and wanted to subdue him based on instinct—not that he had a chance in hell of doing it.

Peter smirked as he continued, reveling in the efficacy of his demonstration. "It was then that the poor soul—or souls—were forced to seek refuge at the nearest wasted scrap of civilization: The Rose Hill Motel. I stayed there a few nights myself. I was not impressed. However, the staff was delightful."

"That's why you put her in danger?" Fleet cut in. "You just wanted her motel for your sick fucking plan?"

Peter threw a hand up over his shoulder. "She was never in any danger. Shortly after the 'catalyst' moved in, she made the rather inflexible demand that young Harlow not be harmed. I agreed, but under the stipulation that the girl remain ignorant of my plans. This held true throughout the entirety of my work, though she managed to become quite the fly in the ointment, regardless."

Peter walked up to Fleet and kicked him onto his side.

"As the plan predicated, over the course of their brief stay, a few handpicked members of my flock whisked the sacrifice away in the night, taking their vehicles and possessions, along with gaining access to their phones. From there, I sent my most loyal servant—God rest his soul—out into the world to write fraudulent texts and use their credit cards, thus destroying any pattern that would lead the likes of you back here. And it was perfect...for the most part."

Peter sat on the carpet and crossed his legs to be closer to Fleet.

"All proceeded smoothly for months. Our only abscondence on record was the infamous 'bungle' by the sheriff. The poor man failed to forfeit his conscience and deflected his duty, despite the fact he had participated in his fair share of abductions. The two gentlemen escaped unharmed, leaving our sheriff quite the pariah among my flock."

Boos erupted from the congregation, eliciting another volley of condemnation at the shaken Denvis. Peter was forced to put up his hand to silence them in order to continue.

"It was not until later that the proprietor developed her good Samaritan streak, repairing the tires and sending potential victims on their way. When my followers came calling in the night, they found the henhouse vacant. This carried on for some time, but I was willing to wait it out and formulate some alternative plan of action. But as I learned, you can only keep such voracious animals on a leash for so long."

Peter slumped his shoulders and tightened his lips.

"Months of planning and reciting the same prattling nonsense over and over for it to come to this."

He gave a backhanded wave to the crowd as he kicked himself to his feet.

"It has become tiresome."

Peter faced them and took a seat on a step leading to the pulpit.

"My initial foray into this whole thing was a tad maladroit, but overall, I would say it was a success. And as with any meaningful invention, it has far eclipsed the true intent of the creator."

He rested his arms on his knees and clasped his hands together to point at the crowd.

"While this lot may listen to my doctrine, they have taken it far past the mere snippets I dribbled upon them. I told them you need blood to ascend, but some seem to consider one soul too meager an offering."

Peter turned away from the congregation with a sneer.

"These fools began setting traps to give travelers a flat tire, or brazenly abducted them with firearms and roadblocks. Some even left town to grab strangers in the night with no adherence to the laws I had set. They took it on their own to bastardize my nonsense to fit their own ends and wanton desires—just like any good religion, I suppose. Perhaps I can take solace in knowing the 'religion' I created has reached such a pantheon. Still, their rash behavior has caused me no end of troubles, and worst of all, they act as if I was ignorant of their actions!"

Peter leaned back and shouted to the crowd.

"Did you hear that, Karen? I know about the contractor you slew in recompense for painting your living room the wrong shade of blue! He was right! You have to look at it in the light first, you silly twat—that is what the samples are for! You as well, Mark! I am fully aware of your Craigslist follies. Being lowballed on some gaudy end table is no justification for eviscerating someone. And of course, how could I forget the Honeysuckles..."

Peter seemed especially agitated by two individuals in the crowd as he pointed at them.

"Three delivery drivers. Neighbors from your very own town. People never even given the choice to join our family. You butchered and befouled them in the community 'atelier' under the school. Not for your God. Not for your 'ascension.' Only to satisfy your own terrible delights."

The two he addressed stood out most from their reaction, as if they were going to burst into flames for their disobedience. Fleet recognized them. They were the parents of Lowy's prom date she had pointed out in the restaurant.

They looked so normal, so common. But they were murderers. Had they always been that way, or was it Peter's fault? Blighted by their own ignorance and emboldened by the lies of a charlatan, how quickly they slaughtered without concern or remorse.

Was it really that easy?

Just as it looked like the couple would burst into granules and blow away, Peter relented his assault with a shrug. "And now here I sit, overcome by the mob which I helped to create. That is how I concluded the end was upon me."

Peter got up and walked back to stand over Fleet.

"I took a 'spare part' from the basement..." he smirked and wiggled his fingers at Fleet, "...before my followers purged the place of human remains in a failed attempt to hide their transgressions from me and placed it on the path jogged by young Harlow."

He turned around to look at the church entrance.

"I only had to wait. Patience, then I could unveil my masterwork. Explain the folly of it all. This time, I *would* get through."

Peter's expression hardened.

"Instead, they sent you."

He squatted and stared into Fleet's eyes with stale bemusement.

"Why are you here?"

Fleet shook his head in confusion. "I don't—"

"Is it to insult me? Is that their intent?"

"Insult? What are you—"

"I have confessed my entire devious plot like the stereotypical villain for your benefit. It is only proper that you return the favor. Now answer me: why are you here?"

Peter stood and motioned for him to speak.

Fleet pushed himself up to a sitting position and said in a firm tone, "It's my job."

Peter rubbed his forehead, unimpressed by Fleet's response. "Very well. We can play this game if you so desire." He made a swift motion with his hand toward Denvis.

"Kill him."

Denvis' head shot up and his eyes bulged with terror as he thrashed about in a futile attempt to free himself from his bindings. It ended with him lying on his back when the chair toppled over from his struggles.

Viv lashed her tongue across her snout as she stalked toward the helpless man.

"What the fuck is wrong with you?" Denvis cursed in hopes the congregation would realize their mistake. "He just told you everything! He admitted he lied right to your faces! The god you've been worshiping is a sentient balloon knot in the sky! Why are you still listening to him?"

Peter sighed and turned to the people. "What is the one thing our Lord despises most?"

In uproarious tandem, the crowd shouted, "ASYMMETRY!"

Peter slapped himself on the forehead and rubbed his face. "Idiots. This...this is why..." He clenched his fists to regain his composure. "All right, what is the *other* thing our Lord despises most?"

This time, the congregation did not disappoint—even Viv barked along with the crowd.

"DOUBT!"

Peter smiled at his handiwork. "I have trained my dogs so well."

All the fight drained from Denvis as he closed his eyes in acceptance of his fate. With a nod from Peter, Viv continued onward to fulfill his original command.

"No, wait! I'll do whatever you want!" Fleet yelled, his desperation rising the closer Viv got to her prey.

"Then tell me! Why are you here?" Peter screamed back in kind.

"I told you! It's my job! I'm a Servunday!"

Viv reached Denvis and put a toe on the bottom rung of his chair. With the slightest push downward from her foot, she jolted him upright.

"I know what you are, boy! That doesn't answer my question!" Peter spat out the words. "I showed my calling card! I should have gotten another!"

To his side, Curtis rocked back and forth as Fleet asked, "What 'calling card'?"

Viv slid one of her claws across Denvis' cheek, followed soon after by a fresh stream of blood.

"My card, you wastrel!" Peter slapped the back of his hand into his palm. "The one ripped down the center! I put it with the severed hand I left for the girl. The second they saw it, they should have known it was me!"

Now that rang a bell. Fleet swore he had seen something like that, but he just couldn't place it. The pressure and fatigue were muddling his recollection, making it a struggle to recall anything at all. While he tried to marshal his thoughts, Denvis gasped as Viv palmed the top of his head like a basketball, her sharp nails burrowing deep into the flesh of his neck.

Perhaps out of desperation, an image formed in Fleet's mind. His eyes widened as he reached out to Peter. "Wait! I saw it! I know what you're talking about!"

Peter held up a hand, signaling a stay of execution. Viv backed away from her promised kill with disappointment.

"It was never in the initial report!" Fleet explained, his voice cracking. "But when I was looking over the crime scene, I found the card! It was farther down the road in some bushes! It must have blown away or something!"

Peter bent down and scowled at him. "In the bushes?"

"That's right!" Fleet confirmed, relieved that he had swayed Peter. "In my intel, there was a picture of the hand, but there was never any card there. They couldn't have known it was you! That's why intelligence concluded this was a basic murder case—no Tryst involved. The only reason I'm even here is because they didn't trust me with a real mission! Can you believe that shit?"

Fleet feigned a chuckle as he gauged Peter's reaction.

"Impossible," Peter whispered to himself, looking off into the distance. "But then again, it was rather windy that night." He slid into a gradual laugh as he ran a hand through his hair. "Your words ring true. I put my card in the hand, but the wind must have taken it alight! How absurdly delightful!"

"See? It's all just one big misunderstanding!" Fleet joined in with the laughter, attempting to placate the madman before him—though calling everything that had happened up to this point a 'misunderstanding' made him want to vomit.

Peter wiped some moisture from his eyes with a thumb. "I did tell the sheriff to report the hand exactly as it lay, and it seems he performed my instructions to the letter. If anyone is to blame, it should be me."

Fleet rolled onto his back and took a deep breath as Peter continued to laugh at the cosmic farce that had been thrust upon him. He had managed to stall the madman for now, but he knew it wouldn't last for long. He had to act, but what could he do? His mind was foggy and unresponsive thanks to his injuries and lack of energy, but maybe if he kept Peter talking, it would give him enough time to think of something.

Fleet propped himself on one elbow and made to speak, but Peter silenced him with a finger.

"Even after all these years, life is still full of surprises." Peter put a hand to his chest and exhaled. "Speaking of..."

He snapped his fingers.

Viv barked in delight and extended her arms out wide.

Denvis looked straight ahead, like a man facing the firing squad. "Tell Buck I love her, and that I'm sorry I—"

The monster squealed as she clapped her hands together on Denvis' head, causing blood, bone, and brain matter to fire into the air like a geyser of confetti. Bits of flesh rained down upon Fleet as he stared on in horror. The remainder of Denvis' body fell limp as the congregation applauded and cajoled his sudden execution.

Fleet screamed and buried his face in the musty carpet as he fought back tears of rage. "Why? Goddamn it, why?"

Peter clamped his palm atop Fleet's head and lifted him to meet his eyes. "Because I need you to understand how serious this is." He turned his wrist to make Fleet face toward the gruesome scene. "Those two had known each other for years, been friends for decades. Yet she ended him on my word alone, with no qualm or doubt. Imagine how much easier it will be to kill perfect strangers."

With a twist of his arm, he tossed Fleet aside and sent him rolling over toward Curtis. Peter then held his arms aloft and addressed the congregation in a booming voice.

"My children, you have done it. You have proven to our God you are worthy of his love and admiration. You are all so close to true ascension. There is but one last task you must perform."

He glanced at Fleet to make sure he was paying attention.

"You must 'cleanse.' Wipe the irreverent scum from this world. Bathe in their blood so that you may stand in his presence clean and free of the shackles they have placed upon you. Begin with these two sheep before me."

Peter pointed toward the church doors with his head held high.

"Once you finish with them, venture into the world to slay and devour all you find until your bellies can hold no more, until your bodies can move no longer, until there are none left standing to profane our Lord. Only then will ascendance be yours!"

The crowd cheered and hooted at his sermon as Fleet trembled at the bloodlust in their shouts. As much as he wanted to protest, he had no more words—pure terror had plastered his mouth shut.

As some of the congregation got to their feet, Peter held up a hand to stop them. "Do pardon? I hope you do not go to feast without saying our prayer—the full prayer."

Those who were already up sat back down so fast the pews threatened to collapse. They clasped their hands in prayer, the cheers for blood now replaced with a monotone humming that permeated the room. Even Viv dropped to her knees and prayed, though it sounded more like disjointed growls.

Peter turned his back on the mumbling congregation.

He then walked over to Fleet and squatted down next to him. "I look forward to your decision, my son."

Then, almost lovingly, he placed a hand on Fleet's head and whispered into his ear.

"Et pereat mundus."

Without another word, Peter strolled down the center aisle, past the congregation, and through the exit to await the finale.

CHAPTER THIRTY-SIX

DECISION

FLEET WAS PARALYZED. EVERY breath he took quaked like it would be his last. All he had the strength to do was look down at the dingy, blood-soaked carpet.

The murmurs of the congregation washed over him like a malevolent funeral dirge that signaled not only his end, but the deaths of countless others. To his side, Curtis' muffled screams broke through the chants as he rocked his chair back and forth.

"I failed, Scriptor," Fleet lamented, his face gaunt and drained of blood. "I'm sorry. I don't know what to do."

With one final push, Curtis crashed onto his side and kicked his way over to Fleet. He yelled through the duct tape on his mouth, though it only came out as a muffled groan.

It was a struggle to even lift his hands, but Fleet ripped the tape from Curtis' mouth in one quick yank. Just as his lips were freed, Curtis hacked up a black piece of plastic in a deluge of saliva.

"The hell is that?" Fleet asked.

Between laborious coughs, Curtis choked out, "It's the detonator!"

Fleet's look of defeat changed to one of confusion. "Detonator?"

Curtis motioned toward his thigh. "I've got a knife in my pocket. Hurry and cut me loose!"

With great effort, Fleet recovered the knife and cut the bindings on Curtis' arm. Curtis took over and set about freeing his other arm before releasing Fleet from his constrictive tape cuffs.

"What's the detonator for?" Fleet asked as Curtis sawed at his last bound leg.

Without breaking stride, he responded, "It's this one! For this church! That crazy fucker shoved it in my mouth and taped it shut!"

"Why would he do that?"

"I have no idea!"

Fleet's eyes went wide. "Does that mean the bomb is still active?"

"Hell, I think so." Curtis freed himself and grabbed the deadly bauble from the floor before helping Fleet right himself, supporting him on his shoulder. "But it's got to be some kind of trap, right? Why else would he do this?"

"I know why," Fleet uttered in a somber tone. "What he said when he left... He wants me to make a choice. I can either kill us all right here, or I can let them go."

"Pretty fucking shitty choice since we die either way!" Curtis lamented.

Fleet looked over at the congregation still locked in prayer. "If I can convince them of the danger, I might be able to bargain our way out of this. But if I do that, more innocent people will..."

The words stuck in his throat. All he could think about was that wall of license plates back at the bar. If everyone here did as Peter commanded, their previous body count would be a pittance compared to the coming massacre. Even those who were unable to shift were still a threat; leveling a crowd with an automatic weapon was just as effective as a transformed Tryst in a short burst. With the conscious freedom of their sacred tenant, who knows how many would die in their unholy conquest?

He couldn't let that happen.

Fleet snatched the detonator from Curtis, held it high in the air, and shouted as loud as his mangled body would allow, "Listen up, assholes!"

Heads popped up one by one in response to his proclamation. Viv snarled at his interruption, forced to abandon her prostration. She got to her feet and stomped over to them.

"I wouldn't do that," Fleet warned, wagging a finger at her. "Not even you would survive such a massive explosion at this range."

This was a bluff, of course. If anyone was going to survive this, it was her, but it wouldn't help the situation if she knew that.

The crowd murmured, prompting one person to ask, "Explosion? What's he talking about?"

Fleet grinned—now he had their attention. "We rigged this church with enough explosives to send us all to hell and back, that's what."

Another parishioner stood up and pointed an accusatory finger at Fleet. "He's a liar! He's just trying to save his own miserable hide!"

The crowd went into a tilt as Viv renewed her snarling approach on the two of them.

"I can prove it!" Curtis yelled as he backed away from her, pulling Fleet with him.

Fleet gave Curtis a questioning glance and whispered, "You can?"

This prompted him to nod and address the crowd. "Under the third pew from the back! See for yourself!"

In the midst of the crowd's audible disapproval, a young man crawled along the floor to search the spot Curtis had said to look.

Fleet had been told that there was only going to be a single bomb placed outside on the propane tank—there shouldn't be anything inside the church itself. Was this a bluff? If it was, it was a terrible one, considering they could disprove it in two seconds. Just what the hell was Curtis trying to do here?

The young man stood back up with a concerned look on his face. "There's something stuck to the bottom! It looks like clay with wires and stuff going into it!"

"That's C-4!" Curtis exclaimed in a threatening tone. "And that's not the only one! There's a shit-ton more scattered around the church!"

Panicked gasps echoed throughout the room at this sudden and frightening revelation. People moved away from the affected area, only to realize that they didn't know where the other explosives might be.

"Why are there bombs?" one woman called from the middle of the crowd.

"Why *are* there bombs?" Fleet echoed, turning to his partner for enlightenment.

"Peter did it," Curtis explained in a hushed voice. "He took our explosives from the motel after he grabbed me. I watched him rig the entire place while I was tied up here. He even made a big show about where he put them to make sure I saw."

Fleet felt a spark of understanding. "He planned this from the beginning."

This was Peter's way to free himself from the rebellious congregation and take out a Servunday in the process. But why? Why all the theatrics and convoluted bullshit? Why bother offering the choice of how it goes down? Even though Peter had explained his entire plan, Fleet still couldn't fathom *why*.

Regardless of that asshole's intentions, they now had a bargaining chip—a chance to avoid mutually assured destruction.

There was a way out—but at what cost?

In the interim, some bold parishioners had checked under their seats as well. A few of them returned with mortified expressions as they shared their findings with the others.

Fleet looked around at the congregation, but soon realized that a madman's motive should be the last thing on his mind right now. "Shit! Don't just tell me, Scriptor! Tell them!"

Curtis nodded his understanding and bellowed, "The bombs are there because your leader put them there! He doesn't give a shit about you! He's gotten tired of you, and now he's tossing you to the curb like garbage!"

Their angered cries ricocheted from the rafters and throughout the building, an audible amalgamation of their combined disbelief and hatred toward his words.

"LIAR!"

"BLASPHEMER!"

"SWINDLER!"

Fleet's expression hardened. This was pointless. Peter had convinced them to murder in cold blood, to eat human flesh. How could something as ineffectual as the truth have any sway upon them?

Fuck this.

"I don't give a shit what you believe!" Fleet shouted to the congregation. "The only thing that matters now is that you are all surrounded by sticky death, and I'm holding the goddamn trigger."

Fleet pointed the detonator toward Viv, causing her to put up her hands and back away.

"Here's what's going to happen. We're going to leave, and if I see a single one of you make toward that exit, I swear I will end us all right now."

"Why would we do that?" someone asked from the audience. "What's stopping you from blowing us up once you're outside?"

Fleet glanced over at Curtis and exhaled before changing the terms. "Then just him. I'll be staying here."

Before he even finished his sentence, Curtis grabbed him by the arm and gave it a hard shake. "The hell you will!"

"There's no other choice!" Fleet grit his teeth and jerked his arm free. "If we both go, they'll try to escape, and no way am I going to let even a single one of these fuckers roam free!"

"You act like I'm really going to leave you here to die."

"I don't plan on dying, but it's taking everything I have to just stand here like this," Fleet admitted as he steadied himself on Curtis' shoulder. "That's why you have to get out and call for help. I don't care how high up the ladder you have to go, just make it happen!"

Despite the grimace of fear, there was still defiance in Curtis' eyes.

Fleet steeled himself as he pushed away from his partner to say in the most authoritative tone he could muster, "This is an order, Scriptor."

"Please, man. I don't want to lose another one today," Curtis begged in a cracking voice.

"The only thing you're gonna lose is your dignity when I whoop your ass at B-ball."

"Goddamn it." Curtis' lip trembled as he fought back a smile. "Even now you're still a fucking goober, huh?"

A wisp of a smile graced Fleet's face, but only on the side Curtis could see; his expression remained firm toward his captive audience.

Curtis swallowed hard. "Okay. I won't let you down, Servunday Hangman."

He walked toward the center aisle as Fleet held up a threatening hand and shouted, "He's leaving! If I see any of you try to stop him, it's fucking over!"

Fleet held his breath as Curtis walked down the aisle, his movements stiff and cautious. The congregation fell silent as all eyes looked toward the one man not bound to this place. When Curtis slipped past the last pew, his pace quickened until he punched through the exit to safety.

As the doors creaked back shut, Fleet let out one last sigh of relief.

"Good luck, brother."

Curtis burst into a sprint the second the fresh air hit his face. His mind was racing even faster than his feet as he navigated through the maze of cars that had gathered in the gravel cul-de-sac.

I have to get a phone and call for help, but where am I going to find one? They took mine when I was caught, but I never saw them grab Sea's phone at the motel. I bet it's still there. That's my best shot.

He looked back at the church, finding relief in the fact that it had yet to erupt into flames.

I'll be back, brother.

His body seized and he fell onto the ground as the transformation began. Even as the agony spread throughout his body, he clawed and kicked his way forward, trying to save as many precious seconds as possible.

As soon as he finished, he exploded into the woods with everything he had. He tore through the trees like they were nothing more than dried reeds standing in his way. He reached the road in seconds, but before hitting the asphalt, he dropped to his stomach when he heard a car approaching in the distance.

Hurry! Hurry! Fuck! Fuck! Should I do it? Should I just go? If they see me, they'll just think I'm a deer or Bigfoot. Nobody believes them when they say it was Bigfoot. Goddamn it, I don't have time for this!

Curtis gasped as the vehicle in question came into view through the dense foliage.

That's Hangman's truck! But who's driving it? I can't get a clear view. It's got to either be Lowy or someone else, right? If it's Lowy, I can use her phone. If it's someone else, then they're probably involved in that church. And If that's the case, I'll kill them.

Curtis darted into the road and planted himself as he prepared for whatever outcome it may be. He breathed a sigh of relief when he realized it was Lowy in the driver's seat—as well as Oreen and BJ crowded next to her.

Shit! Now I've exposed two more. It's fine. There are more important things right now. Once she stops, then I can... Curtis' ears folded down against his head. *She's not stopping.*

To his chagrin, the engine roared as Lowy stepped on the accelerator.

She doesn't recognize me in this form, and based on all the shit that's happened, I don't blame her for trying to flatten me. But if I get hit, they're the ones who are going to be hurt. I've got to do this perfect.

Just as the truck was about to collide with him, Curtis leaped into the air and dug his claws into the roof of the cab. He used the momentum to flip himself around as he flew over the bed and grabbed hold of the tailgate. As he came back down onto the road, he dug his feet into the pavement and held on with everything he had.

The truck dragged him several feet as his claws carved massive divots into the hard pavement. Smoke billowed from the squealing tires as the truck came to a reluctant stop. In the cab, Curtis heard the panicked occupants screaming at their harrowing predicament.

"What the fuck! What the fuck! What the fuck!" Oreen shouted in a shrill voice.

BJ couldn't even bring himself to yell or scream; he only mumbled through his open mouth in disbelief as his gaze shifted between the holes in the roof and the creature behind them. Lowy lost feeling in her foot from how hard she was still pressing down on the gas pedal.

"What are you doing? Go! Go!" Oreen screamed, his eyes watering with panic.

"I'm trying!" Lowy shouted back, hunching over the steering wheel as if it would somehow help.

The car lurched forward when Curtis released one of his hands and waved it frantically at Lowy.

"What is that? What is it doing?" Oreen screeched.

Lowy looked at the rear-view mirror. "It's...waving?"

For a split second, she glimpsed Curtis' tail flick over the tailgate into view. "It's like it's been dipped in a barrel of oil..."

The roar of the motor softened to a gentle purr as Lowy eased her foot off the gas.

"What are you doing!" Oreen shrieked. "What the fuck are you doing!"

Without responding, Lowy lowered the driver-side window, which coincided with the drop of her passenger's jaws.

She stuck her head out and called to the monster, her voice meek and stilted. "Curtis?"

Curtis let go of the tailgate and clapped his hands together, nodding as he ran up to her. Getting on his knees so he didn't have to bend over, he explained the situation to her in sign language.

After he finished his spiel, Lowy shook her head. "I'm sorry. I don't understand."

Curtis clasped his hands over his head. He was so used to conversing with other Tryst like this, he had assumed she knew how to do it as well. He was going to have to turn back if he wanted to communicate.

This was bad. Unlike Fleet, Curtis had never gotten the chance to recharge his batteries after the last fight and the proceeding cover-up. Making it through this last transformation was a miracle on its own, but it had taken a lot out of him.

Curtis repeated a silent mantra to himself as he prepared to revert. *Don't pass out. Don't pass out. Don't—*

Oreen pointed a trembling finger at the monster. "It's using sign language. Why is it using sign language?"

Curtis pointed a finger back at Oreen in excitement, causing him to recoil in fear as BJ lay a protective arm over him.

"That's right!" Lowy exclaimed. "You know sign language! Please, you have to tell me what he said!"

"You were telling the truth," Oreen whispered through his open, unmoving mouth.

"Oreen! Focus! What did he say?" Lowy shouted, rousing him from his stupor.

"Sorry, I didn't really get it," he responded in a trembling voice. "I was a little too focused on shitting myself."

Without provocation, Curtis repeated himself while Oreen watched.

Despite his fear, Oreen stammered, "He says that the Hangman is at the church and that they are going to kill him."

"They're going to kill Fleet!" Lowy blurted out in a panic.

Curtis nodded and continued on as Oreen narrated. "He says that he—guess he means Fleet—can stop them with a bomb, but he'll die too. Umm...now it's asking for a phone."

Lowy pulled out her phone and offered it to Curtis.

He wiggled his enormous digits at her before signing again as Oreen translated. "I can't talk, and I can't type with these fingers. I'll need to turn back."

"No!" Lowy shouted, making Curtis jump like a kitten startled by a bug. "We need you like that if we are going to save Fleet! Just figure out some way for Oreen to do it for you!"

Lowy checked her phone to find it had one bar of service.

"We're out of the dead zone, but it won't last much longer the closer we get to the school."

With a quick prayer that it would hold out, Lowy shoved her phone into Oreen's chest, causing him to fumble it.

Oreen cleared his throat. "What should I do?"

Curtis signed instructions, but Lowy interjected. "Do it on the way!"

"On the way?" Oreen echoed.

"Yes! Get in the back with Curtis and figure it out!" Lowy shouted, tears of desperation collecting in her eyes. "If we don't hurry, Fleet's going to die!"

Oreen glanced at Curtis with mortified apprehension, then looked back at Lowy like she had just asked him to jump from a plane without a parachute.

She grabbed Oreen's hand and squeezed. "I promise on my life that he will not hurt you."

Oreen did not respond as tremors of fright rocked his body.

"Don't worry," BJ consoled, breaking the silence as he wrapped Oreen in a quick hug. "Everything's going to be fine."

BJ stepped out of the cab and jumped into the very center of the bed, sitting with his legs crossed. Catching on, Curtis gave Oreen a thumbs-up and a quick smile—purposely hiding his teeth—before he followed suit.

The shocks groaned in agony as Curtis slid into the bed like he was easing himself into a hot tub and sat with crossed legs against the cab. BJ was nestled against him, keeping a watchful eye on the monster. Curtis gave him an awkward smile and folded his hands in his lap.

"Oreen, please!" Lowy pleaded.

Oreen's whole body shook, but he forced a nod of consent.

Lowy wrapped her arms around him in a tight embrace. "Thank you!"

When she let go, Oreen stepped out and got in the truck bed, taking a spot behind his husband to use him as a buffer.

"Okay, what's the number?" he asked, peeking from behind BJ to watch Curtis' motions.

Alone in the cab, the last thing Lowy heard before the rushing wind drowned out the world behind her was Oreen saying, "Requesting immediate assistance. Zenith level threat. Umm...code white. Yes, code white. Confirmation ID number—"

The engine roared to life as Lowy sped down the lonely road, her knuckles aching from her grip on the wheel. She gritted her teeth and repeated the same thought over and over again.

Just a little longer. Hold on just a little longer.

Chapter Thirty-Seven

FIAT JUSTITA

"Don't fucking move!" Fleet shouted at Viv. He was sure she was trying to sneak up on him, but to be honest, he couldn't tell if she was or not. The blood loss and fatigue had caught up with him, making the room rock like the deck of a boat on open water.

Since Curtis had escaped, the congregation had become restless as they lamented their situation, but Fleet ignored their cries as he focused most of his attention on Viv. In that form, it would be simple for her to leap through the window—or the wall itself—and survive the blast. He wondered if the reason she had not escaped already was to protect the congregation, but then decided it was most likely because she just hadn't thought of it yet.

Fleet swayed before crumpling to his knees. He caught himself from falling on his face with the hand that held the detonator, eliciting a collective gasp from the congregation. He pushed himself back to his feet as the crowd's shock mutated into anger.

"What do you want from us?" a voice cried out.

"To realize what you've done!" Fleet shouted back. "I want you to see that you've been deceived by that piece of shit that filled your head with nonsense and left you all here to die!"

"Why would he do that?" cried another. "Why would he abandon us?"

"Because he doesn't care about you! He never did! You've served whatever sick purpose he had and now he's done with you!"

The crowd fell silent as they considered his words, so Fleet took the opportunity to reason with them.

"But I can help you—because I *am* you. I know how it feels. It's like everything you've ever known, ever believed in has been ripped away, and you're left in the dark, wondering what comes next. But you have to realize that what you're doing isn't right! Please, give me a chance! I can teach you the truth, show you how to make amends for your crimes so you can lead decent lives!"

Fleet studied the crowd after his impassioned speech, hoping to see at least a glimmer of enlightenment among them.

A few moments passed before a lone man stood up to address him. "So, what you mean is..."

Fleet held out an encouraging hand when the man trailed off, and with a hopeful smile, he coaxed him to speak. "Go on, what is it?"

The man's eyes flashed with conviction.

"This is a test."

"What?" Fleet lowered his arm in defeat. "No..."

"You said it yourself! Father Peter knew about the explosives when he brought us here. Don't you see? This is our test! Just like Earl, this is our opportunity to prove our fealty! To pave our way to heaven!"

Fleet's stomach dropped as he glanced down at Earl's corpse. "This isn't a fucking test!"

The unknown man pushed his way down the aisle despite Fleet's constant threats of impending doom. "This man is doing the father's bidding. As he said, he has ascended, same as we have! He is one of us! There is no other explanation! He challenges our faith on the father's behalf to test our resolve! What else can there be?"

Fleet's mouth fell agape as this innocuous man crafted his inane narrative formed of logic tainted by madness. But what scared him the most was that the entire congregation seemed to hang on his every word; it was as if Peter himself were speaking through this random deacon.

Soon his justifications were spreading like a disease throughout the desperate collective, finally reaching a head as they erupted into a deafening roar of approval.

"Goddamn it, please!" Fleet begged, his voice cracking. "Stop this!"

The man fell to his knees as the congregation let out an uproarious confirmation. "We're so close! We can't stop now!" The man convulsed as he screamed, his voice shifting into a growl as he spoke. "One last order! I won't be left behind!"

Not long after, more parishioners fell to their knees and added to the sickening chorus of transformation. Those who were unable to shift encouraged the others by performing Peter's ridiculous choreography. Viv joined in with a blood-curdling howl strong enough to make Fleet teeter on his feet.

They won't listen. No matter what I say, they won't listen. It's over.

He flicked open the plastic cover and placed his thumb on the silver knob.

I have to end this.

His hand was shaking. He grasped his wrist, only to discover it made the trembling worse.

Why can't I do it? This should be easy! I'm giving myself for the greater good! Not long ago, I would have killed to have a worthy justification for it.

Tears welled in his eyes as he hung his head over the detonator.

"Rose... I'm sorry..."

Off to the side, Viv had shaken off her reverie, now intent on fulfilling Peter's ultimate command. She bared down on Fleet but froze in place when she noticed his thumb on the trigger.

Fleet gave her one last defiant glance—and flicked the switch.

There was the gentle sound of breaking glass that preceded the deafening explosion. Fleet found himself compressed into a ball as he tumbled end over end away from the hellfire that his finger had wrought. He skidded to a halt as his brain entertained the morbid possibility that he was now only a smoldering head rolling through the grass.

He let the world stop spinning around him before he noticed the labored breaths next to his cheek that barely won out over the ringing in his ears.

In the distance, he heard an indistinguishable voice that soon solidified into concerned shouting. "Fleet! Are you all right? Fleet!"

He squinted to see who was calling, only able to make out a pair of feet, then knees, and finally a face as the figure bent down to greet him.

"Lowy?" Fleet moaned, still unsure of what was happening.

"You're alive!" she shouted. "Curtis, you did it! Good boy!"

It was only now that Fleet realized it was his partner who was encapsulating his body in a tight embrace. Curtis had grabbed him a second before the explosion, using his Tryst form as a shield to protect him from the blast.

Curtis' arms and legs were still wrapped around Fleet like a quarterback trying to protect a fumble as they lay in the soft grass where they had landed. Lowy fell on top and ensnared both of them in a hug, causing Curtis to groan in agony.

"How did... I don't..." Fleet said, his words filtered through a haze of confusion.

The acrid smell of burning hair wafted from Curtis' back where his skin was charred and cracked. He released his hold and rolled Fleet onto the grass, exposing the pieces of rebar that were jutting from his side.

"What the hell were you thinking?" Fleet shouted before grabbing a protruding bar. He yanked hard, seeing stars as he overexerted himself. "We got to get those out of you."

He tried again, but this time found himself face up on the bloody grass. He felt a hand on his shoulder as he was lifted back into a seated position.

Fleet craned his neck toward the man towering over him. "BJ?"

Behind BJ in the distance, Fleet saw Oreen waving at him from the bed of his own truck.

"Let me help," BJ said as he sat down in the grass next to Fleet. He took hold of one skewer and placed his foot on Curtis' chest. "This might hurt a little."

Before Curtis finished nodding, BJ yanked the rebar from his flesh in a spurt of blood. Curtis let out an agonizing scream as he clutched at the exit wound. Lowy gagged as she covered her mouth and turned away toward the remains of the church.

Curtis' eyes rolled back in his head as the second bar was excavated from his body. He only gave a slight tremble before falling motionless, his breathing labored and uneven.

BJ watched in fascination as the wounds sealed themselves shut, waiting until they had vanished before addressing Fleet. "You should thank her. If we'd been even a second later..."

Fleet turned to look at Lowy, her attention now centered on the raging fire before her. He held out a feeble hand toward her and crumbled onto his side. BJ took the lead and lifted him to his feet, supporting him with a comforting arm around his shoulder.

Fleet called out her name in a raspy voice as his eyelids drooped. Lowy turned back to him, her figure framed in the blazing inferno, and flashed a knowing smile. Even though his consciousness waned, begging him to let go, Fleet returned a grateful smile of his own—one that quickly faded into a look of pure terror.

Behind Lowy, embers swam through the air and flames licked the ground as something burst from the rubble. She tumbled backward in horror at the twisted figure that manifested before her like a demon escaping through the gates of hell.

Viv's entire body was blackened and torn, blood oozing from every rip in her skin as the flesh struggled to mend. Her eyes had melted, creating tendrils of goo that poured from empty sockets, framed by a charred skull with no ears.

A desperate wheeze escaped Viv's throat as she flailed wildly at everything around her in a fit of madness. Her limbs tore apart the earth and slung debris at random, all the while unknowingly inching her way closer to Lowy's position like a thresher out of control.

The words shredded his throat as Fleet yelled out to her. "Lowy, run!"

Lowy kicked at the ground to push herself backward, but it wasn't fast enough to outpace Viv's progression. She pulled into a ball as one of Viv's wild swipes missed cleaving her leg by mere inches.

"Viv!" Fleet cried out as her massive hand arced down toward Lowy.

Viv froze and tilted a hollow ear canal toward Fleet's voice.

"That's right! Over here!" As Fleet spoke, he squeezed BJ's shoulder before hobbling off at an angle toward Viv.

With a nod, BJ bent down and crept toward Lowy's position.

Fleet elevated his voice, hoping that the fire had damaged her hearing enough that she wouldn't notice BJ's clumsy attempt at stealth. "You had one job, Viv. He put his faith in you, and you fucked it right up. Might be hard to get into heaven when you're that much of a goddamn failure."

A frothy liquid oozed from Viv's blistered mouth as she snarled at Fleet's jabs, orientating herself toward the sound of his voice.

"But you know what I think? I bet you never gave a shit about that cult. You were just addicted to the power. It made you feel good—even godlike. Why should one god worship another, right?"

BJ reached Lowy and yanked her out of the monster's path. They collapsed backward in an inelegant heap as Viv passed them by, all her attention on Fleet's insults.

Milky orbs bubbled into Viv's eye sockets as Fleet continued to accost her. "You were already twisted before he ever got his hooks in you. After all, you killed your husband without his consent. This whole charade just gave you the opportunity to be your true self. But you're nothing special, just a Tryst with the taste for blood—and that makes you my prey. I am rescinding my offer of mercy and casting the only sentence appropriate for your ilk."

Viv lunged toward him, kicking up an explosion of dirt. Fleet pointed at her as a rumble grew behind him.

"Fiat Justita."

A deluge of blood erupted from Viv's mouth and splattered on the windshield as the grill of Fleet's truck collided with her chest. Inside the cab, Oreen's leg ached from the pressure he was applying to the gas pedal. He remained focused despite Viv desperately clawing at the truck's hood as they hurdled toward the burning church.

At the last moment, Oreen kicked open the door and jumped from the cab, his body spiraling sideways across the ground. Viv's howl of pain was cut short as the truck crashed through the wall into a sea of flames. What remained of the building collapsed inward, sending out a shockwave of heat and smoke.

Balancing on one leg, Oreen stood up and pried loose a large board that had impaled his shoulder with its rusty nails. BJ ran to him, giving him a once-over as he asked him if he was all right.

Instead of answering the question, Oreen spat at the burning rubble and yelled into the hellfire, "How's that for a cider, you old bitch!"

Got to remember to stay on his good side, Fleet thought with a meager snort as his body went limp and the world around him faded into darkness.

CHAPTER THIRTY-EIGHT

INADEQUATE

FLEET MOANED AS HE rubbed his throbbing temple. He tried to blink away his blurry vision but jumped when a voice next to him cried out, "He's awake!"

Though Fleet had never seen him before, he recognized the man's uniform as belonging to medical personnel. As his vision cleared, he realized he was in the back of a tactical van with an IV needle in his arm. He had been dressed in thin cotton pants and a threadbare t-shirt to replace his tattered clothes.

The medic watched him in reverence. "I can't believe you're even conscious right now after an ass whoopin' like that. You guys are a different breed."

Fleet nodded, choosing to take what he said as a compliment.

Curtis stuck his head through the open door in the back. "You're awake!"

"So I've been told." Fleet winced at a painful throb in his temple. "What happened after I went down?"

Curtis gave a mild shrug. "You and I passed out until the cavalry showed up, but that's about it."

"Better late than never, I guess." Fleet propped up on his elbows. "How you doing? Last I remember, you were looking pretty rough."

"I'm fine. Healed up quick, but I sure as shit want to sleep for a few days straight." As if predicting Fleet's next question, Curtis said, "The others are fine, too. Oreen sustained some minor injuries, but he'll be all right."

Relieved, Fleet let his head fall back on the pillow and closed his eyes. "Good. That's good."

"Don't get too comfy." Curtis covered his mouth and muttered in a hushed tone. "The boss is here."

Almost as if it were an introduction, the door next to Curtis swung open. "Even in whispers, refer to me by the proper title."

The woman that stood before them was dressed in black and exuded an air of authority that was almost stifling. With a nod of her head, she motioned for the attending man to leave, and he did so without question.

"Servunday Vuota!" Curtis stuttered. "Servunday Hangman has regained consciousness!"

"Thank you, Wayman Scriptor, for that apt summation of what I can plainly see."

Curtis gave an awkward bow and bit his tongue.

"Hello, Violet," Fleet said, choosing to use her code name. "Glad you could make it." She narrowed her eyes at him for the informal greeting, but Fleet was undaunted as he asked, "So, my first case. How'd I do?"

"Yes, what was it again?" Violet touched an index finger to her cheek, counting each point made on her other hand. "Three civilians exposed. Massive property damage. One agent killed in action. Over sixty confirmed executions. And you let the primary instigator escape."

Each time a finger went up, Fleet seemed to shrink back further and further into his bed.

Violet closed her hand back into a fist. "But considering you were up against 'Him,' I would say that you came out on top with this one. Well done."

Fleet's jaw dropped with such ferocity that it risked detaching from his skull. "Are you serious?"

"I am. If anyone is to blame here, that should fall on me," Violet continued, ignoring the fact that Fleet had gone comatose from surprise. "I set you on this case believing it to be benign while I took on a mission that I was certain was authentic. As such, you were understaffed and ill prepared. Even when you asked for my help, I ignored you on the pretense that you were simply nervous. Therefore, in a way, this is my fault."

Fleet held out a shaky hand toward Curtis. "I-I think I'm having a stroke, Scriptor. This is it for me. Please, after I'm gone, go to my place. There's a hard drive I need you to destroy. It's mostly toilet cam stuff, but I'd just gotten a Brazilian wax and I was feeling cocky."

As Fleet finished, Violet reached inside and grabbed the pinky of his outstretched hand. With a quick twist and a loud pop, she dislocated his finger. Fleet let out a yelp and jerked away to nurse his crippled digit as she backed out of the van without a word.

"If there's anyone to blame here, it's me," Curtis blurted out. "If I'd only listened—"

"I do not care," Violet interjected. "Your failure or success is no longer my concern. Servunday Hangman and I share the same rank now. If there is any punishment to be administered, it is under his authority to discern what that may be."

"She's right," Fleet agreed, still cradling his hand. "Regardless of the circumstance, I was in charge. Everything that's happened here falls on me and no one else."

"Well said," Violet concurred. "And since you are in charge, we must compare notes to discover the link between our respective cases."

Fleet gave her a puzzled look, prompting her to explain.

"I had my team investigating a rash of disappearances. Though they were from all over the country, they had one thing in common: one of the last transactions on their credit card was at a barbecue restaurant about nine hours from here."

"You thought people were being picked off at the restaurant," Fleet said after putting it together.

"Correct. I will not speak to the gory details, but there was a case very similar to this one in the past, so we surmised it may be a resurgence. It is impossible that all these missing people having their last meal at the same location was mere coincidence. While it could have been human related, the fact no bodies were ever found led to the possibility of Tryst activity."

Fleet nodded. "I get that, but what's it got to do with my case?"

Violet pointed at nothing in particular. "Based on testimony given to us by the young woman—Harlow, I believe—we investigated the bar where you were attacked and discovered the license plates. As it so happens, many of those we have run through the system match with the missing persons in my case."

Fleet began picking at his memory. Hadn't he heard something about a barbeque restaurant earlier? The natural reaction would be to write it off as a coincidence, but after everything that had happened, he had to at least consider the possibility.

He patted his hips, remembering that he lost most of his pants during his fight at the bar.

"I assume you are looking for the contents of your pockets." Violet pointed toward a small metal table at his side. "We recovered your wallet from that ramshackle pub. Once again, nice job on that. I see you took my lessons to heart when you engaged those men."

Fleet reached over toward his wallet but quit about halfway as pain surged through him. He gave Violet a pathetic look. "A little help..."

Violet groaned and stepped into the van to grab his wallet, which she tossed onto his lap. Fleet thanked her and set about flipping through its contents.

The card Earl had given him was still miraculously tucked away in the folds. Fleet pried it out and flicked it toward Violet. She snatched it from the air between two fingers just before it hit her face. He received a perturbed glare before she gave the card a once-over.

Fleet took great pleasure in the look of confusion that manifested on Violet's face.

"This is it," she scoffed in disbelief. "This is the restaurant! How did you get this?"

"From Earl."

"Earl?"

"Yep. You see, I know exactly what happened."

The fact that he was one step ahead for once must be giving her a conniption—and he *really* wanted to rub it in her face.

"Tell me!" she demanded, her voice rising.

He couldn't help but give her a shit-eating grin, breaking it only when he saw her anger approaching its tipping point. "Earl: an amateur taxidermist and self-appointed connoisseur of cooked meats."

"Fuck Earl. I don't give a shit about Earl. Tell me what you know! Now!"

Cursing? Oh, he had her good. This was just too sweet.

Her stare of daggers persuaded him to continue, though he had to stir the pot just a teensy bit more. "You mean you haven't figured it out? The answer's right there in your hand. Look at it this way: each hole in that punch card represents a person's life."

Violet's expression softened as she turned her attention back to the card.

Curtis tried to look over her shoulder. "I don't follow."

Delighted that he had caught Curtis as well, Fleet explained his esoteric theory. "That asshole told us himself, remember? He sent Earl out with a victim's credit card and phone each time to throw us off the scent." Fleet pointed at the punch card in Violet's hand. "Then Earl took it as an excuse to visit his favorite barbeque joint and used their credit cards to buy his food before branching off somewhere else."

Violet let out a sigh of defeat. "We used their GPS data and purchases to track the last location of each missing person. While they never ended at the same place—some even multiple states away—that restaurant was the single common factor between them all."

Though her face was still stern, there was a tinge of regret in her voice.

"We assumed they were covering their tracks just as you said, but we should have gone back further. We would have noticed that they came through this area at some point."

"I don't know about that," Fleet said. "From what I gather, they were grabbing people from different towns as well. You could have mapped it to a general area maybe, but it's not as appealing as a single overlapping point. I think you would have gotten there eventually, but not before a few dead ends."

Violet turned away. "That means nothing. We were hasty and paid the price. I will personally review this case to identify our points of failure to ensure they are not repeated in the future."

Curtis stepped back up to the door. "Did Peter do all this to lead our main force away from his cult? It worked out perfectly that everyone was hours away when shit hit the fan."

"I don't think that's right." Fleet clicked his tongue and shook his head. "I'm not sure why, but Peter wanted us to show up when we did, and having everyone go to the wrong place goes against that. It's like his true intent was to have some kind of big showdown or something—us versus his followers."

"And why do you say that?" Violet asked.

"The calling card…" Curtis interrupted.

"Peter told me as much himself," Fleet added, his eyes narrowing at Violet. "He put his tag with the hand because he knew we'd come running, but a twist of fate meant that we never even saw the damn thing. He was expecting more than just the new guy to come after him. Funny thing, he was super pissed that only I showed up in particular, like it was an insult to him somehow."

"That's enough for now," Violet said as she turned to leave. "We can do the official report later."

Fleet leaned forward and called to her. "Tell me who Peter is! If he's this fucking dangerous, why have I never heard of him? If Scriptor and I had the intel, even just known about his damn calling card, we could have stopped all of this!"

Curtis looked ill at his inclusion in Fleet's words.

Violet halted mid stride and peered over her shoulder. "Get some rest. You earned it."

He threw off his sheets to go after her, forcing Curtis to step in and catch him before he face-planted out of the vehicle. "You said we were equals now!" Fleet yelled. "One and the same, fighting for justice! After everything I've gone through, do you still doubt my conviction?"

Without acknowledging him, Violet walked off toward the first person she saw and began barking orders.

"The fuck was that?" Fleet cursed as he steadied himself against Curtis.

Curtis puffed his cheeks out as he exhaled. "My guess is she's bummed that you outshined her on this one."

Fleet nodded in agreement, deflating when he realized he didn't have the energy to pursue the matter with her any further—but this sure as hell wouldn't be the end of it.

"I don't know, but something's off. She only dislocated my finger instead of breaking it." With a quick jerk, Fleet popped the bone back into its socket and shook his reconstructed hand. "I wonder if she's feeling guilty about this whole thing. She did admit she was wrong and even apologized to me. That is literally the first time she has ever done that."

"Do you think she has the emotional range for regret or compassion?" Curtis asked.

"She does. It's just kind of hard to tell sometimes," Fleet sympathized. "This job messes with your head, and she's been doing this since forever. How many people has she killed? How many friends has she lost? Shit, look at us: we've already lost one, and it's only our first case."

Fleet bit his tongue when he saw Curtis lower his head.

"I'm sorry, man. I didn't know Sea that well, but he seemed like a good guy."

"Yeah," Curtis whispered back as he cleared his throat.

Fleet struggled to find something that would comfort him. "It's not your fault. He accepted the risks when he took the job, right? It could have happened to any of us. This whole thing was shit from the get-go."

Curtis gave another hollow 'yeah.'

Fleet sighed, knowing full well that there was nothing more to be said. Instead, he wrapped his arms tight around his partner as Curtis struggled against him.

Just as he was about to break free, Fleet said, "You saved my life again, brother. Thank you."

Curtis sobbed into his shoulder as Fleet continued his embrace in silence, fighting back his own emotions. They had faced incomprehensible peril and come out on the other side, but it had not been without cost—it was a burden they would both have to carry.

Curtis finally backed away and wiped his face. "The boss didn't see that, did she?"

"See what?" Fleet asked, feigning ignorance. "By the way, I noticed you getting a little boned up in that hug. Is this something we need to discuss?"

"Fuck you!" Curtis coughed with a laugh as he rubbed his wrist against his nose.

Fleet joined in the laughter until Curtis cleared his throat and blinked his puffy eyes. "Wooo. Uhhh, okay. I'm good. I'm good," he said, more to himself than anyone else. "Well, I got shit to do. You should check on the others."

He pulled something from his pocket and handed it to Fleet.

"We found this in the rubble. I figured you'd know what to do with it."

Curtis departed, leaving Fleet to inspect the object he had been given. He ran a thumb over the metal plate to clear away the soot and found he held the singed remains of Denvis' badge. Fleet's grip tightened as images of Denvis' final moments flashed through his mind.

"Damn it..."

Fleet sighed and tried to slide the badge into his pants pocket, but dropped it in the grass, forgetting that the ones he now wore had none.

Before he could pick up the badge, a voice called out to him in the distance. "Hey, asshole! We need to talk!"

"Thanks for your concern, Oreen. I'm doing fine," Fleet responded as he righted himself to face him. "How are you—whoa, shit!"

Fleet's tone changed when he saw Oreen's sorry state. He was shirtless and had bandages wrapped around his torso that were dappled with blood. His face was covered in cuts to complement a black eye, and his arm was wrapped up in a sling. BJ followed him close behind along with an agent Fleet had never seen.

"What's all this about mandatory detainment?" Oreen demanded, more concerned with his circumstances than his injuries. "They keep telling me we have to be held for questioning. This is against my rights!"

"It's standard protocol," Fleet confirmed. "You've seen some things you shouldn't have. We have to make sure that you won't go blabbing about it."

Oreen narrowed his eyes at Fleet. "Is that some kind of threat?"

"No, it's common sense. We're supposed to be a secret, and we need to make sure you can keep it that way for all our sakes. Also, don't forget that you killed someone. Even if it was to save us, did you expect to walk away from this without at least talking about it?"

Oreen frowned. "I suppose. But I'm going to have some questions of my own."

"And I don't blame you," Fleet sympathized. "Now, before you say something that makes me regret it, I just wanted to thank you—both of you. You saved my ass back there. So...yeah."

Oreen's truculence abated in response to Fleet's gratitude. "I didn't do it for you...but you're welcome all the same."

Forgetting Oreen's injury, Fleet extended his right hand before switching to his left. Oreen accepted, and the two shared a quick but firm handshake. BJ and Fleet then shared a nod of respect, a mutual understanding that transcended the need for a physical embrace.

"So, where's Lowy at?" Fleet asked, looking around. "She's the last person I need to thank."

Oreen's expression softened at his question before pointing off into the distance. "By the trees over there. She's in a pretty bad place right now." He gave Fleet a concerned look, one that showed his disappointment at not being able to console her on his own. "It would help if you talked to her."

"Yeah, I'll do that," Fleet agreed as he bent over to retrieve the badge.

Fleet started in the direction Oreen had pointed out, then stopped short. "Oreen. This probably doesn't mean shit coming from me, but..."

Fleet struggled with the words, trying to decide if they were the right thing to say.

"I think Rebecca would be proud of you."

Oreen's face tensed up as he bit down to keep his lip from trembling. The facade was almost believable, broken only by the tears streaming down his face. Oreen gave him a nod of acceptance, which Fleet returned in kind.

He gave them one last wave as he made his way over to Lowy. However, his pace slowed as she came into view, sitting behind a tree with an agent standing not far away. His forward movement ceased altogether as he pondered what to say to her.

She had lost everything. Her friends and neighbors were all gone, snuffed out by his own hand in a single moment. All she had left was her life, and he had almost cost her that as well.

This was all his fault. Any form of apology would never be enough.

Fleet's eyes fell from Lowy down to the dirt below his feet. *I'm sorry, Lowy. If only I hadn't been so weak and stupid. Can you ever forgive a fuckup like me?*

Fleet fell backward onto the ground as something crashed into him.

"You're all right!" Lowy yelled.

Her arms were clasped around his abdomen as she lay across his body. Fleet stared into the crystal blue sky in stunned silence as he placed a hand on her head and stroked her hair with his thumb, her tears soaking through his threadbare shirt.

"I was so worried when you passed out!" Lowy said through the sobs. "It looked like you would never wake up!"

Beginning with a laugh, he joked, "Well, I was until you speared me in the gut."

He did not get the reaction he was expecting. She didn't push away in embarrassment. She didn't apologize for hurting him. Instead, her grip around him grew tighter as she asked, "Is it true?"

Fleet propped himself up with a grunt. "Is what true?"

"Is it true...about Denvis?"

Fleet was now all too aware of the badge that he still grasped.

"Is it true about the murders?" she continued. "That he was a part of them?"

Fleet's grip on the worn and battered badge tightened. "Yeah."

Lowy drew her legs into her chest as she shook. "Why? I don't understand why he did it. How could he do something so terrible?"

Fleet placed his free arm around her. "I can't speak for him, but I don't think he did it out of pleasure or malice. It was ignorance—something that none of us are above. He was scared, so he latched on to the first person who acted like they understood what to do in a world where nothing made sense."

Lowy's sobs seemed to subside.

Thinking his words were doing her some good, he continued. "But in the end, he realized that what he was doing was wrong. He fought against everything and everyone he knew to redeem himself. He gave his life fighting for all our sakes—to make it right."

Her sobs started back up again.

"Lowy, I can't tell you how to feel. I can't even tell you how *I* feel. But the one thing I know is that I respect him for learning from his mistakes, for questioning the 'truth' that was forced on him. Denvis was a good man; it just took him a little while to understand what that meant."

Lowy became full-on inconsolable, and Fleet figured the best thing to do was to let her ride it out. Several minutes passed before he ushered them both back to their feet.

As Lowy wiped the grass and dirt from her clothes, Fleet held out the badge for her to see. He wasn't sure if she was ready for it, but it had to be done. "Here, you should have this."

Lowy squinted down at his hand. "What is it?"

Fleet looked at the badge, then at her. "Really?"

"My glasses got cracked when the monster attacked me."

"Didn't even think about it. My bad." Fleet took Lowy's wrist and put the badge in her palm.

She brought it close to her face. "Is this…"

"Yeah," Fleet confirmed. "The last thing he said before he…was how much he loved you."

Lowy swallowed hard as she pressed the badge to her forehead and nodded, her lip trembling. "Thank you. Thank you, Fleet."

He watched this moment of catharsis with quiet content until a thought scratched its way into his mind. "You said you broke your glasses. How did you know it was me coming up here when you tackled me?"

Lowy gave a timid smile and confessed, "I took down three other people thinking they were you."

"Are you kidding me?" Fleet laughed.

Lowy covered her face in embarrassment as Fleet brought her in for a hug. "Man, it's going to be fun having you around, Buck, that's for sure."

Feeling awkward after he realized how invested the agent was in their display, Fleet broke off the embrace.

"Come on, let's go grab the others. We can carpool back to headquarters, and I can fill you guys in on everything along the way—if I manage to stay awake that long."

Lowy nodded before sliding Denvis' badge into her pocket, but stopped when she realized it was already occupied. She extracted the tiny red car that Fleet had given her. "Here, I want you to have this back."

"Holy shit. I almost forgot about this," he scoffed with amusement as he accepted the toy. Fleet swirled his thumb over it several times before it dawned on him. "Wait, so this means…"

"I trust you," Lowy finished for him. "But I'm still trying to process everything that's happened. It's like I'm drifting, moment to moment. Everything feels so surreal. Like reality itself is just some sort of fever dream."

Lowy wiped her eyes as she looked at the blob standing in front of her and held out her free hand.

"But knowing that you're there for me. That you'll be with me. It really… It just…"

Lowy simply looked at him and smiled.

Belonging? Victory? Comfort?

It wasn't even close.

Fleet was experiencing some joyous conglomeration of feelings he had thought long abandoned, and he wished for her to know it—to share in it. He wanted to tell her how much that simple smile meant to him.

But there were no words. Everything he could think of felt...inadequate; perhaps unnecessary is the better word.

So instead of trying to explain himself, he took her hand in his own—and smiled back.

EPILOGUE

"WHY THE HELL DID you bring me out here, ya daft sock!" cursed the masked woman.

Peter stood in the dense thicket, pretending to listen to her complaints as he peered upward at the last tendrils of smoke still visible from the ashes of the church. He held a phone in his outstretched hand, its camera pointing toward the carnage he had vacated a short while ago.

"Sure, the fiery burp was a lick, but you nearly got us locked!" The woman continued to chastise him from behind the mask of some nondescript animal with large ears. "I lean ya some pepper, and this is how you blow it? You've finally lost it, then?"

"You have not performed the favor yet," Peter corrected, his eyes still trained to the sky. "You are here so that I may ask the favor in person. Consider the show a bonus."

"You're a real lunker, you get? I got a bloody phone."

After a momentary smirk, he replied, "I am also going to continue borrowing those two. I have plans for them."

The woman shrugged. "I'm caught ya kept 'em on straight for as long as you did, truth."

Peter looked at her from the corner of his eye. "I have a way with people."

He switched his satellite phone off mute and orated to those watching.

"There is the truth left smoldering before you. A fledgling community of peaceful citizens, utterly razed. Given the chance to foster kinship, they instead chose to burn them all. They rather remain puppet masters, undulating their fingers among the shadows as we dance about for their amusement. They are cowards. Murderers. Every one of them."

Peter pointed in accusation at those tending the church.

"The Servunday: self-proclaimed keepers of the peace—dogs of the elite. They care for nothing else save the pleasure of their masters, trading in their very humanity to live on their knees. You saw him. You saw how quick he was to slaughter. To those like him, we mean nothing. Our freedom is a blight upon their very existence, and they will not surrender us even the right to live."

Peter watched himself on the tiny screen as he continued.

"But we are not chattel for them to feast upon. We have strength and wisdom to match our tenacity and our will. The time draws near, my friends, when equality shall be ours, if not by diplomacy and understanding, then by tooth and claw. And if events tonight have not solidified your resolve, I suggest you bow your head now in the hopes your masters do not strain themselves as they clamp the shackled collar upon your neck."

Thumbs-ups and smiley faces populated his stream as his followers voiced their support. Peter fought the urge to roll his eyes at the colorful show on the screen; proselytizing in person was so much more entertaining.

"Very good." He gave them a small bow. "This is why I have placed my trust in you. I know none of you will ever betray me or the cause. Walk safe, brothers and sisters. I shall be in touch soon."

Without turning off the phone, Peter crushed it in his hand over and over as small plumes of smoke rose from his fist. He dropped the ball of plastic and glass onto the ground before setting his eyes on the mysterious woman.

"You sure can load them pockets," she said with a laugh. "Almost got me thumpin' too."

He beckoned her over with his index finger, which elicited a similar response from her middle finger.

"Must you always be so combative?" Peter complained.

"I'm not like them bunglers you got. I can right think for myself without having to put in a call to his worship."

Peter sighed but relented, stepping in close as he whispered something into her ear.

The woman crossed her arms. "Anyone ever told ya you're a real burnt sally?"

Peter cocked his head. "I am not familiar with that one."

"How 'bout a scumbag piece of shit?"

"It is all for the greater good, I assure you. So, what will it be?"

"Whatever. Let's be even," the woman declared as she backed away. "You got where I'll fix."

With those parting words, the woman leaped straight up, leaving nothing behind but the momentary rustling of grass and limbs.

Peter reached into his pocket and took out a piece of red licorice, which he dragged across his lips. "Well, my boy, you have certainly made things interesting. I believe I will see how this plays out."

He took a large bite from the chewy stick before turning away from all he had wrought.

AFTERWORD

Thank you for reading my book! I began writing this during the night shift of one of my three jobs at the time in an attempt to keep my brain from atrophying like an old stump in a swamp. By some miracle, I managed to fart out a rough draft, which for one of my ilk (i.e. lazy), was an accomplishment in itself.

Life got in the way and I ultimately shelved it for a long while, but the thought of it never really left my mind. I eventually returned to my magnum opus with the belief it had aged into a ripe vintage, but found it had fermented into a giant barrel of cringe.

I attacked it with renewed fervor, and looking back, what must have been the basest understanding of my own native language. It was one of many rewrites, with enough edits to compose two or three more novels, and enough poor grammar to make English teachers across the country commit suicide en masse.

After 12 years, my book sees the light of day, more because I feel I have to do it for my own sanity instead of spending another year chasing that imaginary dream of "perfection." While it may still be 'cringe', it is my 'cringe', and I am proud of it.

I hope you enjoy reading it far more than I did writing it. Do not take that last remark as my withdrawal from the written word; I still plan to do more. I am already hard at work on the sequel, so hopefully you won't have to wait long to find out what other zany antics Hangman and company get up to.

That being said, knowing that there are people out there who care about my work would light a fire in my heart, so to speak. If you have the time, please leave a review on Goodreads or Amazon, and spread the word on social media if you are able.

Once again, thank you for taking the time to read my book, and I hope you enjoyed it.

-Christopher Harvard

JOIN THE FREE MOUSE MAILING LIST FOR A FREE BONUS CHAPTER!

OFFER.FREEMOUSELLC.COM

JOIN THE MAILING LIST to get updates on future books and recommendations from other authors. Membership includes a free bonus chapter that sheds a bit more light on the 'atelier of horror.' Also, you may be graced with some bonus material or funny stories like 'Buttery Justice' below.

Given the opportunity, I always thought that I would step up and do the right thing. I wonder if you too have fantasized about being a hero, fighting the bad guys, and taking a stand against injustice. I believe it is human nature to play at being the hero, though it is often relegated to our daydreams, unchallenged, until that one day when it is tested—and you are found wanting.

Dear readers, I experienced just that circumstance recently, exposing myself to one of my deepest fears:

The knowledge that I am a coward.

I witnessed an atrocity, and I stood by and did nothing save lower my head in shame. I had the chance to make a difference, but I fell craven and let my baser instincts prevail to avoid any social awkwardness.

On the precipice of my dreams, I still hear her calling out,over and over, the cadence escalating with each baleful screech.

"EAT YER BUTTER!"

While that may have caught you off guard, allow me to explain.

Not long ago, I found myself at a greasy spoon; the food was passable, but it had a nice homegrown atmosphere. During the meal, I noticed a family sitting to my right; two parents and a child still blessed by the innocence of youth. While it took a moment for me to realize what was happening, once I did, I nearly expunged my bacon and eggs.

The mother was spoon-feeding this poor lad straight butter.It was not as a side, or a topping, but as a main course. Just butter. She made it through three spoonfuls as I watched helplessly from the sidelines.

And perhaps the worst part was that it wasn't even good butter like Kerry Gold. It was that cheap lactose spread that every restaurant has, the kind they cannot legally call 'butter.' Basically, it is the butter equivalent of someone who shows up at the family reunion, does a line in the bathroom, then makes a pass at their cousin. What next? Were they going to wash it down with those little cups of creamer you get with your coffee? (You know who you are)

But here is the crux of my failure, dear readers. At this point,the child actively rebuked his next serving of butter, slapping it away. It was then that the mother began her banshee wail:

"EAT YER BUTTER! EAT YER BUTTER!"

Human decency demands that I stand up for this poor, abused child. To scream, "He doesn't want any more of your damn butter!"

But I remained silent, drowning my fractured ego in another glass of sweet tea with too much ice. The butter consumption soon resumed, and I could swear I heard the boy's arteries clog in real time like an engine with sugar in the gas tank.

But it was then I was given a moment of respite; something that gave my inaction meaning. After his last spoonful of spread, the little shit stood up, ran over to me, and coughed right in my face.

Fuck you, kid. Have fun getting through kindergarten after your triple bypass. I'll send you some Power Rangers stickers to slap on your oxygen tank so you look cool when you wheal it around the playground; careful bringing it with you on the slide, it'll take your head off. At least now they can just get you an IV of that shitty spread and put it straight in your veins to keep you from going in public to cough on decent folk like me.

Little butter-eating ass bitch.